A Spark of the Fire

Previously Published Books
by Steven WinterHawk:

Title: *This is a Circle*
Published by iUniverse Bloomington, IN.
Date: 12/12/2011

Title: *SHILOH – A Native American Jesus*
Published by iUniverse Bloomington, IN.
Date: 11/13/2012

Title: *Queen Anne's Lace*
Published by iUniverse Bloomington, IN.
Date: 12/13/2013

Title: *My Sister Cathy*
Published by iUniverse Bloomington, IN.
Date: 02/04/2014

Title: *Arrows of Truth*
A Book of Poetry and Prose
Printed by The Printing House
for WinterHawk Publishing
Date: 05/29/2015

A Spark of the Fire
When Star Woman Fell to Earth

A collection of science fiction fantasy stories
About space, time and dreams with a common
Theme of relationships
"We are all Related":
An Aboriginal theory of Relativity

by

Steven WinterHawk

A SPARK OF THE FIRE
WHEN STAR WOMAN FELL TO EARTH

Copyright © 2016 Steven WinterHawk.

All rights reserved. No part of this book may be used or reproduced by any means, graphic, electronic, or mechanical, including photocopying, recording, taping or by any information storage retrieval system without the written permission of the author except in the case of brief quotations embodied in critical articles and reviews.

This is a work of fiction. All of the characters, names, incidents, organizations, and dialogue in this novel are either the products of the author's imagination or are used fictitiously.

iUniverse books may be ordered through booksellers or by contacting:

iUniverse
1663 Liberty Drive
Bloomington, IN 47403
www.iuniverse.com
1-800-Authors (1-800-288-4677)

Because of the dynamic nature of the Internet, any web addresses or links contained in this book may have changed since publication and may no longer be valid. The views expressed in this work are solely those of the author and do not necessarily reflect the views of the publisher, and the publisher hereby disclaims any responsibility for them.

Any people depicted in stock imagery provided by Thinkstock are models, and such images are being used for illustrative purposes only. Certain stock imagery © Thinkstock.

ISBN: 978-1-4917-9439-5 (sc)
ISBN: 978-1-4917-9440-1 (e)

Library of Congress Control Number: 2016905750

Print information available on the last page.

iUniverse rev. date: 04/15/2016

Dedication

I would like to dedicate these stories in part to the memory of my recently departed friend, Bonnie. My life partner and I have known Bonnie for about 30 years so her passing into Spirit was a tragic experience for both of us, even though the three of us were strong in our beliefs of life after death.

I also dedicate these stories to my Soulmate who is also my life partner, who I met (in this reality) the same time I met Bonnie.

I would also like to thank my friend and Editor, Heather Embree, for helping me to transform these stories and my dreams into a readable book.

And last but not least, I dedicate this book to my grandchildren, and great-grandchildren in hope that they and all children are inspired to follow their dreams.

* Additional Credits for:
A Spark of the Fire
Hi-Res Digital photo purchased and downloaded used in the creation of a cover for this book.
Wallpaper Stock Photo - ID-1009949.jpg from FreeDigitalPhotos.net.

Introduction and Disclaimer

These are Science Fiction stories, born of imagination, a flight of fancy and dreams. The usual disclaimer stands, preceding any such stories even if the stories originate from the author's dreams. I need to point out that none of the people are intentionally meant to represent anyone living or deceased. Some, like the Jinn (a mythical creature made of fire) are, however, a Smoking Mirror of someone I have met in my waking life. Just the same, they are all unique to my Dreamtime. This will be similar for the names of the places, of the towns and cities and organizations in my stories. There is a somewhat common belief among dreamers, that everything in our dreams can be seen as some part of us calling out to be recognized.

The stories in this book while being my dreams are partly inspired by: "Sky Woman who fell to Earth," a Native Creation story. When Native stories like this are told, the stories are expandable and based on a Female Divine Presence. Our stories are told orally, so that they can be adapted and learned from in the world in which we live, day-to-day. With this in mind, there is the Native belief that we are all Sparks of the Original Fire.

This book is a collection of a life time of dreams. Not all of my dreams to be sure, because a life time of dreams is more than one life time could hold. Therein lays the paradox. As my dreams and the stories began to play out; it became evident that something or someone was missing. A key as given to me to unlock a certain dream that I named *"Hot to Trot"*—at the time in somewhat dubious respect of the fire. This story is at the end of this book, so in the tradition of the mystery, the first is also the last. A journey begins that religion might deny and logical scientists will tell us is impossible—a journey beyond the speed of light, and time.

...what if there was another dream?

When my good friend Jinny passed into Spirit she left behind more unanswered questions than answers. First and foremost, Jinny, as the name suggests, was – is a jinn, and a jinn is not susceptible to dying like the rest of us of mortal birth. In Islamic theology, jinn are said to be creatures with free will, like humans and unlike angels, made from smokeless fire as humans were made of clay. The jinn, humans and angels are said to make up the three sapient creations of God. Now this may seem to be a strange statement by me, a supposition, considering that Jinny was not of any religion on the earth, but it is meant to say that my friend was and still is a mystery.

A day after Jinny's passing, I experienced a dream that either discounted or reinforced my original belief that she is a fairy tale creature beyond my needing to understand. In this dream, I was sitting with Jinny at her computer table in Guelph, in the midst of a rousing discussion about my latest dream (a dream within a dream) and out of the blue, she handed me an object, and said: "this will help you to understand." And I woke up.

I woke that morning with the urgency of a trip to downtown Toronto. My life partner asked me to drive her downtown for a follow up for some tests she had at the Woman's College Hospital. I dropped her off at the door and continued on circling the block for a parking place to wait until she called to be picked up again. On the fourth drive around, I took a turn and ended up on a small side street – a circle in itself, and parked in front of an aged house with a sign that proclaimed it to be "The U. of T. Faculty of Law".

I looked for the book I had intended to read while I waited, but found that I had left it at home. So I sipped my luke-warm coffee and attempted to nap. I was unsuccessful (it seemed) to nap or meditate as my kidneys began to call out for my attention. What to do? I opened the door to my car and searched up and down the street with my eyes to locate a possible restaurant or Johnny-on-the-spot in the park on the other side of the street, to no avail. Nature will have its way with our bodies, and I was embolden to take a route that I might not have chosen otherwise. I locked the car, and with a sidelong glance at the man on the riding lawn mower who was gathering up the new fallen leaves, sauntered casually in the direction of the House of Law, then purposely up to the front door.

    I tried the door, and found it unlocked, so I decided to go inside, acting like I belonged and, for a moment that seemed true. I followed stairs to the basement level, meeting only one person in the hall. A young woman (a student?) paused to enquire of me: "Professor?"

    "No, sorry," I replied, and she went her way. I followed the stairs down to the lower level, and easily located the rest room. Having been relieved of the situation that had made me so bold, I exited the toilet, and followed the corridor in the direction of a side door that I somehow knew about. On the way, the hallway took a turn, and so did I, to come to a wall that seemed to have no purpose except in a memory that didn't make sense. I searched the wall with my hands, and found nothing, but a small vertical slit, just right for a…? And the dream that morning popped back into my head. "What had Jinny said? Better yet, what had she given me?" I took the wallet from my pocket and opened it to find a computer key card! Operating strictly on instinct now, I inserted a key that I had been given in the dream into a slot in a wall in a house that I had no real reason to be in. And it worked! With a hiss, a door swung open, and somewhere, a quiet air-conditioner started up, dispelling the first gasp of stale air.

    The hidden room that I stepped into was some sort of classroom at first sight. My right hand found a switch, and banks of florescent lights began to come on, one after the other. The door closed automatically behind me, but I was in no way alarmed to be trapped. In fact, I felt right at home. I walked purposely to the front of the windowless classroom, where a sign hung over the teachers' desk:

"NASA – U. of T. Joint Venture - Department of Quantum Law." A lengthy title that still did not ring a bell, until I took a seat in the professors' chair. This was my chair! It hit me like a ton of bricks. "I am..." I turned around the name plate on my desk to read "Joseph Champion," and in smaller script: "Professor of Quantum Theory." Well, that explains it all! But it did not. There were memories flooding into my mind that were not mine, but they were!

Instinctively, I pushed the "on" button of the antique-like computer under my desk and turned on the old tube monitor to listen as the PC churned and the screen crackled to life. The computer in question was a "dumb terminal." A "green screen" appeared with the title similar to the banner above my desk: "NASA – University Of Toronto Joint Venture – Quantum Theory Programming."

"Programming? To what end?" I wondered and at the same time I knew. I typed in my password, and waited for the connection to be made with an IBM mainframe located somewhere in the building – and still active after all these years and dust. How is this possible? Does the U. Of T. know about this? How could they not? And as the monitor came alive with the numbered lesson plan that I was teaching the last time I sat in this chair, I heard other computers begin to start up in the back of my mind – no – in real time - in this time, in this classroom as my students arrived. I raised my head to watch the remaining students file in. I knew all these young people, by name. They had been handpicked and personally interviewed by me, for a particular aptitude, a leaning toward Quantum engineering – especially. I sought out a particular student and found him, waiting for his terminal to connect. Our eyes met, and he smiled, and at that moment I felt that something was wrong. It was too early for him to be there. Too early, meaning the class was too new. Shane would not join us 'til later in the program. Until a certain event caused us to meet – and a certain destiny brought us together. Shane was the only Native American student in the class, and was selected because of his unique ability for lucid dreaming...

...And wait! It was all wrong! My mind filled with memories that belonged to — him! I am that young man! I am Shane. How could this happen? I must be losing my mind! I got up and stumbled to the door, amid concerned voices: "Professor Champion? Are you all right?"

I mumbled about needing air, and made my way up the steps to the front door. Outside, it was unusually bright and sunny, and the cars that were parked at the curb were square blocks – from some old movie out of the early sixties! I fell to my knees in the lush green summer grass, and was aware of thinking that I must be going insane!

The Forest

Dreamtime

... the beginning?
There is a place, the child said,
Where magic is alive.
Where Spirits walk, deer can talk,
And all our dreams survive.

Just take my hand, I know the path,
I've walked it many times.
Please come with me, she said with glee,
He thought she spoke of rhymes.

But went he did, and he exclaimed:
I've found another me!
Their dreams were blessed, with time compressed,
Into reality...

...WinterHawk
Another Time and Place

ONE

<u>Shane</u>

Shortly after his birth in a nursing home on the edge of the New Credit Indian Reserve, Shane contracted meningitis. Meningitis is an inflammation of the membranes (meninges) surrounding your brain and spinal cord. His parents took him to a nearby hospital in Hagersville, where they discovered that a number of babies with this disease were infected and the chance of survival at that time was not good. His father, being of Native Indian descent was a young man – fresh out of the Canadian army, but still in contact with his Native roots as an Ojibway. His father had a strong belief in other ways of healing, so he took Shane to a woman known to be a healer on the New Credit Reserve. In this woman's care, the boy was healed, but not before certain memories (dreams) were ignited, that would smoulder in a young child's mind, and come to life when Shane began to think on his own.

As Shane grew up, he became a dreamer – that is someone who could easily remember his dreams and sometimes found those dreams as real as his everyday life. He was in fact, a constant day dreamer as well. One of the first impactful dreams he had as a young boy was of being taken some place and having people – Native people drumming and chanting over hium. Later on, when he told his parents they (including his father) were at a loss to explain this dream and advised him to let it go as just a fanciful daydream. Just a few years into being a new parent, his father was quickly becoming disenchanted with the world and the way anyone who admitted to being an "Indian" was treated as a second class citizen of Canada and the world, even if that person gave part of his of her life to the preservation of our freedoms in the Second World War that had just ended. Native people were just above (or equal to) the black people, especially in the USA where slavery had been abolished by law, but not in the minds of many US citizens. In Canada, we were in fact, less than blacks, even though we had been on this land before those who made the laws.

As Shane neared the age of beginning school, his father took it upon himself, to change the families last name, and declare that he was a gypsy from Montreal, claiming this was the reason his family did not show up in the record books. Shane never found out how his father pulled this off, as the boys birth certificate – and the birth records for the two much younger sisters showed their true last name, and when later in Shane's life he decided to apply for a Native card, that true name as an Ojibway of the New Credit Reserve was required. The first alternative branch of Shane's tree of life, started at school with a slightly altered last name. This was his first true Spirit Name.

Shane started school with the name LaFlame. His new last name was to be quite appropriate, in that it spoke of a fire that would not be denied. The first "test" came part way into grade one in the form of a no-nonsense teacher who threatened to blow his cover, so to speak.

"I don't know what your father and mother are trying to pull off," his teacher exclaimed in class at the beginning of grade one, "and I am frankly surprised that it got this far, but I recognize you and your family. I taught on the reserve for a while and a couple of my students were your cousins. And your aunts had a different last name than you do now. How do you explain that?"

Shane shrugged. "If my dad says he came from Montreal and he is a gypsy, then it must be so." Shane had been told by some Elders that his original family, three Aboriginal brothers had migrated from Quebec to form the nucleus of what would become the "Three Fires," first in Port Credit, and then moved to New Credit on part of the Six Nations Reserve. So he was not really telling an untruth, and neither was his father.

His teacher never did pursue the problem of his last name. Perhaps this was because he gave her other things to think about and was living up to his inner desire for knowledge. His curiosity was insatiable. He borrowed and read every book in the small one room school library. Shane had learned – been taught to read by his mother, who supplied the nightly entertainment for Shane and his sisters by reading aloud most of the books he brought home from school. One morning during bible class, taught by the one and only teacher the subject was Genesis and how God created the world in seven days.

"Class? Do you have any questions? Yes, Shane?"

"Is it possible that God's time is different than ours? And the part about the seven days was written because we could not understand it otherwise?"

"Sit down Shane. No, it is not possible. The Bible was written to be the truth for us to believe, without question." She hastily put away the book and shuffled the papers on her desk. "Now we will get on with our day. Please take out your math books. Where did we end up yesterday?"

Shane's mind did a double take (if you didn't expect questions – why did you ask?) Do the math. One and one does not add up to seven in any person's mind – no matter how you figure it out.

As time went on, the child remembered - more than he should have, and things that no one else present could confirm. The child received a wake up, in the form of a memory of being some place where helpful, caring beings had assisted in healing him, until the sound of singing called him back. Neither of Shane's parents could recall any place in the hospital, or anywhere else that they had visited with him, as being the place that stood out in his memory. His father did recall that the singular Indian woman in the hospital on the reserve had held him for hours on end, and chanted "Spirit songs" to help him become well - and it had worked. How the healing worked was not important. One of Shane's relatives later remarked about how lucky he was to have lived past the age of two — relatives do have a way of speaking, — to wake up a seemingly ungrateful child.

The boy's father and mother had met in the army, and at the time when motherhood became Catherine's primary concern, her husband still had to fulfill his obligation to his country. Edward and Catherine lived with his family in a big, rundown, rented house on the Indian Reserve. This arrangement was partially due to Edward being away a lot and the fact that they had very little money. They could have lived on army grounds, but Edward was very close to his family and thought that Catherine and the baby would be better off with someone to look after her until he was out of the service.

Catherine's acceptance into the family, her being white, would have been nearly unbearable, had not Edward's mother been of English decent. The Elder woman understood some of the problems of communication that arose. These people seemed stuck between worlds - the world of the white man, and that of their ancestors. Most of Edward's relatives were, in Catherine's eyes, red-skinned individuals who lived white skinned lives. They possessed some remaining Native pride, but had little knowledge of their ancestral heritage. Catherine had only her history books to help her understand why she did not fit. Shane later began to believe that perhaps it was not so much her colour, but the fact that she, at least it appeared so, knew who she was. Catherine had been brought up as a Christian and her religion was important to her. Here was a People whose spiritual beliefs, once the driving force in their lives, were now mostly lost - or taken away by the white man.

Catherine's gentle way of teaching and of raising her son would have fit very well with the early Native methods of child-rearing. She helped to instil in him the belief that he, and everyone else on the Earth, was a special being, deserving of love. Catherine's God (her personal image of the Christian God) was kind, loving, and forgiving. A story that stuck with the boy for some time was shared by his father: One day while they were living in Ottawa, before Shane was born, his father and mother were crossing a street and discovered a sparrow that had been killed by a car. Catherine stopped, and found a place nearby to bury the tiny bird.

As a toddler, Shane was an inquisitive child. He might often be caught staring into empty space and sometimes pointing where others could not see anything. Although his mother allowed the child the free rein to explore and grow, it was partially due to his Grandmother's influence that Shane did not stop "seeing." Shane's grandmother came from an English family and did not completely discount the existence of "wee folk" or fairy people. She also knew, that many children often have unseen playmates up to a certain age. She had raised eleven children of her own. Shane had very pleasant memories of his grandmother. She was grandmother, baby-sitter, and protector to numerous offspring - her own, and subsequently those of her children. She was an important piece of the puzzle. Perhaps it might be more appropriate to say, that in the tradition of Elders before her, she helped keep the "magic" alive for her grandson.

TWO

The child continued to see someone that was never seen by anyone else, and confided only in his grandmother. All the while, his Mother did her best to teach him the religion that her parents had passed on to her. He accepted her teaching with a nod of his small head, and then went back to playing with his invisible friend.

One night when a summer wind swept through the old farm house that the family rented, when everyone else was fast asleep, five year old Shane thought he heard his name being called.

"Come out and play," the voice echoed.

"Can't, I'm too tired," he answered sleepily, rolling over on the bed.

After a while, the wind quieted down and all that could be heard was the creaking sound of an old house going to sleep for the night. Shane's relatives often told him that this was the sound of ghosts walking. His Father's family was extremely superstitious. Oddly enough, these "ghost stories" didn't bother a small boy as much as it seemed to frighten the teller of the tale.

As he was just dropping off to sleep, he noticed a movement in a darker corner of the room that he shared with his parents. A girl stepped out of the gloom into the light of the moon, framed on the floor.

"Howcum you're here?" Shane asked. "Don't you know its bedtime?" He whispered so that he would not wake his mother.

"'course I know," his sometime invisible friend answered him with a giggle. "It's the best time for you to come and see my forest I told you 'bout."

Shane's friend had said that she lived in a great forest part of the time with her grandmother and other teachers; and that she would take him there sometime, to meet "Ourman".

"Don't worry. No one else can hear me, and they won't hear you." She explained that she was in his dream.

"You're silly!" he blurted out. He slid quietly out of bed and walked over to shake his finger at her nose. "I'm awake...can't you see that?"

"Oh you are smarty pants! Then look who's sleeping in your bed!" She deepened her voice in her imitation of one of the bears in "Goldilocks" and giggled as she pointed.

Sure enough, someone who looked exactly like him was curled up asleep beside his mother.

"You're tricking me somehow, like you always trick me." He was laughing now. "How come I can see you sometimes and sometimes I can't?"

"That's 'cause you don't know my name, and I do know yours," she riddled. "Ourman says that we must never tell anyone our real name, because if someone knows all about us, then they can call us to them from the Magic place and use our magic. He didn't say magic, but that's what I call it. Come on. Don't be a spoil sport. Let's go, so that I can show you my forest."

The boy finally shrugged his shoulders, took his friends outstretched hand, and followed her onto the patch of moonlight, which was framed by the darkness of the bedroom. The darkness fell away, to be replaced by a moonlit forest that was nearly as bright as day. The smell of pine needles filled the air and the trees stood tall around them like protecting soldiers, making the boy feel calm and secure almost at once.

"Wow!"

He exclaimed, and then when his voice echoed in the stillness, he continued in a whisper:

"Is this really your home? Do you live here all alone?"

"'course not silly," she giggled. "I told you before. I come here to play, and Ourman is always here with my grandmother – and an old Indian Medicine Woman who is teaching me. I'm learning to be a Wood Sprite. This place is full of Magic like the stories your mom reads in your books."

Shane had previously told her some stories, as he remembered them that his mother read to him nightly. This forest certainly had a feeling of Magic about it. You'd almost expect to see Alice chasing the white rabbit through the trees. Suddenly, a rabbit appeared on the path ahead of them. The boy jumped back, startled.

"Don't be so surprised!"

The girl laughed at him. "You called the rabbit, didn't you?" She bent down and picked up the tiny creature.

"I did not!" he retorted, thinking that a joke was being played on him.

"'Member what I said about knowing someone's real name? Well, it works a hundred times better in this place. You know the smell and the feel and all 'bout rabbits, so when you thought "rabbit," it came. Ourman taught me that just the other day. 'Cept maybe you cheated, because there's lots of rabbits in these woods and he didn't have far to come."

Shane looked at her in awe.

"Do you mean if I knew your name, I could really call you to come and visit me at my home whenever I wanted? Tell me, I'd like that." He said this excitedly.

She opened her mouth to speak, but a gentle, commanding voice interrupted her before she could utter the name.

"Not right now. You can tell Shane your name all in good time. Remember how I taught you how to know when the time is right for something to happen?"

"If it is right, there will be a feeling, like a little voice in my heart," she recited. "Oh, hello, Ourman; I was telling Shane about you."

A man dressed in a plain white robe stepped out of the shadows. He had obviously been watching and listening since they had arrived in the forest.

"Hello Shane, you can call me Arbrin. Until you showed up here, I had given Sprite and her grandmother another name to call me by. I have collected many names in my travels but Arbrin will be fitting for you to share—and the reason will become known when you are ready. I have watched over you since you were born.

Sort of like what your mother calls a Guardian Angel, except I'm not an Angel."

The boy stepped back.

"Are you God? Am I In Heaven? My Mommy told me..."

"No I am not God, and you are not dead and gone to Heaven. I am with you to guide you and to be your teacher. This is simply a safe place - a place of learning. Have you heard about school?"

"Oh yes I have. Mommy said that I might go next year."

"Well," Arbrin continued, "this is like school, a special school. If you had not continued to "see" and play with your friend, you might not have come until you were grown up. You can thank your grandmother, and your friend, that you are here now, but it was mostly up to you."

The boy thought hard. His brow became furrowed as he tried to understand all that Arbrin had said to him.

The man's laughter sounded like a running brook in the field near where the boy lived. He reached over and tousled the child's hair.

"Don't try to figure it all out at once, or your forehead will be wrinkled like an old man before your time. We take things slowly around here. Learning should be as much fun as playing, if you're learning the right things. That is really your first lesson, right Sprite?"

The man, whose age would have been difficult even for an adult to guess, turned and winked at Shane's friend. Then, in a semi-serious and with a proud tone to his voice, he continued.

"Your friend," he addressed the boy, "Your friend learned to go to your home from this forest. She was lonely and wanted a friend to play with so much that she began to believe she could do it - and she did!"

"Two more important lessons have already been shown to you by your friend":

"First, if you really wish to do something - so strongly that nothing can stop you from believing in it - you can do, or have almost anything you wish! Your friend proved this."

"The second and also very important thing that "Sprite" has shown you should be remembered along with the first. Learn to listen for a little "voice" in your heart. This is really a feeling like "good" or "bad" - this is how you will know if something is right or wrong for you to do at this time."

"An example of this might be - if you are wishing for something, the voice or feeling in your heart might say, "Good! There is no problem!""

"Another time, this feeling in your heart might tell you "Something is wrong," which could mean: whatever you are wishing for, or about to do is not good for you or someone else - at this time. In time, you will learn to "hear," and not to disobey the voice in your heart."

The boy nodded his head, but his forehead was a mass of wrinkles again. The "teacher" smiled, and spoke again to the boy in a gentle reassuring voice:

"You also did well because you were able to see your friend, and did not stop seeing and playing with her, though some other people told you that no one was there just because they couldn't see her. I think that you both have earned some time to play."

Arbrin dismissed them with a gentle wave of his hand.

The rest of Shane's first trip to the forest went by all too quickly and soon it was time for him to go home.

"Think of how good your bed at home feels."

Arbrin told him. "Close your eyes, and remember your bedroom. When you open your eyes again, you will be home."

The boy did as he was told and felt like a strong wind had taken hold of him and swept him off his feet. He heard a rushing sound, and when he opened his eyes, he saw the sunlight peeping through the blind of his bedroom. He was rested, as though he had slept all night.

THREE

"What is this Army like where my daddy works?" young Shane asked one day after another dreamtime journey to the forest. He had overheard his mother talking with his grandmother about the current state of the world.

"Is there shooting and killing?" he was wide-eyed with wonder and concern.

"No, thank God. Your father is not stationed overseas; and besides that, the war is over. There will be no more shooting and killing like that taking place, (at least until the next war mongers come along)." His mother added the last bit to herself. She paused from her task of preparing supper to look down at the five- year-old tugging at her skirt.

"Your father will be able to come home to visit us soon. Do you understand what I mean if I were to tell you he will be home in one week?"

The small boy shook his head "no."

"Why can't he come home to see me now? I want to see my daddy now!"

Catherine reached down and picked up her son, shaking her head in dismay.

"I'm sorry, but, there are rules that everyone must live by, and right now the rules say that your father cannot come home until next week. I don't like it anymore than you, but we have to live with this fact, for now."

The boy looked like he was about to cry and continued to talk to his mother as if she could do something about the problem.

"I don't like those rules. Who made them? Not me. Did you mommy?"

"No I didn't son." His mother sighed and hugged him to her.

"But someone did and until we change them, we have to live with them. I don't know what else to tell you."

Suddenly the boy's face brightened.

"I know. Why don't you just call daddy to come home to us?"

"Call him home? I don't think you understand. We have no telephone here. And anyway, the army won't let him come home right now." Catherine was rapidly becoming exasperated by this conversation as it represented a very sensitive issue for her. She was fed up with other people running her, and her husband's lives (most notably, the army, and her husband's relatives. The latter being mostly due to a pent-up feeling of having very little personal privacy).

"Please run along and play. Before you know it, the week will have gone by."

Shane decided that if his mother would not "call" his father home, then he would. He proceeded to follow the appropriate steps as he remembered being taught in his dream. His mother noticed that for the rest of that day, he was extremely silent, spending most of his time gazing out the window, as if watching for someone or something.

When his father did not show up the next day, the boy became agitated. He felt as though someone had let him down. Later that evening, he suddenly started crying for his father, and could not be quieted down. Within an hour, a knock was heard at the door. Shane's mother opened the door, and his father walked in out of the cold.

"Strangest thing happened yesterday," the boy's father said. "I got the strongest feeling that something was not right at home. I guess I could have put it out of my mind, but you know how I'm fed up with this "playing soldier," especially now that the war's over. So I just walked out. I went A.W.O.L. The Military Police will be looking for me tomorrow, but I had to come home to see my family tonight."

Edward picked up his son who was trying to hide the fact that he had been crying, and said: "What is this child doing up past his bed time?" Then rumpling the boy's hair, he kidded his son. "Did you know that I was coming home tonight to see you?"

Catherine simply stared for a moment at the child in his father's arms, and then hugged them both.

The boy could barely go to sleep that night, after the excitement of having his father home. He anticipated visiting the forest in his dream. He had a lot to tell his friends.

Sleep finally came. He was already standing in the middle of the room when the little girl walked out of the shadows to greet him.

"You were waiting for me tonight," she noted.

"I would have called for you, but I still don't know your name. I 'member the forest but I don't know the way there," he finished, almost out of breath.

She led him by the hand once more to the moonlit path that had not been there one second before. Tonight, a crescent moon with a clear, star-filled sky made the forest a welcoming place to be.

He wondered out loud:

"Is it ever day here? Every time I come here the moon is out."

"Are all boys this silly?" She pretended to make fun of him. "'course it's not always night-time here. You came here in your night dreams, but people also have day dreams, you know." She puffed out her chest and announced proudly, that she knew how to "medicate", so she could come there during the day time.

At this last pronouncement, Arbrin who had been standing behind the little girl, laughed, and gently corrected her.

"I believe the word you meant to say is meditate. Just the same, I am very proud of how well you have learned since you first dreamed of this forest."

Arbrin turned to Shane.

"You seem about ready to burst. Do you want to talk about what happened to you?"

In a single breath, the boy related how he had called to his father to come home. Arbrin listened patiently, patting the boy on the back. He slowly explained a difficult lesson for such young minds.

"Shane was able to send a message to his father; and because his father also wanted to do what Shane asked, his father came home. The love between children and their parents is the same as knowing your father's or mother's "secret name," your own "secret name," is held in your heart from the time you are born and has the power to call you even in the "awake" world. When you think of a person's everyday name, and if you know their "secret name," you know all about them - enough to call them to you or to send a thought into their head. One of the few times that you cannot put a thought into a person or animal's head, is when they are on their path and know where they are going. You cannot call them off it."

"Do you mean how the rabbit was on the path when I called him?" Shane wanted to know.

Arbrin laughed and soon all three were laughing, although the boy sensed that the joke was on him.

"There are other meanings to the word "path" and I will tell you about them another time," Arbrin finally said. Arbrin felt the children did not need to hurry. They were handling all they were able to for the present, but he also needed to caution them about the use of names.

"As I explained to Sprite..." Arbrin began:

"... every minute that you spend in a place like this forest, you are not only learning - you are storing up something like magic. The magic, if you like to call it that, is now part of you. If someone can call you, your magic comes with you. Tell your name only to those you are sure you can trust - and then only when the time is right. Also be careful in calling others, because they have put their trust in you!"

FOUR

The nightly visits to the forest became more frequent, and the boy quite often shut himself off from the ordinary world in favour of playing and learning with his friend. During one visit to the dream forest, Shane asked: "if the little girl was learning to be a "'Sprite," whatever that was, "what was he learning to be?"

Arbrin pointed out that the little girl enjoyed speaking of the forest as a place of Magic, the way she liked the nickname "Sprite." The teacher finally conceded that, "maybe being able to communicate with all the small animals that fill this forest and play with them is really what Magic is all about. Sprite is learning to love and trust Nature and herself."

"You, Shane, are here to learn how that same Love could heal much of the problems in your outside world. Right now you won't really understand, or remember all that I am teaching you until you need to use the lesson. But you can both help each other and learn the right way through play."

"Your father's people, his ancestors, were always great healers. This is part of your inheritance. What I mean is, the old-time Indians were relatives of yours and they have given you the gift to be a healer. Do not worry too much about all of this right now. Healing can be done in so many ways: from touching, to simply telling a story to someone. For now just learn to be yourself."

All this was too much for the young child to digest at one time. Shane remembered, however, that being born an Indian was important to his life. When the Council, that Arbrin attended some nights, met in the grove to conduct a Shamanistic journey to help someone, the boy was all ears and eyes. His friend watched with him from behind the trees.

"See that old Indian man coming out of the steam house?" She did a play by play, "next they're gonna wave smoke all over his body. My grandmother says that they are cleaning all the bad things out of him, so that he can go to the Spirit world and not get hurt. Arbrin said that if we have bad things in us, it brings bad things to us faster than if we are clean."

The young girl described a sweat lodge ceremony that initially induced a cleansing sweat in the person participating. Afterward, the person about to make a "Spirit Journey" would bathe in the pool in the center of the forest. A further cleansing was done by wafting smoke, from burning sage or sweetgrass, over his body.

Throughout all of the ceremony, a steady drum beat reverberated throughout the trees. When the person was ready to make the journey, the drum beat increased in intensity. To one side of the Council circle, there stood an extremely old tree. This tree dwarfed all other trees in the forest and was so tall that its top could not be seen. At the base of this tree there was an entrance, a hole in the trunk that Shane had not noticed before tonight. As the drumming intensified, the size of the hole grew, until it was big enough for a man. Shane turned to look inquiringly at his friend.

"Arbrin told me that the hole in the tree can go up to the High Spirits or down to the Lower World. Lots of times the old men go down through the hole in the tree to bring back some part of a person that is lost; to help heal them." She was very proud of all that she remembered.

At the mention of healing, Shane's ears perked up. "Wasn't this something that he should be learning?" Shane leaned over and whispered in his companion's ear:

"Have you ever been down the hole? What do you think it's like in the Spirit world down there?" He was full of questions.

"No." She had never gone into the hole in the tree. Her grandmother had taught her to listen to the little voice in her heart when she was not sure about something and until tonight, the little voice said "stay away from the hole in the tree!" She experienced an uneasy feeling even as Shane asked his question. Maybe when the time was right, the voice would say: "OK!"

Shane was too caught up in his own excitement to hear her warning. He was set on finding out where the hole led to. Also he was a little put off since his friend seemed to know so much more about the Dream world than he.

"I'm going down the hole!" he announced in a whisper.

"I don't think you should!" she warned again.

This made him even more determined to prove himself.

"You won't tell on me, will you?" he asked.

"'course not, but I'm afraid for you." Her continued insistence awakened an odd sensation that began in the pit of his stomach. He did not want to back out though, in case she thought him to be a "fraidy cat".

The little girl would not let him go through the Spirit door by himself; so, hand in hand the two children crept stealthily around the outer perimeter of trees that surrounded the glade, until they stood beside the tallest tree. She looked imploringly at her friend to try one last time to change his mind, but his face showed only the dogged determination of one that would not be swayed. They stepped into the light of the campfire only for a minute and slipped quietly through the opening in the tree trunk.

The darkness that greeted them was accompanied by a cool wind, heavy with moisture. They stood in a close tunnel, just large enough for their heads to clear. Except for the wind, there was only stillness; not a sound to be heard. At this point, Shane reconsidered the folly of his actions, but upon turning around, even the few steps they had taken left only darkness behind, as though the entrance that they had come through was now miles away. If anything, the passageway took on a dim light in front of them.

"Come on, it looks like daylight that way."

He tried to sound brave.

Sure enough, the further they walked along the slow, downward slant of the tunnel, the brighter the light ahead became, until the children stepped out into a grassy meadow, where the sun shone at midday. Tall grass waved in a warm breeze, even birds sang. The very air was clean and sweet with the fragrance of flowers. They both breathed a sigh of immense relief.

Shane having gained back his bravado spoke to his friend:

"See I told you everything would be OK! This must mean that I'm really learning to be an Indian Doctor. What else do you remember I'm supposed to do?"

"Well," she answered hesitantly: "Arbrin said that the old people always bring back a gift, something that has magic in it, like a feather, or a shiny rock — you know, the kind of rock that makes rainbows in the sun."

Just as she said this, they came upon a busy stream gurgling up through a hole in the ground. There were crystal stones along its bank.

"Look!" the boy pointed excitedly and let go of her hand to pick up a stone. After letting go of her hand, he had barely enough time to grasp a crystal and, for him, the whole atmosphere of the meadow changed. Feelings of loss, and bleakness, struck him and he could not regain his balance. The girl reached out for his hand, but was too late to stop him from falling down the opening where the water came out of the ground.

Blackness closed in on him. It was as though he had gone blind - if it were not for the small stone in his hand. The crystal produced a faint light in the heavy darkness; just enough to illuminate shadows, moving shadows! He was not alone! The shadows shied away from the light of the stone in his hand as dim as it was. Fear gripped him and the light dimmed even more. The shadows moved toward him. A hand formed in the blackness and reached out to him, asking — wanting — what?

The light from the crystal was now very dim. As the light flickered, the hand reached more boldly — for the very crystal itself. He grabbed his hand back with the stone in it, his heart pounding in his chest.

"No you can't have my light!" he tried to shout but managed only a raspy voice. He thought about the girl in the meadow. For just a moment he forgot his own plight and worried for her safety. Was she ok? Or would she come down the hole looking for him. The crystal blazed to life in his hand, its light cutting through the darkness, sending the shadows back down the tunnel.

The boy retreated in the direction that he thought was back to the meadow, holding the shining crystal out, to guard his retreat. He walked backward, looking now and then to see if anything followed him, until, without warning, he tripped and the stone went flying from his hand. The light from within the crystal quickly dimmed to a point that it was barely discernible on the floor of the cavern.

Shane jumped to his feet and lunged to retrieve what he had dropped, while the shadows closed in about him. As his hand touched the crystal, a strong arm circled his waist, lifting him off his feet.

FIVE

Even in a state of deep meditation, Arbrin was awake to his duty as a Guide and Protector. He sat rocking in time to the drum, and his eye caught a movement on the other side of the circle, closest to the large tree. He saw the two children step around into the light, and disappear through the entrance in the trunk. There was no time to inform the rest of the Council, just time to act. He bounded across the circle and followed the children down the Spirit tunnel. He knew that haste was imperative - time in the Spirit world is not linear; it does not always follow a set pattern. His only hope was to come out below, sometime or somewhere close to the destination of his two young charges.

As luck (?) would have it, he came out on the far side of the grassy meadow. Not a soul was in sight, however Arbrin sensed the presence of the girl, and fixing her in his mind, stood next to her in a moment. She sat cross-legged on the ground, her eyes closed. Before her was an opening into the ground from which a stream gushed forth. She broke her concentration to look up at Arbrin.

"Shane fell down there," she explained breathlessly.

"I tried to call him back, but he doesn't come!" She looked very worried.

Arbrin knew then, whatever had happened had been one of those quirks of fate called destiny that places a being somewhere they are meant to be. Otherwise, the children could not have gotten anywhere near the tree without his knowledge, and the boy would have instantly come back at the girl's summons. The opening was too small for him to fit down, so Arbrin used the same method that he had used to come to where the girls now sat. Both times, he was able to concentrate on either of the children, and go to their side.

Arbrin had to accustom his eyes to the darkness in the next instant. When he did, he saw the boy diving across the tunnel, to grasp a glowing stone that provided a faint light in the gloom. Arbrin was also aware of shadowy beings advancing as though pulled by the dimming light. These beings could steal life-force from anyone that did not know how to protect themselves. The boy's hand touched the crystal and Arbrin was at his side, scooping him up. The Guide quickly transported the boy and himself back to the girl in the meadow.

The boy and girl hugged one another while their tutor issued both of them a warning not to let go of each other's hand. He said with a wry smile: "I'm not taking any chances that Shane may have some other reason to be here today. We've learned enough for one day!" A Guide must not only be ready to guide and protect; it seems that he too must be ready to learn.

Once all three travelers were safely back in the forest, Arbrin asked the boy to tell him all that had transpired before he had been rescued. Both children talked excitedly, until Shane finished with: "And this is what I brought back."

The boy showed Arbrin the crystal that had caused so much trouble in its acquisition, but had also protected him.

"You were meant to have this stone." Arbrin explained to the boy. He produced a cloth bag, while telling Shane: "After you clean the crystal in the pool, keep it in this bag. A crystal is an important healing and meditation aid."

Shane washed the crystal in the pool in the middle of the forest glade. Along with the Spirit tree, the pool was of special significance to the Shamanistic Council and anyone who visited the forest. The children played in the shallow water and as they both grew, the pool grew with them.

Arbrin taught them that whenever they had a problem, they should gaze into the water, and quiet their minds - letting their mind become like the calm unrippled surface of the pool. He also taught them to drop stones into the water, as a way of letting go of things they no longer needed. With the calm undisturbed, mind the answer, or a way to find the answer would rise to the surface. Later, as they were able to understand more, Arbrin taught them to look for the cause of the problem in the water's reflection. Knowing that they would see their own image, he chuckled out loud:

"This does not mean that you cause problems for yourself knowingly," he assured them, "it simply means that you cannot see past yourself."

Arbrin and the grandmother adapted the lessons to meet the understanding of the children. They kept the promise of making the "lessons" fun. He and the grandmother also encouraged their pupils to follow their own intuition, to learn to listen to their own "voice." Sometimes, these self-initiated lessons proved tough - as with the unplanned journey down the Spirit tunnel.

Shane sat up in his bed. The boy awoke from a nightmare in a cold sweat. It had to be a bad dream. He still shook from its lingering influence, but he could not remember much of it. All that remained was the memory, as silly as it seemed, of one of his relatives who had quite innocently peered through a piece of stove pipe to frighten him when he was a small tot.

Shane would check the next morning with his mother, who confirmed the stove pipe story. He kept his reason for asking a secret. A dream, or a memory, of someone peering down a "tunnel" at you, is not something that nightmares are made of! Even the lingering cloak of darkness - that hid the real dream, should not be enough to put such dread in the mind of a seven year old. It was the hidden, the unknown, that troubled him. A resulting fear of the dark would follow the boy for some time. In the meanwhile, he got out of bed and moved the coal oil lamp from out in the hall way, nearer to his door, to dispel the shadows.

SIX

Shane blinked his eyes. The sunlight was brighter all of a sudden.

"Don't you think its natural magic the way the water refracts the sunlight and creates rainbows?" The young girl at his side always noticed beauty in nature. She was unusually bright, with a vocabulary quite advanced even for a child nearing teenage. The two children lay on their stomachs gazing into the pool in the middle of the forest.

This was quite a different forest than the one in which Shane had gone to sleep in only moments ago. He had mastered the art of travelling to the dream forest about a year ago, through meditation. He was recalling less of his dreamtime during his "normal," waking life however. Upon asking Arbrin about this, his teacher reassured him that this was necessary to enable the boy to cope with the reality that he was living in at any given time. Arbrin also told him that his "lessons" would be available to him when he needed them. It was not the lessons that he was afraid of losing; it was his friends.

"I wonder what will happen in the future for us."

The boy spoke more to himself than to his friend, as he attempted to clear his mind and focus on any images that might appear on the calm surface of the pool.

"Arbrin says that the future is uncertain at anytime, because it depends so much on the choices that we still have to make," she said. She answered the question that he posed, although she knew he did not expect her to.

"Still," she continued, "if it's also true that time is only something made up by us, as the old Shaman says, and yesterday and tomorrow are part of now, there must be something that we can find out? It can be very confusing! What do you think?"

He did not seem to hear anything that she had said; he was so deep in concentration. His mind quieted, becoming like the surface of the water. Images started to swirl before his eyes. Tall buildings came into view, only to be replaced by the darkness of an underground cavern. A shadowy hand pointed at him - or rather past him. He was about to exclaim that he hoped this did not mean he would have to go back down the Spirit tunnel again, when he saw himself, sitting alone on a hillside. Suddenly the image of him in the pool ducked. A black shape as large as a small airplane swooped out of nowhere and flew straight upwards from the depths of the water toward the surface. He jumped back from the edge of the water in fright.

"What did you see?" The girl asked him, in alarm.

He breathed a sigh of relief.

"Wow that was too real! Maybe I shouldn't try to see the future after all until I understand more. I'm afraid that someday I might forget this place and how to get here. I might lose all of my friends here, especially you and Arbrin. It's so easy to think of our time here as only a dream, when I'm awake back home."

"Don't worry, I'd come after you again." She reassured him. "I think we're better off living in the moment of now, as Arbrin taught us."

"You're probably right," he agreed, cautiously bending over the pool again.

"Look here, I can see myself asleep by the creek back home! What a strange feeling it is, being in two places at once! Have you ever tried this?"

"No." She answered. "I haven't ever seen my other self in the pool. I don't remember much about home when I'm here. I just know that one day I woke up, or went to sleep —whatever — and I was here. Arbrin told me once that is one of the reasons that I learn so fast."

"I don't understand." He looked perplexed.

"All that happens here is built on what you believe, right?"
He nodded.
"So if you don't have old memories to tell you that magic does not work, it will work for you, and at least it will while you are here."
The idea excited him.
"But you told me that you learned to meditate to come here, the way I do now!" he pointed out.
"Right," she agreed, "but I just remember that I know how to get here. It's the opposite of you. I think that I'm more awake in this forest than I am anywhere else. When I want to return home, I think of an old grandfather clock that stands in the hallway back there, and – zap - back I go! For some reason the clock sticks in my mind."
She bent over the edge of the pool, to see what he was looking at and the images changed. Instead of a boy asleep by a stream, an ocean scene came into view. A broad expanse of beach emerged, the surf pounding away with such ferocity, that although there was no sound accompanying the vision, the action of the waves on the sand produced the illusion of the breaker's roar. One solitary figure, a small person sitting in a wheelchair, with their back to the two children, occupied the beach.
"What do you suppose...?" Shane started to ask his friend what she thought the image in the pool represented, but stopped in mid-sentence. Her face suddenly turned pale and she drew back. "Is something wrong?" He asked, as it became his turn to be concerned for her, much the same as she had for him earlier.
"I don't think that I want to see any more!" She blurted out. "This game is no fun anyway, and Arbrin says that learning should always be fun."
Before he could reply, a noise interrupted the silence of the glade, a loud crashing. Someone or something was coming toward them, noisily through the bushes. Neither Shane nor his friend had ever questioned the safety of the forest, the serenity was never broken, so they didn't know what to think. They didn't have long

to wonder, for in about a moment, a ragged furry animal came into view, plunging out of the trees and straight across the clearing for the boy. The girl gasped in alarm, as the creature jumped upon Shane, nearly knocking him to the ground. The boy wrestled with the animal, laughing all the while.

He exclaimed:

"Streak, old boy, how did you ever get here?"

Then he turned to his friend who was beginning to imagine he had lost his mind.

"This is my dog, Streak. I didn't know that animals dreamed the same as we do."

The two children laughed as the dog ran back and forth, between them, barking all the while. The appearance of the dog made both children forget the incident around the pool. When the dog calmed down a little, the girl turned to Shane.

"I'd like to run. Do you think that Streak will bother the other animals here? They're all so tame."

"Only one way to find out," he answered:

"I'll hold him while you call a deer."

Her natural ability to communicate with the animals in this part of the forest had led to her "calling" a deer to accompany them whenever they jogged or ran, for fun or exercise. Sometimes a majestic buck answered her call, but this time a small fawn responded, poking its nose inquiringly out from behind a tree. The forest had the same calming effect on the dog that it had on every other being, or was it a case of the dog being "ready" for the forest that he came there? Either way, Streak did not attempt to chase the deer, but accepted its presence non-chalantly, much to the relief of the children.

The young girl lived to run! She was in her element when she was running through the forest and spending time in the company of the animals that lived there. Today was no exception; she could hardly wait to be off — still, she paused, knowing that something else should be done first. But what?

She turned to Shane and said:

"There is something I must tell you today."

She leaned and whispered a single word in his ear - his face brightened with understanding. In the next moment, she bolted and was off through the trees with the small deer at her side. The boy and his dog followed. Although he had not a hope of catching his friend, they always enjoyed the chase.

They stopped now and then to rest and catch their breath. When he was old enough to notice that he still became tired, or out of breath while in the dream forest, Shane reasoned that there must be more to tiredness, or for that matter maybe even sickness, which happens to your body. "How much of it originates in your mind?" he began to wonder.

The girl was in a particularly mischievous mood today. Just when the boy thought he was about to catch up with her, she would sprint on ahead, close on the heels of the fawn, playing hide and seek with the boy and his dog. As they ran on and on through the forest, the trees about them changed. The stately pine was replaced by a wide variety of other trees, some of them ragged. At times, Shane found himself having to jump over fallen tree trunks. The forest began to resemble any other woods that the boy might have found back home - except that the dense undergrowth added a touch of wilderness and uncertainty to the area, giving Shane an uneasy feeling.

The boy and dog stopped for another rest. The dog sat on its haunches, his tongue lolling out, panting in the heat while Shane listened for any sign of his friend. The forest was quiet, except for the far off calling of some type of bird. The dog abruptly came to attention, as though hearing something that Shane could not. A low rumble came from the animal's throat and in the next moment, he tore off through the trees at a right angle to the path that they had been following. The boy felt compelled to follow, since he was uncertain at this point as to whether the girl had doubled back to catch them by surprise.

"Was it his imagination, or had the already quiet woods taken on a deathly stillness?" Even the birds had stopped calling. It was as though nature was holding her breath.

Shane stopped at a small rise in the ground and his blood froze at the scene before him. In a small clearing about one hundred yards away, a drama was being enacted. The girl, his friend, knelt with her arm around the neck of the deer. She stared directly into the face of a wolf, a mere twenty or so feet away. All that separated them was Shane's dog, his hair on end, trying to look twice his size, growling deep in his throat. Most of the show on the part of the dog was bravado, however, because the dog was still only half the height of the wolf. The wolf barely acknowledged the dog's presence. Instead its gaze was fixed upon the deer.

For a brief moment, the boy was also transfixed. The wolf took one step forward and the dog growled louder. Shane knew that he must do something, but what? Then he recalled something that Arbrin had said:

"There are no coincidences, everything happens for a reason."

Several noteworthy things had taken place at the beginning of this day, one of which included the dog showing up in the forest. Shane's friend had picked this day to let him in on a secret. The boy cleared his mind as much as was possible. He then filled it with memories of his friend; memories of times they had played together, strong memories, emotional ties. He had to be sure that what he was attempting would work - he might only get one chance. When everything felt right, his mind and his mouth formed a name, the very name she had confided in him that afternoon.

"Kitt. I would like it if you would call me Kitt."

In the next instant, Kitt and the deer she had held onto stood beside him, a safer distance from the conflict with the wolf. The wolf blinked in surprise, looked at the dog and snarled. Then, he backed up a few steps, and disappeared like a grey ghost into the surrounding trees.

Before the girl could thank her friend, or either of them had really recovered from the shock of all that had transpired, a familiar voice called them to alert. Arbrin appeared beside them.

"The surprise will soon be gone and the wolf will come back," Arbrin cautioned. "It's best that you all get back to the pine forest. Shane, please collect your four-legged friend and we will go."

The trip back to the glade with the pool and the Spirit tree was relatively quick and simple. They all held on to each other, the two friends grasping onto the animals - and remembered the safety of the pine forest. This aura of complete calm and safety was the feeling that Shane "hooked onto" when he meditated to make the journey to the place of dreams. Now he had found a place in Dreamtime that could be just as threatening as some of parts of his everyday waking world, if a person was not in harmony with his or her surroundings.

"If you walk in balance within yourself, no place in the universe will feel threatening to you. Wherever you are, you will know that it is your choice to be there. You will no longer be a victim, but a Spiritual Warrior, taking part in an incredible adventure that we call life!"

These words were spoken by an old man of the Council later that night, as the day's happenings were discussed around a campfire. The children only partially understood their meaning at this time. Life did, at times, seem to be an adventure; but much of it still seemed to be happening to them haphazardly, catching them unaware.

"Do you really mean everything that happens is our choice - even being sick and dying?" It was all too mind-boggling for Shane to understand. This was not the first time he was faced with this question, nor would it be the last.

"Perhaps—," Arbrin spoke up,"— you are still too young to really appreciate this lesson. You will, in time, see most sickness as a sign that some part of our life needs looking after. Let me tell you a fairy tale to show you what I mean."

SEVEN

"Once upon a time, there was a beautiful young princess and a handsome young prince," Arbrin began.

An old Indian man sitting next to Shane around the campfire playfully nudged the boy in the ribs. Shane pretended not to notice, as Arbrin continued with his fairy story:

"These two thought that they would live happily ever after if they never grew up. As they played, however, they found that life was very boring if there was no adventure in it. So they decided to go looking for adventures and found that they were learning from these adventures. At times it seemed they were lucky to live through some of these adventures, but they did not want to stop enjoying each new day and the wondrous things it brought. The only part that was a downer," Arbrin winked at Kitt, concerning his choice of words, "we can use more upbeat vocabulary — after all, this is a modernized fairy tale!"

"The disturbing part of their lives was that frightening things happened to them, just when they least expected, and without any reason that they could see. It seemed beyond their control. They had been told that their world was a magical place; but if that were so, why did they not have a choice - except to learn the hard way. Wasn't life and learning supposed to be fun?"

"Who was working the magic?" Arbrin asked, and then continued.

"One day both the beautiful princess and the handsome prince fell into a deep sleep, in which they were both suddenly awake.

"Which is the dream, and which is the real world?" they both asked at once. In one world, people did not believe that magic could work, so it did not....or so it seemed. In the other world, people believed in magic and it did work."

"What is the difference?" they both wanted to know.

Being the adventurous types, they decided to try an experiment. "Let us try to remember the feel of magic at work - the way it does in the place of magic. Both of us can remind the other about what we really know, so that we do not fall asleep in the non magical world."

The experiment worked, only too well. When the young prince saw his world through magical eyes, he saw more than he wanted to see. He saw a terrible dragon swoop down and carry off many of his friends and family. Where the dragon took them, he did not know; but when he realized that he was seeing the future, he did not want to see any more in case it might be real. Because of this, he would not have his friends and family around him anymore. So he immediately stopped "seeing," as nearly everyone else in the world had. He said to himself so much that he did not want to see, it affected his eyes and he soon needed glasses. Very soon he could not even see many of the friends that he had feared losing.

A similar thing happened to the young and beautiful princess. There were also events in her life that she did not want to see. She decided to be awake only in the place of magic, and not to remember the so-called non magical world. She even forgot how beautiful she was in the non magical world, even though she was the same person in each!

As luck, or magic, would have it, this fairy tale is not finished. There is a possible happy ending: The prince and the princess, who now seemed to live in different worlds, because each did not want to see the whole truth, were visited by a giant. This giant was tall enough that he could see far, far away in many directions. The giant could not see forever, but he could see far into many lives. He saw many people, including the prince and the princess that would not accept responsibility for the use of magic and their lives; pretending not to see the truth. These people pretended so hard that they even fooled themselves.

The giant took pity on the prince and princess. He knew that they both enjoyed life and had tried so hard to learn. He told them a riddle, which, if they were to solve it, would help them escape the problem of being separated, and make them free to enjoy more of the adventures of life.

"This riddle is named: The Traveller", Arbrin explained.
"I am a traveler. But I have not gone.
As I see myself start, I can see myself done.
Awake with the moon, while asleep in the sun.
Am I the dreamer? Or a dream of someone?"

The fairy tale and the riddle completed, Arbrin turned to the children. He smiled at their perplexed looks.

"The fairy tale might give you some hint why everything seems to be '"happening"' to you," he told them.

"Do not try to figure out the riddle completely. The answer is not something that can be said fully with words. When you think that you have the answer, talk about what you are feeling at that moment, but be ready to let your answer lead you to the next question."

The old Indian Shaman, that had earlier kidded Shane, stroked Shane's dog and said to the boy:

"It looks like your four legged friend will be coming to stay with us for a while." He looked directly into the boy's eyes with a gaze that implied more than he had said. His face was kind, but the boy avoided his eyes and said nothing in return.

Unlocking the Wisdom
(Between You and I)

The Lie
By
Steven WinterHawk

Between you and I
It's not just the telling
That hurts
It's the believing
That is passed along
With the whisper
Of the Lie.

When I was told
My grandmother died
I rushed outside
In the middle of the night
I fell to my knees
On the wet grass
And I prayed.

I prayed that it was not true
But between you and I
I believed what I was told
It was not until much later
I met my grandmother
In a dream
That I became aware of the Lie.

What? – I asked God
And whoever else that
Would listen
What is the reason
For this Lie?
Between you and I?

EIGHT

When Shane awoke, it was dusk. The small woods were rapidly filling with encroaching shadows. Although he assured himself that there was nothing to fear, the call of a loon sent shivers down his spine. Some shadows appeared to move, reminding him of something that he blocked - a memory attempted to surface, like a bubble rising to disturb the calm surface of some clear pool of water. He called to Streak and set off for home in pursuit of the loping stride of the dog.

"That dog! He's never still," Shane thought to himself as he recalled that the dog had recently taken to chasing cars.

"Why should that bother me more now — out of the blue?"

There was something that he could not remember, try as he might, about the dog — something important. He attempted to keep the dog in the house the following week, or at least away from the road that passed within about one hundred yards of his home. He had to give up. You cannot pen in a farm dog. It was an unfair thing to do, especially when he could not recall why.

On one particularly humid day, shortly thereafter, the boy and a friend were tossing a ball over a shed to each other. Shane was on the side of the shed away from the road. He stopped for a moment, and removed his glasses. He bent over a nearby rain barrel, to splash some water onto his perspiring face. Something moved in the water — at least something appeared to move! He stepped back, but curiosity made him look again, his glasses still dangling from one hand.

A scene, so familiar that he gasped and stood transfixed, came into view. A boy and a dog sat together on a grassy hill top — a picture of serenity. In the next moment, the boy in the rain barrel vision ducked. A large dark shape swooped towards him and his dog. When the dark shape vanished, the boy sat alone.

Shane ran for the front of the house, knowing that he would not - could not be in time. The screeching of a car's tires stunned him with an impact that stopped him in his tracks. He did not even have to look, he could not bring himself to look. His father ran from the house to curse the driver who had killed his son's dog.

The boy stood in a daze. A feeling inside told him that the dog was not dead. He refused to accept that the animal was not alive - somewhere, but where? Life plays strange tricks sometimes. In his dazed condition, he would have searched anywhere. A relative came by a short time later and Shane hitched a ride to his Grandparent's house. He was not quite sure why. Was he attempting to run away from a truth, or was he still looking for the dog? He was confused.

It wasn't until his father, who followed to pick him up, arrived, that some sort of realization hit him. He broke down and cried, before replacing his eye glasses, which he had been clutching in his hand since the dog's accident.

A split occurred that caused a further separation of the part of him that was to live in the dream forest, away from his logical self. He did not really quit "seeing," but rather pretended that he could not.

NINE

Shane lay flat on his back under his favourite shade tree on the front lawn of the ramshackle dwelling that he and his parents called home. Like many houses that his parents rented, the outside resembled any rundown shack that you might find on any Indian Reserve. Inside their home, however, was always a spotless indication of his mother's tenacity. She never accepted the old adage: "you can't make a silk purse out of a sow's ear." His mother was never idle! She never sat still, except while she was reading. He had many fond recollections of stories that she had shared with him, through reading out loud when he was very young.

Shane had been taught to read by his mother, before attending grade school and he was never seen without his nose buried in a book of some kind - unless he was taking part in his second favourite pastime, daydreaming. As soon as he was old enough to earn a few dollars allowance by cutting wood for the family cook stove, he lived in the fantasy world of comic books and science fiction.

The science fiction pocketbook that he was reading this day absorbed his attention as usual. A combination, however, of the warmth of the sun and the flickering of the sunbeams through the tree branches overhead, made him increasingly drowsy. Finally, he succumbed to the desire to catnap, resting the book over his eyes. Peacefulness, and a sense of complete security, soon led to a familiar feeling that settled over all of his body. He "hooked onto" this feeling and his "automatic pilot" took over.

"I've been waiting for you to answer the message that I sent to you. It sure took you an awful long time!"

A Spark of the Fire

Kitt stood in the clearing near the middle of the pine forest, her hands on her hips in a mock scolding manner. Both of them were fifteen now, if you were to measure time according to the logical, "real world." Shane knew without saying that any scolding from his friend had to be play-acting. She never had an unkind or negative word for anyone. Her bright, happy outlook on life buoyed his spirit every time he stepped into the glade and in no time at all, he was laughing and feeling amazingly uplifted.

"I was sure that you had forgotten how to get here! I was about to come after you again."

Kitt continued, with a twinkle in her eye: "Maybe I should have sent you a "'wake up'" call earlier!"

She laughed at her little joke, knowing that Shane only remembered the forest these days when he daydreamed, or was in a meditative state during his normal waking hours. He was still able to make the journey during some night dreams as he had as a child, but his conscious, waking mind convinced him that the time spent with Kitt and Arbrin in the forest, was "only dreaming."

"I can see why we are drawn together," Shane told her. "We are two sides of the same coin. You forget your other self when you are here, and I have trouble accepting this place as real when I am not here. If it weren't for you, I just might forget this place for good."

Kitt blushed, confiding in him that he was also the key that kept her on track and working toward sorting out why she chose to not remember her "other home."

"My only connection is a memory of that old grandfather clock — maybe time is also part of the puzzle, as well as knowing that both of us live in those different worlds."

Listening to her speak and seeing her blush for perhaps the first time that he could recall, it struck Shane that he had never thought of her as anything more than a close friend, nearly a sister, and they had grown up together. He was starting to notice girls, but was extremely shy and withdrawn around them. Kitt had never seemed the typical "girl" as Shane saw them.

"Let's ask Arbrin, if there is some way to know both worlds like when we were little," he suggested. He had already guessed the first thing that their teacher/guide would say:

"To do what you ask, you must be able to face the truth in both worlds, without turning away," Arbrin answered. "Children can do this because they are so trusting and have so few fears, until adults convince them differently. I do not say this to put down your parents and other adults. Everyone has their own unique way of seeing life; that is their truth."

"Mankind—and womankind," Arbrin added, with a smile "have gotten together as a whole and decided that there is only one reality. Those who open their minds enough to let in the belief in magical realms are ready to see more. You are such beings. All that you need to do is to relax that strangle-hold that most people have on their minds, and pay attention to what is really going on, moment-to-moment. The minute that either of you see anything that shakes you, you immediately shut down—please relax and trust."

Arbrin had hardly ever given the teenagers a lecture in such a serious tone. His face changed quickly back to his normal smiling self.

"Above all," Arbrin continued in his regular light heartened manner, "do not feel pushed for time. It will all work out if you relax and treat time like you did as children. Enjoy every moment, especially those that you spend together. This will help you both, as you have already discovered. The universe works mainly on Love."

Both of the youngsters looked slightly uncomfortable, while Arbrin laughed, enjoying himself immensely.

"You are hooked on the everyday concept of the word "love". He explained: "There are many meanings for the word, but they all have the basic root in Spiritual Love. The best example of this is the ways both of you have trusted and worked together since you both were little children. Enjoy this relationship as it is. Do not think that it has to be anything else."

Shane breathed a mock sigh of relief.

"I didn't think that I was ready for marriage yet!" He joked, and received an elbow in the ribs for his effort from Kitt who also laughed out loud.

Arbrin also chuckled. "You have passed a major hurdle—a test, which is one of many that involves both of you and your special friendship. There will be a time that both of you will forget all about me, this forest and all that you have learned here, although I will still guide you in ways that you may not recognize. When this happens, it means that you are ready to put into action, in the logical world, the lessons from the dream world. In truth, you will not really forget, and your main link with other worlds will be your memory of each other."

"Other worlds?"

"Do you mean there are other worlds that we might visit someday?" Both of the teenagers asked the question nearly at the same time.

"Yes - no one knows how many. Probably as many for each being that they can stretch their beliefs to include."

This last bit of information really excited the teenagers.

"Then the fairy tale that you told us about two people going on all these adventures and travelling to far off worlds did have some truth in it." Kitt observed. "I guessed as much, but it was mostly a feeling I had inside."

Arbrin smiled. "All fairy tales have some basis of truth, or teach some lesson for those who are wise enough, and innocent enough to see."

"Is it possible that Shane and I have already met, or will ever meet somewhere in the "real" world?" Kitt wanted to know.

"Which "real" world are you talking about?" her teacher inquired, with twinkle in his eye.

"I'm sorry," she laughed. "I should have been clearer. I mean the logical world that most people think is the only real one; where nearly everything is physical and earthy—oh—you know what I mean!" Kitt became momentarily exasperated, trying to make herself understood. Arbrin and Shane both laughed and she joined them in appreciating the joke.

"You are starting to understand my riddle. When reality and dreams both start to seem real to you, you are on the verge of realizing a truth. You must both remember, at this point, not to try to think it out logically, or you might cease to believe what you now know to be true. Your logical world may even be turned topsy-turvy. You must accept that both realities are right, in their own particular way, for you to walk a balanced path."

"Now to answer your question: At the present, the two of you will not meet in the logical world, unless you both work out many problems and relationships that you have now, and are planning in your probable future. However, the future is a matter of choice, as I have taught you, so do not discount anything. Besides that," Arbrin smiled slyly, "you are both here together now; and believe me (you must already suspect); this is as real as you might wish it to be!"

More than a year passed quickly by in the "outside world." The young boy and girl turned sixteen, and approached their seventeenth birthdays. One day, Arbrin came to them with a mysterious look, one that he reserved for his major announcements.

"Come with me," he said. "I have something important to show you."

They both followed their guide and teacher to a path they had not seen until today. "Things appear when the time is right," Arbrin reminded them. "Follow this path and see where it leads." They followed close behind him, and soon came out at the edge of the forest.

"Do not question, just tell me what you see," Arbrin instructed.

"There's a big city out there!" Both Kitt and Shane spoke at once. Sure enough, beyond the fog-like mist at the edge of the forest, modern buildings reared their heads, skyscrapers reaching towards the sky. A very large, sprawling city.

"We have seen this city – your grandmother and I, in the distance for some time," Arbrin explained. "The very closeness of it and the fact that you both can plainly see it has confirmed something for me. It appeared here only this morning. This city resides in what you may call another reality, one that both of you are meant to meet. This is an answer to questions that you both asked me one morning, concerning whether you would ever meet in the world outside this forest. This answer was waiting for you to be ready for it. Sometimes a verbal answer to a complex question, as you had asked, is not enough to understand. We must sometimes experience it."

Neither of the youngsters could see any relationship between what he had said and their questions regarding their ever meeting each other in physical reality. Arbrin was quick to say that he could understand this.

"But you soon will. Within this world that you see before you, lives, shall we say counterparts of yourselves. Before you let this confuse you, let me explain further. This is another dimension, like the forest, another step outside your physical world. Many people in your logical world live there, experiencing life in a slightly different way than they do in their waking world. The old Shaman might even say, "walking a different path.""

"Some people might remember this world as you do the forest," Arbrin continued, "as a dream - they might even be helped to solve problems in their daily life by what they recall. Another term to describe this place that I am talking about is a parallel world. I ask you again, to refer to my riddle, before deciding something is 'only a dream.'"

"What are we to do there - how do we get there? Can we just walk out into this city?"

Shane and Kitt both had many questions.

"Hold on," Arbrin laughed. "One question at a time. First, those young people that are similar to you — if not another you, have come to a certain point in their lives of awakening. They have earned the knowledge that you will take to them by your going there."

"Think about the possibility of what your grandmothers and I have told you. Don't attempt to decide whether you believe or not; just expect something to happen— and it will."

TEN

"The fault, dear Brutus, is not in our stars. But in ourselves, that we are underlings." She closed the book she had been reading – Shakespeare's Julius Caesar, and pondered the recent newspaper article about Stephen Hawking. Hawking was definitely not an underling! He was a young genius, who seemed to be eclipsing Albert Einstein's Theory of Relativity, explaining it in good hard mathematics. The article described Stephen Hawking's work in terms of the new discovery of Quantum Mechanics. Hawking had just written "*A Brief History of Time*," and was working on "The Theory of Everything". The article went on to describe a young man who was bound to his wheelchair, and as his theory was being formulated, his body became progressively immobilized by the disease that had struck him down in the flower of his youth.

The young girl dropped her hands to the wheels of her wheelchair and turned herself around to face back into what had once been her family's summer house. The breakers roared behind her, but she was oblivious to anything but the thoughts that were running through her mind. Her world was changing, and so was she. That was at the top of importance – in her mind.

The wheelchair had been her only companion on the old veranda for nearly as long as she could remember. There she sat, watching the sea and contemplating her fate in life. Her father had died in the car accident that had left her in the wheelchair when she was a very small child, and her mother had elected to live in the summerhouse year round. All she really remembered about the accident was her mother screaming:

"It's your fault! If you had only known enough to sit still!"

Her mother had regretted the outburst almost immediately, but it stuck in the child's mind. Perhaps it had contributed to Katherine not caring to try to get well, when the doctors later said there was a chance that she might walk again if she had the determination. She asked her mother about the accident later. Her mother explained that she was very energetic as a child and would not sit still, even in a car. Consequently, in the middle of a business trip that her father took the family along, she began to jump up and down on the back seat. Both parents tried unsuccessfully to calm her. Katherine's father reached back to sit her down. He had been driving at the time, and took his eyes off the road for just a second. That was all that it took for the car to swerve and hit another car head on.

Katherine remembered her mother's hysterical words, spoken before the doctor could calm and quiet her. The child was being wheeled down some hospital corridor at that moment. Her mother tried afterwards, to do everything she could to make her daughter's life easier, but Katherine refused to take any interest beyond the wheelchair and the seaside.

Katherine could hear her constant companion, the grandfather clock, ticking away just inside the hallway, as she wheeled past. She stopped before the full-length mirror hanging beside the ancient clock, and shook her hair over her pale shoulders. It pleased her to see the fire sparkle within her honey colored hair. Katherine's hair always possessed a shimmering life to it. She was a close cross between a blonde and a red-head.

"You know you're not all that bad looking."

She mused: "If only—?" At one time, she was given to extreme bouts of self-pity, but lately she had begun to feel prettier; more worthwhile. She wheeled on past. Her mind slipped back to early memories: of dreams that had gradually taken on such a reality of their own that she eventually had to simply let them be, lest they be swept away by doubt.

A child who could not run and play had a lot of time on her hands. During a daydream about some fairy tale her mother had read her, Katherine had dozed off and woke up in the forest. In the forest she could run and play, but she became lonely for someone her own age to play with. She went looking, with methods taught by her grandmother, to find a playmate. Life from that point became a blur passing by her mind's eye. Here she was - ready to make the jump of belief again, but this time with company.

"Mother, I'm going to my room to nap now, OK?" she called to her mother who was in the kitchen.

"Alright dear, are you going to have some supper with me later? I'll wake you if you want me to."

"Thanks anyways— I'll eat when I get up." Katherine answered. She led a life of doing nearly anything she was allowed, according to her own timetable. It had taken her a long time to get her mother to agree to this arrangement, but the older woman finally conceded, that: "Even a cripple should have some control of their life," as Katherine put it.

With the aid of leg braces, the young girl had long learned to maneuver in and out of bed and some other places that she wished to, when it suited her purpose.

Stretched out on the large bed, Katherine contemplated Arbrin's words, while she counted down her meditation. Having made the journey to the forest so many times in the past, it was relatively easy for her to reach a semi-trance state so familiar, from which she could feel the pull of her destination. A comforting darkness closed about her and the bedroom fell away.

A pool in the forest:

How deep the pool
Within that forest glade.
How ever green
The stately pines that shade.

The wind still whispers
Promises we made,
The moss remembers
Where I reclined to gaze...
Into her eyes...
Into the pool...
How deep the pool...

...winterhawk

ELEVEN

"Oh God!"

"Kitt— you really belong here!"

Shane expelled his breath, in a moment of inspired amazement - of enlightenment. Shane and Kitt stood on the path near the middle of the forest. Caught in transition while returning together from a distant world, the sweet memories of their reunion were fading fast from his mind. This forest, this enchanted place, had grown in their hearts and minds, and had become so important to their lives, in ways that they might never have imagined. The numerous visions they had relived would now prompt them to wonder at its time compressed mystical reality.

In that very second of his exclamation, the object of Shane's wonderment and awe, stood materializing at his finger tips. Kitt was no longer a teenage girl child, but now a young woman. This slender, young woman with fairy-like beauty held his out-stretched fingers in a clasp that was closer to a caress. Her fine honey golden hair, with its touch of fire, billowed over creamy white shoulders, floating, moving in one of the many breezes. These same breezes filled with pollen from dandelions and flower blossoms, swayed the pine boughs, and whispered their secrets to him, in the stillness of this mystical forest. She was the same young woman Shane had witnessed growing up with his own eyes, except that now, she possessed an aura of enchantment as the very forest itself.

Perhaps it was the transition, of passing from one world to another, or perhaps it was the emotions still present. She was, after all, the same young woman who had surrendered her love to him, as sure as he, minutes ago, had held her in his arms.

"Or was she— how could she be—?" Even now, Shane was struck dumb with self doubt: "How could he even dream of this vision, this magical creature as being his lover, his Soulmate?"

"You really belong here!" It was all he was able to say.

"....And so do you," she answered him.

She was still dreamy-eyed and maybe she did not really comprehend his meaning— or did she?

And now the memories faded. Forgotten by him were the years of growing up together. Forgotten as well the many times they had played as little children, laughed as teenagers and shared secrets few people would dream of - much less consider the dream as real.

"I— I don't know—?" He was at a loss for words, until the forest and the beautiful young woman with arms outstretched faded from his eyes.

* * *

Shane lay on a hospital cot, outside the operating room. Waiting for the anaesthetic to take effect, he mulled the past year over in his mind - it had flown by so quickly. He recalled leaving high school quite clearly, but after that, everything was nearly a blur — especially the last half of the year, following Christmas.

In his mind, he relived his memories – back to the moments that had brought it all down.

His father's magical transition following the changing of the family name had run its course. Edward had appeared to have solved his drinking problem, and with the new name, had gotten a full time job at the Gypsum plant in Caledonia. Then a new car followed, and the land and house that the family had rented off the reserve in Nanticoke, had been offered to Edward to buy, at a modest price. It all seemed magical – change your name, and change your future. But old habits die hard, and the alcoholic addiction was not that easily conquered. His father gave in to his old fears, and turned the offer down. A year later, the local Government decided to build the Nanticoke Hydro Generating Station on the land and the magic had been lost. Shane's mother meanwhile was becoming progressively deaf while listening to so many broken promises.

For his father, it was old hat – and he seemed happy, staying drunk and on the verge of losing his job and his new car. But it was not finished for Shane. One day, during lunch hour, he left the school with thoughts of joining his long time Native friend in a game of pool just off the main street in Hagersville...

The events that had changed his family's lives were playing on his mind, when he woke up in the hospital with memories that did not match or make any sense at all. Bits and pieces floated back to him. "Where had the time gone?"

A greater part leading up to this moment had been spent meditating, drawing and writing his usual obscure poetry. He now recalled putting in a few months working part time on a dock in a small town named Port Dover. Cheap pay perhaps, but there was something there that felt right - something he could never put his finger on!

And then came the tobacco harvest— tobacco was still grown as a major crop around the village of Simcoe and the town of Delhi Ontario in 1966. Both rural communities being located close to the Six Nations Indian Reserve resulted in the yearly tobacco harvest becoming Shane's regular summer job.

Now some six months since Shane's last dream journey to the forest, he found himself in direct contact with the plant he had been taught to use as a bridge, a link to the Spirit world. Shane finished the season of the tobacco harvest by taking a job in a plant that bailed and shipped tobacco out of the village of Simcoe itself. For only one evening shift, eight hours, he handled bales of tobacco, where he stacked and moved the bales from here to there.

Before this, his first— and destined to be his last shift in the tobacco plant was over, Shane came down with, tonsillitis so severe he could barely talk.

"I think it is past time for you to get those tonsils out!" Shane's father had advised him when he picked Shane up after work that evening.

"Funny," Shane wondered to himself at the idle thoughts that pop into a person's head at moments like this— "what happens to your mind while your body is under anaesthetic? Is your mind asleep as well (whatever being asleep really means), or do you go somewhere else until your body wakes up? What a silly thought!!!"

A spacey feeling was settling in. He blinked. "That light up there in the ceiling is getting as bright as the sun— now, what was it I was thinking about? Oh yeah— something I read in a science magazine— that must be where it came from— or was it on TV?"

He struggled to remember: "going somewhere— and then I remember something about sickness being related to an imbalance between our physical and Spirit bodies—that even sounds a little far out to come from a science magazine— I'll have to ask— that's even crazier— and who the heck was I thinking of?"

The hospital gradually drifted away, out of his view. The overhead lights merged into a blazing sun. Either he or the hospital became part of another reality. He blinked against the glare of that sun in a clear, cloud free sky.

Shane rolled over onto his stomach, propped up his chin with his two hands and thought long and strong about the problem at hand. He recognized the forest at once, the pool as well. He stared into the pool, calming his mind, intent on finding some answers. All of his memories of his childhood spent in the forest, with the fair haired girl flooded back.

"How long have we been together—and where do I get some of these weird visions, the darker stuff from?"

Many questions remained unanswered, but these two in particular, had bothered Shane in his quest to understand himself, and his relationship with this girl. Kitt did not appear in what he called "physical reality," yet Shane could see her inspiration within his poems. She was also his constant companion in this "dream world".

Images swirled within the pool. Shane watched a play in which a small boy accompanied a man dressed in a golden robe up the side of a mountain. The winding path was nearly as treacherous as the man in whose footsteps the boy walked. He felt an instinctive uneasiness about the man in the sun colored robe, even as Shane became one with the boy. He knew at once however, that this man was his teacher, or at least would be in years to come. The small boy had been selected to be the man's apprentice.

"If you are to be my pupil and perhaps my helper one day, I must be certain that you will not have a single thought in your mind of ever betraying me. I am about to show you your fate should this ever enter your head."

Having said this, the man pointed to the next peak not far away. He and the boy had reached the summit of the small mountain. On a flat but rocky surface, in front of a cave, sat a small girl, about the same age and the same brown-toned skin as the boy who was Shane.

Information flowed into Shane's inquiring mind. The man who Shane had followed, partly out of duty, and out of curiosity about becoming the man's magical apprentice — had lured the small girl up to the peak. The golden robed man had learned her name, and all he could about the girl. He then used this information to gain her confidence and aid him in some form of hypnotism. Shane's view of the future of this event did not answer another question. Perhaps he had to seek the answer in other ways: did this man really possess any true "magical powers" or had some form of hypnosis been employed on both children that day?

Shane was mentally pulled back to the scene at hand. The boy recognized the girl as a sometime playmate from the village where he had been born. The magician had obviously expected, and waited for this to happen. He raised both arms skyward, and a rift, a hole appeared above the plateau on which the girl played, seemingly unconscious of the man and the boy. The boy attempted to call out— but his throat seemed paralyzed.

Through a door-way in the sky, a huge dragon like creature flew to snatch up the girl, and carry her back from where he came. The magician lowered his hands, and the hole in the sky closed up.

The images swirled again, but before Shane was himself again, he became a man— the boy from the previous vision now grown. He sat on the spot where the girl had vanished. Years of training flowed through his mind, fuelled by thoughts of revenge at first, until he had discovered a secret, unknown even to his teacher. He sat cross-legged in a circle of wooden carved sticks, on which odd glyphs had been etched and painted. Shane recognized the runic symbols that had drawn his curiosity. He had watched a "monk" at a psychic fair do a past life reading with these same runes— for Katherine!

This circle of runes in the vision before him now, Shane felt at once to be another method of Spirit travelling. He was a driven being, driven to search for a childhood friend with dedication— evolving now beyond vengeance, leaving no stone of knowledge unturned in his quest.

Shane found himself, now an observer, apart from the man in the vision. "How deep do these visions go?" he wondered. "Does this Quest have an end?"

A soft hand touched Shane's shoulder, bringing him back to the reality of the path in the forest.

"You've always inspired me to be my best!" he told her.

"And you have always remembered me and found some way to find me again." Kitt knelt and put her arms around him from behind. There was no incrimination in her voice, at him for experiencing his self-doubt. She was happy to see him again, but sad that he had not returned sooner—sad they had to part at all.

With a sense of fear, of repeating his "disappearing act" upon seeing her again, Shane turned slowly around. "Had she anticipated this fear? After all, she could read his thoughts!" If so, she had dressed appropriately— attempting to downplay her mystical appearance. She wore a loose fitting white blouse, and blue jeans. He sighed and hugged her.

"This is me, my true Spirit self would never forget you. Nothing can separate our Spirits," he stated emphatically. "We are also living keys for each other's lives. When I can see my Spirit body and its life as being more than a dream, I am sure I will be in balance. Then the self doubt will never be able to sway me, and I can be with you here or anywhere and whenever I please."

"I thought that I really had it for just a little while one day," he continued, in a reflective frame of mind: "I was lying under the shade tree back home, and I mentally wrote this poem about us. The poem is called *Dreamtime*— "He recited it for her.

She repeated the last two lines: "Their dreams were blessed, with time compressed, into reality."

"What did you mean when you said that you thought you had it? It sounds to me like you saw through the veil!"

"No," he shook his head. "I might have, until—well, the last half of the poem came out, and my mind shut down." He recited the last half with a somber face. "There are my old fears (in the last half of the poem), my fears of losing you. If only I could believe that I have already passed the hurdle, and forgotten you for the last time - but it still gnaws at me; you remember the reading that the gypsy at the psychic fair gave us?"

She agreed: "We both have other lives to face."

Kitt sat down beside him on the grass at the side of the path and the pool and stretched out at his side, leaning on one elbow. "I've given a lot of thought to that myself. Look into the pool again—what do you see?"

"I see myself," he laughed, not fully understanding.

She giggled girlishly: "no—yes— I mean tell me what you see. What does your reflection look like?"

"Well... I am tan-skinned, with long hair— could be I look like an Indian. What do you think? I feel the adventure, the excitement and unlimited potential, when I'm this person, when I am here with you!" He began to understand.

"And what do you look like back home in the physical world?" she encouraged him.

"I'm a short haired boy— man with Native blood— a trifle boring perhaps." He laughed at his description of himself. "Well, maybe not boring but I am awfully quiet—a dreamer."

"And which is the real you?" She smiled and a thought crossed her mind to change the smile into a frown. "Instead of answering that question, can you tell me who is the real me — the one you see in front of you, or..."

Shane knew she avoided mentioning the girl in the wheel chair, the other self Kitt chose to forget.

"They are both you! And here in the forest — this is the real you, and me that we can be if we chose. Remember what being in that "other world" taught us: we are each other's reflection!"

"Am I really that girl — she must be grown up now— the one in the wheel- chair? How can I go back to being her, although I know I must?" Kitt sighed.

"You must learn to love her," he said: "as I would, if I were to meet her. I think you're being hard on yourself. We both have a lot to face - we'll be able to grow if we first love ourselves for who we are. I remember something Arbrin told us: that, one day we would forget this place and him, to live our other lives with the love we have learned here. The only consolation is we will still be Spiritually linked."

"If only..." he drifted into thought, he became lost in her eyes. He then continued the "conversation" through the link of their minds: "If only we could be as children again, innocent—able to run off and play together for eternity. But no, I want to see, and grow, and Love." Thoughts of another city, another world took him back to a cold winter night.

"We can always be children," she assured him: "that part of us will always be. To enjoy each other's company in a more complete way, we must become more complete within ourselves."

"You read my mind!" he joked. He touched her mind again, with a very human thought.

She returned the thought: "What would happen...I've wondered myself, what would happen to your doubts, and my incomplete self, if we?"

Shane could see in her eyes, along with their Spiritual bond, that she was also wondering if making love would bring them into the harmony they both wished. "Cannot love conquer all? Is this a human failing, wishful thinking?" He was ready to accept the responsibility that came with true Love, but a thought remained in his mind:

"What if?" He heard her breath quicken, her heartbeat sounded in his ears in time with his own. Their minds were as close to being one, without losing the joy of love as expressed through being two.

"Can Love conquer all?"

"Yes, Love can conquer anything!"

"Even doubt and feelings of incompleteness?"

"Love dispels doubt, and heals incompleteness!"

"Can Love reach across time and space?"

"True Love knows no boundaries!"

"And can Love come in the form of a dream?"

"Love is that which dreams are made of...."

The fragrance she drew through her presence in the enchanted atmosphere of the forest filled his senses— the part of him that remembered his separateness.

There are few sounds like the mournful call of a wolf in the wild: eerie, lonely - a call for kinship, sometimes much more. The call shook the young lovers out of the serenity of their moment. It touched more than their ears. It sounded again, again, before the call received an answer - from its own kind.

"In the woods, outside the forest!" Shane lept to his feet, extended his hand to help her up also. He felt drawn by the call, summoned.

"Hurry...." Kitt also sensed the urgency:

"They're headed for the peak where we did our vision quest."

The special spot she meant was a bit of land jutting out from an otherwise flat top of one of the higher hills, a plateau, and a peninsula jutting out into a sea of clouds. The first visit for both of them to this special spot had been as separate beings. Each had visited the spot to partake in an old tradition that the Native People call the Vision Quest: where they seek a personal vision from the Great Mystery. Shane and Kitt returned many times together to meditate and enjoy a breathtaking view of the valley below from the precarious edge, a drop off into thin air.

When Shane and Kitt came within sight of the special spot, "they" were there—waiting for them. Out on the edge, his back to the chasm stood a proud buck. The majestically antlered deer stood with his head down in a menacing gesture. The buck faced the pack of wolves that had run him to this point, to the edge of life and death. Wolves and deer stood frozen in time—to catch their last breath.

The leader of the wolf pack advanced. Shane recognized the large grey wolf. He was sure it was the same animal he had first encountered that day shortly after Shane had first learned of his friend's secret name. That day, a small female deer, a fawn protected by Kitt, had been the wolf's objective.

Shane had glimpsed that same wolf a number of times after, during games of tag, in which Kitt had lead the young man in endless pursuit. He recalled seeing the wolf again, after they had achieved the balance enough to run unharmed through the wilder parts of the woods outside the forest. The major difference today was that the wolf had always appeared to Shane and Kitt as a singular creature, alone. Now the wolf stood at the front of a pack of its own kind.

The ghost-like leader did lead the pack to this spot, but somehow it still stood apart, advancing now, as the other wolves held back watching, taking cue from the lone wolf's actions.

Recalling how he had rescued Kitt and the fawn, Shane tried to call the buck, to transport the animal to safety. Nothing happened, the animal refused to come.

"You cannot influence in any way what they do not wish, any man or even animal that is firmly balanced on their own path!"

His guide's words rang in his memory, but became lost in the young man's jumbled thoughts. Shane could only think at this moment of stopping that which he did not understand. The drama being enacted was real for the animals involved — but had he caused it, or had he drawn the scene from another moment, which waited for his commitment to acknowledge it. Either way, this meant facing a decision within himself.

Shane had sat in meditation on the very spot many times, so it was easy for him to travel via thought, to stand in front of the buck in hope of touching the animal and thus transport it to safety. To accomplish this, the deer would have to let Shane touch it. The animal lowered its head and warned him not to come any closer. He stood between the deer and the wolves.

Shane turned as if to somehow influence the action of the wolf pack. The large grey wolf met his eyes and briefly halted. The message of their eye contact was clear, though not in human language. The wolf began to creep forward again, until, like the uncoiling of spring - he leapt.

Shane blinked — in the next breath, he found himself in Kitt's arms. He shuddered, and buried his head in her hair, against her neck. Above them on the cliff, the leap of the wolf carried the buck and itself, as one, over the edge to their death in the valley below.

Kitt hugged him close and stroked his head, comfortingly. "I "called" you back," she whispered. "Please understand - what I did, was for both of us. If you truly became who you are to be with me before, that was an act of innocent love. It might be your decision, but I couldn't let you take the chance again. I might lose you, or we might be parted longer than either of us would care to imagine. You don't have to die, to prove to the world how much you care - or especially to prove anything to me."

Shane hugged her and kissed her in appreciation. "Thank you," he said: "I guess you did the right thing. After all, I gave you the right to try and help me anytime you feel the need, the moment I let you into my heart."

"There's only one way open for me," he sighed in resignation. "You were right about that earlier—although we hoped—I've learned too much to do otherwise. I'm ready to face my truths and my life—freely and with as much love as I'm capable of. It's the only way I can be with you forever."

Kitt shook her head in agreement:

"That goes for me as well. Somehow, I must heal the other me—become more of a whole being again." A look in her eyes carried a message, which because of Shane's personal decision, he was able to interpret.

"I don't know why I didn't see it before," he exclaimed: "Men and women —you and I represent each other's questions and answers! For me, you are the clue to my wholeness—and so much more! So many of my answers can be found through my closest friend—my Soulmate."

"It works both ways. I guess you can see that too?" she hugged him. "Or you wouldn't be thinking what I'm reading in your eyes? But are you sure?"

"Yes, he hugged her back, to assure her of his intentions." I would like to go on a healing journey to the Spirit world to help you - if you will let me." Shane spoke as one whose personal decision had now lifted a veil, as confirmation that his choice had been correct.

"You mean to say that you would do this for me?" She hugged him even tighter, knowing how much Shane feared the dark world of the Spirit tunnel.

"And for me," he reminded her. "I've got a lot to gain in this too. Let's go and tell Arbrin and your grandmother what we have decided to do. I'm almost sure they'll approve." Then he felt the tug of the anaesthetic wearing off his physical body. He had journeyed to the forest by chemical means. The tug, like some choices we might make in a moment of passion, if ignored might have been final for his physical body. Having made his decision, however, he no longer feared that he couldn't come back. His commitment to her would bring him back. Shane assured Kitt of this. In more ways than one, they had made the leap together this day, into the Mystery, and together they had survived that leap — of Faith and Trust.

TWELVE

"You can make the journey to the Spirit world the next time both of you come to the forest."

Arbrin spoke to Shane, who sat beside him, to his right around the Council campfire. Kitt sat beside the Elder Shaman woman who she knew in the Dream as her grandmother and her personal instructor - much the same as the old Shaman who taught Shane in matters dealing with his Earthly Shamanistic path.

"There is much preparation for something like this," Arbrin continued. "You have much to think about before attempting this, no matter how good your intentions. Do either of you have any questions for me? Tonight is like the night before your graduation, if this were an earthly school. We are here to celebrate."

"How can we celebrate before the final test?" Shane wanted to know. "Suppose I fail to do what I am setting out to do? Isn't this presuming too much?"

"There is no fail or passing mark in this school, or in life itself. We graduate to our next step of evolution, when we instinctively know we are ready." Arbrin smiled at him. "The healing journey that you are to undertake is your own decision entirely. It was both of your decisions to step forward with trust - to leap into the unknown with faith."

"You decided it was time to face your real selves; to "see" and act with responsibility. You have decided to walk the balanced path of the Shaman. To take this step, you must realize that the tests, and there are more to come, will come to you when you are ready. You decide when the time is right to grow. Your Higher Spirit Self is always in harmony with the Great Mystery. You are a Spark of the Living Fire. Your Higher Self calls the tests, to help you grow in Love. Think what this means to your lives back in the "physical world." Will you choose to remember this truth? If not, who will you or any of us, blame for our fate?"

Arbrin smiled. "Do not for one minute take any credit away from who you are right now. This is a big step - an accomplishment to be celebrated!"

"There is something that still doesn't seem fair!" Kitt spoke up: "Shane and I are so right for each other. Someone called us Soulmates. Yet it seems we have no choice but to live other lives on earth, forget each other, possibly even marry someone else?"

"If you think about all that you have learned about time and space, you must know that you will never really be apart." The woman who was Kitt's personal teacher spoke up. "Also there are debts that both of you have incurred through ignorance of karmic laws in the past, that have to be balanced."

Arbrin turned to Kitt and smiled. "Tell me," he asked, "what do you see wrong with this fellow sitting across from you? What would you be able to tell him about himself that needs improving?"

Kitt blushed and looked over at Shane. "I'm sorry I can't really tell you much that I don't like about him, because I love him for who he is."

Again Arbrin smiled knowingly, and turned to Shane.

"And what about you, do you notice any imperfections, can you tell this young lady some way that she might improve herself, so that she could evolve?"

"Kitt is the most perfect friend that I could ask for; I also love her for who she is. I would not ask her to change at all." Shane's face also colored, as he answered.

"For this reason," Arbrin told them, "we learn to love and interact with other people. It is true, your Soulmate will always bring out the best in you; but to become further evolved, we must also learn to love everyone unconditionally. Most beings will love many others in the process of finding their Soulmates. Some people that you are attracted to, will be similar to that one being that will make you feel whole. For this reason, many can be unhappy with love. They have such high expectations for the one that they love and marry. You may never be sure in some of your Earth Walks, if this person you are with is your Soulmate or not. Your lofty expectations may not be met."

"In truth, we should recognize that there are no mistakes, and the person that we are attracted to has a lesson to teach us. As I have already pointed out, to evolve to the point that we are ready to experience the unconditional love of our Soulmate, we must be willing to give that love to all other beings."

"I am not telling you," Arbrin was quick to point out, "that we should let anyone degrade or mistreat us. There is little to learn from that type of relationship, except that we must have a very low image of ourselves. This relationship might be a sign that we need to learn to love and respect ourselves. If there is no way that this person is going to change their attitude toward you, then respect and love that person for himself, and say good-bye."

"Just leave?" Shane was taken completely off-guard by this statement. "What about if the reason that they are treating you so badly is due to karma from some past life?"

"Then you must do all that you can to right any wrongs through love, and a mutual understanding that it was a much more ignorant you that acted wrongly in the past. You should try to make the other person aware that you are now a more loving and contrite being, and it is to their advantage to forgive. As I have suggested, you should do everything possible to make it up to them, except submitting to physical or mental punishment. If all else fails, then return through meditation to your safe place, which for you and Kitt is this forest. On this journey, invite this person's Spiritual Self along. Once here, mutual forgiveness can be arrived at - but remember you must be sincere for this to happen."

"We—" Arbrin indicated the Council, and himself — "do not believe that the old "eye for an eye" belief in karma ever did anything to further the evolution of sentient beings in this or any other universe. Revenge only perpetuates the cycle of karma, and no one evolves. If a being forgives and acts in unconditional love,

A Spark of the Fire

the cycle can be broken. Hence the old adage: two wrongs do not make a right."

"Everyone get up, and stretch your legs." Arbrin instructed. "We have a surprise for you. Two of our group will entertain us with a song, after we have a break."

Shane wandered about, and finally sat down again next to his Shamanistic teacher. The old man grinned and threw the younger man a pear: "Here; have something to eat, they're sweet and good for you."

"So ask your question," the old man prompted him.

"You knew that is why I sat down here beside you?" Somehow, Shane was not surprised. "Do you also know what I am going to ask?"

"More or less," the Shaman replied, followed by his contagious grin. "The answers that Arbrin gave both of you are all true and right, but they are never enough for young people in love — so, go ahead, ask."

"About all of this karma talk and loving other people?" Shane began: "— why can't we, Kitt and I, just work together and help other people that way. At least we would not be apart."

"Think about what you have just said." The old man replied. "Now that you know that each other exists - and that you are not just part of each other's imagination, nothing can keep you apart, except your own denial of love in the universe. I can say very little about this, except that it involves facing your true self, and that brings us back to the moment at hand."

"As for working together, that will never cease. I am going to ask you a question, that I am sure Kitt's teacher friend is asking her at this moment."

Shane glanced over to where Kitt sat talking with the old Shaman woman. Kitt looked up, and they exchanged smiles.

"Suppose when you go back to 'normal reality'" the old man spoke: "you were to meet Kitt there, and although you had done all that you thought possible to help heal her, she was unable to heal herself. If you met her there, still confined to a wheel chair, would you look down on her, as though she were a failure and not evolved as you? How would you react? Think very carefully before you answer this."

Shane stole another look at his friend. She met his gaze again, this time with a questioning look on her face. The look was quickly replaced by her familiar smile. He knew that it was more than a physical form that attracted him, it was the understanding—and something nearly like electricity or fire that passed between them.

"I would understand that she was handling her life lesson, as best she could; that there is no such thing as failure. I would love her for who she is at that moment. Then I would offer more help, but not force it on her." Shane surprised himself at the depth of his answer.

"I could not have answered it better myself!" The old man slapped him on the back. "This is what the connection with our Soulmates teaches us. Now you must apply this answer to everyone else that you meet in your life. You must be able to love other people — even those that are obstacles — with the same degree of compassion that you would give this one person who makes you whole. All other beings deserve this love also."

Shane admitted that this was a big task and he could see now, the reason that one day he would have to go back to "normal reality" — not just clear up karma, but to face himself.

"Don't look so serious!" the old Shaman told him. "You resemble the Wolf in one of Arbrin's stories. In case you have not already guessed, this Wolf is one of your totems. The Hawk represents your personal Spiritual self, and the Wolf is your physical self. This is the reason for the conflicts that you have involving Wolves and your mistrust or even fear of most dogs. You must also learn not to judge yourself too harshly. At this time I give you your name and this."

The Shaman produced a necklace made of alternating Wolf's claws and Deer antler. Shane felt sure that it had been collected from the scene of conflict, where he had tried to stop the wolf pack from killing the buck. In the middle of the necklace was a sunburst, made from the feathers of a Hawk. The old man hung the necklace around the younger man's neck and announced solemnly, but quietly:

"I give you the name that you were born to in the Sharing Dream that some think is the only reality. You are to be called: Wolf Dreaming Fire."

Shane felt, this must be what it was all about. Now that he was given his name, formally, this must be a graduation. Even as he experienced the high of the moment, he heard the old Shaman say:

"Now that you have some idea of who you are, I will give you a hint about who you can become."

Shane became alert. "What could he mean? Everything seemed so complete. Well, nearly so. At least I thought I was on the road to facing who I am —and that's what it's all about. Isn't it?"

"What do you mean—?" The young man stammered.

"First, I must tell you again not to take everything so seriously. Now that you have learned to act responsibly, do so. But enjoy life as well." The old man grinned, and then went on talking, kindly but firmly:

"Learn now to trust your own actions. You might act in a manner that might be considered incorrect at times, but, on the whole, you will not act in a hurtful way now that you know better. We all make small mistakes. It is the big ones that are more difficult to correct. There are secrets you are beginning to "see," that will enable you to enjoy life and the relationships within it as they should be enjoyed: There is a part of you that is thought to be of the physical by most - but is more than physical! You can journey in this "body," even to the so-called higher worlds. This part of you, knows itself as your Spirit form, and, at times, is close to being as one with the spiritual energy we Shamans call fire. This Fire is also Love. It is the warmth of Love that we share with our own kind, like the Wolves and the Deer. Love has many forms from respect, to passion —but love is most kind, when it is warmly given."

Shane sat very still and took all of this in, until he felt compelled to speak:

"This love that I've learned to feel. Isn't this real Love? I walk on air when we are together or for that matter every time I think of her."

"It is real. It is one of the warmest types of love, but you have denied its full expression in the past. That is why you identified with and feared the Wolf, which is your physical totem. But I have not given up hope for you." The old man grinned and winked a sly wink.

His pupil looked down at the wolf-deer necklace that hung about his neck. He had been holding it thoughtfully the whole time. The young man dropped his hand away quickly, wondering how much the old man could really "see".

"—And that is why," the old Shaman continued with a serious but gentle face, "that, although you learned to express love for Kit in another world, when the comforting warmth kindled into a flame, you stopped short of fully recognizing your Soulmate in the "physical reality." This is the responsible thing to do! Consider also an important part of the lesson of facing yourself, as learning to trust yourself. You have learned to listen to the voice of your heart, so that your actions will be correct and loving. Learn to experience the fire that is the Spirit!"

Arbrin called everyone back to the Council Fire. Shane could hardly keep his mind still, it was so full, with so many questions that he had thought to be answers—that would lead to questions not yet asked. Still the surprises of this night were not over yet.

"In honour of this occasion," Arbrin began, after everyone was seated again: "two of the members of our council have composed a song. They will now sing and play it for you."

After the song was sung and everyone had finished applauding the two performers, Shane asked Arbrin if the Council held this type of celebration for all of their pupils. It made him feel important or special.

"Yes, we do," Arbrin replied. "Everyone is equally important. Occasionally, however, the celebration is something else. We feel the need to commemorate some pupils' accomplishments in a grander manner when you know the person is so close, yet does not see the love in life, or take time to smell the flowers."

While the song was being sung, Shane noted that Kitt was now left alone to her own thoughts. He went over to sit by the fire beside her.

"So, what did your Shaman friend have to say" she asked Shane.

"He gave me a Spirit name. He named me "Wolf Dreaming Fire."

"Neat!" She congratulated him. "So what are you going to do now that you have your name Mr. Wolf?"

"Don't forget the rest of my name," he replied, surprising her with a quick kiss. "I am Wolf Dreaming Fire."

"No doubt," she smiled. "And whose fire are you dreaming about, if I may be so bold as to ask?"

"Your fire," he replied, for the moment just as bold.

"I think I like that," she returned the kiss. "But I seem to remember a story about your people's customs of courtship. I remember that if you want my hand in marriage (and the rest of me that is attached), you will need to give my mother and father some ponies in return. How many ponies do you think I am worth?"

He thought for a moment, and was inspired by a memory, if that is what it was. "I will give your parents one pony in return for their daughter's hand."

"Only one pony?" She pretended to pout.

"Yes, but this is a special pony, like no other now or ever has been. This is a Spirit Horse that can take them to the Stars."

THIRTEEN

Throughout the cleansing ceremony, Kitt stayed at Shane's side. She joined him in the sweat lodge. They both were blessed by the smoke of the sweetgrass. She also shared the pipe with him.

The cleansing ceremonies were complete, and the sound of deep rhythmic drumming reverberated in the night as a steady heartbeat in the forest. Kitt sat across from Shane, around the campfire.

"There is one more thing that must be done to ensure your safety and the success of your healing journey." The old man who was Shane's Shamanistic teacher, looked first at Shane and then to where Kitt sat beside her grandmother.

During the ceremonies Kitt had been dressed in buckskin leggings and an elaborate doe-skin vest. She had explained to Shane that the costume was made with her help, by her teacher. The old woman had assured Kitt that no animal had been killed to make the vest and trousers. "Any animal skin we now use for clothing comes either through the animal dying a natural, evolutionary death, or an "accidental" death. We know there are no coincidences. We realize this is then a "gift" from our four legged brothers, to remind us of the fragility of each physical body and the new evolved skin our brothers and we will wear after death."

A question passed through Shane's mind which he forgot to ask this time around: "Obviously the word 'death' does not hold its same meaning for these dwellers of the forest, but how long might life be if lived here?" He bagun to think of these beings as immortal. "However, evolution of the form must happen here also, but how—when?

A Spark of the Fire

In the light of the campfire Kitt stood up, and turning her back in modesty, removed her doe-skinned vest with the help of her grandmother. Shane appreciated the view of a slim, white back, shining in the flickering light. He quietly drew in his breath as Kitt stood with her back to the campfire, nude to the waist, until she slipped a white cotton dress over her head. Turning around again, she held the vest for him to see. She blushed slightly, knowing he had watched her every move — unable to look away, drawn as a moth to a flame. Her thoughts sent to him were far from scolding, as his were far from shame. Kitt walked around the fire to give the vest to him.

"You must wear this 'Ghost Shirt' your friend has helped her grandmother to make and that your friend has worn. This is part of your friend now that she has worn it close to her skin. This shirt will help to protect you and remind you of your purpose."

Shane accepted the vest from Kitt and admired the fine bead work. The Ghost Shirt was decorated with pictures of both their personal totems, Physical and Spiritual - animals and birds. He stood and Kitt helped him to slip into the vest. She embraced him warmly before returning to her place on the other side of the fire.

The drum beats gained in volume, pulsing in Shane's ears; touching his body—gently and now firmly, until his personal vibration would be in tune with the Spirit World of the shadows. A chill came over Shane's frame, as he received his last instructions, this time from the grandmother:

"Remember to think only of your purpose, by concentrating on the shirt we have made you. At first we were not sure that you should ever journey to the Lower Spirit world again. Your first encounter was an omen. Your Grandfather and I have seen a mark on your back from the day you came to us, and that first journey showed the mark to be a danger to you. I am not attempting to frighten you; just urging extreme caution. Every sign now points to success in this healing journey you now undertake. The balance hangs upon your reason for making the voyage: it is this reason, this undying love that you must concentrate on to ensure your safety and success."

Every step was a beat of the drum as Shane entered, for the second time in his remembered life, the Spirit tunnel through the hole in the ancient tree. The entrance was large enough to let a young man crawl through and then stand erect in the darkness.

Already the dank, moist air within the tunnel seeped into his body, while he waited for his eyes to adjust to the darkness. Shane knew that if he were to turn around, the entrance would be far behind, even though he had barely stepped inside. Before the dampness could gain hold on his body, he became aware of comforting warmth dispelling the dark feeling; warmth emanating from the vest, being supported and fuelled by memories awakened within his own heart. He was ready to go on.

In the dimness, mostly with his feet, he sensed the gradual downward slope of the tunnel. With so gradual a slope, thoughts that the descent might take a lengthy amount of time ran through his mind. Then, as he proceeded, the ground dropped steeply away and he had to move cautiously - so that he did not slip on the treacherous rocks under foot.

A cool wind touched his face, blowing from somewhere far below and at times he imagined forms moving past him in the tunnel, out of the corner of his eye. When he turned to look, no one was there. With the wind came a feeling over his skin, as though now and then, feathers brushed lightly against parts of his body. His concentration wavered for just a second; he lost his footing and plunged down the shaft.

In what amounted to more of a slide than a fall, Shane ended up in a small cave at the foot of the tunnel. He sensed almost immediately that he had reached his destination. From his sitting position on the ground, he saw a hand reach out to him, as though to help him to his feet—he knew better. A traveler of this lower world, Shane had been cautioned, about accepting any form of help from these shadow beings, except that which you have come looking for—as it might require some kind of payment.

With great resolve, he gathered the vest about him, his sense of purpose once more strong in his mind. He declined the offered hand and returning to his feet by himself, standing on firm ground again.

"Now—how to let this shadow being know of his mission—?"

Shane held his hand to his heart and once more envisioned his purpose, the need for healing. He thought with love, of the young woman he wished to help, by returning that which the shadow beings had taken. In a moment of weakness, she had given up to them a portion of her soul, something she had felt unworthy of possessing.

Sometimes a Shaman will make a healing journey to this land, when he has sensed the need. He will attempt to retrieve a part of someone's soul, or ownership to their essential life-force that they have given to this shadow world. This part of the self must be given for these beings to be able to possess it. Shaman the world over have discovered that many people, in moments of grief, fear, or doubt, often give away a beautiful part of themselves to some "shadow hand"—and once given, it is difficult to regain.

Shane held his hand out this time with strong resolve, not in giving but with unmistakable intent, to that of retrieving in the name of Love. So intending, he could not be refused.

The shadow being's hand was turned and it pointed to the far side of the cave where a radiant light illuminated the wall. There, barely growing, but undying, was a delicate flower which proudly dispelled the gloom. A small garden was illuminated by this one brilliant, crystalline petalled blossom.

Shane put the shadow being out of his mind with a strong intent and bent over the glowing flower. He carefully dug around and under the roots, so as not to leave any of the plant behind. He also was careful not to cause any damage to this delicate symbol, of love and whatever else that might be part of a young girl's soul. While he unearthed the flower, Shane began to wonder how he would transport this fragile bit of life back up the Spirit tunnel in one piece. He knew that he did not dare to let even one petal of the flower become lost or damaged.

"There is only one way—" he resolved. Having completed unearthing the plant, he stood to remove his vest to wrap it in. Even the thought of taking off the Ghost Shirt, brought a chill. A cool breeze touched the nape of his neck, making his hair stand on its end. As he inched the vest off, a flurry of feathers brushed at his body—gently, making him aware of their presence.

The vest was off in his hand. The feather touches became frantic - then stopped as suddenly as they had begun. There was a presence in the small cave with him, maybe more than one being. He filled his lungs with the cool damp air, ready to proceed with his mission—waiting to see if his audience, the watchers that hid in the shadows, were going to make any further move. He wondered if they were finished testing him, or if they would take any action he might have to respond to. He wondered at the same time how he might be able to deal with these nebulous beings.

Shane was about to conclude that they had only been attempting to frighten him, when something touched his back near the base of his neck; something, or someone with some form of claw.

From within his being, a power surged into readiness, a power whose existence Shane had not been aware of until this moment. This power waited for him to unleash it, to turn and confront his tormentors, to initiate a battle that he felt more than confident of winning. The feeling of confidence originated in his solar plexus, surging with personal power, threatening to strike out with a force Shane could only guess at. This power was initiated by knowledge he had not known was his, until this moment. The claw slowly and methodically inched down his back, teasing and daring him. The power grew.

"This feeling of Power is not connected to my heart!"

This thought struck him even as he hesitated, in the act of striking out. He steeled himself once more with resolve, and looked within his heart to listen to his spiritual voice. Almost at once the vest in his hand and the radiant flower drew him back to his purpose. The claw inched down his back, testing for a second more, and then was gone. The intense coolness of the cave dissipated, and though he still detected company in the small confined area, there was no longer a feeling of unfriendliness.

Shane wrapped the brilliant flower in the vest and with the glow of the petals emanating like a lantern, he made his way up the tunnel, back the way he had come. This time the ground was no longer slippery and the slope did not seem as steep. He was no longer bothered by any of the shadow beings, and his ascent to the world of the forest was easy and uneventful.

Shane stepped out of the opening in the tree, and the drum beats that had accompanied his journey stopped. They had been with him throughout the Spirit journey, but he noticed them most, when the pulsing sounds became silent. The drummer and the rest of the council turned to look at him in expectation. Kitt leapt up and ran to greet him. Before she could hug him, Shane motioned with caution to his bundle. Without a word, he held it out to her.

Kitt carefully unwrapped the precious package. She caught sight of the flower, and her eyes widened - she drew her breath in sharply. "It's so beautiful!" she exclaimed, bringing the blossom up to her face to smell. With a deep breath of the fragrance, she reminisced with delight:

"I remember my home! I remember both of my homes!"

She flung her arms around Shane and showered him with kisses and thanky-yous. Her words, referencing to "both of her homes," held him mystified. Before he could inquire as to the meaning of her exclamations, the two musicians (the woman and man who had sung so sweetly and played the Spirit music) — approached the embracing couple.

"—And do you remember us—?" They asked hesitantly.

The joy on Kitt's face resembled the brilliance of the flower she held to her bosom. She ran on winged feet to hug each of the musicians with her free arm.

"Mother!"

"Father!"

Tears of joy streamed down her face. Shane was struck dumbfounded. Arm-in-arm, the three came to stand before him. His words echoed back at him from months ago. He had spoken with sudden illumination but without full conscious understanding:

"Kitt, you really belong here!"

"You do belong here!" he agreed. For a moment he felt almost cheated, lied to. Had she fooled him all along? Of course not! The very thought was unthinkable!

"Then what—?" Shane began...

"Remember the fairy tale with the rhyme, that I told both of you while you were children?" Arbrin spoke with fatherly kindness: "I have often advised you that these stories hold much truth. Kitt did not remember her heritage, her beginnings, any more than you do at times even now. She did not lie to you. When she came back to the forest as a small child, she did not recall these, her Spiritual Parents, or any previous time spent as the "Sprite" she so aptly nick-named herself—the Sprite she began learning to be."

Arbrin continued: "To us, who remembered her here, she is one of the true Fairy folk, as the "physical" world would call them. Kitt was born of Spiritual Parents in this mystical place. She has spent most of this life with you, learning to be herself, as you and everyone else that the Great Spirit has created, are doing."

"Another riddle for both of you." Arbrin looked at Shane, and then a joyous Kitt. "Most beings in the world, that is, the logical world, think of an important Spiritual truth in the reverse that it actually is—although they know better. Spirit came first, and then created physical form. Can you now guess why?"

Shane answered for both he and Kitt: "Love must be shared to be truly experienced."

Arbrin agreed: "We believe that to be so—even the original creation of mankind was not so the Great Mystery could have someone to bow down and worship him, but so that He/She could experience the Love that is Itself. The beauty of Love needs duality to share itself."

"So how many lives, or lifetimes does it take for us to remember who we are?" Shane asked, not expecting an exact answer to a question he had grown fond of asking.

A Spark of the Fire

"I have once hinted—how many lives and how many beautiful worlds are you ready to believe in?" Arbrin replied.

The female singer and flute player, who Shane now knew as Kitt's spiritual mother, stepped forward and hugged him:

"I am called *"Song of the Robin"*," she told Shane: "We have met before, and my Spiritual mate and I have played and sung for you—for both of you. We wished to bring you both together for your own happiness. We also could "see" that it was part of your path, though your own choice, to restore our daughter's memory of her true spiritual beauty."

The male singer now spoke in his husky melodious voice:

"I am called *"Loon who sings at Midnight."* I sometimes sing in people's dreams, to help them remember. Though my songs sound sad, it is my voice and these songs that bring deep memories to the surface. We are a perfect match, my mate and I — for the bright, happy songs that *"Song of the Robin"* sings, will lighten anyone's day."

"I remember so much more now." Kitt reached out to take Shane's hand. "Growing up in the forest the first time was beautiful, but lonely. I always felt something was missing. Then one evening, my father sang for me, and his song carried me into one of your dreams. I remembered us, and I called out my name, hoping you would also remember. I hope it was the right thing to do - I would still take the chance again." She looked to Arbrin for assurance.

"Who can say what your heart will tell you?" Arbrin spoke gently. "— If it comes from the heart, the voice will never lead you wrong. Sooner or later, Soulmates will remember each other. It may take many lifetimes, some spending only moments together in passing."

"You . . ." Arbrin spoke to Shane" — had already begun a life; had made a commitment to another being, when your Soulmate called out in your dreams. You have been blessed with making decisions based on Love — that, at the moment, were innocent of the responsibility — still, this universe, and all of creation for that matter, depends on balance. Although you were both able to meet outside the dream — at the moment of your births, other compensating lives were begun for both of you in one of the so-called "physical realities."

"Your decisions were based on Love and in innocence, so neither of you is experiencing a set-back as such. You have an opportunity to balance your physical and Spiritual selves, and to do it with the same Love that the former decisions were based upon. It is not the Shamanistic view that the physical reality is some kind of punishment for sins. This life on the Mother Earth is a chance to experience, as you have already guessed, the joy, and the Love that is shared in the duality of male and female, with all our brothers and sisters, man and animal." Arbrin seemed about to say more, but saved whatever this may have been, sensing another choice to be recognized by the young couple. Arbrin stepped aside, as Kitt's and Shane's teacher Elders were speculatively examining Shane's back.

"Arbrin is certainly right about one thing," the old Shaman, Shane's teacher-friend exclaimed: "You have definitely been blessed with the luck of innocence!" The old man smiled a huge smile. "It may be more correct in this particular circumstance, to say it was not luck, but actions based on unselfish love that has been your saving grace."

"Indeed—" Kitt's teacher chimed in. "When we saw the sign of the Hawk on your back, we could only speculate how you would receive this mark. The omens based on the first time it appeared, warned us of danger. We can see probable futures, but we cannot make the choices, or face the tests that were for you and you only."

"You are saying that I was in great danger, if I hadn't acted correctly?" Shane was shaken. He remembered the confident feeling, that he could have triumphed - had he chosen to confront the shadow beings.

"You could have lost much of what you have worked so hard to accomplish with Love-based actions, if you had resorted to the darker side of magic to face your tormentors. You would have won the battle, but would have initiated a war that no one can ever win.

The use of magic for aggression or personal power, only serves to separate its user from his oneness with Creation. It makes him less, and less powerful, because he must then depend only on that personal power that he can store inside himself and disallow his link with the one Great Mystery."

"Soon the very beings that the battle was fought with would become your allies, and you would depend more and more on them, until in effect they would surely own you. You would have given yourself over. It is true; we have painted the worst picture. Some Shaman do manage to walk the thin line, but considering all that you had to lose—"

The old Shaman smiled at his student, then at Kitt. "We were very worried for you."

"—But the mark?" Shane asked.

"It remains on this Spiritual body as a sign that you have passed the test. You have learned "Earth Magic" in a previous lifetime, in which you wished to employ it in revenge against a malicious teacher. Now, you may use it to help others, if that is your choice. This mark now allows you to go unharmed on journeys to the lower Spirit world."

"Ideally, a Shaman will learn to walk in many worlds, spiritual and physical, but try to remain non-judgemental. He will not try to "correct" what he does not understand, because he cannot live someone else's lesson. He may, however act as a true guide, one who may lead someone to the answer the person seeks, by pointing out the signs they may not see, hinting at warnings, but leaving the final interpretation up to the seeker. Please remember this: some of the most powerful healings have been accomplished simply by the telling of a Shaman's story."

"As I experienced this remembering—" Kitt spoke to all present—"the part of me that is Katherine, remembers my other mother in the physical world. I have unanswered questions concerning her early departure from my life. Are any of you able to help me with these questions?" Kitt gazed imploringly at her friends.

"What is the last recollection you have of your "other" mother?" Instead of answering Kitt's question, Arbrin replied with a question of his own. In his role as a guide and teacher—this meant drawing the answer out of the questioner. Should she be ready, the answer will be waiting for the seeker to discover.

"I have a memory and feeling that I would be seeing my mother again and she might answer for herself. Of course! I should have known—I do now—I must go to wherever she can be found to have my questions answered!"

"There is another level of a Spirit journey that you may take, if this is your choice," Arbrin confirmed. "This is a journey to the upper spiritual worlds. One of the reasons you may wish to make this journey is to meet the Spirit of a loved one who has passed on. Even if they have returned once more to the Earth, the Spirit holds the essence of their former self, and can be visited on a higher plane."

"I have cautioned you often in these matters of complicated thinking in logical terms. This is beyond logical reasoning. If you attempt to pursue logical thought to arrive at Spiritual truths, you may get lost in disbelief. If you wish to see your mother, to visit her, you must simply accept the possibility and not reason it out."

FOURTEEN

Shane was only too glad when Kitt agreed that he should accompany her on her journey to the Upper Spirit World. He was sure that Arbrin and the rest of the Council – including her grandmother had foreseen their making this journey together. He recalled the cleansing ceremonies they attended together. There was no one lesson, Shane insisted that either of them could experience that might not be meaningful for both. He was experiencing an uneasy feeling that he and Kitt might soon be parted, and he was not about to let her out of his sight. A part of him also looked forward to meeting Katherine's mother.

The drums were much faster in tempo for this journey. The travelers would enter, as part of the age-old ritual, through the hole at the base of the Spirit tree. The drum beats and the shakers raised the traveler's vibrations, until Shane found himself within the tree itself, in a different Spirit form, clutching Kitt's hand as the two streaked skyward. The speed of their ascent could not have been measured, except by thought. One moment he could "feel" her hand in his, as everything blurred, and the next second, they were in the sky. They were both Spirit birds flying together towards the West, the place of departed souls, and into time itself.

The actual journey was a haze in Shane's mind. He could not even be sure if the body of a Hawk he felt himself within was real, symbolic, or both at the same time. The same applied for the radiant white bird that flew at his side.

The mist cleared ahead, and a distant mountain came into view. On the mountain top, on a small plateau, a woman in green robes stood quietly waiting. Her arms reached skyward in the act of requesting help - perhaps in the form of a vision from the Great

Mystery. As the two Spirit birds flew closer, she reached out in greeting to them.

They descended to stand before her, once more in human form. Almost at once the woman's faraway look changed. Recognition came into her eyes. She was no longer some unknown high priestess from some future (or ancient) race seeking a vision for her people; she was Katherine's mother, and it was her daughter who now stood before her.

"I would recognize my daughter anywhere, even if she visits me in the form of a bird! A mother's love will not let her forget her children!"

The woman cried very real tears of joy, as she hugged her daughter, the older woman's long black hair blowing out behind her on that windswept mountain plateau. The moment of mother-daughter love created an oneness within Shane.

When the tears of reunion ebbed down, Katherine's mother greeted her "son-in-law to be". She felt kin to Shane, but couldn't put a label to the relationship. She began then, to tell her story as simply as possible:

"As you might know, in my lifetime, the earth was the site of a growing terrorist threat. And to make things worse my generation abused the earth, taking and not giving back. Many of us felt responsible for this threat upon our children's lives. I realize now that there are many levels of awareness, and many worlds that think of themselves as "The Earth." Perhaps what happened to us may be taken as a warning to others and it may not need to happen elsewhere.

One day, far into the future as you would know it, but far in my past now, Our sun went Super-Nova and its power was so devastating, it created a chain reaction throughout our solar system. A good many events led up to this test for humanity—a test that we failed."

Katherine's mother continued with the story: "I recall hearing of a "big bang" theory as the beginning of our universe. This must have been similar to the magnitude that many scientists envisioned as birthing our universe. We went to sleep and dreamed a new dream—and woke up on this planet that had been deserted – mined out and raped by its former inhabitants – left fallow, you might say. And in our Dreamtime the sun of this world was re-kindled with new life.

It is believed that the original people, who colonized this world, came from an ancient race. And when it became unlivable for human kind. They went to the stars searching for a new home. Though this happened a long time ago, the story of our new world's birth has been passed down — and as to its accuracy, we can only look to the sky for any substantial proof."

"But what does this have to do with your presence here?" Katherine asked.

"This world, as you see, is still in its infancy - forests and grasses are still like hairs upon a baby's head. We see it as our duty to pay back, to balance creation. Though we may not have personally neglected and given up on this planet, we were gifted with this new home and have become a race of planters, to be incarnated upon this new Earth, to help in its rebirth. Our original ancestors brought with them seeds and from those seeds, trees and grass now grow, which provide more seeds for us to sow and look after. One thing we do not understand, more than anything else, is that, animals started to appear one day. Perhaps our Foremothers are responsible in part for this as well. But we believe that the animals that mankind once wiped out from the original Earth, are now, like us, seeking incarnation here—returning home to Terra."

"Foremothers...?" Shane noticed the wording.

"Yes." Katherine's mother, now with mystic eyes, assured him the phrase came from her now home world. "We are a race of new beginnings—new birth is all around us. Our religious beliefs are based lightly upon a female deity. This is all in the name of a new race of intuitive, gentle, loving beings, of which I am a spiritual representative, a high priestess."

Katherine looked extremely thoughtful, letting it all sink in—an important question had still not been answered for her: "I have come to the belief that time is only relative. Was there another reason, for you to leave dad and I when you did?"

Her mother sighed and repeated the question: "Why did I leave when I did? I could not have answered that question at the time, but now—" she smiled. "This body of mine has learned the secret of Spirit travel. Please accompany me in the form that you journeyed here."

The lady of the twilight planet sank cross-legged to the earth, and soon rose from the top of her head in a Spirit form - a vague bird shape. When the three flew out over the valley, Shane was somehow not surprised to be following a Robin!

They rode the gentle breezes, over forests and meadows, to circle above some people near the base of the mountain. None of the workers looked up; and Shane realized then, that the bird forms, in which they travelled, were for Spirit eyes only.

"They can't see us, can they?" Katherine asked.

"Wait a moment," the reply from the mother sounded in Shane's mind.

Off by himself, one man toiled diligently, planting small evergreen trees on the hillside. He worked intently, with obvious love for his task. For some reason the scene brought a thought to Katherine's mind:

"If only my own father could have loved the Earth enough to work in the garden like this man — perhaps we might have —"

The man looked up.

"He can see us!" Shane exclaimed.

"Katherine," the man below them whispered, "this time I can see you." He stood with arms outstretched.

"Daddy!" This was all Katherine could say. In one motion, she spread her Spirit wings above her head, and alighted on the Earth transformed into her physical form. Where he had sensed Katherine's presence — and saw her with his heart, the man could now see her physical likeness but he could not touch her.

Katherine's father chuckled: "I guess I still have to do a lot of growing. It is still too much for me to take the next step of belief.

With a little patience and understanding on your part - perhaps the next time we meet I will be able to hug you again. If you can forgive a hard headed man's stubbornness, you will be able to hug me all you want back there in time."

"We have all grown a lot since the three of us were last together!" Katherine's mother smiled. "Otherwise this reunion could never have taken place. Now you know one of the main reasons I left when I did. I was fulfilling a promise to your father—to help him wake up, as he would say, in his words. This was not the "supreme sacrifice". I didn't even consciously know the why of my choice. Our Spirits planned this—so that we could grow together."

Shane went for a walk to look around and to think over the words of Katherine's mother, while the family talked and enjoyed their reunion. When he came back, he sensed Katherine (Kitt) was ready to return. This twilight world had made a great impression. Planted within both of their hearts was a seed, a desire to do whatever they might be able to, no matter how little, to promote love and harmony in mankind within their own time. Perhaps they could help to avert the neglect resulting from distrust and lack of love.

"Though it was a terrible way for this world to become what it is today, but it's now so very peaceful," Katherine told her mother. "I am sure we will return. Perhaps we will make this our home one day." Katherine had picked up the thought from Shane, and agreed with it completely. Shane did not attempt to sort out if the thought had been all his, as they were both in harmony at this time.

They left Katherine's father to his task of love, and returned to the mountain top.

"You were seeking a vision as we flew here," Shane noted. "What will you tell your people about our visit, if at all?"

"I have received my vision," the woman answered him. "Though this is an extraordinary happening — the answers — the visions are all around us, if we know where to look. Consider what I am going to tell my people, and wonder not how visions that uplift a race are constructed. I will say":

"I fasted for many days, lifting my eyes and my thoughts up to the Great Mother, the Great Mystery. One morning, as the Soulmate of our Earth rose in the sky; and their daughter, the symbol of his love when he is not present, slipped away to rest from her twilight vigil, I saw two birds fly out of the great beyond. They flew down toward me — and even before my eyes, the two radiant birds alighted on this Earth we are calling Terra. One of the birds, a Dove, became my daughter from birth, and the other, a Hawk, my daughter's mate — they had found eternal love in each other's company."

"My daughter and her mate told me that they felt instantly at home in the harmony of our planet. They vowed to visit us again, perhaps to live with us forever, to enjoy the peace that they found in our world. They then flew back to spread the message of peace and love to people of other lands."

"I will tell my followers this simple true story. Though the wording of my vision might be changed, it will stand as a prophecy of peace for our planet in years to come."

"Anyone can be responsible for furthering Love and Peace. Even the smallest act of reaching out to another, to offer help, or simply to express love and kindness is meaningful—it does not have to become an earth-shaking vision; it is in the eyes of the beholder, the way it touches the heart. *From hand to hand and heart to heart, the seed is passed that will one day grow and cover a world.*"

The woman, who was Katherine's mother transformed during her speech, and became the mystical eyed high priestess again. A parting message reached their ears as they circled, seeking the spiritual winds that would carry them back:

"As High Priestess, I am also the Keeper of Memories. Sometimes I think that I remember too much. Your visit here today has given me faith that some memories can be healed. I remember a world where nearly every race imagined themselves to possess the "One and Only Truth". This way of thinking makes everyone else wrong by comparison, and makes a world of Peace and Love nearly impossible. It is not surprising that the one "vision" that all races did have in common, prophesied of doomsday!"

Her words were now carried on the same winds that bore Shane and Kitt away: "A caution about things planted in the minds that might find their way to the heart: look closely at the prophecies that are told. Do not most people believe in them, although they might pretend not to....? And do you not now know of the strength of belief, especially if it is world-wide? It is wise to be wary of considering prophecies of disaster and destruction more than a warning of a probable future - lest we make them come true with our belief in their unchangeability."

FIFTEEN

"Will this reunion with Katherine's mother be more than a remembered dream for Katherine? She was there with me. I mean really present, though I left with you."

Shane asked the question that pulled at his mind all of the journey back to the forest. Now the two travelers stood watching their friends. The members of the Council were enjoying themselves, eating, sipping wine, and dancing in the fire-light. The young woman who stood and watched the merriment at Shane's side had golden hair. Her hair was as long as Katherine's, but with a slight wave, there was a curl to it. Waiting for her thoughts, Shane noticed the way Kitt's blonde hair caught the light from the campfire.

"You are right," Kitt replied. "The lives of our other selves are at once part of and separate from ours. As I am her, she is me—I have had a feeling—that part of our lives are on hold, waiting for something to happen."

Kitt moved at this precise moment, to step between Shane and the campfire. She turned to face him, and waited. A log within the fire cracked, and sent sparks into the night sky. Her hair caught the light again, and might just have been part of the flame. Shane recalled the "fire," the feeling that had accompanied her presenting him when with the "Ghost Shirt." He now wore the embroidered vest that he had wrapped the precious flower in, but there was another change in her apparel. Kitt had modestly pulled a white cotton dress over her head, to replace the vest she gave to Shane. Now she stood before him, her blonde hair ablaze with the fire-light, clad in an ankle length white dress, with long swaying fringes. He guessed that the dress was made of doe-skin, as was the vest. Shane had not seen her change, yet his eyes did not lie!

The next move came without thinking. Shane guided her to the fire to join in the dance. Soon they were circling the flames, along with the other dancers. He twirled her in his arms in a smaller, quicker circle than the others. Catching sight of the full moon overhead shining down through a cloudless sky, Shane recalled that this particular moon was the last key to the magical dance.

The musicians and their music paused, to draw a breath—for the drum to sense the heartbeat of the forest—and continued...

On bare feet, another couple danced, through time and space, unto the grassy carpet covering the glade in the forest. From the Spiral dance taking place around the fire, Shane and Kitt reached out and met their other selves half way. Four became two, and the circle was completed. The link that had kept them so close—even to making them almost one at times—closed in upon itself.

Throughout the dance, the beat of the drum had increased in tempo, setting the rhythm for the flute and the guitar-like stringed instrument. When the four became two, the pace of the dance was that of a timeless afternoon another couple danced "alone" on a deserted street. In the next moment, however, that breathtaking tempo was surpassed, and yet another barrier breached. While dancing on solid ground, the couple felt themselves drawn upwards, toward the full moon. As in meeting themselves—their Spirits reached out again, to become:

numerous other children, teenagers, adults, and faces without names flashed quickly by—too many in number to know—except that they too were the eyes for Shane and Kitt. It was now too fast, and far beyond understanding. For just a moment now, Shane saw Kitt, as separate from all of this, separate from him, until their thoughts blended and became:

- a wise teacher and guide,
    - a Council of Shamanistic friends,
        - an enchanted forest,
            - and a pool...

The two being now one, for a brief, but eternal moment touched oneness with All—only to fall apart, and like Autumn leaves, float gently back to earth. The second their feet touched Mother Earth, Shane and Kitt were themselves again. The other couples returned via the moonlit path to that distant world—to share warm embraces in another form of the Dance of Love.

Arbrin's gentle voice whispered in the minds of all four young people, barely discernible in the high of the moment, but with a message they would not soon forget:

"The oneness you have experienced is the true spiritual link with that which the Shaman calls 'The Web of Creation', The spiritual fire that is awakened with passion in physical love-making can be another link with the Web, another way to experience the brief touch of Oneness with the Great Mystery, but only if the fire of physical love is transmuted with unconditional Love and complete Trust. All lovers sense this, and seek to attain that feeling of ecstasy—of being one with each other; the stars; and the Universe. There is a reason the Great Mystery allowed this Oneness to be experienced through a seemingly ordinary act of love: we must realize that we are all actually one; all are part of Creation. It is unloving and selfish acts that separate us, and create disharmony."

The forest was silent - except for the drum.

The clear voice of the flute player Shane now knew as *"Song of the Robin"* and also Kitt's spiritual mother broke the silence:

"The music halted, as it does at this moment, of its own accord. Even if we were to attempt to pluck the strings and blow on the reed, no sound will be produced for this Dance. The Drum, the pulse of creation will go on forever. Any further music will be symbolic of your relationship and will be present in both of you as long as you acknowledge your spiritual bond. The music can be sweet and beautiful, or whatever you both wish to create and experience."

"It seems to me, that we have already gone through this at least once before," Shane whispered to Kitt as they sat beside Arbrin and their friends around the fire.

"....Except, the last time we didn't find the time to join our magical friends for a going away party."

When everyone had tired themselves out by dancing, they sat once again to share a small sip of wine. *Song of the Robin* spoke with her clear voice, sounding like wind chimes ringing in the stillness:

"Arbrin—" she implored,"—please tell us one more story, one with a happy ending, before we go about our ways. It will be dawn soon and even the best parties must end."

Arbrin smiled, as though sharing a secret joke, and agreed. He spoke to the Council, all friends, around the flickering campfire:

"The story I am about to tell you will require the help of the two newest members of our Council, as well as the rest of you all."

Arbrin produced a shining crystal decanter filled with a liquid so clear that the bottle seemed empty. Next, he took out two exquisite crystal wine goblets. He motioned to Kitt and Shane to come forward, and handed them each, one of the goblets. He then went around the circle and put a little of the clear liquid in the other members glasses.

"And now the story—" Arbrin began. "This is the story as it was passed down to me by my own teachers, of how the original concept of Soulmates was initiated by the Great Spirit:

At the beginning of time as we know it, the Creator made all things out of Fire. They were part of the Mystery, yet knew duality. Love was shared by all two- legged, winged, and four-legged brothers, including all plants — everything on the Mother Earth. All were aware of being brothers in Spirit. Then, as you know, many forgot the brotherhood, forgot to share their love, even with their own mates within their own tribes.

To remind all of the sharing of Love, the Great Spirit called two of his most loving mates."

Arbrin motioned to Kitt, who was blushing at the attention, and Shane, to step forward.

"I have given both of you crystal goblets to share this Spirit with each other." So saying, the Great Spirit poured a small bit of water from his infinite Source into the glasses, and asked them to sip from one another's goblets in sharing. *"I now make this pact with you and promise - that your glasses will never be empty. The more that you are willing to share with each other and with your brothers and sisters, the more will I give to you.*

Now, pass around the circle—each from a different direction and share this wine, as you have already shared, with all of your brothers and sisters.

At this point," said Arbrin, who played the part of the Great Spirit in the play, *"your purpose is dual"*:

First to make your fellow members aware by example, of my pact, and of their part in this pact which involves being willing to share of the wine that I have also given them.

The Second and equally important part of this journey: as you pass around the circle, something about these, your fellow members of the tribe of the Mother Earth, will remind you of the One you seek—and you will glance across the fire to re-establish contact.

You will meet half way 'round, and rejoice at the reunion before proceeding, each in your separate directions, back to your beginning. Who knows how many times you will go out, until you are aware that you are seeking each other. You will meet again and again until you realize that you were never forced to be apart—but went willingly to learn to Love, as your Creator meant Love to be, and to teach this Love by example. You will teach everyone; and everyone in turn will be your teacher. At that moment, you will meet one last time never to part."

Shane and Kitt met back at Arbrin and the grandmother's side in their part of the story.

Arbrin continued to speak his part, playing the role of the Great Spirit:

"Now, you will go out together, with this Pipe that is ever-burning. Together you will share the smoke, the other form of Spirit, with all of your friends — friends you have met many times. You will be as part of a big family.

And as you pass in a clockwise direction, carrying the Pipe, and sharing the smoke, do not be surprised if you meet either or both of yourselves coming from the opposite direction

I will now confide a secret:

Though sometimes in your journeys you may have felt lonely and sought that which you knew not—you were never alone. Not only did I always accompany and watch over you, but in the magic of Shamantic time, in Dreamtime—at that same moment in time that I first sent each of you out in different directions, seemingly alone—at that very same moment in time, We sent both of you out with the Pipe, together!"

"That was certainly a beautiful story Arbrin told last night."

Shane spoke quietly, as though any word above a whisper would disturb the peace and stillness that enveloped he and Kitt. They were finally alone in the forest. They sat with their backs against the tall Spirit tree, gazing into the dying embers of the fire. They were a scant few feet from the calm, unrippled surface of the pool.

"It still makes my head spin to think about it all, though." He pondered the complexity. "It makes me wonder what, or who is real sometimes — do you know what I mean?" When he finished speaking, a thought crossed his mind; a memory that brought a smile to his lips.

"Yes, I do know what you mean—!" Kitt laughed. "—You mean, like the time you pinched me to prove how real we were, and all of the time; your mind was on more 'interesting' ways to prove our reality."

"You were reading my mind again, weren't you?" he pretended to scold, while he turned to face her, drawing her to him.

"Umhummmmmm—" she answered, as their lips met. It was a long and tender kiss, followed by silence. They gazed into each other's eyes, revelling in the mental spiritual contact that many lovers who trust each other enjoy.

"This is for you, so that you will remember me, no matter how far apart we may be—and until we can be together forever." she whispered—offering him a petal of the Crystal Spirit flower, the same flower he had retrieved from the Lower Spirit world. She continued:

"Keep this, a symbol of my childhood spent with you, which I now give to you with my Love and Trust. Keep this near your heart."

They were in the pool, which seemed so deep now that they had grown. As they dived and swam in the water, his mind replayed images of her—one in particular: she had stood nude, completely unashamed, pausing before diving into the water: She looked for the entire world like the lithe fairy spirit that he knew her to be, and at the same moment, possessing the beauty of a 'physical' woman. Her long golden hair draped over her shoulders hiding not much of those physical charms.

"Are you going to join me for a swim—or what?" Kitt raised one eyebrow, a challenging smile on her lips.

"OK—" he laughed, getting up from the mossy bank. "I was enjoying the view."

She smiled, still waiting.

"This is an enchanted place, you know—" he remarked: "—Especially now, with the sun coming up—and all."

She had left behind her laughter, before he followed her into the pool.

They dove and swam like dolphins, touching, caressing, then laughing when they broke the surface for air. It seemed they only needed to come up for air in this enchanted pool, whenever it occurred to them to do so. He remembered this same pool as being just deep enough for two small children to splash in, at one time, and now it seemed bottomless.

"I wonder how deep this pool really is?"

He gasped breathlessly. She treaded water beside him, her long hair sleeked back, her skin glistening in the morning sun.

"You had better watch out," she warned with a laugh. "Look where your curiosity has gotten you already! Aren't you about ready to get out yet?"

"Forever might pass before I would get bored with this pool, as long as I can share it with you. One more dive and we can rest on the bank," he promised.

They dove, searching for the bottom of a bottomless pool. He led the way, playfully—checking now and then to be sure that she still followed. Instead of finding the bottom of the pool, a light appeared ahead. Shane stopped, waiting for her to catch up and grasp a hold of his hand. He pointed to the light and felt Kitt tug at his hand as if to pull him away. For some reason, he felt drawn to the light ahead—he could not look away.

They swam closer and a familiar sight greeted his eyes. He had seen himself sleeping beside the water, the creek bank back home, before, but this time something was different. He couldn't look away, no matter how hard he tried, even though he felt Kitt's hand in his, tugging - attempting to distract his attention, to draw him back.

Then he knew what was different this time! The figure on the bank before him, started to move!

"NO! Not now—not yet!" His own voice echoed inside his head — despair at the sight, at the knowledge—and then, overwhelming doubt.

"This can't be happening—!"

"I'm waking up—!"

SIXTEEN

The young man stirred, gradually waking up from a beautiful dream. It was hard to shake. He hovered half in and half out, wondering at the feeling that someone was tugging at his hand, trying to catch his attention. The sensation disappeared when he opened his eyes wide and shook himself.

"Wow! That was some realistic dream!"

It left him wondering at its reality. He looked around the small woods, the clearing through which the quiet stream wandered. His senses drank in the sights and smells of an autumn day. The smell of the leaves and fall flowers especially entranced him—they lingered, and were extremely pungent. The fragrance filled his very being, imprinting upon his senses...and became a quest for him for the future.

Memories flooded his mind. Upon gazing down into the water near the shore of the small creek, where the stream ran clear and quiet...he saw a face. Was the face in his mind or in the stream itself? A name tried to form in his mind, on his lips—a name to match the face. The image in the water reached out to him.

At this point Shane did something that only much later, years later, he would learn the folly of. Instead of attempting to go back into the "dream," he reached for physical evidence of a mystical event, perhaps by reflex. Later he would recognize many physical confirmations of his dreams. But now, doubt, and an elusive quality of the moment itself held sway—he reached out to the hand in the water. The second his own hand touched the water, ripples disturbed the mirror-like surface and swept away the image of the strangely familiar face, a young woman's face, and her outreaching hand.

A tear formed in the corner of one eye as the memories of his dream receded. He shook himself, and recalled that it was past time for him to get on back home. He felt a pressing need to "get on with his life."

On the edge of the small woods, he halted one last time and looked back toward the clearing. Was his imagination acting up again? He could almost be certain he had heard — the laughter of children at play.

Dreamtime:
(...continuing)

The children played, too soon they grew,
They learned of Fire and Love.
As he had grown, a thought was sown,
Small doubt, but strong enough.

They're only dreams, some voices said,
Though warm was love's embrace.
I know her name, am I insane?
I can't forget her face!

He reached for her, but doubt grew strong,
The dream was swept away.
He saw love fade, this vow he made:
I'll return somehow, someday.

THE END?

A Spark of the Fire
(When Star Woman Fell to Earth)

A Spark of the Fire:

When Star Woman fell to Earth
It was where she wanted to be
"I want to be with my People"
She said.
She had Courage
She had the Courage
to know who she was
"I am a spark of the Fire!"
She said
with the Courage
and Conviction
of someone
who will know!

When Star Woman fell to Earth
the Earth was Water
the Earth was Her Womb
Her Fire did not die
"I look for someone"
She said
"Someone with Courage"
who does not fear
to stand so close
to the Fire
that all is untrue
will be
burned away!

When Star Woman fell to Earth
many tried
to build her a home
a new lodge
on the back
of a Turtle
But many failed
to go deep enough
to the depths
of themselves
to find the Earth
to build a new lodge
for Star Woman

One small creature
who was not afraid
to know who he was
in Water and Earth
and Fire!
He dove deep
into his depths
and faced his Fire
He stood so close
To Her
that everything
that was not True.
was burned away

When Star Woman fell to Earth
he had the Courage
to scoop up Earth
and build a new lodge.
for Star Woman.
on the back
of the Turtle
to share with
Her
And had the Courage
to call Her his mate
When Star Woman
fell to Earth.

When Star Woman fell to Earth
some people
who might,
not believe
would ask:
"How can this be True?"
How can anyone know
if this is True?
How can anyone
have the Courage
to stand so close
to be set aflame
by Her Fire?

and He will answer
in a small
humble voice
"the one who
has the Courage!"
he will know:
that He too
is a spark
of the Fire!

...winterhawk

ONE

Shane lay on a hospital cot, outside the operating room. Waiting for the anaesthetic to take effect, he mulled the past year over in his mind - it had flown by so quickly. Everything was pretty much a blur - especially the last half of the year. In his mind, he relived his memories – back to the moment that had brought it all to fruition.

His father's magical transition following the changing of the family name had almost run its course. Edward had appeared to have solved his drinking problem, and with the new name, had gotten a full time job at the Gypsum plant in Caledonia. Then a new car followed, and the land and house that the family had rented off the reserve in Nanticoke, had been offered to Edward to buy, at a modest price. It all seemed magical – change your name, and change your future. And it worked. Somehow it all worked. For the moment at least. Shane's father agreed to buy the house and the bit of land attached and when the government came with an offer to buy the land to build the Nanticoke Hydro Generating Station a year later, his father agreed. Edward worked out an agreement to sell the land except for a small package near the fence by the road. And with the money they made from the sale of the land to the government, a new modest but modern home was built to replace the shack that was torn down. Shane's mother found a specialist to operate (successfully) on her ears. With the assist of hearing aids, Shane's mother soon had a driver's licence, a part time job in the nearby town of Simcoe, and then a car.

But it was not finished for Shane. One day, during lunch hour, he left the school with thoughts of joining his long-time Native friend in a game of pool just off the main street in Hagersville. The events that had changed his family's lives were playing on his mind, as he walked slowly up the quiet street to mid Hagersville. And then low and behold, he was transfixed at the crossing. Standing on the other side of the street was someone he was almost sure he knew—but she seemed older, more mature. She was attired in a formfitting diaphanous green jump suit that made her look like someone out of a Sci-Fi movie. As he moved to cross the street, the woman rushed to push him out of the way of an oncoming van, and the vehicle that struck her, gave Shane a glancing blow. The two of them lay prone on the highway.

Shane came to with an awareness of a throbbing in his legs and knees. The van that was responsible for the damage, had continued on over the train tracks, and burst into flames. Shane crawled over to the woman lying in a heap in the middle of the street. When he touched her hand, her awareness was ignited and she raised her head to make eye contact.

"Come find me again," she said, and Shane blacked out. He woke up later in the hospital with memories that did not match or make any sense at all.

Bits and pieces floated back to him. "Where had the time gone?"

"What am I doing here?" His throat was sore, and his voice squeaked.

"You shouldn't try to talk just yet." A nurse that passed the door to his room stuck her head in. "Do you want some ice cream? You just had your tonsils out you know. You must still be a bit groggy from the aesthetic."

He was groggy, but that didn't account for his having a private room, and why. If he was here just to get his tonsils out, why did his knees and legs hurt so much? And what were these strange memories that included...

"What happened to the woman in the green suit?" Shane asked the nurse the next day, when he was able to talk better.

"What woman?" the nurse replied. "You were brought in here alone – by ambulance, and your room paid upfront by a Mr. Champion. There was only you in the ambulance."

"I don't know any Mr. Campion," Shane insisted. "And there was a woman who saved my life. I just want to thank her." (and find out why she seems so familiar), he was pondering.

"I will ask the head nurse if she can be of help in contacting Mr. Champion," his nurse replied. "You are to be released tomorrow."

"Released?" he wondered. "Why do my knees hurt when I try to stand up? What is that all about?"

"I don't know anything about that either." The nurse was becoming agitated. "Let me get back to you after I talk to the head nurse."

His nurse did not return. Shane's father paid him a visit on his way to work. Then later that evening just before the end of visiting hours were up; Shene heard a gentle knock at the door to his room.

"Can I come in?" A man that Shane did not recognize came in, closed the door behind him, and sat on one of the visitors chairs. "I am Professor Champion," he announced. "Do you have any questions for me?"

Shane had no end of questions. The first concerned the woman in green.

"Officially, there was no woman or anybody else but you at the site of your accident in Hagersville."

"Well, we both know that is not true." Shane replied. "I want to know what happened to her – officially or unofficially. She is someone that I recognize."

"How could that be so?" Champion asked with a look of incredulity. "You can call me Joseph by the way."

"OK Joseph – uh Professor Joseph, I'm guessing? what do you mean by saying that? Are you suggesting that it isn't possible for a Native kid like me to know a woman like her?"

"Yes, I believe I am. And it is not just because she was older – more mature than you, or no better than you."

"Then you are admitting that there was a woman – a woman in a strange green body suit?" Shane shook his head, thankful to no longer be doubting his memories. "I was beginning to believe that I dreamed her up."

103

"Officially," (there was that word), "she did not exist." Professor Champion scratched his head, wondering where to go from here. "But if she did – if there was such a woman, where did you know her from? Where did you meet her?"

"You might find this hard to believe..." Shane paused.

"Yes – go on."

"I met this woman, I know this woman from my dreams! Even though she was much younger then, I am almost certain that she is the one I dreamed about. And she said something to me after the accident that confirmed this belief."

"She said something to you? In English? What did she say?"

"Yes, in English – why not?" She said "come find me again.""

There was silence in the room. "Tell me about your dreams?" Joseph requested. "Tell me about the dreams that this strange woman in the green body suit appeared."

"Well," Shane hesitated. "She did not have the strange green suit on when I dreamed about her, and as I said before, she was much younger. But I am more than sure that she is the same one." And Shane gave the professor a synopsis of meeting Kitt in his dream, being sure not to divulge her name and a few other personal memories.

"So you believe that you met a young woman in your dreams –and then again on the street where she was older and gave her life to save you?"

"She gave up her life?" Shane's eyes began to fill. "Are you telling me that she is dead? Why couldn't you help her?"

"We took her body to a special clinic in Toronto when we checked her over at the scene and found no life signs. And before you ask, we did try everything in our power to revive her there on the street. And personally, I would give my right arm to have been able to talk to her, because my colleagues and I believe that she was not of this world."

"You mean an alien? From a UFO?" Steve halted with tears flowing down his face. "My dream friend is from another planet?"

"It appears to be true. But we cannot be sure, because when we took off the green filmy body suit, her body went up in flames – there was no smoke mind you. But she just turned to a pile of ashes on the operating table. We have the strange green suit, but except for the idea that it somehow preserved her life, we have not even the foggiest idea how it worked or if it will ever work again."

"So what makes you think she is an alien? Did you find a spacecraft or anything else?" Shane wiped his tears away as his curiosity overcame his grief at losing her.

"Visiting time is over." Professor Champion rose to leave. "I will get in touch, or one of my colleagues will, as soon as you are back on your feet. I got your address from your father when he came to visit you the other day." And with that, the man called Joseph Champion would be temporarily gone from Shane's life. But not before telling the boy once again: "There was no one but you on that street in Hagersville. No one! Please do not mention a woman in a green suit, if you ever want to hear from me again."

Shane limped out of that hospital with the aid of a cane, minus his tonsils. His legs, especially his knees hurt like hell, but the hospital had checked them out to find that: "you are good to go. Your legs will heal with time, but you will need to use a cane for support in the meantime. Sorry, you will also have to give up any aspirations, if you had them, to run in the Olympics. Otherwise, you are healthy and ready to get on with your life."

"Get on with my life?" he mused. "No Olympics in the future, and that crosses out roller skating, I guess." Shane had taken a liking to roller skating in the small rink in Simcoe. Once or twice, and he was hooked. And he had been an avid runner as long as he could remember.

"Now what?" His 13th semester at school was interrupted, and he had already missed a lot of days just pretending to be sick so that he could stay home and daydream. Life seemed to be sending him a message. Be careful what you wish for, because you just might get it. And he did – in spades. Now, he had all kinds of time on his hands, but a desperate longing to move on, cane or no cane. "Come find me again." That was all she had said. But how? The school year was shot, and he was anxious to get on in another way – yet to be revealed. Who needs a 13th year at school anyways? It was for someone that might go on to University, but the kind of logical teaching that they would provide did not interest him in the least. He wanted more – and at the top of that "more" was the girl (now woman it seemed) that was disappearing from his logical memories, and his dreams seemed in jeopardy of being lost as well.

One day, as if in answer to his reaching out to the Universe for an answer, a dark car rolled into the family driveway. Two men got out of the car and knocked on the door of the modem bungalow out in farm country,

"I believe you are Shane LaFlame?" they asked.

Shane nodded sleepily from a nap in the middle of the day. His father was at work, and so was his mother. His sisters and younger brother were at school. "Who are you? What do you want?"

"Joseph Champion sent us. It seems that he believes you are technically qualified to join our electronics studies at the University of Toronto. This is only open to special students that have a certain aptitude – and Joseph has picked you for a chance to take the course."

It was like a dream come true – almost. "What do I need to do? he suspected that there must be a catch.

"The only catch," the man seemed to be reading his mind, or had heard this before, "is that you have to impress our faculty that you want this so much that nothing will stop you from succeeding. Professor Champion must have seen something in you to believe that you are a candidate for this special project. The rest is up to you. If you accept our offer, we will arrange for a part time job for you in a suburb of Toronto, and give you help at finding a place to live."

"It sounds too good to be true." Shane answered. "Can I call you in a couple of days with my answer?"

"Of course." The second man gave him a business card with a telephone number to contact the office in Toronto. "But don't wait too long to call. That is part of the test to see if you are up to the challenge." The two men got into their car and sped off, leaving Shane with his mind full of questions.

"If you want to follow your dream," he told himself, "the first step is up to you." His mind was at once filled with the memory of the woman in green, and her last words. "I would be out of my mind," he spoke to himself again, "not that I haven't been told that before, to turn down this chance of a lifetime."

Later that evening Shane shared the good news with his father and mother. "Go for it!" his mother said immediately. "What do you think Edward?"

"Uhhhh, yes," his father answered. "But where will you be staying? And will you OK so far away from us? Won't you be lonely?" Shane's father was never one to stray too far from his family on the reserve, and was devastated when his mother passed away.

"I will sleep on it." Shane answered.

The very next day, Spirit gifted Shane with another "offer that you should not refuse," in the form of his high school friend Wiley who he had not talked to for some time. Wiley was the chief's son on the Six Nations Reserve.

"After you left school," Wiley began, "I got to thinking about how short life is and how things can pass you by if you don't make a move. I went to Toronto and got a job in a shipping department for Caterpillar of Canada. Just like that, I took the clipping out of the paper, walked in, and was hired on the spot. I found a room too. It is a small room in an apartment in Mimico – rented out by two brothers that had a car accident. They are living off the accident claim and going to the track, but they need the money from the spare room to help pay the rent. I asked Jimmy, that is the older brother, and they said it was okay if I got another border to share the room. It has two small beds. What do you think?"

"When can we go?" Shane's friend agreed to pick him up at the end of the week. "OK! I hear you!" Shane shouted to Spirit. He phoned the number on the business card, and talked to Joseph Champion's assistant. "I will be in Toronto at the beginning of next week," he told her. "And please thank Professor Champion for the once-in-a-life-time chance to prove myself. Oh, and I already have a place to stay, but would appreciate help in finding a job."

His friend picked him up as promised, and that Sunday evening, Shane paid for one month's rent ahead of time with some money he had saved from working in the Tobacco harvest to Jimmy and his brother. The next morning, Wiley was off to work and Shane went across the street to a pay phone to set up an appointment to meet with Professor Champion.

"Professor Champion will be available to meet with you after class this evening." The assistant informed him, and gave Shane directions to the University of Toronto's Law Faculty, and Shane caught a ride on the "Red Rocket," which the woman called the Toronto Transit's streetcar. And later that afternoon he stood in front of the building that he hoped would provide an answer to his dreams.

"Professor Champion will meet with you in one of the rooms down the hall." The woman Shane had talked to on the phone told him to wait on a nearby chair until his appointment. She did not seem surprised at the quick meeting that was arranged. "Joseph likes to get right to whatever he has planned, and he personally interviews each and every one of his students, before he takes them down to the 'dungeon.'" She chuckled at what seemed to be a private joke.

"Please come this way," Joseph's voice broke Shane's train of thought. "Were you dreaming?" The older man led Shane into a nearby room and closed the door. The professor seated himself behind a large wooden desk and motioned his future student into a chair. He had a big smile on his face.

"I was thinking—wondering how this all comes together. It is almost magical, like a dream come true."

"Well, if you know how it ends up, please let me know so I can be prepared," Joseph replied.

"It ends up the way we want it to, with the Creator's help of course, and in its good time."

"In its good time," the professor agreed. "And with the help of people that we meet and have yet to meet. The old story about, when the student is ready, the teacher will appear? I am not talking about myself as much as I am saying that we are all students of the Universe and each other."

"For sure! I have been lucky to have dreamed some amazing teachers on the way here."

"Tell me about them. Tell me about her?" Shane had shared a bit of the dreams, including his meeting the girl who he believed to be his soul mate.

"Amazing. More amazing if you knew the other side of the story that has been given to me. Can you tell me her name – the girl in your dreams, and where does she come from? Where does she live?"

"You are thinking that my Soulmate might be the woman in the green suit?" Shane's brow became furrowed. "I do, too, and that has me more than a bit sad, 'cause if I believe that, then she died right before my eyes on that street in Hagersville."

"But you told me that the last words she said to you were: "'come find me again.'"

"That much is true – I have not been able to get these words out of my mind. But how, and where? Where is she – is she real in this reality? Then how do I find her?"

"I believe I may have part of the answer. The part about where, Professor Champion answered. "At least not.in a very logical way — from a non-logical source."

"How so?"

"First, let me fill in a bit of the details. If I were to reveal to you in strict privacy, that I am a representative of NASA, you might wonder why we have set up this classroom in Toronto Canada. This part of the story, including meeting you, began with someone who lives near here, in a suburb of Toronto, sending me a message that something would be coming down – literally from outer space to a set of co-ordinances North West."

"A space ship I guess?"

"That is what we believed too" The older man continued. "And since I met you the first time, and saw the woman in green turn to ashes before my eyes, we were able to find the ship – intact. And....

it is identical to a ship that crashed in the USA about 10 years ago. We have been able to reverse engineer a lot technical devices from that damaged ship. But even with an undamaged ship now in our possession, we have not been able to discover how either of them must have worked. Imagine – a ship that must have journeyed many light years from some planet out there among the stars. And have the pilot, on both ships survive the journey and not be hundreds or thousands of years old! Your woman in the green suit? If I recall how she appeared to you that day on the street of Hagersville, and to us until we removed the suit, she could not have been much over—fifty of our years—about my age, if that!"

"You said that someone told you that the space ship would be landing here in Canada?" Shane asked. "How could they know? And where do I fit in?"

"In the beginning, this someone who contacted me sounded like they were part of a hoax—an elaborate prank, or just a loony. We get them all the time – calling NASA to say that they were abducted or have seen a UFO land in their backyard. We have since become a bit more tolerant, since the whole population could not be outright loons! There have been a few that defied logical explanation. I digress. This time, the person was able to give us information that was provable – even before this ship came down. And then there was the matter of the other ship we have that crashed in the USA. And, she was able to give us other coordinates – a destination to search the night sky for a planet in a solar system that is sometimes not visible – on the other side of our sun."

"She? You said she. She, this person who lives near Toronto and has been providing you with provable information is a woman?" Shane became alert.

"Sorry. That was a slip of the tongue – maybe? Yes, a few years ago a woman who would not give up, left messages for someone to check out at NASA, and I was the designated contact when her information proved true. We were able to use a long range telescope and see that planet beyond the edge of our solar system, and ultimately receive an S.O.S. A call for help. That is where you come in. This woman in green appeared to know you. How do you explain that?"

"I dreamed her," Shane replied. "Remember me telling you that she was identical to the girl in my dream, except older."

"And she told you to come find her again." Joseph smiled a sly smile. "Would it surprise you to know that the woman who gave us the information that up 'til now has been correct, admitted to me, that she dreamed it all?"

"Not at all. I believe in my dreams. My ancestors lived their daily lives, hunted and fished and traveled our Mother Earth as though their dreams were as real as their waking reality. So there is a woman who dreams like me living close to Toronto. Can you tell me her name, and how I can get in touch?"

"Sorry, no can do. She asked to remain anonymous. But I might be persuaded to provide some more information about her, if you tell me more about the mysterious girl that you dream about – maybe her name?" The professor appeared to think there might be a connection, and so did his future student.

"Sorry again," Shane replied. "I am sworn to secrecy, at the cost of losing her. And that is something I never want to do ...again."

"So, we are at a stalemate of sorts, but it is also quite evident to me at least that we were drawn together to answer an S.O.S from the stars. How about if we go looking for the woman in your dreams?" The professor did not wait for an answer; he stood up and motioned Shane to the door. "Come with me down into our 'dungeon', our hidden lab and the classroom that you will be working in."

The dungeon was in the basement of the Law Faculty, with a hidden door that could only be accessed by a coded key that was like the new credit cards that the bank was starting to use.

"By the time you come back, you will be set up with your own access card, and a computer account and password." Professor Champion told Shane. "I will need to get you to sign the necessary forms and the agreement to be part of our team." When the secret door opened, a quiet air conditioner started up. Joseph flicked a light switch, and banks of overhead lights began to come on. It looked like any classroom that Shane had seen, except there were no windows to the outside. Over the desk at the front of the room where the teacher would sit was a banner that read: "NASA – U. of T. Joint Venture - Department of Quantum Law". Joseph sat at one of the desks, and showed his new student a box he said was a computer—attached to a small tube like screen that resembled a TV.

"I won't go any further right now, one of the other students can show you how to turn it on and login with your password. This is just a terminal – a dumb computer that connects by RJE – Remote Job Entry, to an IBM mainframe in the NASA office in the States." Shane's eyebrows went up, and Joseph smiled. We got a good head start with what we learned from the electronics in first ship that crashed that I told you about. But we and IBM were already a good way there. We now have a satellite that keeps pace with the earth, orbiting out there in space. It transmits the signal remotely and it is like we are working on the Mainframe hundreds of miles away. This is the most secure way we can do this. The data we send and receive is encrypted in case anyone that might have equipment like us stumbles on our signal."

"So, you don't have any intention of having your own main computer here in Canada?" Shane asked.

"Not at the present time." His teacher replied. "The U.of T. has a mainframe on site but if we do see the necessity, we will be buying one of the newer, smaller models that IBM is working on."

"Like an AS400?" Shane surprised himself as the information popped into his head.

"Yes!" Wherever did you get that from? IBM is keeping any information about their new models secret to anybody but the Space program.

"I don't know," Shane was being absolutely truthful. The name came out of the blue. Maybe I worked with one in a past life or something."

"Or something," the Professor agreed. "Maybe you dreamed about it? But if you did, then dreams must be somehow outside the control of time, because much of the technologies we are using have not officially been created yet. And that my friend is why I decided to bring you on board. I wonder how long it will take for you to get up to speed with computer programming. I have a few starter books that you can take with you tonight to read up. But treat them with the same secrecy that you do our lab here in the basement of the U. of T."

TWO

"There is someone, a woman, out there in a Toronto suburb that has dreams like me!" Shane went home to his shared room that night with the computer manuals tucked safely under his arm. He sat up late that night devouring the pages. Meanwhile, his friend Wiley slept like a contented baby in his bed on the other side of the room.

Wiley was gone off to work as usual when Shane woke the next morning. Their landlords, Jimmy and his brother were already off at the racetrack where, according to Wiley, they earned most of their money to support themselves, having survived this way for a couple of years on a settlement from an accident – a devastating car crash.

Shane bought a newspaper from the convenience store across the road that he learned was called Lakeshore Boulevard. He went through the classified section until his eyes were blurry. He saw many openings that all required a diploma or work related experience, none of what he had. In the late afternoon, he made the trip across the street, and phoned the number for Professor Champion's "secretary". Actually she was the only means of contacting Joseph. as the professor did not have a secretary. Shane wondered, what would the effect be to a project that had been instigated by an S.O.S from the stars, if anything bad were to happen to a man who kept his secrets locked away in his head?

"The Professor left a message for you." The woman Shane had talked to the other day passed on the information. "He told me to apologize for not giving it to you when you were here. I guess you know he has a lot on his mind. Any ways, he told me to give you the information about a possible job which he promised to do when he asked you to come to Toronto."

Shane took out the note pad and pen that he had learned to carry for just this kind of situation. He jotted down the name of the company and the person in HR. that the professor must have talked to, and the directions to get there by bus. "Thank you!" Shane said to his new and future teacher, and checked the clock to see that there was still time in the workday to get there and apply for the job.

"Your Professor from the University of Toronto gave you a glowing reference. So we agreed to give you an interview for an opening in our shipping department, even though you do not have any previous experience," the woman who worked in the HR. of Boyle-Midway explained. Boyle-Midway was, as it turned out, a middle-to-large company that produced and sold house hold chemicals. The interview was quick and complete to both Shane and the woman's satisfaction, when she realized that she was hiring a young man, without much experience, but a curious and intuitive mind. "When can you begin?" She smiled and handed Shane's signed acceptance to the man from the shipping department that came up to meet his future employee.

"As soon as possible," Shane replied, "How about tomorrow?"

Shane was so filled with satisfaction and joy, that he missed his bus stop as the vehicle turned south on Lakeshore Blvd. and he got off across the street from a building called "Mimicombo". It was a roller rink that was just a few blocks down from the apartment that Shane now called home.

"A roller rink?" It would have interested him more, before the unfortunate accident that left him with the part-time use of a cane. Shane had left the cane behind for the job interview. He decided that any potential employer might shy away from hiring someone who might not be able to carry their weight. Rightfully so, as at this moment in time a so-called "disabled" person might be given the chance, but would be seen as having one strike against them, and be relegated further down the list. He tested his legs and knees. They were still fairly strong, but extremely tired. He hobbled noticeably in the direction of his lodging, deciding to check out the roller rink another day.

Luckily, the decision was agreed upon that Shane would be starting at Boyle-Midway the next Monday, so he had time to exercise his knees, and get them in shape before then. "I remember a dream about a young girl who was able to get out of her wheel chair and walk – and run, with my encouragement. If Kitt is as real as she seems to be to me, I can be inspired by her and do the same!"

By Saturday, Shane hits the computer books, and decided to venture out. He had already read and digested most of the information, and the how and technical information of the computer's working and the programming theory was fully alive in his mind. In theory, anyways, it was like remembering something he knew before – somewhere. He also recalled a small restaurant down the street just before the roller rink, and decided to treat himself to a light evening lunch. With the aid of his cane, he arrived at the restaurant hungry and energized.

Shane ordered and as he waited for the food to come, he watched the beginning of a hockey game with the Toronto Maple Leafs playing the Montreal Canadians on a small black and white TV on a corner shelf. Shane's food arrived, and as he ate, the first period in the hockey game ended, and an advertisement came on for an Ice Show that would be coming to Maple Leaf Gardens. Shane watched in awe as two dancers glided in perfect harmony across the surface of the ice.

"I can do that!" A voice came from the table across the way in another booth. Hello, my name is Rudolph Winchester. My friends call me Rudey. It's an old German name that means famous wolf." He moved over into the seat opposite Shane and extended his hand.

"Interesting," Shane replied. "I am a Native and one of my spirit totems is a wolf ". He held out his hand to the other young man. "Pleased to meet you Rudey," but the other man snatched his hand back with a sly smile.

"I did not say that you could call me by my nick name." And then he laughed at his private joke, and grasped Shane's hand and shook it vigorously. "Just kidding." You can call me whatever you want. But

A Spark of the Fire

I think that Rudolph Winchester would look good on a marquee. Don't you? The Olympic team of Rudolph—and his partner.

"You are part of an ice dance team?" Shane replied.

"No I am part of the future roller-skating team that will be in the Olympics. The Olympics are really close to adding roller skating and I plan to be there. Me and my skating partner that is."

"Well, I wish you well." Shane was genuinely enthusiastic. "I had hopes of learning to roller-skate better, like I did back home in Simcoe, but as you can see, I had a little set back." Shane motioned to his cane that was in full view of the other man.

"I saw that," Rudey replied. "Too bad. Maybe you would like to come down to the Mimicombo to watch me—and my partner skate sometime?"

"I would." Shane replied and shook the hand of his new friend. "Pleased to meet you Rudolph."

"That's Rudey to you." He smiled broadly, and got up to leave. "I need to go to practice now, but the invitation is open."

"Strange!" Shane mused. "He did not seem to want to tell me his skating partner's name."

* * *

That following Monday Shane started working in the shipping department at Boyle-Midway, minus his cane. He walked strong and proud as he was escorted down by the HR. woman to be re-introduced to the shipping manager. On the way he passed an open pit where another man about his age was dumping chemicals into a mixing bin that he later learned was part of the process of making one of their flagship products – a well known toilet bowel cleaner, made up mostly of a corrosive chemical. The dust filled the air so that Shane had to cover his mouth and nose, and was thankful to Spirit that he had not been hired for that job.

"He should be wearing a mask." The HR person noted Shane's reaction. "It is part of the safety requirements."

As the woman led Shane on to the other side of the plant, he thanked the Spirits again, that his father's job at the chemical plant in Caledonia was mostly outside – moving and unloading flat bed transport trucks. Still, it must be in the air at both places. "I am thankful for the job, he mused, but I'll ask Wiley to be on the lookout for an opening in the Caterpillar plant where he works."

After a brief introduction, and description of his duties by the Shipping manager, Shane was shown how to read packing lists and where the product was to be found in the racks and sent out on rollers into a waiting transport truck. At first he was running around, searching for the produce to put on the make shift track out to the truck where another man helped the truck driver to stack the boxes in the van. It didn't take long for his legs and knees to become painfully numb. Then, just as he was getting the hang of locating the product in the boxes, one of the other workers that were out among the racks with him came up and spoke in a low voice.

"I can see that you are in a bit of pain?" He smiled in a friendly manner. "You will get used to it – I can also see that you don't give up easily. Why don't you switch with Mike in the Trailer? Pat, that's the name of the truck driver, is a real hoot to work with, will show the ropes. If the boss says anything, I will say I told you it is good to see how both ends work."

Shane went home stiff and sore, to collect his cane, and grab a bite from the restaurant. And then he boarded the Red Rocket to downtown Toronto. His schedule for the time being was 4 hours an evening at the U. of T. on Monday, Wednesday and Friday. Shane arrived at the Law Faculty location in Toronto and met with the woman who was Professor Champion's part-time secretary.

"The Professor will be right up to take you to the classroom in the basement," she informed him, and within minutes, Joseph Champion appeared to shake his hand and welcome him as a student.

"We have created a computer key card for you," he explained, and presented his new student with the access card. When they reached the hidden door, Joseph advised Shane what to do – to locate the small slit into which the card was to be inserted. "Go ahead and give it a try," he suggested.

The key card worked perfectly and a door opened where there did not appear to be a door the moment before. "We try to keep this lab a secret as much as possible, but most of the Law School's teachers and personnel have enough knowledge of it to be able to contact me, and anyone who might be inside in case of fire or any other disaster. If anyone were to see you open the door and ask, just smile and leave them to their thoughts. If they are really curious, they will contact someone here that will kindly tell them that it is none of their business." The Professor seemed to enjoy the ability to keep a secret that the conspiracy seeking public might want to investigate.

The windowless classroom was as Shane remembered from his previous visit, except there were four other people, two about Shane's age and two others nearer the Professors. Joseph introduced Shane to the other "students" who were working at their computer terminals, and explained that "we are all students here." We are all learning to interact with what the scientists in NASA and others in Canada and around the world call Quantum Physics, or Quantum Mechanics. This is theory only! Although there have been men and women who have worked out the hard mathematical equations, it is all still theory. One of the things we have discovered is that when anyone observes an experiment that involves Quantum Physics, the very act of observation affects the outcome. Something like your dreams Shane? Everyone—Shane is a Native person who has dreams similar to the woman who helped in the start of our project SOS from the stars."

The other students smiled and one woman, somewhat older than the others shrugged, "I guess you might think we are a bit loony to try to go to the stars based on someone's dreams."

"Well I have my doubts sometimes, concerning my dreams, but for me, this is a personal and often intimate thing that is usually proven true. I have found my soul mate in my dreams, and I have seen her appear in this reality for just a few minutes. I have a soul yearning to go find her again." When the words left his mouth, Shane wondered if he had said too much.

"We have no secrets from each other here," the Professor replied. "Well not technical secrets anyway. We do not need to know the intimate details unless they apply to the project at hand. Now, perhaps Stephanie can help you to get booted up and signed on so that you can get a first-hand look at what we are doing here." Stephanie was the woman who spoke earlier.

"Call me Steph." She sat down beside a computer terminal and motioned Shane to join her.

"Shane," he replied, and pushed the button that she indicated would turn on the computer under the desk. In no time at all, he was typing in and verifying to change the password he had been set up with. And he was online, connected to the main computer in NASA.

"You are an old hand at this," Stephanie chuckled. "Did you dream it?" He blushed. "If you take this menu you can select a personal library that we set up for you containing some of the programs we have been working on. Don't be timid about trying what you have been reading in the study books. You will be able to change anything in your personal library, but for those changes to become operational, they would have to be transferred to our live system by me, and authorized by another senior programmer, or Professor Champion." She left Shane to play around with the code on the screen as he saw fit. When she saw, him again, he was immersed in the work, and indeed he was rapidly looking like this was "old hand" for him. Meanwhile, Shane surprised himself.

Slowly it all came back to him, but where did it come from? True, it was basic programming, and basic control language, but last week this was only part of a dream for him, and words in a text book. Now the dream was becoming real. He wondered how much more would materialize. Maybe a woman who dreams like me? A woman who lives close to the Toronto area? Or despite what Joseph said "sorry, I can't reveal her name," may be revealed by Spirit, all in Good Indian Time.

Shane boarded the Red Rocket for home that night mentally and physically exhausted, but high in the sense that everything was going according to plan. Maybe not his plan, but then he did have a choice as it appeared, according to the Quantum Theory in the way he can affect the outcome,.

Wiley was in bed when Shane quietly opened the bedroom door. "Kind of burning the night time oil aren't you?" Wiley sat up sleepy eyed.

"You could say that. My first day at the new job and my first real evening for the night course I am taking." Shane had explained part of it to his friend from the reservation, but the other young man just shrugged it off. "You do what Spirit guides you to, and everything will work out." Wiley had told Shane that the Native Elders were always open to share their wisdom with young people, except for the situation that might cause injury; but it was up to the young person to take the initiative and ask.

"What are you doing tomorrow night?" Wiley inquired. "After work I thought we might go shoot a few games of pool if you are up to it?"

"Sounds like a plan," Shane agreed. "I have no class tomorrow. I think I will stay over this week end, hit the books, and check out the roller rink just down the road." When Wiley had asked if Shane wanted to come to Toronto with him to look for a job, he had told Shane that he drove back to the reservation every weekend to be with his aging parents.

Shane went to work that week minus his cane. His legs were getting stronger, but he attended the lab in Toronto that Wednesday and Friday evening physically exhausted though emotionally charged. Joseph checked in to see how his new student was coming along, and was pleasantly surprised with Shane's progress in gaining an understanding of what they were attempting to accomplish. The Professor placed a longish crystal on Shane's desk. "This is from the ship that crashed," he explained. "We believe it had something to do with powering the craft, though we don't know for sure. I brought it here for inspiration for our team. Keep on the way you are, and let me know if you have any more dreams."

That Saturday, Shane got up early and went to a nearby park to study. Before he was aware of the time that passed, the sun was going down over the nearby lake. He gathered up his books and cane, and resolved to take up his new friend's suggestion to check out the roller rink. After a light meal at the nearby restaurant, Shane found himself on the upper level of the Mimicombo, overlooking the wooden skating surface. The local roller club was practicing below, and he saw Rudey and a young girl that must be his skating partner going through their routine.

"They look pretty smooth! They seem to be a great team." He said to himself and to no one in particular.

"They are good together," a voice answered at his elbow. A woman who came over to watch. "Might be better if he was not so pushy. Ooops that is just my opinion. Hi, I am Sheila, I work part-time in the snack bar. I once was a good friend of Melanie's, before her partner showed up."

Shane shook her hand and noted, as young men do, that Sheila had a wedding ring, and also a good sized cross around her neck.

"Oooops again, don't tell Rudey that I told you her name. He gets upset if he catches anyone talking to her – especially another man." The woman chuckled and then frowned. "He is paranoid! There I said it." She turned to check that no one was waiting at the snack bar.

"Why would that be?" Shane pondered. "I have met Rudey in the restaurant and he seemed friendly enough."

"Might be that they are suited for each other." Sheila continued. "If roller skating really makes it into the Olympics as a demonstration sport a couple of years from now, Rudey and his partner have a good chance to be there. A lot of water might flow under the bridge before that happens though." She smiled pleasantly and returned to her spot behind the counter. Shane followed her over and asked for a coke.

"You seem really interested. Is that cane a result of a skating accident?" she asked, handing Shane his drink.

"Sometimes I wish." He replied. "I used to skate back home in Simcoe, but I am still recovering from being hit by a car while walking across the street. In Hagersville. I am Native – born on

A Spark of the Fire

the Six Nations Reserve. For most white people it was easier to say the Six Nations, like when he crossed into the USA, rather than to tell them he was actually an Ojibway from the New Credit which is part of the larger Reservation. Long story not needing explanation, except to another Native person. But then to the Natives, on the whole, they were all part of the Red-skinned People and the borders do not exist except in the minds of those who created them. His mind was wandering – remembering.

"Do you know much about adjusting or fixing roller skates?" Sheila broke his train of thought. "We could use help part-time in the skate rental if you are interested."

"That sounds good to me," he replied. I have some spare time that could be spent on other things than working and going to class three times a week."

"Whoa there! Sounds to me like you are pretty booked up. What are you taking?"

He thought for a minute. "Computers," he replied.

"Computers? Like in Commodore 64 of those game machines?"

"Kinda. Some people believe that computers might become a personal thing someday. We might have a computer in every home."

"Yeah – right! And I will be working at the Royal York serving the elite instead of a snack bar at the roller rink."

"You shouldn't sell yourself short," he replied before going back to watch his new 'friends' dance on skates. "You might just take this job as far as it goes, and then you might be a personal secretary to the Manager of the Royal York, and a computer would be just one of your tools when it replaces the typewriter."

"Or I just might be the Manager of the whole damn place." She shot back with a chuckle. "Yup! That's what I am about!"

"Yes, you could." Shane said to himself. "And I just might be on a ship to another world to meet my soulmate. I need to keep my wild ideas under wrap, at least for the present." He watched as Rudey and his partner finished up, and the lights dimmed to let everyone know that the evening session would be opening for the public in a few minutes. Shane finished his drink and made his way down the stairs. The two dance skaters changed below, and disappeared out into the night, without so much as a wave. And Shane was almost sure that Rudey had seen him watching from the balcony.

The next Saturday, Rudey met Shane in the restaurant again and offered to buy a coffee. Rudey was quiet and reserved at first then, seemed unable to contain himself. "What did you think? I mean, I saw you watching. We are going to the Olympics, I feel it in my bones."

"I was impressed." Shane answered with genuine praise. "You make a great dance team, you and your partner. I wish I could skate again, but as you can see, my wings are clipped, so to speak."

"The cane." The other man managed a wry smile. "Too bad. Yes we do make a great team. We are so much alike, and I love her more than I can tell you. But she frustrates me sometimes. She is so timid that I almost feel like I am pulling more than my share." He stopped as though he might believe that he had opened up and said more than he wanted to. After awhile, Rudey continued talking, but it was all about himself and his "dreams." Shane could not get a word in edgewise.

As the other man talked, Shane had a momentary "memory" of a vision that came to him one morning while he was waking up. An Elder and aged Native woman appeared to Shane and said: "do not tell anyone about your experiences here." And she was gone. It applied, to the circumstance of this man and his partner, and even more so to the time he spent in the classroom in Toronto. And it became evident that he should not let on to Rudey about his going to work without the cane. "I have a girlfriend – a Native Girl back home who I believe is my soulmate." Shane told a small lie but not entirely untrue lie.

"You have what?" Rudey stopped his monologue. "I am happy for you." And he really did seem happy to learn that bit of information. "I should tell you, that Melanie is my soul mate. She told me so the other night. And we are planning to get married one day. Did I tell you that the company I work for has a branch opening in Calgary? I am thinking of applying for a position out there – it would be a step up for me, and for my future wife."

"Do they have roller rinks out West, in Calgary I mean?"

"What? Of course they have only the best roller rinks in Calgary." Rudey was silent for a minute, and then said with a large grin. "I guess I should go now! Got to keep in practice you know. Practice makes perfect."

Shane dropped into the roller rink that Tuesday night. He took Sheila and the management up on the offer to work part-time in the skate rental shop.

Rudey had not come to the restaurant that evening. So Shane was surprised when his skating partner showed up early to get her skates adjusted.

She sat on a bench while Shane checked out her skates. "They seem OK to me," he informed her. "The action was a little loose but everything is ship shape now."

"I am Melanie," she smiled and offered her hand for Shane to shake.

"I know," he returned the smile. "I have been watching you and Rudey skate. You are a great couple."

"Have you ever skated?" she asked.

"Yes I skated back home, in Simcoe. I am Native – from the Six Nations."

"I know that, too." She patted the bench beside her offering him a seat. "Rudey told me that you have met your soulmate. Is that true?"

"Yes, I have. I dreamed about her."

"Have you ever wanted to dance skate?" She changed the topic of the conversation in mid-stream. "I could teach you."

"Sorry," Shane could almost see where this was going. He motioned to his cane leaning against the bench. How could she not see it? "It might be a while before I can think of skating again."

"Too bad," she replied, and then the conversation was interrupted by Rudey, who showed up unannounced and late.

"Time to go Mel" His eyes sent daggers of fire in Shane's direction. "We need to practice, remember."

She got up and dutifully took Rudey's hand. "See you later." She smiled as they descended the stairs. Rudey did not have his skates on yet. In a few moments, Rudey marched up the stairs to confront Shane with blazing eyes. "Do not...I mean, do not speak to my girlfriend again. If I catch you even so much as looking at her when she is not with me on the floor, I will shoot you! Do you understand?"

"I understand." Shane was not impressed or afraid, just surprised at the other man's burst of temper. "Look over there." Shane pointed to his cane. I am not a threat to you or your partner on or off the skating floor. And you know what? I am learning to walk without the cane at work, but it will be some time if ever, that I get back to skating again."

"Well bully for you." Rudey was calming down a bit. He walked to the stairs and turned to face Shane again. "Just remember what I said." And he made a mock shooting action with his hand and finger, before stomping down the stairs.

THREE

Rudey and Melanie came, skated on Thursday and went, and then Saturday and the next week as well, avoiding any contact with Shane like he had something that might be catching. Then neither of the couple showed up at all. And Rudey did not return to the restaurant again. A couple of weeks went by, and Sheila only shrugged. "No Idea. When Melanie and I were good friends, we used to hang out every chance we got, but Rudey put the kibosh on that."

Meanwhile, Shane was attempting to come up with a connection, any way that the programming the team that Joseph had put together in Toronto and in the USA could be used to interface with the ships from another world and help them to travel to the stars. The ability for a person on earth, bound by gravity and the speed of light to travel to another solar system was out of the question according to Einstein's Theory of Relativity. Nothing can go faster than the speed of light. That was the accepted limitation. But Einstein was also quoted as saying: "Imagination is more important that knowledge."

"How about Dreams? Shane wondered.

Shane sat one evening holding the crystal from the ship that had crashed in his hands. "How about Dreams?" he wondered. "When I dream, there is no limitation. I can be in my bed at night, and in the next instant, on another world somewhere out there in space, maybe?" His eyes blurred and his thoughts turned inward. In that next moment, he was in a different place. Hagersville? Any way, he stood by a railway track, and watched as a sleek train out of some science fiction novel whizzed by at a speed beyond anything on Earth. And when the wind from the train was all that was left, a young woman in a green uniform stood waiting on the other side of the tracks. The smile on her face was extremely inviting. And then the vision, of the daydream faded away.

"Something?" Professor Champion stood by Shane's desk.

"Yes," Shane replied. "I was there. I am sure it was another place, another planet, even though I started out at that crossroads in Hagersville. And she was there too except she was much younger, like I remember her in my other dreams."

"And?" Joseph breathed a sigh of anticipation.

"And she had that look in her eyes – like she was asking me to come find her again? Crazy, don't you think? A young man's fantasy," Shane blushed.

"Not at all." The professor sat at the empty desk next to his student. "That is why you are here. There is something about dreams that speak to those who can open up to them that is like the mystical side of Quantum Physics. The woman who gave us the coordinates to look for knew something that we did not. She said it was like she was there, and part of the team on that other planet sending out the message to us light years away on the other side of the sun. And when we intercepted the S.O.S., it was in four of the languages that we speak here on Earth. Either they have been here before, or have watched the messages that SETI sends out, looking for life on other planets. Life like us. The logical downer of all this, is that the messages we continue to receive are from so far out there – so many light years, that as they would be long gone – their sun will have went supernova by now. They are long dead and gone."

"Except if the speed of thought, of dreams, is used as a substitute for the limitation that the Theory of Relativity implies." Shane replied.

"Yes! Yes." Joseph patted him on the back. Keep thinking like that. "If they can make that journey, and still be as young as she appeared, then we must be able to make the trip back.

"Maybe she was in a cryogenic state, and made the trip frozen and woke up here? And what about the other ship?"

"There was no evidence of a sleep chamber on either ship," Joseph replied. There was room only for two people. Did I tell you that? But only one person made the trip each time, as far as we know. And you know what happened to her?"

"And the other ship –that crashed 10 years ago? Was there anyone in it?

"It was empty. We have a theory, though, that the person from that other ship was driving that van that tried to run you over in Hagersville."

"What would make you think that?"

"We traced the driver who rented the van back to a room in Hamilton. And we found a copy of the green suit left behind in his closet. Apparently he was thinking of coming back after doing the dirty deed."

"He?" Shane was astounded. "How did you know it was a he? Didn't he turn to ashes like the woman?"

"No – we found human remains in the fire that burned most of the van. Either he found a way to live without the green suit, or maybe he was able to take over a man's body here on earth. And I am beginning to sound like a conspiracy freak now. But this is so out there, I mean having the two ships, and the information that the woman who dreamed it has become as real as this crystal you are holding. All I can say to you at this point is, keep up the good work."

Tuesday night at the Mimicombo was a practice night for the club so Shane dropped in to see if there was any sign of his former friend and his partner.

"No sign," Sheila informed Shane. "But I heard a rumor that one night I was off, Melanie had a fall. She fell and injured her arm, and that is why they have not shown up for practice."

"I guess that Rudey only comes to the restaurant before practice?" Shane wondered to himself. "Who was I kidding about ever being able to be friends with someone who is deathly afraid of you or anyone stealing his girlfriend?" When he thought about a bit more on the way home, he also remembered that the other man had talked of nothing but himself and his grandiose accomplishments. "Some friend!" Still there was some kind of bond, something like a past life connection between the three of them—Rudey, Melanie, and himself. He had felt it watching them skate. It was like he was out there skating too. He resolved to himself that he was not going to let it go, and when his newfound friends came back, he would be there to cheer them on. So whenever he could, he showed up to work in the skate shop and carry on a conversation with Sheila.

A week passed by, and the next Tuesday, Shane was in the skate shop at the roller rink, and Rudey and Melanie walked up the stairs. He was holding on to her right arm to support her, and her left arm was in a sling with a cast from the shoulder to the wrist. His face was quiet and down cast, like someone who was about to ask forgiveness, which might have been Shane's imagination, since he doubted if the man even forgave anyone in his life.

"I want to ask you all to forgive me." Rudey spoke like he really was sorry for his past actions. "Especially Melanie," he said. I was pushing her too much. I only want the best for her though and we have made up and have a big surprise. You can tell them Mel."

"Rudey and I are getting married. As soon as this cast comes off and I can get the ring on my left hand. My ring finger is swollen right now. I have a crack fracture from falling on my hand, but it will heal and we can get back to skating soon. Meanwhile.... your turn Rudey," she nudged her partner.

"Melanie and I will be having an engagement party at her mother's apartment next Saturday and we would like to invite the both of you to the party. Sheila and you, too, Shane. Can you come?"

Sheila agreed. "I can come for a while, but my little one who is just about to turn two, is too much for my husband to manage on his own. I will be happy to come though."

"I will, too, if you are sure?" Shane replied.

"Of course we are sure." Melanie chirped up. "Aren't we Rudey?"

"Yes, of course," he replied, his face a bit flushed. "We want all of our old friends to celebrate our engagement. We will be inviting the rest of the members of the skating club when they show up down stairs.

Melanie handed out the information cards with the time and location on it to Shane and Sheila, and the two descended the stairs arm in arm.

"Well, that beats all!" Shane exclaimed. "One night I am threatened to be shot, and then I am invited to their engagement party, like an old friend no less. What do you think of that?"

"I think he got a bit of a wake up when she broke her arm," Sheila replied. "My guess is that he became angry out there on the floor and pulled too hard on her arm, and was responsible for causing her to fall. I will go just as a show of support for Melanie, and I will use my beautiful bouncing baby girl as an out to leave early. What about you Shane?"

"I will probably go," he replied. "I want him and Melanie to know that I have no hard feelings. I hope, for her sake, he makes a good husband."

"I would not hold my breath," Sheila managed a grin. "And you will get to meet Melanie's mother. That woman is a saint! Divorcing from a man who was so much like Rudey, and looking after three young girls all by herself. And to make it worse, her older daughter seems to think the divorce and everything is her fault. Don't know where that came from, but Melanie is walking baggage for a broken family. And a constant flirt – as if you didn't notice. But she will always be my long-time best friend."

On the Saturday of the engagement party Shane walked to the location on the invitation. It was a long walk along Lakeshore Boulevard to the intersection of Royal York Road. Shane might have taken the streetcar, but he was using the opportunity for additional exercise for his knees and legs. On top of that, he had time for a good thought about whether he really wanted to go. At the corner of Royal York, stood an old multilevel apartment that might once have been a home. He walked to a side door and knocked.

The door opened and Melanie was there, all bright eyed and gushing with excitement. "Oh! I am so glad that you came." She hugged Shane and kissed him on the cheek, much to the chagrin of Rudey, who shook his hand and welcomed him in. "And this is my Mother." Melanie introduced a tall rangy woman who was almost a twin of her daughter, except for shoulder-length red hair, and about 20 years (maybe older than) her daughter's age. Shane (and the woman) both hid their surprise.

"I know her!" Shane said to himself, as he shook the hand of this woman of his dreams, or....? "Great Spirit? How many versions of my soulmate will I meet? Will my real soulmate please stand up?"

"I am Kathleen." Melanie's mother let go of his hand after an awkward moment. "Please forgive my daughter's lack of protocol in introducing me. But then, she did say "here is my Mother." "Didn't she? Can I get you a coke or something harder? Wine maybe?"

"Would you have tea?" Shane was still awe struck. "If only this woman was a few years younger...? There is a lesson here for me that I am obviously missing! First the woman in the green suit, who dies in front of my eyes, and then comes back in my dream on another planet. And then the daughter from the roller rink, and now her mother? And they are all, spitting images of Kitt, except for being different ages! What gives?"

"Here is your tea." Kathleen interrupted Shane's train of thought. "My mother had an old Irish saying "it will all come out in the wash.""

"My grandmother, too," Shane agreed. "There seems to be a few other things that we might have in common."

"All in good time," she smiled. "If you hang around after the party, we can find a quiet time to talk, and maybe I can help you sort some of these coincidences out?" She had a knowing look in her eyes, and Shane realized that she may actually know more than she let on to the rest of their friends, including her daughter.

"What do you think of my mother?" Melanie and Sheila came over to where Shane sat sipping his tea and looking out to the Lake beyond the living room window. "She is really a saint! Isn't she?" Sheila said. And Melanie continued with her bubbly and almost flirting way. "Instead of wanting to date the daughter, maybe you really needed to meet her mother? How about that?"

"It is about Respect." Shane replied loud enough for Kathleen to hear. "In the Native tradition, we are taught that all women are to be respected first and foremost for who they are at the time that they are part of our life. Don't you agree?" Melanie's mother raised he tea cup in a salute. And Shane excused himself to talk with some of the other guests that he recognized from the roller rink.

Later, all the other guests had left, and Melanie's two sisters were playing music in their room with the door closed. Melanie walked home with Rudey who lived further down Lakeshore Boulevard. Kathleen told her to phone and she would walk to meet her daughter when she was ready to come home. Kathleen made Shane and herself another tea, and motioned him to follow her outside, down to the lake.

"You are a very understanding mother," he noted, taking a seat away from her on a rock, starring out to the lake.

"Because I let my young daughter go home with a man and probably stay overnight? That borders on a mother who doesn't know how to enforce morality."

"I believe that morality is not something that we enforce, and rather we model it," Shane replied.

"So how am I modeling, is it my divorce which is forbidden in the eyes of my Religion that makes me a bad role model?"

"It makes you a good role model when you do what is right, no matter what society says. You told me, that your older daughter is head strong, and will do almost anything to get her way. I agree, and that would include running away to marry the man she thinks is her soulmate, or is her destiny."

"So I condone her actions so that I can be there to help her, and catch her if she falls? Is that about right? You don't need to agree or disagree. I have made my bed—and my daughter will lie in it?"

"And what about that idea of destiny, anyways? You are right I have no right to judge someone like you who is centered in this reality, when I live for my dreams," he pondered.

"I used to believe that opposites attract—my previous husband and I were like night and day. But when I see these two interact, I see two that are like peas out of the same pod. They fulfill a need for each other. Maybe they will help each other to see that? I want my daughter to have a better marriage – all three of them to have a better life than I have had up until now. And that has to include the dreams that I cannot or refuse to remember."

"Those dreams, however strange and out of time they are, helped you to stand and walk tall. And to say 'enough' when you knew it was time to walk away." Shane noticed. "You are the young girl that was trapped in her wheel chair, aren't you?"

"That much is true. But I am not the one that you are looking for. She is out there somewhere among the stars."

"With all due respect, I agree with what you are saying," he replied. "But within that respect, and in the mystery that we call time, you were a young girl who ran and played with a small boy in a forest."

"Yes…and no! How could I have been? The timeline is all wrong. I am almost old enough to be his mother. How would any of this be possible?"

"It is possible when there is a great lesson of love and respect for ourselves that we need to learn. That is almost a word-for-word quote from the lips of our teacher, isn't it?"

"It might be, if I could remember. Or choose to. I remember a young girl that was not like me in any way, who inspired me to stand on my own two feet, literally! But she must have 'possessed' me while I was weak. Because now I have dreams of her in another place – on another planet that is slowly dying, and now she is asking for my help – our help."

"Maybe we can go on in a good way – a better way, if we could learn not to be wrapped up in someone else's judgment of right and wrong." Shane was speaking from his heart.

"How does that apply," she came over and sat on a large stone next to him.

"I mean that in the ways of my People, the Christian idea of possession is not the only answer when Spirit communicates or shares our life in this dream. There must be a more respectful way of seeing something that was, and is still, good for both of you. Maybe the new age idea is not all that wrong, that "we are all One." That would work for my Native ancestor's, too."

"I agree," she replied. "We could not be having this conversation if you had not said that respect was so important to you, when I met you at the door earlier in the evening."

The sun was beginning to set over the lake. "Read my tea leaves," Kathleen requested. "Out of the blue, I remember a boy who told me that his father once read tea leaves in Ottawa. How do we do this?"

The Big Bang Theory:
How do I know God as a Woman?
The Big Bang Theory was born in the minds of Men
Who could not imagine taking the Time
To Know Her Infinite Love!

...winterhawk

FOUR

"I remember a boy who told me that his father once read tea leaves in Ottawa. How do we do this?" Kathleen said to Shane. They had finished their cups of tea while they talked by the lake.

"You already have a start, since you made our tea with loose leaf tea. There will be a few tea leaves left behind in the bottom of our cups." He instructed her to turn her tea cup upside down on one of the large rocks by the water. "Now, turn it around four times, and give it to me. And I will see what I can see."

Shane recalled that when he turned sixteen, his father had agreed to read the tea leaves for him, like he had done in a fortune-telling tea room in Ottawa. "Hmmm —" Shane's father had exclaimed, "I see a chair with wheels. You will meet and marry a woman in a wheel chair some day. What do you think of that?" Shane had not given it much thought until finding more about Kitt in his dreams, and now, today.

"Hmmm—" Shane stared into the cup that Kathleen offered to him. "I see...I see a bird, an Owl. An Owl is the symbol of the feminine, the moon, and the night. Sometimes, to hear the hoot of an Owl can be warning of illness—"

"—or death." She completed the sentence for him. "During my last checkup, my doctor sent me for an x-ray. The x-ray showed a spot on one of my breasts that has not yet developed into a lump."

"You should remember that the Owl coming into your life is more often a warning to pay attention – your subconscious is trying to get your attention." He was quick to reply.

"A warning to pay attention to my dreams?" She picked up the cup and rinsed it in the nearby lake. "I am doing just that. I have been sharing my dreams with a Professor that I tracked down – because

the woman in my dreams gave me information to pass on."
"Professor Champion?" Shane asked, although he now knew the answer to a question that had been dogging him. "I am studying with Joseph Champion three times a week. He and a group of students, including myself, are working on a way to answer that S.O.S. from the stars."

That Monday evening, Professor Champion informed Shane that since his student was making such surprising progress at becoming familiar with computers and programming, he was keeping his eye out for a better job for him, one that would suit his newfound skills. "How would you feel working for a firm that might require a computer operator? I think it would be beneficial for all concerned."

It had occurred to Shane too, that having the money to buy a car might be a good thing, since his friend Wiley drove back home every weekend. Shane was quite happy with riding back and forth with his friend, and helping with the gas, but he believed that nothing is by chance. The appearance of an Owl in Kathleen's tea cup held a message for Shane, too, even if she said that "she was not the one he was looking for," there was a connection none the less. The coincidences were far too many. First there was the shared, and new dreams that she passed on to the man he was studying with. And then there was the startling image that appeared in her tea cup – when he agreed to do a reading for her "like the father of a young man she had known". Shane had already checked into the cost of borrowing money for a car. His present job would allow him to do that, but not much more. A better paying job plus the chance to work with computers appealed to him a lot.

That weekend on impulse, Shane rode home with his friend. "I tried to get in touch with you," the older one of his sisters informed him when Shane walked into the door in Nanticoke. "I left a message at your work, but you had left for the day."

"What's up?" he asked.

"Our Father went for a checkup last week. He was coughing but the doctor said it was probably nothing since he gave up smoking over ten years ago. Anyways, the doctor sent him for an x-ray. And the prognosis is not too good. He has cancer, and it is so far advanced that any treatment will not help."

"How much time?" Shane sat down on the nearest chair.

"About six months at the most." Shane's sister began to cry.

Shane's father spent a short time in the hospital and was sent home with the prognosis that they had done all they could, and it would be better for him to spend the time he had remaining with his family. And when his father came home, the man who had let alcohol do most of his talking was a changed man, a man who recaptured the Native ancestry that he had denied.

When Shane returned to Toronto, he bought an old Mustang so that he could come home twice a week and on the weekends when he was not still joining Professor Champion and the rest of the team in the hidden workshop of the University of Toronto. When Shane's father returned home, Shane would be treated with conversations with a man he barely remembered as a small boy. Shane learned to listen to his father in a way that he either could not or would not when his father could not let go of his previous addiction to alcohol.

One afternoon, Shane visited his father and his family back home, he was greeted by a strange pronouncement: "I heard a bird in the tree outside the window call my name." This became the norm, rather than the occasional outburst of spirituality from his father, and one day he told his son that he was seeing his relatives that had passed into Spirit appear at the foot of his bed. The months passed quickly, until one evening on his way back to Toronto, Shane obeyed an impulse to stop and phone home.

"I was sitting talking to father, his sister told Shane on the phone, and in the next minute, he quit breathing. The ambulance is coming to take him to the hospital. Your father—our father—is gone!"

Shane's life was on hold, and before he could hardly think, he was attending a viewing in the local funeral home. There were people, and relatives that Shane barely recognized. "Why is it always like this?" he wondered. In the vestibule outside the chapel, a woman walked up and hugged Shane like an old friend. "Who are you?" he asked. "I remember you, but I don't know from where or when."

"My name is Jinny," she answered. "I am a long-time friend that you met in another dream." She smiled at his look of wonderment. "I am a jinn, as my name implies – a being created by God out of Fire. I cannot die, and neither can you, or anyone else. The difference being, I know who I am. In the final outcome – we are all One." She looked to where Shane's father reclined, looking like he was asleep. "No one is ever lost when you remember them – you will meet again, like you and I right now."

"I believe what you are saying, and I do know you but—there is someone else missing." He returned her hug.

"Someone else?" She laughed. "Yes there is. God sent me here to tell you: 'When you are searching for God, search for Her, instead of Him.' She is closer than you think. The stars are closer than you imagine." With that the strange woman walked to the nearest door into the night.

Shane walked inside where his mother sat watching. "Who was that woman?" his mother asked. "Is she the one that you told me about?"

"No mom," he replied. "But she is helping me to find the one from my dreams."

"Well," his mother hugged him, "when your father is laid to rest, do what you need to do – go to the stars if you feel the need. I will be OK. The mortgage is paid on our house; I have a car to get around when I want. And I have your sisters and brother to look after me. Do what you need to do to follow your dreams."

After his father was cremated and his ashes buried in a wooden container so that his remains could return to the Earth, Shane returned to Toronto. The roller skating was now a part of the past that had served its purpose. Shane had a car, so he could visit his mother and the rest of his family when he chose to, and his respectful friendship with Kathleen. Kathleen provided him and the Professor with occasional bits of information that seemed to come as Kathleen suggested via something like possession, or channeling, as the new age people might call it. Shane began to imagine, that had he not met Kathleen in the flesh, they would have communicated in the dreaming as they had in his boyhood. Her sense of urgency about the SOS from the stars and the woman in green would not have been easily dismissed.

"I have a new job prospect for you, Professor Champion informed Shane one evening. "One that might help you hone your computer skills." The job was with a division of Caterpillar Tractor, the same firm that his friend Wiley worked for in the shipping department.

"I have heard that our company is opening a new plant in Brampton." Wiley told Shane. "I asked my Elder on the reserve whether it would be good for me to apply for a job there, and she told me that the new plant will only stay in Canada for about 10 years. I checked and sure enough, they signed a lease due to a government incentive. I will be staying behind at the shipping department in Mississauga for that reason." Wiley also told Shane that he was looking for another place to live, and would be moving out of their shared room soon.

"Ten years?" Shane shrugged, and decided it was a good move for him and he would apply for the job at the new plant in Brampton with the recommendation from Professor Joseph Champion as soon as possible. "In ten years, or less, I hope to be on a ship to the stars," he smiled, and remembered reading something that Richard Bach had written: "What the Caterpillar sees as the end, the Butterfly sees as the beginning." The synchronicity of the quote, as he recalled it, was amazingly right on!

After his friend moved on, Shane did, too, finding a one bedroom apartment on a farm in Brampton that would be closer to his new job as a computer operator in Brampton. With his newly acquired car he was still able to take the subway down town, or the Red Rocket to continue his work and study with Professor Champion. The Professor was open to Shane doing shift work and coming down town at different times because the computer operator job was mostly babysitting an RJE operation through a satellite connection to the company's home in Peoria Illinois. Shane was able to study during the quiet times he was alone on the night shift.

One day, after a day shift at his new job in Brampton, Shane decided to check out a Drum circle that a person at the Native Community Center in Toronto recommended. The Four Colors Drum Circle drummed every Wednesday evening at the Heart Lake Conservation area. The Circle at Heart Lake was in a part of the park where a Native Medicine Wheel had been created. The Four Colors Circle was, as the name implied, made up of people from all four colors skin. One evening of drumming using a borrowed "Community Drum" had Shane hooked. The Circle was led by two people who might have had their credentials questioned by a stricter Native organization, but their spiritual rights could not. The co-leaders had Native ancestry despite the fact that they both originated from England and had come over at different times in their life to discover their passion for all things Native, and had assisted in creating the Medicine Wheel in Heart Lake. With the help of the two leaders, Shane attended a drum-making workshop and joined the group in Heart Lake whenever Spirit permitted.

It was as a result of this Spirit-inspired drumming that Shane made a breakthrough in solving the part of the problem of journeying to the stars and beyond the speed of light.

FIVE

"Do you have a memory about re-gaining part of you that makes you feel whole and worthy of a magical life?" There was a thought that had been bothering Shane since he had read the tea leaves in his friend Kathleen's cup. And then there was the part that she had revealed about her trip to the doctor who described a black spot on her x-ray that had the potential of becoming a tumor.

"I have a vague memory of that dream," she replied. "But now it seems to have happened to someone that is no longer me. I have a shared memory, if that makes sense?"

"It does for me," he acknowledged. "At times I feel like the dreams are so real that they replace my memories of my everyday life. And there are other times they are more like waking up from a memory of a different me. The reason I asked, is if this were somehow real, then it should have an effect on our everyday health."

"I see where you are going," she replied with a sigh. "That dream did have a lot to do with inspiring me to walk away from my wheel chair. But now after all that has happened with my life – my failed marriage and my responsibilities for raising three children on my own, it is a distant memory. Like you put it, it is like something that happened to someone else – maybe more so for me than you."

"Your marriage did not fail, and you will not fail to be the best parent that you know how." Shane and Kathleen were sharing a tea down by the lake behind her apartment. "Our shared dreams, with the help of the girl from the stars, have a reason. I believe that everything that happens is for a reason. And now, our respectful friendship is about helping those people on that far off planet, who may be another version of us. I met a woman at my father's funeral who claimed to be someone I know in a different dream. She told me that, ultimately, we are all One."

"That is a common new-age belief." Kathleen replied. "And while it may be spiritually true, there is something missing in it for me."

"Strange!" Shane agreed. "That is what I said to her, too."

"It is a beautiful belief, but it neglects to speak to the reality of my life that I am living now." She replied. "I am a Christian at heart and I believe in free-will. I believe that I have the questionable right to make mistakes."

"That rings true for me, as a follower of the Native Traditional Path, having converted from my mother's Christian religion. The respectful question I have for my previous religion is the concept that the Earth is somehow a lesser place to live – as though our only purpose were to 'ascend' to Heaven. I have to ask my former self, if he still exists, is who created the Earth? I believe that God created the Earth, and anything God creates has a sacred purpose."

"And the scientists that thought up the Big Bang Theory did so because they were unable to imagine the Time to appreciate Her Infinite Love?" Kathleen blushed as she said this.

"I could not have said it better," Shane agreed. "So we, and the others who think like us, are somehow in the middle of a paradox. To help the people on that far-off star, and ourselves, we need to accept that there must be another way of experiencing our life on this planet, and the rest of the Universe."

"So where do we go from here?" Kathleen sat her teacup down on a nearby rock. "Another tea cup reading would only tell us what we already know, that we are here in this world at this time, and even if it is another dream, it is very real."

"I recently made a Drum." Shane announced. "And it helped me to remember another part of the healing ceremonies that I learned with the help of my Spirit guide and Native teachers. The Drum is my Heart, and when I sound it I am briefly taken to a place where I am more whole, more alive than I can ever remember. Next time I visit you, would you be OK if I brought along my Drum? I think it will help to connect to our Heart. And…with respect, the Drum may help you to heal what the x-rays are suggesting may happen." Kathleen agreed that this was a good idea, and Shane left for home wondering how many more memories Drumming could help him understand. "What if we have done this all before, in another dream, and we just need something that will help us wake up? Or maybe time is an illusion, too?" That last thought made his head swim.

His drum helped Shane to access dreams and it transported him to worlds that seemed beyond understanding, except through the oral stories that his Ancestors handed down from generation-to-generation. "How much of this is real, and how much comes from my imagination?" He wondered, and this led to creating a recording – 20 minutes of drumming that he used to meditate. On impulse, he took the drumming tape to the lab in Toronto, along with a small tape player and headphones.

With the headphones on, Shane sat at his computer terminal, and scanned the lines of programming information. He was getting more familiar with the programming and computer control language and as the drum tape played in his ears, he could almost see a correlation. It almost came together, it almost talked to him. He even heard voices in his mind: "This is our daughter, would you like to see more of her?" Two women and a man stood on the other side of a set of train tracks, and the woman (probably the mother) was talking to him. As he stepped forward, their faces became a blur. A panorama of stars filled his head and he was racing through the Galaxy. It was pleasant at first, but then he was soothed into a deeper meditative state, and a part of his mind brought him back to the computer screen in front of him. The connection, the purpose was lost. He took off the headphones and rewound the tape to the beginning and glanced around.

"Stephanie?" He called out to the woman who sat at a desk a few rows over, immersed in the code on her terminal screen. She looked up, breaking her concentration. The look on her face said: "You called?" There was not a hint of annoyance at being disturbed. On the contrary, she was always helpful. Stephanie was a master programmer, and this was her profession, when she was not here in the lab.

"Can I borrow the crystal for a few minutes?" he asked. The Crystal was on her deck beside her monitor.

"Of course." She picked up the crystal and got up to sit at an empty desk beside him. "You have an idea?"

"I do." He answered. "I have been using this tape I made with the sound of drumming on it at home, to aid my meditation. But here, I am going everywhere and nowhere at once. I am wondering if the crystal will help me to focus." He took the crystal from Stephanie, held it, and tuned on the tape player again. Almost at once, the drum connected to his heart, and the crystal came alive in his hands.

"Have you seen the latest transmission?" A man's voice awoke Shane to a brightly lit room.

"What is it all about?" He heard a voice reply.

"More of the same, broadcasts from something they call TV and the like. News and information from all parts of their world. If I were to believe that this is all they are, I would be recommending that we keep away. They can seem to be totally focused on war, taking from each other, and polluting their world without regard for the environment, as though they were the only species that are important."

"Luckily, we know different." The person who was Shane replied. "And if it had not been for your daughter's dreams..."

"If we had not believed in my daughter's dreams, we probably would not have even known they and their planet existed." The other man opened the door of the room they were in – and Shane followed him out into a large area that resembled an airport hangar, complete with strange, sleek vehicles that were in various stages of completion.

"How are the latest tests proving?" Shane asked.

"Our crafts are faster and faster, but they might as well be going in reverse when it comes to escaping the boundaries of our universe. We hit the same wall, that our scientists claim is the speed of light. So far, they are correct and we are trapped on a dying world, unable to find another home before the predicted death of our sun."

"And what about the world that your daughter helped us to locate? Are they any further along?" Shane surveyed the vast airport hangar, and experienced occasional gusts of frigid wind as a door opened and quickly closed, letting one of the experimental aircrafts move out to the runway.

"On the surface, if we only had their broadcasts to go by, they would seem to be on a parallel road. They might even be a bit behind us in technology, if it were not for certain scientists that are on the verge of believing in Imagination."

"Imagination?" What does that have to do with our physical ability to go to the stars?" Shane's voice echoed in his ears.

"One of their prominent scientists, the one called Einstein, who is also a proponent of the Speed of Light Theory, is credited with having said: 'Imagination is more important than knowledge,'" the other man replied to Shane.

"And dreams? I can see how the dreams that your daughter has is helping us to find our way to the stars, and to these people so many light years away, but seeing the way and going there, is a different matter." Shane followed the other man into one of the crafts, a two-seated version, and they moved soundlessly toward the hangar door. Shane noted that the pilot, who sat in the right seat, had his left hand on a series of crystals, with one finger on the first of four crystals. "This is our cruising speed," – he explained to the other man who Shane shared a bit of consciousness with. "Any speed you can 'imagine,' he smiled and continued as they raised in the air from the compact runway. The ground fell away and became a blur. "Are you game for more?"

"Show me the works. Show me what she can do." Shane was breathless. Some part of him was mindful that this man might have an inkling of a thought, of knowing, who he was speaking to.

"And this next crystal will send us to a speed many times that of sound." The pilot pressed his second finger to the second crystal, and Shane's mind went giddy as the clouds evaporated around the ship. And the next, God only knows, we have not been able to measure this. "Nothing seemed to change, but Shane felt suspended, weightless, as the blackness of space closed around.

"And the last crystal?" Shane was almost afraid to ask.

"We believe that this last crystal will propel us to the Speed of Light, but we have, again, no reference to prove that, or if it is actually beyond the limit."

"How so? I am open to find out if you are?" Shane watched as the man's fourth finger poised over the last crystal."

In the moment that the pilot's finger came in contact with that fourth crystal, the ship was on course to a waning sun. Space and Light exploded around them and like a mighty celestial hand that was closed and opened to release the two men and the ship into...

"Have you seen the latest transmission?" A man's voice awoke Shane to a brightly lit room.

"What was that all about?" he heard his voice reply.

"That is our predicament," the other man replied. "And this is the Paradox that we are trying to solve. We are hoping that you and the people on your world can help us to solve it before our sun goes completely cold."

The tape player stopped, and Shane removed the headphones.

"What was that all about?" Stephanie and Professor Campbell asked in unison.

"I was there!" Shane replied blinking in the incandescent light. The lab was unusually bright, but the light was pale compared to what he had seen – where he had been. "I was on the other planet, in an experimental lab, and a man took me on a test flight in one of their spacecrafts. And he told me – rather showed me the problem they are having getting off their world – to find another planet beyond the stars before their sun dies."

"You were in one of their spaceships?" Joseph was breathless. "And you saw how they flew it? We have yet to have even the foggiest idea how that is possible, even though we suspect that the crystal is part of what makes it happen."

"Yes," Shane confirmed. "There were four crystals, and when the pilot touched each in their turn, the ship accelerated until the last one sent us to what they believe is the speed of Light. And then...we were back at the hangar, as if we had not gone anywhere at all. And that – is their problem. He called it a paradox."

"Only four crystals?" Joseph frowned. "Are you sure? Please describe the cockpit to me – especially the placement of the crystals."

Shane described the interior of the spacecraft in as much detail as he could remember. "The pilot sat in the right seat like you would when driving a car in England, and he flew the ship by pressing each of the four crystals, one at a time, with his left hand. There was no engine sound, but the speed blew me away, and eventually back where we started."

"Only four crystals?" The Professor was puzzled. "Both of the ships we found – the one that is on the Reserve, and the one that crashed and is in the NASA hangar, have eight crystals. I wonder what the second bank could be for? It is positioned exactly where the pilot's right hand could access it. I am guessing that the version of the two ships that we have are from a point in time that they found out how to overcome the paradox. Maybe with our help. Great work Shane...and Stephanie. Both of you keep it up and I believe you will solve this together." He put his hand on both of their shoulders.

"I didn't do a thing," Stephanie shrugged.

"I have a feeling that, since the space craft is built for two people that there is something in that construction that is related to the two banks of crystals. Just a crazy thought. But then, Shane would not have the computer know-how and be where he is today without your help."

"Arête de dire bêtises!" Stephanie was flushed. "Sorry, I revert to my native tongue when I get flustered. I didn't mean to say that, excuse me Professor, but that is nonsense. All I did was help Shane to get started and he took to the computer like he was just remembering something he already knew. And today, all I did was hand him the crystal."

"Oh, sorry, I apologize. I seem to have hit a nerve," the Professor smiled. "I was jumping ahead of myself. I really meant to say that it might be interesting if someone else tried the experiment using Shane's headphones and tape."

"OK, but not me." Stephanie moved back to the safety of her own desk. She was red-faced and flustered, but eventually joked and tried to play it down. "I am a single girl and intend to stay that way. No matchmaking please."

"Hooo K," the Professor shrugged. He seemed to be enjoying himself. "Anyone else? How about you Diego?" He asked a young man of Mexican- Spanish heritage. "Are you willing to give it a go?"

"Si. I am ready to go to the stars," Diego responded with enthusiasm.

Diego was fitted with the headphones and held the crystal in his hands. Shane turned the player on, and stepped back. A few seconds passed, and the young Mexican man's eyes went large, and his mouth followed suit. When five minutes or so had passed, his features became softened, and his eyes gained a faraway look. "Bella!" he exclaimed as the tape shut off. "Beautiful!"

"Where did you go?" the Professor asked.

"I went to…the Big Bang…and followed the universe as it expanded…on and on…it was beautiful. I could never stop," he sighed and handed Shane back the earphones. "You should make a meditation tape with this," he smiled.

"I might," Shane responded, "but I would need to include this crystal with the tape."

"Let me try?" A hippy young man called Alfred requested. "I am really ready to get turned on by the stars."

"That might be the generic trip," Shane suggested. "When I used the tape, I had an intention. I think that may have been the difference. Or maybe I am the different one here? I am a dreamer, and let me be very honest, I have found my soul mate in my dreams, so I would like to apologize to our friend Stephanie and say that I have no reason to pursue a friendship with anyone who does not think I am being respectful." He looked at Stephanie and saw that she was blushing.

"I can relate to love." Alfred replied. "But as for intent? Any ideas Professor?"

"How about wanting to connect with someone working on the crystals like the one you will be holding?" Professor Champion replied. "After all that is why we are together here."

Alfred held onto the crystal, put on the tape, and was transported. His eyes were large like Diego's at first, and then they took on a thoughtful gaze. His eyelids closed, and his eyes moved like someone on REM – dreaming sleep. When the tape ended, he opened his eyes, and shrugged. "Yes, I was a man – almost like I possessed him – with his consent of course. I was installing crystals into one of the spaceships. He knew I was there, and explained everything he was doing in great detail, but it was not anything we have not already guessed. Confirmation I guess."

"Were you able to ask him anything?" The Professor inquired.

"I tried. But I don't know if he understood me. "That is all I know," He kept repeating. He seemed to be talking to a group of similar technicians. Who watched in the background? It was as though I was one of those men watching."

"How many crystals was he installing?" Professor Champion asked.

"Only four. The mind of my man did not have any memory of having done this installation any other way."

"This is like my dream," Shane commented. "It may be happening now, or has already happened, and these people are long gone and exist only in our memories like passing waves of light. I prefer to believe that the Theory of Relativity is as it implies – a theory, but the Relative part of it is alive for me. This is something that may be hard to understand for someone who is non-Native."

"I tend to believe as Shane does," the Professor replied. "Or we would not be here today. There would be no reason for us to think we can answer the S.O.S. unless…unless any of you think this is all for scientific or military gain."

"I, for one, would like to think that there is always hope," Stephanie replied. "This touches a painful memory for me, about a sister that I lost. That is personal but it is a good part of what drives me, and keeps me here to find answers that are beyond our present knowledge. What can I do to help?"

"Maybe you can have a try at the crystal and sound meditation, and help Shane to put it together in a program or application that can be used by any of us to connect and pilot one of those ships that we are building at NASA?" the Professor suggested.

"Sorry, I am not ready for the crystal meditation just yet. I have my reasons." Stephanie, but I can offer my programming and computer skills to create an application or device that will."

"That sounds fair to me." Shane replied. "Is there anyone else that wants to take a turn at the crystal – with the intention of contacting one of the engineers on that planet that may or may not exist?"

There were three other students present that had not tried the crystal meditation. Those three, and then Diego were able follow the drum beat and use the crystal in a successful attempt at contacting someone else in the hanger on the far away planet. The intention was somehow a key for what could be a mass shared dream. But whatever the truth may be, they all had a renewed focus and a common goal. Stephanie was just not ready yet, and that was to be respected. Their Professor however, was game to see it his students were unique in a way that young people can be, before life shuts down their imagination.

"Imagination is more important than knowledge," Joseph repeated his favorite quote from Einstein – his mantra. But, after a few minutes of listening to the drumming tape, the Professor shut it off, and removed the headphones. "I have the intention, but this is more than this brain of mine can handle at this time. I concur with Stephanie. Everything in it's' time. But there's the Shakespearian rub. "'It is not in the stars to hold our destiny but in ourselves.' Time is a construct, perhaps of men, a coping mechanism created to avoid living in the moment. I will try again, or just go along for the ride."

Working with the other members of Joseph's team became an enlightening experience for Shane. In the beginning he had been under the impression that Joseph had invited him to learn about computers and the IBM system for Shane to become a programmer. Shane learned quickly that he was not about to develop a way to interface with the engines of the spaceships from the stars using the programming skills he learned, and neither were the rest of the team. They each had their individual expertise that would, possibly with time, create a workable method of making the crystals that powered the ships work in earth-based ships. It was it seemed, another method that the people at NASA chose to reverse-engineer the technology that was light years ahead of them.

Upon taking a closer look at the people like Diego and his fellow students, they were not being trained as programmers. They were engineers, working on advanced concepts that their professional counterparts in the USA might have trouble adjusting to due to a closed minded approach of how a system that might power a ship to the stars might operate. In short, the Theory that stated that the speed of light was unsurpassable would prevent those with that limited belief from accomplishing the task and the reality of the physical evidence that the ships from the stars seemed to present. Someone had piloted those ships – without cryogenic (sleep) chambers. And they had survived to tell the tale, as evident in the woman dressed in green, and the "man" who became human and attempted to put an end to the project at its inception – or so it seemed. Like attracts like. If there was any truth to the crazy idea of possession, then the man who was traced back to the apartment in Hamilton was a perfect candidate. In addition to the green suit, his apartment also contained the remnants of a bomb. The van that he had been driving did not explode of its own accord.

And then there was Stephanie. Her job was also more complicated than it appeared. She was a computer and programming wiz, homegrown, with a logical block that was a result of having lost her older sister. Stephanie was being fed new concepts via the Professor and NASA. She refused to pack up and move to the USA because her remaining family who migrated from

A Spark of the Fire

France now lived in Canada. The new concepts that Stephanie now brought to the table, to help Shane create an interface with the crystals, was due to a major jump in the IBM system as a whole. The IBM system that she connected to with her terminal in Canada had been upgraded to an "iSeries" and then an "eSeries." She had the technology at her disposal, and the expertise to create an application and possibly a device that would make use of sound and light to interact with the crystals to power any ships that NASA might be in the process of constructing.

"And why?" Shane wondered at first, had the lab and the students been brought together in Canada? Why not in the USA – at the NASA headquarters? Maybe part of the answer lies in the complete and potentially working ship that was hidden away in the protective hands of the Six Nations reserve. Joseph was open to tell Shane in the beginning, that they had requested that the ship be moved, but the Native Chiefs realized that they had a prize given to them from the Star People. Perhaps physical evidence of their story about "How Sky Woman fell to Earth?" Joseph laughed at the irony. These people were able to use the threat of revealing their prize to the Canadian government, if needed, to protect the ship. And so the lab was set up in Canada, and bright young minds were recruited to make the impossible possible. This bit of irony and loss by politicians (on both sides of the border) was made clear to Shane when his Native friend Wiley informed him of the plan by the company he worked at to take advantage of the financial gifts that resulted in the use of the land in Brampton. And this was a common thread for big companies in countries that open a subsidiary someplace that might benefit from the sharing of their resources. And then the potential butterflies that might have resulted in sharing are lost when the obvious natural resources have been minded out - except for those who are able to see this as the precise and correct time to exit their cocoons.

And then there was Kathleen. She was not about to give up her knowledge to just anybody. The Spirits of the Stars had pressed her to find the right person to benefit from the S.O.S. That someone proved to be Professor Joseph Champion, and the rest was becoming history. Kathleen's history, however threatened to come back and affect her personal health and her family. One afternoon Shane visited Kathleen, thanking her for the opportunity that she and her daughter had given him to learn Respect – otherwise his "working friendship" with Stephanie might not have been possible. Kathleen informed Shane that day that Rudey and Melanie, having been married, were planning to move to BC.

"Melanie told me this week that Rudey has a chance at a good promotion if they were to move to Alberta. I told her, as any good mother would, to think about it, with her heart and not just her brain, and if it seems right to take the chance for a better life. Do you think I made the right decision?" she asked Shane on the rock out by the lake.

"That would not be up to me or anyone to judge," he answered. "I believe that if she knows that you will be there for her even if she makes what might seem to be a mistake, it will turn out right. How did your last x-ray turn out?"

"I am holding my own. The spot has not grown much, but I am fearful that I will not be around to see my future grandchildren." The Drumming helped me to connect with that little girl who was healed in the forest. Can we do more of that?"

"The drumming helped me, too," Shane replied. And he shared the insights that he had as a result of his new job, and working with the team at the lab in Toronto. "Let's continue to share the drum. And there has been a new memory that has come up for me. I wonder if you remember working with stones in the forest. When our teacher showed us how to search for answers meditating by the pool in the forest, he showed us another way using two stones."

"Something comes up," she smiled and asked him if he would begin the drumming. "I remember someone telling the little girl and boy to still their minds like the surface of the pool, and the answers would rise like bubbles to the top."

Shane began to drum, lightly and methodically and he was drawn into a dream of distant yesterdays. He wondered if this memory had been there before, or if the past were not still alive somehow.

"Take two small stones," their teacher said. "Hold one in both hands and play with your imagination. Imagine that the Grandfather Stone in your right hand holds the memories of how things are (good or bad) in your life at this moment. Try not to judge. You can learn from things you do not like as easily as those that you feel good about. And then there may be things that you want to change, or learn more about. The Grandfather stones are about concrete knowledge. Things we need to survive and prosper in our everyday life. But there is more. The Grandmother Stone that you hold in your left hand is about compassion – learning with our Heart. Sometimes this may mean letting go, and sometimes the teaching of our Grandmother is about opening up to new ideas to solve problems that cannot be conquered."

"Think. Meditate on the Grandfather Stone in your left hand, and the Grandmother Stone in your right hand. And when your mind is as still as the water before you, hold out both hands, and drop the stones into the pool. And just watch as both stones create circles – concentric circles in the pool. And watch as those circles meet, and seem to cancel each other out. That is the answer to your problem at hand. Do you understand?"

Shane continued to drum until it seemed right to sit in silence by the lake.

"I thought that the answer was about me being the creator of my own problems." Kathleen spoke after a while. "I am part of it to be sure, but it is not about getting stuck in self judgment and guilt either."

"Thanks for sharing that." Shane replied. "There is something there for both of us. Are we done for today?"

"My tea is finished." She smiled. "And I do not need a tea cup reading to tell me that whatever might show up at the bottom of the cup or at the top of the pool of water, is not something that cannot be changed."

SIX

"Have a look at this," Stephanie said to Shane. She was now sitting at a desk beside him and openly sharing her accomplishments, while respecting his ideas at the same time. "I have been able to set up an application that can be turned on with a button to activate a sound stream to connect with the crystals."

She was visibly excited.

"Could we use this as part of, say, a helmet worn over the head – something that a pilot might wear?" Shane asked.

"Why yes, that would work," she agreed.

"That is a great idea," he replied. "Would you be able to use that helmet to control the ship?"

She shrugged. "Possibly, but not in my present state of mind. And then there is the paradox. Do you think that the other four crystals have anything to do with the problem that comes up when the ship reaches the speed of light – presuming of course that this is all true. I hope you don't think I am doubting what you witnessed as a passenger."

"No problem," He replied. "It is a bit far out for me too. But I am able to accept my visions and dreams as real in a way that most people might not. And I recently shared a dream with my friend Kathleen about using two stones and two hands to create a belief in which magic can take place."

"Magic? Really!" And Stephanie giggled in a way Stephen had not witnessed before.

"What is magic, if not something that imagination and intention makes happen in real life?" he smiled. "Magic can be used to heal. For my Native ancestor's, the Shaman used Ceremonies to heal and bring about positive changes for their tribes."

"I could use a bit of that magic." Stephanie sobered up.

"How so?"

"Do you remember me telling everyone about losing my sister?" She sighed and leaned back in her chair. Tears were beginning to form at the corners of her eyes.

"You don't need to talk about this if it is too painful," he replied.

"Thanks, but I do. It's time. And I trust you enough to be the one to share this with." The lab was coincidently empty. The other "students" and the Professor had gone out to lunch. "My sister, Lizzie, died when I was much younger – before I decided to devote my time to this project with Professor Champion. I left school and was just moping around the house, and then one day he showed up and asked me to come to Toronto to work with him. Out of the blue." She sighed deeply, remembering.

"That was pretty well the same thing that happened to me," Shane said, when Stephanie did not continue. "Lizzie? Is that short for Elizabeth?"

"Lise," Stephanie woke from her daydream. "I like to call her Lizzie. She was just a year older than me, but we were like twins. And we still are, except she is gone. Lizzie had a dream, too. She had her life all planed out. She shared it with me every day, how when that cad…I don't even want to remember his name, but I remember how he asked her—to marry my sister. And they planned a big wedding together, at least she planned it. I don't think he could have been in on the planning though. And Lizzie had even picked the names of her children. She could see their faces—a boy and a girl. It was so real for her, that when at the last moment, the day before the wedding, he disappeared. He disappeared like he had never been part of her life. And Lizzie was devastated." Tears were now flowing down Stephanie's face.

"I am so sorry," was all Shane could say. "That would be a terrible thing for you and your sister to live with."

"It would have been, if it had ended there." Stephanie straightened her shoulders in the chair and wiped away the tears. "How could we know? How could I have known? Lizzie moved out and got an apartment of her own, and when I visited her she was taking pills to be able to sleep. And then one day, she did not answer my phone calls and when we found her it was too late. We took her to the hospital but it was too late to save her. Our father cried, but you know what bothered him the most? He and my mother were told that a person who dies like this will not be allowed into heaven. God! That blew me away! What kind of God would make that kind of rule! And what kind of man would do that to someone like my sister?"

"What about your mother?" Shane asked. "She could not believe a terrible thing like that. I certainly could not believe in any God like that."

"My mother just cried. I think mothers' always believe the best of their children. Our mother only said: "'I don't believe that! I don't believe that my Lise would do that – it is a lie!'"

"I agree with your mother," Shane replied.

"I do, too," Stephanie replied. "I believed in my sister too, and I still do."

"What did you do?" he asked.

"I asked my mother and father where the priest was."

"He returned to the chapel," my father replied with tears in his eyes.

"Well I went down there to see about this – to set it right., Stephanie told Shane. "I calmly asked the priest: "'What right do you have to talk to my mother and father like you did in my sister's room? And who gave you the right to pass judgment on her?'"

"God gave me the right," he answered, and turned back to his candles and incense. And when I didn't leave, he said: "didn't you read the death certificate.""

"I know what it says," I answered.

"Then you know that the cause of death is Unknown. And we both know what that means."

"Oh we do, do we?" It was hard to hold my temper. "If WE had a scrap of decency, we would know that it means that my sister died of a broken heart. Due to a snake of a man who promised to love her forever and betrayed his commitment at the last moment."

"There was no signed commitment," the priest answered.

"There was an agreement before God. Isn't that enough?"

"Unless there is a signed marriage document, it is not enough," he answered.

"And the document that is the death certificate? Can we believe it? It was signed by a doctor who wrote "'cause unknown.'" Or isn't a doctor's signed certificate to be believed?"

"I will make it right," the priest replied.

"And did he do as you requested?" Shane asked.

"Yes! And he apologized to my parents as well. But now I am stuck with a fearful belief as to what might have happened to my sister's soul, and a paradox — a real threat to my sanity."

"What do you mean?" Shane was even more puzzled.

"All that I just told you did not happen! Yet I remember it as though it did. You see, I do not have a sister called Lise or Lizzie. I am an only child. But I remember her like I have always known her – she has been my playmate, my older sister since as long as I can recall."

"Wow!" Shades of my dreams," Shane exclaimed. "I have lived that same scenario all my life, but as a Native child, it is pretty well accepted that we dream. Then, what does the rest of your family – your mother and father really think?"

"My father has always thought that I need to see a psychiatrist, since I was able to talk about my invisible sister. But my mother has been steadfast in her support. And now, my mother is using this to convince my father that she was right in the beginning, and we should never have immigrated to Canada. My mother, by the way has refused to learn the English language. She does not feel at home here. She says that "these are not my people'." And my mother thinks this will all go away, and everything will be made right if we return to France."

"So what do you think?" Shane asked. "I don't think you are any crazier than me."

"Now that IS a statement in itself." Stephanie managed a smile. "I do not think I am crazy, either, except maybe like you. But my vision of my sister will not go away, and I have lost my faith in the God that I was taught about from birth."

"At my father's funeral," Shane replied, "I met a woman who claimed to be a friend that I met in a different dream. She appeared out of the blue, just when I needed her, and told me that no one is lost. And she also said something really strange. She said "when you are searching for God – look for Her, instead of Him."

"What does that mean?" Stephanie was drying her eyes on a Kleenex. The other people were returning from lunch.

"For me – as a Native man, and someone who has found his truth in dreams, that means to search for a Female God – the compassionate, loving and forgiving part of God."

The Professor and the rest of the team returned and the dark feeling was lifted for Shane and Stephanie, as she began to share her ideas with the rest. And then when everyone was packing up for the evening, Stephanie came over and offered a newspaper clipping for Shane to see.

"I have had this for a while," she explained. "See what you think."

It was an advertisement for an Edgar Cayce meditation group. A "Search for God" group in Mississauga.

"Would you like to come with me and check it out?"

"I sure would," he replied. "I have read positive things about Edgar Cayce and I think I could benefit from a closer connection with Her – God I mean. I hope you will excuse my Native way of looking at Spirit."

SEVEN

"Have you read some of the prophesies by Edgar Cayce?" Stephanie asked Shane on the way to their first meeting with the *Search for God* group in Mississauga. She had picked up Shane at the farm in Brampton in her car.

"About?" He had a good idea what she was going to say next, because the idea had occurred to him that there was a connection between the crystals and..."

"Atlantis," she replied. And he nodded, waiting to hear her take on it. "Cayce made a prediction that the lost city of Atlantis would rise again from the Ocean. The time is about right, don't you think? And there is the not-so-strange coincidence of the crystals. Atlantis was supposed to have perished beneath the ocean due to a misuse of the powerful crystal that they used."

"I have thought a lot about it, along the same track of mind," he replied. "In our case, the crystal is real. We can hold one of them in our hands, and access the ship hidden somewhere intact, on the Native reservation. What if, this is the same crystals that Atlantis used? And what if Cayce's prediction was symbolically in meaning, that Atlantis, whether it existed in our reality or not, would rise again in our consciousness?"

"The part of the crystal that we have in the lab excites our brains," she mused. "Haven't you noticed? It wakes you up – that is unless you are a Native man who is already awake to his dreams, then you are already awake to the potential that we can become. Anyways, I need to apologize for not being fully truthful with you until I learned that I could trust you. I have avoided handling the crystal, because I have dreams that I don't want to face. Dreams that include losing my sister. And of course there is more, but I don't want to go there yet, until I am ready – if ever."

"I understand. I really do," he agreed. And he also realized that he could not divulge anything about his friendship with Kathleen. Kathleen had agreed to continue passing on whatever information she received to Joseph and now Shane if she was able to remain anonymous. It was partly due to this respect that Shane was now about to embark on a possibly different friendship— a relationship with Stephanie. And he was not asleep to the possible similarities of Kathleen's life and Stephanie's lost sister.

The Search for God group was a registered affiliate of the ARE, the Association for Research and Enlightenment, dedicated to caring on Cayce's work after his departure into Spirit. This group in Mississauga was facilitated by an Asian couple who led the group meditations once a month. They began with a reading from Cayce's *Search for God* book, and proceeded onto a group meditation on the reading. It was a pleasant couple of hours that both Shane and Stephanie enjoyed.

"So, what do you think?" he asked Stephanie on the drive back home.

"I felt right at home," she replied. "A good part of it must be due to being in the company of people who don't think I am crazy because I believe in a sister that I have not met in this world."

He smiled and agreed silently that this was so true for him, except it was not a sister that he was looking for. In the Native Tradition, a man has many sisters and brothers – all that are due the respect of being who they are, and not needing to be changed into something or someone that fits his needs. "I will be interested in seeing what Professor Champion thinks about the idea of Atlantis and the crystals that are located on that planet way out there among the stars."

"Maybe they are the same, and then again we may be at fault for the way our brains process things. Like a computer, we can only see things that we have been programmed to accept. People say: "garbage in, garbage out." But one man's garbage, or fearful idea of possession, may be another woman's contact with Angels."

"Very true!" He found himself agreeing with a lot that Stephanie was sharing.

* * *

"I am feeling peaceful as the ripples from the stones come together," Kathleen whispered. They had shared the healing ceremony on rocks behind her apartment. The only sound other than her voice was the pleasant lapping of the waves on the rocks. The traffic on Lakeshore Boulevard was far and distant, like in another world.

Shane was drumming, and his mind was in another place. In that other place, he was a participant in a ceremony that involved a journey to the world that existed down the "rabbit hole" – down an opening that was appearing at the base of a large tree in the forest. This was to be part of the healing journey that might involve him bringing back something that was precious to his friend and constant playmate since birth. That something (his mind recalled in a timeless state) was a beautiful crystal that would help her remember who she was. And at this point in his remembering her, he was confused. This confusion brought him back to the present, and the Lake, and his grown friend Kathleen. "Are we all really a spark of the same fire — are we, in truth, One?"

"How about if both statements were true?" Kathleen replied.

"Sorry, I didn't mean to interrupt your healing meditation," he blushed.

"No apology needed," she replied. "I have my answer and I guess in your way, so do you. You were off somewhere? Care to tell me about it?"

He sat the drum on his lap, and gave her a brief description of his vision dream, being discreet as to her part in the ceremony. "And….as I was coming back, I heard something that I must have missed before. There was the constant and comforting sound of the drum in the forest, and something else. I just can't put my finger on it, but there was another sound – something that was almost as important as the drum…it's gone now."

"It will come back, when the time is right." Kathleen reassured him. "I thank you for your help. I am feeling much more confident about the future. I will be there for my daughters, I know that now. I had what could have been a setback earlier this week. Melanie and Rudey packed up and headed for BC. I thought for a while that I had failed her. But now, I know it is all part of letting go, and I told her to make sure to remember to keep in touch. I told her I am here for her, and we hugged. I remembered what you told me about the Ojibway good bye. I did not say good bye. My daughter is not lost – she will be just a phone call or a plane ride away."

* * *

Stephanie was much more peaceful after a few shared meeting with the *Search for God* group. And she worked elbow-to-elbow with Shane in creating a first demo that contained an energetic equivalent of his drumming music attached to the back of a helmet that could be worn by any member of their group. While wearing the helmet, and further incarnations of the same, any member of the team could connect with an engineer who worked with the crystals and the associated paradox on a planet light years away, that may or may not still exist in so-called real time. In the beginning, unfortunately, the person in the lab in Toronto still had to have physical contact with the crustal. But they all reported increasing vivid dreams as a result of the experience.

"I want you to keep your dreams a secret for now, and not share your experiences with anyone out of the classroom," Professor Champion urged. Shane had heard this somewhere before.

"What about the remote connection to NASA?" Diego asked.

"That, too,." the professor replied. "Keep working on the engineering part of the ships that we are constructing as we speak in the USA. That is, in part, what this lab in Canada is about. But there are more important reasons for our being here than was within the scope of the original project. I have come to believe that the S.O.S. is real, in some way even I do not understand. NASA,

A Spark of the Fire

however, is becoming aware of the far-reaching technology that the real ships only hint of."

"This is for your ears only!" The Professor came out from behind his desk and gathered everyone around. "The people in the USA, my people, and my higher-ups, have been able, with your help, to construct ships with the potential of going into space. But there is one thing missing — the crystals that will power these ships. In the USA we have one crashed ship, in disarray and in many pieces, lacking a cohesive ability that it was created for. It is like a human body that all parts will work and express life together, but when disassembled, the parts do not match the capability of the whole."

"We," the Professor continued, "have been covertly searching the Earth for crystals like those that might conceivably power our ships like that one that crashed and the one that is in safe keeping of the Native people. But the only thing we have found closely resembling those crystals was in underground caverns beneath Hiroshima and Nagasaki, and Chernobyl. And beneath other sites where atomic explosions have occurred. We have found crystals growing there that are almost identical, but are for all sense and purpose, unusable."

"Why are those crystals not usable to power the ships that NASA has built?" Stephanie asked.

"The potential power is evident," the Professor replied. "But there is also residual radioactive energy that would be completely and devastatingly harmful for all life. Somehow, those crystals that were in the ships from the stars have the correct energy balance that ours do not. We need to know more, or...do not let this out... we need to go to that planet and bring the crystals back to power our ships, and then the technology that we in this lab are only dreaming about."

"But to go to that planet, as NASA intends," one of the other lab members spoke up, "they would need either the ship on the Native Reserve or the crystals that are in it. Am I right in assuming this?"

"Correct, on both accounts," the Professor replied. "I am a loyal American, and I support most of the endeavors my country has envisioned, like going to the moon, and helping countries that are in need here on Earth. But this seems to have taken a greedy turn. They want those crystals and the technology they represent beyond any idea of sharing or responding to the SOS. The easy and logical answer is based on the theory of relativity, in a non spiritual way: the people that sent this message and the planet that we can see with long range telescopes, are long dead and gone. But the crystals that they used to send the ships will still be available. That is if the star has not gone super nova. Then we are seeing images of objects that no longer exist. There is the paradox that we have in our hands."

"But those people do exist in Spirit," Shane answered. "And the difference between the ships that we see in our dreams, and the physical ships that came to Earth with a second group of crystals, seems to indicate that someone—maybe we helped them. That is the real paradox."

"I believe that may be true, too," Professor Champion shook his head. "But my government, my President is talking to your Canadian leader. And I am wondering if your politicians and leaders are either soft in the head or greedy beyond their own pockets. This would not be the first time this happened, by the way. In the recent past, the Avro Aero that was a super-fast jet of Canadian origin was dumped at the request of our president in the USA. He convinced your Prime Minister that Canada should not have any ship that was capable of speeds that your friendly neighbors did not have. Now, no matter how stupid that seemed at the time, history is about to repeat itself."

"Do you think our government knows about the ship that is hidden away in the Native Reserve?" Shane asked.

"If they do, whoever is in charge is thinking about his own ambitions. And that, maybe, is to sell out his country to the demand of the USA. I make this statement even in the light of loving my home country." The Professor was silent for a moment. "I do not know what to believe, except that I am hearing from reputable sources that the Government of Canada is going over old Treaties that will enable them to confiscate land along the Grand River, that rightfully belong to the Native people."

"I heard that, too," Shane replied. "My friend Wiley told me that the natives are getting ready to blockade any intervention into our lands. That makes sense, even for the few of my people who might know about the ship from the stars."

"So what can we do?" Stephanie inquired. "That ship belongs to the Natives. It is a gift from Sky Woman. And it is a physical message — a cry out for help."

"For the present, I am asking all of you to keep secret the information that you learn that isn't related to the actual building of our ships in the USA, until we can see our best course of action."

When Shane visited Kathleen later that week, she informed him that she had talked to Melanie and her daughter told her that she was pregnant.

"That must make you feel good – to know that you are going to be a grandmother," Shane replied.

"Yes – and no," Kathleen said. "Yes I am happy for her – and me. But I didn't have to read between the lines. Rudey and Melanie are going through a difficult time with their relationship. I am thinking seriously about moving to BC to be a support for her, and Rudey. In fact it is more than just a thought. When I told Melanie about my idea, she cried over the phone. She needs me, and a change of scenery would be good for all of us – my other two daughters too."

"I feel good about your decision either way," He replied. "Joseph and I will miss your input on our project, but a mother's love here at home is more important than sending a ship out into space. If you don't think it would be intruding, can I ask you if you are an only child?"

"No problem," Kathleen replied. "I do have another sister, in Ireland and I have been thinking a lot about her lately. In fact that was part of my healing prayer when I did the ceremony with the stones. I imagined my sister being part of the healing as the ripples of the stones came together. It was for both of us – healing a family that has so many differences but is so much alike. And that includes Melanie too. Melanie has the gift, too. I used to think that it was a curse. We were brought up to believe that being what some people call a medium is someone who has crazy dreams, but I believe now that it is a gift from God."

"I take it that your sister in Ireland has the gift, too?"

"Yes – she paved the way for me, even though I didn't know it, until it began to happen to me. My sister in Ireland was deserted by her husband and when she filed for a legal divorce, our church excommunicated her. What a stupid senseless thing to do. All because she believed she was a reincarnation of Joan of Arc. There are a lot of women that have had that belief you know. How can they all be Joan? It had me almost believing that there was something wrong with her. No – I don't believe that I am Joan of Arc, but there are mysteries that we don't know about until it happens to us, don't you think?"

"I agree," Shane replied. "I have dreams in which I am someone different that I can't explain too, as you are aware. Someone told me once, that if it is impossible, it must be true."

"That sounds like good, advice, even if it cannot be logically proven as true."

"But sometimes it can be proven, when it comes true for us," He reminded her. "My people tell stories about logical things that have proven true in this world time and time again. One story we tell is about *The Three Sisters*. I guess you've heard that one?"

"*The Three Sisters'* story is about three different kinds of plants that have been grown together in a group to feed your people. That's what I heard. How does that apply?"

"It is a logical story that has been proven to be workable and useful for the Native people," Shane replied. "But it might have a deeper meaning for someone who dreams, and sees that Spirit, body and mind come together to make up the Fourth world that we live in."

"Hmmm? Kind of like the Holy Trinity?" she guessed.

"Yes, a female expression of God's Love. When you see our world through Native eyes, like I do, the Fourth World is a reality where we are all brothers and sisters working together for a common good."

"And the three sisters help this to become real," she smiled. "But I only have one other sister…unless? Unless you think that the woman on that other planet is really my other sister?"

"Stranger things have happened, and become real. I would like to wish you well in telling your daughter that she comes from a long line of special women who have helped to change the world."

EIGHT

The drum beat was soft and almost monotonous, intended to soothe and capture the mind in a safe circle of non-involvement. But it was involving. It drew Shane in, and prepared him for a journey of healing. This dream took him back to the forest that he had visited so many times during his life. Off to one side, beyond the fire but with the drumming circle a tall oak tree was going through a transformation. As the drumming continued, a hole appeared at the base of the tree and enlarged to the size that would accommodate a man (or woman) on their knees. Paying homage to the Spirit of the Journey. The ever present drum beat prepared his heart and mind – brought them together for One purpose...but something else was involved in the working of the Magic. Another sound that persisted in the background - opening the mind to the other worlds of possibility and imagination. He attempted to find, and isolate that other sound and found that this action caused him to wake from his dream.

"Where were you?" Stephanie's voice brought him further awake to the quietness of the clicking of the keyboard keys in the lab.

"I almost had it," he replied, shaking himself. He moved his neck and shoulders and looked around the room. The clicking sound persisted. "I was in a dream that I had many times before, in the forest. The vibration of the drum helps take me places, but I am only an observer – not able to participate."

"The Theory of Quantum Physics says that by being an observer of the experiment, we change it. We are attached to the outcome. Does that make sense in Dreamtime?"

"It does," he replied. "We become aware and awake in a way that we know that we are part of All that is. Some people call it

A Spark of the Fire

Lucid Dreaming, when we are able to be awake in our dreams. I have experienced that many times, and knew that I am another person in the dream. There is another state of consciousness, another state of being that I remember from my dreams. A state that involves being present – risking being "real" in the Shamanic journey. And the drum however important and almost necessary is one part of the ship – the canoe that will transport us in a way that is equal to the physical experience of being there. I am sure that there is something that I am missing that makes it possible to go there – to that other world, or planet, beyond the speed of Light and make the journey a real physical experience. I was so close to finding the answer and then something snapped me back."

"It will come." She was becoming more relaxed in her approach to the paradox and the problem at hand. And their friendship was on the verge of becoming that trust without borders. It was all part and parcel. Meanwhile they had a second prototype – a new helmet that a pilot or a lab worker could use to help in the journey. "Try this," she suggested, offering him the helmet.

He held the crystal and used a moment to relax into the vibrations of the "Inner Drum". He was immediately involved in a conversation with one of the pilot trainers in that hangar on the other world.

"It is time that you learned to pilot the ship, if you are ever to make the trip to the stars." The trainer directed Shane (or the person whose body and mind he shared) to get into the pilot's seat on the right side of the ship. He gazed down at the controls, and mentally noted that there were still only four crystals – not eight like the ships that had been used to make the journey to Earth. "Focus! You need to focus on the crystals beneath your left hand," the trainer smiled encouragingly. "Focus your intent as you push down on the first crystal. If you don't focus, you will run into the side of the hangar wall instead of out the open door."

There were no other controls. No steering wheel or joy stick like in a plane cockpit that Shane had seen on TV. He pressed the little finger against the first crystal and imagined the ship and himself to be moving forward out on the runway, and it worked.

"Good – so far," the man in the passenger seat congratulated him. His previous practice in a mock-up flight simulator was basically useless to him now – and in simulation. It had only been able to give him the feel of the controls, but not the experience of the "real thing".

"What next?" Shane asked rather timidly as they sat on the short runway. The ship was like a living thing, a horse waiting for him to give a command. "What if I crash? What if I shoot us like an arrow into the sun?"

"This training ship has another bank of controls like the ones at your finger tips, in case of an emergency, just sit back and I will take over. And then there is an ejection button and a parachute to bring us down safely. But one day soon you will be required to fly solo, with no other means of escape than your wits. This will be a simple short flight to give you a feeling of what the ship can do. I cannot stress how important it is for you to get the hang of flying, because we need you and your team to help us solve the paradox that will take our people safely to another planet before our world dies."

It became evident that the trainer/ pilot knew who Shane was inside the shared body and mind. Shane took a deep breath, and intended the plane to take off, and it did, smoothly and swiftly into the cloudless grey sky.

One finger at a time, one imagined, yet focused intent he was instructed to put the ship through its paces. The earth and sky became a blur, until the instructor, said clearly and distinctively: "Now the last test for today. Press on the fourth crystal and imagine the Speed of light."

"I don't think I am ready for that." Shane hesitated, and lifted his left hand from the controls.

"Neither are any of us." The trainer chuckled and took over the controls, pressing his index finger to the fourth crystal. And in a mind-boggling flash, the ship and its two passengers were back in the hangar where they had begun. And as the hanger and the other world faded away, Shane heard the trainer's mirthful voice: "It will come".

"It will come," Stephanie repeated. Meanwhile, they shared the new prototype with the rest of the team. "This new version is more finely tuned to the frequency of a drumming that Shane and I recorded at a meditation circle that we go to once a month. I think it is appropriate that the mediation group is called *The Search for God*."

All of the other members of the lab shared the dreams that they were experiencing at home, away from the University building. And to a man (and woman) they reported moments of "being there" in the hangar on the other planet without a crystal in their hands. "It is like the other person is reaching out to me," they explained. "They are asking for our help – sometimes desperately asking only that we promise to do all that we can. And I feel so connected that I would be letting down a brother or a sister if I didn't."

"I am glad that you told us about *The Search for God* group." One of the other students said. "I feel like an important part of our group here along with the people we are helping who are only a thought away."

"You are all an important part of this project," Professor Champion assured them. "And in the months to come, we will be challenged to complete our parts – here and in that far away place, and in the headquarters of NASA. I am hoping it will not come down to us doing something to protect the integrity of our project here in Canada – no matter what curves the politicians throw our way."

"There are new housing projects going up along the Grand River, as we speak," Shane noted. "And the ire of my people has been aroused. My people are vowing not to remain idle while the Treaties are being ignored. There is more to this than meets the eye."

"I agree," the Professor replied. "And we need to do all we can even if it might mean helping the Native people to move the ship to another safer hiding place where prying fingers and eyes cannot confiscate it in the name of what is good for all concerned."

"That would be Spiritual robbery," Stephanie spoke up. "I am up for one or two of us flying that ship back where it came from, if need be. And that would really be for the good of all concerned. We could answerer the S.O.S. like we committed ourselves to do, and bring back crystals to satisfy the hunger of the people on both sides of our border. If they had more crystals to power the ships that NASA is building, then they could learn to evolve and make the journey to the stars themselves."

"Which one or two of us do you have in mind? To make the journey to the stars?" the Professor asked with a broad smile. "Maybe you and Shane?" he winked.

"Why, yes," she blushed. "We could do that couldn't we?"

"Yes you, could." He was frankly surprised at her bold statement.

There was a moment of silence, and then the room echoed with applause. There was hardly one of them that would not, if asked, do their part whether it might mean continuing working with the scientists and dreamers who were light years distant and a thought away – or embarking on a spiritual quest to the stars. The flush of the moment fueled a commitment in which each would discover the strength of imagination and inspiration.

"When is that Pow-Wow at the New Credit Reserve that you told me about at Nia?" Stephanie asked Shane as they walked out of the front door of the U. of T. Law Faculty, to the park across the street, and walked to the street car together. Shane and Stephanie were sharing many experiences now, beyond and including *The Search for God*." They danced together in a Nia class once a week and Shane had remarked how the exercise to music was so much like the Pow-Wows that he enjoyed dancing to with his Native Brothers and Sisters.

"The New Credit Pow-Wow is usually near the end of August," He replied. "It is a traditional gathering in the sense that the dancing is not competitive. Not that the others are any less. We dance for the joy of dancing. I am really looking forward to it."

"So am I," She surprised him, this time, by locking arms as they strolled leisurely to board the Red Rocket and to their respective homes.

Spring turned into summer, and the local news reported an increase in confrontation between the Natives along the Grand River close to Caledonia. There was a blockade set up by the Natives to halt the construction that encroached on the land that the Treaties proclaimed as belonging to the "Indians". First, the land that was theirs was given to the rightful owners, and now that same government were looking for loop holes to take it back. There was more to this than met the eye. And those eyes became dark SUVs that prowled the gravel roads searching for what must be hidden in plain sight.

There was no evidence of the blockades when Shane took the 1st Line—the road off highway 6 that led into the New Credit Reservation, and the Three Fires Homecoming Pow Wow. It was called the Three Fires in honor of the original three Native brothers that came from Quebec to settle in Mississauga, before the Natives were moved off that land in Port Credit and offered a place to call their own on the eastern edge of the land of the Six Nations.

It didn't take long for the sound of the drums to call Shane and Stephanie to dance – an intertribal-dance that anyone could join in, side-by-side with the costumed Native dancers. Stephanie was a natural, letting go of her inhabitations and letting the music move her. "Don't you think the fancy shawl dancers are like butterflies, floating, hardly touching the earth?" She smiled broadly and breathless. Shane agreed completely. He danced without agenda, until Spirit called him to the Chief's side, taking a break to watch Stephanie mingle like a sister with the other dancers.

"I am Shane," he greeted the New Credit chief. "My father was born here."

"I remember your father, and your family." The chief shook his hand. "And I think we might be related – we are all related, but I mean by name. Though it beats me why he chose to change his. What are you calling yourself now a days?" The chief did not seem accusatory, just curious.

"My driver's license says Shane LaFlame, but my birth certificate and my status card have my original family name. It is a holdover from a time that my father did not really know who he was. But it occurs to me that when he was telling everyone that he was a gypsy from Quebec, he was not all that wrong. Our family roots must be in one of those three brothers."

"LaFlame?" the chief chuckled. "Do you have aspirations to become a writer? Or are you saying that you are a spark of the Original Fire?"

"You are very keen in your observation," Shane confirmed. "I am also a friend – I work with Joseph Champion. Have you heard of him?"

"Can't say that I have. Should I have?" The Chief continued to stare straight ahead, watching the dancers.

"May be, maybe not," Shane replied. "I was hoping to get a look at the ship. The one that came from the stars." If the chief had heard, he gave no indication. "I can only ask, that if you have not heard of this, could you please ask, as my Chief and personal representative, if one of the head Chief's from the Six Nations might grant me a minute of their time?" The last part of the conversation was at a low level, almost whisper, but an Elder, an aged woman standing by, seemed to reply for the Chief.

"Look at that young woman dance," the Elder exclaimed. "She moves like someone who came from the stars. If you both are here tomorrow, I think one of the Chiefs of the Six Nations will also be. And maybe you might get a chance to talk to her."

"Miiguetch," Shane said to the Chief and the Elder woman. He gave each of them a small packet of tobacco that he had brought for the occasion and joined Stephanie in the dance circle.

"How would you like to come back tomorrow?" he asked Stephanie.

"You just try to keep me away," she smiled. "I am addicted. I could dance 'til I drop. I will sure sleep well tonight. And have lots of good dreams."

When Shane picked up Stephanie the next morning to go back to the Pow- Wow, he asked: "what did you dream about?"

"That is for me to know and you to find out."

After the Grand Entry, both Shane and Stephanie joined in the first intertribal dance and she was off again, stopping only to rest, and when only the regular dancers had use of the circle. An older man danced beside them for a while, and then asked: "Would you like to go for a walk?" Shane joined him on the path out of the grove and sat on a bench beside the monument that was inscribed with the names of the war veterans.

"I am a chief of the Mohawk," the man said to Shane, and offered his hand. "I was told that you have an interest in common with a mutual friend in Toronto? I phoned him and he says that you and your lady friend are to be trusted."

"I am a student of Joseph Champion," Shane confirmed. "Joseph told me that it might be a good time to talk with you about moving the canoe."

"Moving the canoe?" The man smiled pleasantly. "Yes, it would be a good thing to consider. But we like to call it Pandora's Box. Appropriate don't you think?" and when Shane nodded, the Mohawk chief continued. "If I am to trust you, you will need to tell me how I might open the box?"

Shane's mind went back to his pilot training on the day the instructor showed him how to get inside the cockpit of the ship when it was in lockdown. "There is what appears to be a decal of a hand-print just under the hatch – I mean the top to the box. It is encoded with the owners...DNA...actually attuned to the vibration of those who have the security clearance to open it. I am aware of this, but even so, unless I was one of the previous pilots, I might not be able to open the cover to this Pandora's Box. But I would like the chance to try."

"How could you be one of the original pilots?" The Chief rocked back and forth, drawing out a small pipe and accepting Shane's gift of tobacco. He filled the pipe and lit it, then offered it to the younger man.

Shane drew a puff of the smoke and handed back the pipe. "I have dreams of being present when these magical things were being created. And I have been inside and seen them work their magic. And, yes, I have been trained. But the magical thing has been changed since then, and it is possible that I flew to another world before that was completed. Would it be possible to see this Pandora's Box?"

"If you were to stay after the Pow-Wow and the Giveaway, we will share a feast, and some of us could take a short ride." The Chief puffed at the pipe as Shane rose to rejoin Stephanie in the dancing circle. "My partner will come too?" Shane asked. "She knows everything that I know – and maybe more."

"Of course," The elder man replied. "If it was not for your dancing friend, we might not have taken your request to heart. One of the Elder women had a dream that the Sky Woman would return for her canoe. And yesterday that Elder saw her dream come true."

The Pow Wow came to a pleasant close with the retiring of the flags and the Giveaway, and then the feast. Shane sat beside Stephanie and his curiosity once more got the better of him. "What did you dream last night?" he pestered.

"You will see," she smiled, and later her face was flushed as she rode silently, pressed against him in the rear cab of a newish pickup truck. On the other side of the bench seat near the roadside sat the Elder woman that Shane had met the day before. The Mohawk Chief and the Chief of the New Credit sat in the front two bucket seats.

They drove west along the Grand River further into the Six Nations land, and then turned on a dirt and gravel side road north and then west again. "They are getting close, but so far no one has found our hiding place." The Chief at the wheel said. "You are right, and our friend Joseph is too. We will need to move the ship to a better place before that happens."

Further along the road, they were about to pass a cornfield, and the Elder woman leaned out the open window, and said: "Stop here." The driver pulled over beside a rusty fence. There was a rundown barn in the far distance beyond the cornfield. The Elder got out and walked to the fence and the moment she touched it, a wire gate appeared, and a laneway was there among the corn. "It is all here," she cackled. "But someone would have to know what to look for." She undid a twisted wire and pulled aside the gate. The Mohawk chief turned the truck and drove over the shallow ditch and onto the previously hidden lane The Elder closed the gate behind them and they drove through rows and rows, and mounds of corn, squash, and beans planted together. "The Three Sisters protect this secret," she announced.

The lane made a sharp turn as they approached the barn, and they stopped at the dilapidated eastern door. The Chief of the New Credit got out and swung the doors wide to allow the truck inside, and closed the door behind them. At first it seemed pitch black inside the barn, until Shane's eyes became accustomed to the moon light that shone through an upper window that must have been for hay at one time. The barn was now bare of hay, except one object in the middle, covered with a large tarpaulin. The shape of the object was unmistakable.

"There it is." One of the Chiefs pulled the tarp off to reveal a sleek plane – a ship that shone in the moonlight like it might have been newly constructed a couple of days ago. He walked over and shone a flashlight on a particular spot just below the glass dome. "We have all tried, but no one's hand will open the hatch. You are welcome to give it a go." He pressed his hand against the corresponding picture to demonstrate. Nothing happened. The Chief shrugged in frustration. Shane stepped forward in anticipation and pressed his hand where the Chief's hand had been, like he had done many times in his dreams. A breath of time went by …and nothing! Just like the man before him.

"What???" Shane took his hand away in dejection. "Maybe they changed it with this build? Or did I remember wrong?"

"Let me try." Stephanie walked over, and fitted her hand into what might have simply been a decoration on the side of the plane…and the domed hatch hissed open above her. "Just needed a woman's touch," she smiled.

"Or the hand of the rightful owner," the Elder woman replied with a smile that filled her face in the moonlight.

"Can you fly it out of here?" the Mohawk chief asked.

Stephanie shook her head. "I don't think I am meant to be the pilot this time around. That is Shane's job. Right?"

"It appears that is what I was trained for," he replied. "Mind if we give it a try?"

"I remember an old green man in the *Star Wars* movie who said: "don't try – do." The New Credit chief laughed.

"Yeah." Shane replied. "How about it Stef?" And she crawled up inside to sit in the passenger seat with his help. Shane went around and stood on the edge of the wing like he had done so many times before, and eased himself into the pilot's seat. "Wait," he muttered, and fished out something that was wedged in between the seat and the backrest. Something that sparkled in the moonlight. He gave it a quick glance, and put it in his pocket for later. He pressed his finger to the first crystal, and the hatch came down and locked into position. "Hold on to your hat," he smiled at Stephanie who was busy fastening her seat belt. "Oh yeah," he followed her example. "I am a bit over excited. Or haven't you noticed."

When he pressed on the first crystal a second time, the ship raised. "Take off wheels," he announced. The two Chiefs opened the door to the barn and as the moonlight streamed in, the sleek ship streaked out into the night under the pilot's sure command. "How about a quick trip to the moon?" he suggested.

"I am ready. Go for it." Stephanie settled back in her chair. One amazing thing that Shane recalled, there was hardly a hint of g-force.

He piloted the ship low, across the sea of corn stalks, out over the Grand River in the moonlight, turning left to follow the river and up, up into a steep climb above the clouds, and turned, to level out. Hamilton was a disappearing flickering of lights below.

"Faster," Stephanie urged, and his finger was on the second crystal. No earth-bound ship would catch them now. "Faster!" No radar could track them as his finger touched the third crystal, and the moon was an easy choice and what if? His finger poised over the fourth and last crystal as something in his pocket brought up a memory of a distant dream, in the grove in the forest. The drum reverberated in his ears, and another sound took hold —.and he knew the answer — it shone in his memory, and became a vibration in his mind. And that one second of chance, he resisted the warm glow of the second group of crystals beneath his right hand, and pressed down on the fourth crystal that might take the two of them beyond the speed of light.

In a moments flash, the ship was back in the barn where they began, and the other three – the two Chiefs and the Elder were outside the open door gazing up at the stars.

"Ohhhh!" Stephanie pretended disappointment.

"Next time," he promised. "We have other things to do first."

"What things?" She undid her seat belt as he was reaching into his pocket.

"Well, this for one." He held out a sparkling ring embedded with crystals. "Stephanie? Will you go to the stars with me?"

"I thought you would never ask," She replied, holding out her left hand. "Yes - to the Moon and the Stars."

He slipped the ring on her finger and was not surprised how well it fit. They sealed it with a kiss.

The dome opened and the Elder woman stood at the side of the plane. "That was some test flight," she smiled. "If I hadn't been ready, I would have thought you never left — and oh! Should we be planning a Marriage Blanket soon?"

The kiss went on and on. "Soon," Shane and Stephanie spoke in breathless unison. "Very soon."

NINE

"I believe that I have the answer – or part of it." Shane told Stephanie on the drive back from the Native reserve where they had left their car.

"The answer to what?" She asked, having pretty well guessed what his response would be.

"When we were in the ship, about to make the jump to 'Faster than the Speed of Light', I remembered a healing ceremony in the forest. There was the drum, that would guide us on our journey, but there was another sound that I didn't recognize until that moment today. The other sound was produced by the Shaman's shaker."

"Please explain," she requested.

"In the tradition of my People, we use the drum to set up a vibration with our heart, because our drum is a physical representation of our Heart. With the drum we imagine and we intend the destination of our journey. But there is something else needed to open the veil between the worlds. My people believe that our rattles – our shakers can be used to do just that. And this has worked for my ancestors since the dawn of time."

"So, let me be clear about this," Stephanie replied. "We have already discovered how to use the vibration of the drum to travel to that other world that is light years away. And the other members of our group – the other students are able to connect with the minds of the engineers on that other world and work together to construct the ships that will be used to take them to the stars before their sun dies."

"Right," he agreed. "It is a collective effort. And as we share in helping them, we will gain the knowledge to advance our society here on Earth."

"Sharing is the key word," she continued. "And with the use of the crystals that seem to be only found in a safe and usable form on their world we will both be free to explore anywhere among the stars. Although, there is another part of the paradox that raises its head. How can we intend to go somewhere that we have never been before?"

"Unless we have been there before," he replied. "That may be for future explorers to meditate on."

"But the answer you say you found, which is in some way connected with this ring on my finger, will be a vibration, like a Shaman's rattle, that will open a doorway to our destination."

"That is about it, in a crystal nutshell."

They continued on in silence until Stephanie spoke: "I think it is time for you to meet my parents..."

"Especially if I am going to take their daughter to the stars. Take is not the right word. I know I've asked for your consent for us to go together, to the stars, and if that does not happen, even though I believe it will, to spend the rest of our lives together on Earth."

She sighed and grasped his hand. "It sounds so final...don't you think? The rest of our lives," she trembled.

"Are you getting cold feet?" he asked. "Cause if you are, please remember that I am not asking for your signature on a piece of paper, I am asking for a heartfelt commitment. And if either of us was to die, or you feel a change of heart, then you are free."

"You believe that we are destined" This was not a question. "However crazy this seems. If God created us to be together, I agree, and it's what I want too. And if that stern Christian Father God that I was raised to believe in is not in agreement, then I will be trusting in Grace and Free Will — which seems to be the support of a compassionate female God. So you have my answer. Yes, for a second time! I do want to go to the stars and beyond...together." She leaned over to kiss him and he attempted to concentrate on the road ahead.

"Mom, Dad. This is Shane. I've told you about him. He gave me this ring, and asked me to go to stars with him." The minute the words came from her mouth, Stephanie realized how strange that must sound to a pair of logical French Catholics who had vowed to "love, honor, and obey, till death do us part." But then there were a number of die-hard Christians that were rethinking that vow as well.

"Young man," her father responded, "you did not even ask for my daughter's hand in marriage. Never the less, I will agree, simply because Stephanie is strong-willed and will do as she pleases no matter what her parents think." He took a closer look at the ring. "It does not even appear to be inlayed with real diamonds," he shrugged. "What do you think about this mother?"

Stephanie's mother replied with a tight lipped smile. And Stephanie translated the exchange in French for Shane.

"Evidently, my mother understands more than we might give her credit. My mother said: "Young man, wherever you take my daughter, treat her right – be good to her, and protect her or I will come after you."

Shane nodded in agreement. The rest of their afternoon spent in the company of Stephanie's parents was pleasant enough, and everyone shared a glass of wine to commemorate their engagement. Near the end of the evening, Stephanie's father announced that her mother and he would be returning to France as soon as plans could be made. "It is the best thing for your mother and I do care for her more than the financial gains I hoped for in Canada. And if you have a change in mind before we leave, we would be happy if you came back home with us."

"Well, at least I know where your mother and father stand." Shane said as they walked together, and said warm goodbyes in the moonlight. "See you tomorrow at class?" Shane was scheduled to work the afternoon shift, so he would be going downtown to the lab for the morning session.

"I will be spending a few days with my mother and father," Stephanie replied. "If you remember, I arranged for the week off from work, but I will see you on Wednesday morning for the early class."

As fate would have it, Shane received a call later that evening on his answering machine, asking if he could come into work for the day shift, as the person who was scheduled had called in sick. Shane worked Monday and Tuesday and the other person called in to say that he would be OK for Wednesday, if Shane still wanted to resume his regular scheduled shift on Wednesday.

On Wednesday morning Shane met Stephanie for the trip downtown on the street car. "What do you think that was all about?" he asked her. "I believe that everything that happens is for a reason," she agreed.

The Professor was absent when Shane and Stephanie walked into the lab that morning. "Professor Champion had some sort of accident the other evening. He was taken to the hospital," one of the morning students told Shane. Shane and Stephanie went up stairs to find out more from the receptionist.

"Professor Champion will not be coming today." The receptionist informed Shane. "We don't know how long he will be off. As a matter of fact we contacted his office in the USA, and they are sending a replacement."

"What happened?" Stephanie asked.

"No one really knows. He came in on Monday morning, and early in the afternoon, he walked out the front door and collapsed on the lawn. He is in the hospital but they cannot find anything physically wrong with him. But the real strange part of this is he has forgotten who he is. He seems to have had a mental relapse. He does not remember anything – not even his name."

"Is there anything we can do?" Shane asked.

"Nothing. Classes will be canceled pending the arrival of Professor Champion's replacement. Oh — there is this letter." The secretary fished out a brown paper envelope from her desk. "Maybe this will explain something? The Professor gave it to me about a month ago with strict instructions to give it to you or Stephanie only – and no one else, in case something were to happen to him. Maybe he knew something that he was not letting the rest of us know about?" Shane accepted the letter and took it down to the lab where he opened it and after giving it a quick scan, handed it to Stephanie.

Her eyes widened as she read the letter, and she sat on the Professor's desk and said. "I think we should share this with the rest of the class?" Shane agreed.

"As you all know, or don't know, Professor Champion is in the hospital. He left this letter for us to explain the circumstance of his unfortunate mysterious illness. There is no date. It begins:"

"To Shane and Stephanie, and the rest of my students: I call you my students although you are all really my peers in this shared project. But then, a good teacher does not teach, he or she leads, to facilitate the students including himself in a process of learning together. We are all students, in the study of the mysteries of Life. Therefore I will remain your teacher until such time that you come to the realization that you are teaching yourself.

I shared a bit of what I knew about the future of our project in the beginning and as it changed. But I know more than I have shared. Much too much I fear. Lately I have begun to remember the future. Yes, the future! And I can see at least two outcomes. I have attempted, rightly or wrongly to influence the outcome for the best of all concerned, but it seems that I am thwarted in doing so. My view of the future changes as our interaction – as your interaction with the events that we are exploring changes. Let me tell you about one of those imagined futures.

I am about to be taken out of the picture, so to speak. I can see myself reaching a point that my mind will no longer be able to cope, and if you are reading this letter, that may have already happened. This is part of putting the ball, or should I say the crystal, completely in your court. My well-meaning associates in the USA will most likely send a replacement and he or she will put in place the next step in NASA's plan to equip a ship or ships to travel to the planet that is light years away. The foremost part of their plan will be to acquire the crystals that are needed to travel to the stars. The one thing I can see is their intent will be limited – even in the possibility of exceeding the Speed of Light. If they are able to get their minds to function beyond that limitation, the intent will be a logical destination in time in which those people on that world are long gone and are beyond saving.

I have remembered another possibility, one in which my students are to discover a way not only to go to the stars, but to surpass the limitations and to arrive in time (no pun intended) to help the people who sent the S.O.S. How you will do this – with or without the help of NASA — I do not know and that may be part of the reason I will not be there to guide or help."

"It is signed: *Your teacher and friend always, Joseph Champion."*

"Anyone?" Stephanie asked.

"The Professor hinted that something like this may happen," Shane told the small group of students that were present. There was another shift of six people that were scheduled to come that afternoon. That made up the entire group of thirteen who had been studying and working on the project with Professor Champion. "Do you think we should tell everyone where we went last weekend?" he asked Stephanie.

"Yes, but we are vowed to keep the other destination a secret. Shane and I went to a Pow Wow at the New Credit Native Reservation. And from there, we managed to look at the ship from the stars."

"Wow!" Diego exclaimed. "I wish I could have been there."

"I wish you all could have been there." Shane replied. "That ship is one of the major focuses of our project. I was beginning to think it was just another story. Not that I doubt my people's stories, but some are told to inspire and are otherwise symbolic."

"But this ship is real," Stephanie replied. "And beyond that, Shane believes that he has discovered the answer to pilot it to the other planet or even the stars. You have all had success with the induction helmet that we put together. Well beyond that, Shane believes that the next step is another level of vibration like the sound of a Shaman's rattle. I will ask Shane to tell you what he found out and believes to be true."

Shane then told his version of the story about the vibration of the shakers that his people have used in healing ceremonies down through the centuries. He stopped at telling the rest of the class that they had flown the ship, for the time being, until the replacement for their teacher arrived and showed his hand, so to speak. Later that afternoon, Shane had to leave for work, and Stephanie stayed behind to read the letter and discuss her and Shane's new ideas about piloting the ship, or any ship with crystals installed, beyond the belief of current science.

Joseph's students agreed to hold off meeting at the Toronto lab until the replacement teacher arrived from the States. That would most likely be the next Monday morning; they were informed by the receptionist. She had all their phone numbers so she promised to let them know if there was a change in plans. All of the "students" went to visit Joseph in a nearby hospital (for the mentally ill) in small groups, during the rest of that week. Joseph was physically well but did not recognize anyone, and did not remember who he was or what had transpired in his life up until the time he became a patient in the hospital.

On Monday, Shane was back on the day shift at work. When he arrived at the lab that afternoon, he was greeted by a man, called Jack Wiseman who had come from the States to take over the project.

"You are the Engine Man, I'm told." He shook Shane's hand.

"Engine Man?" Shane was not sure how to take this.

"You have been working on an interface between the crystals that power the ship and the actual propulsion unit. So I will call you my Engine Man, and that fits, since you are also an Indian Man – are you not?"

Shane felt a bit put off by this man from the start. It was a sore point for him from earlier in his life that he had been the object of teasing that bordered on bullying, since his father had changed his last name, and "everyone in the high school" knew Shane's real family name and that he was an Indian. Some called him "Injun boy". "All of us here, all of the students have been working together to discover how to activate the crystals that are both the control and the power system for the ship," he replied with a firm mouth. "It was Stephanie that really created the way to integrate the vibration of the drum into a unit that anyone can use to activate the crystals."

"I know that," Jack replied, patting Shane on the back. "But it was you who discovered the vibration that is like the sound of a drum. And now I hear that you might have found how to use the second group of crystals to open a mini "black hole," so that the ships we are building can exceed the speed of light and jump through time. Isn't that right?"

"You could put it like that," Shane shrugged. "It is a bit more about the spiritual way that my ancestor's have used in their ceremonies." He was beginning to think it was not such a good thing to have let out the information about the vibration of the rattles so soon. "We have not tested that yet." He was also glad that he and Stephanie had kept the part of the test flight in the ship to themselves.

"It is only a matter of time now." Jack was all smiles. "Once we get that ship down to our headquarters in the USA we can begin the next phase in the testing, and go to that other planet to get more crystals. We are proud of how you all worked on the project with our engineers in NASA so far. This is just the beginning – you will see. And that is why I am here – to offer all of you a job in our headquarters in the USA."

"What about the lab here in Canada?" Diego asked.

"With Joseph out of the picture, we will be phasing out this lab and offering a green card to any of you that want to come to work with us in the States. As you should be aware, all of your hard work and exploration is documented in our database on the main computer in NASA. When we are ready it will be a simple step to shut down here and continue without the satellite connection in our facility in the States."

Shane was on the verge of asking "then why have the lab here in the first place," and then he remembered that the undamaged ship with its crystals intact was here in Canada – in Native hands actually. But that was about to become a moot point if this man and his organization had anything to say about it – and the Canadian government did not seem to care, or they had been bought out. So he asked instead: "How long will it be before this lab is closed down."

"It might be a couple of months, at the maximum, give or take how long some loose ends are cleared up," Jack replied.

"The main loose end being the moving of the ship from its hiding place in the Six Nations to the main headquarters in the States," Shane guessed but did not say out loud. He smiled as his eyes met those of Stephanie. She nodded.

The new instructor noticed the exchange. "Oh come on now – it will not be such a terrible thing to work and live in the USA, will it? After all, according to Shane's people, that border between our two countries does not exist. And what we will be doing will be for the good of all mankind."

Later at the evening break Shane walked in the park across the street with Stephanie. "For the good of all mankind?" he wondered. "What do you think about that. It may be partially true, since the technology that the crystals will enable will change our world. In fact we will potentially no longer be held back from traveling to other planets. But is mankind ready for that, or better yet are the stars ready to be seeded with our lack of caring for our world and the other species we share it with?"

"And what about those people that sent the S.O.S. asking for our help?" Stephanie replied. "I think what Joseph said in his letter about his associates being so logically- minded that they will miss the spiritual implications of helping someone who is light years beyond our reach. I have this sinking feeling that once they have the crystals to power their ship, they will be hell-bent on getting more from that planet that is already dead in their minds."

"I agree," Shane replied. "But you and I can still do what is right – before our governments bend the laws to allow them to take what is not theirs. History has a nasty habit of repeating itself."

"We can go to the stars – in Spirit Time." she agreed, squeezing his hand. "Will the Native People allow us to use the ship – do you think?"

"The other day on the Reserve, I believe that both Chiefs and the Elder had given us the OK to go then." Shane replied. "I think all we need to do is get in touch with them – a short visit to buy some tobacco, and set a date in Native time."

"How would Native time be for a date for us, in the Eyes of the Creator to travel to the stars together?" She turned to embrace him face-to-face.

"In Native time, things happen when we are ready. Are you ready for a Native Marriage ceremony?" he asked the second time.

"I am," and she kissed him in confirmation.

Stephanie and Shane visited his mother to show her the ring, and to tell her that they had set a date to go to the stars together. She did not blink an eye, and appeared to understand, and was completely in agreement. Shane's mother, a diminutive woman, showed great strength, hugging Stephanie so hard that she lifted the younger woman off her feet.

When Shane visited his friend, Kathleen, she was packing up to move out west. When the two women met for the first time, they immediately exclaimed "I know you!" and they spent most of the afternoon talking down by the lake behind Kathleen's apartment, while Shane skipped stones. "How about if we hold a going away and an engagement party together here in my house?" Kathleen asked Shane. Stephanie thought it was a good idea and the two women had discussed it in great length, including many other things that Shane would learn about later. The discussion by the lake fit into that "you will see when it is time," reply that Shane had come to accept from Stephanie.

That week, Shane arranged for time off work to get married – at the end of summer. He asked for the last two weeks in September during the autumn equinox. He agreed that it was short notice, since it was already the first of September, but he explained to his supervisor that they wanted it to take place at a time that was sacred to his people. He had discussed this with Stephanie, and although the Equinox was September 23, her choice was during the Full moon on September 27th. "It will be our honey moon," he joked.

"I have a feeling about this," she replied with her wise and illusive smile.

"It is rather quick, don't you think?" Shane's supervisor nudged and winked. "Do you have to get married?"

"If you mean is my wife-to-be, pregnant," Shane replied. "no we do not have to get married for that reason. It is just that we found out that it is the best time to take our honeymoon."

"I will see what I can do," his supervisor replied. "I don't really see a problem, unless one of the other men cannot cover for you until you return."

Secretly, Shane believed that he would not be returning. It was time for the Caterpillar to be transformed into a butterfly.

In the weeks to come Jack Wiseman attempted to endure himself in the eyes of Professor Champion's students, while encouraging them to move to the facility in the USA, as he confiscated the helmets and the crystal that they had been using to connect with the engineers on that other world. Despite his efforts to please, however, his enduring nicknames for most of them served to further the cause toward Shane and Stephanie's journey. He kept referring to Shane as his "Engine Man".

At Shane and Stephanie's engagement party in Kathleen's apartment overlooking the lake, first Diego, and then other members of the team that had worked together in the lab shared a secret that they withheld from their new Professor. "We have not stopped dreaming and visioning a connection with the people on that other world, even without the helmets and the crystal." Diego told Shane and Stephanie. "I think the vibrations of the helmets that Stephanie created have conditioned my brain to be in sync with the thoughts of that other man who asked for our help.If you both are successful in physically traveling to that other world in the ship, we will be there with you in Spirit." The two future honeymooners had shared their plans with a of couple close friends.

Shane and Stephanie shared a drumming ceremony with the Four Colours Drum Circle in Heart Lake to celebrate the Autumn

Equinox. One of the leaders, an English/Native man, spoke about the Full Moon that would be on the coming weekend. "It will be a good time for a joining ceremony," he said. "We will be drumming for a good journey for our friends, here in the Medicine Wheel."

And then the time had arrived. The Sunday of the Full Moon came in along with the experience of no-time, one minute they were waiting patiently and anticipating, and then, like magic, they were standing in a circle beside the ship with the light of the moon streaming through the window. Thirteen people made the trip from Toronto and nearby homes on the Reservation to witness the joining ceremony and the first step of a journey to the Stars. "This is a good number for a Ceremony in the Harvest Moon," the Elder remarked as she cleansed the circle with smoke from sage.

While there was a small convey of truck and cars driving into the Six Nations on the dirt road, the Mohawk Chief had answered his cell phone and reported: "We are being followed. That was one of the men at the blockade near Caledonia. I asked them only to delay the police cars and the men from the USA, not to do anything to cause harm."

"The marriage ceremony will be quick," the Elder woman assured them. "As it always is for our People. We only need to speak to the Great Spirit and ask that the walk together will be a sacred journey. You have the gift of a pony for her family."

In the Circle, the Elder read a passage from a book of Ojibway Ceremonies by Basil Johnston, ending with three lines:

"You will share the same fire.

Be Kind to one another

Be Kind to your children."

"...and now, do you want to go with this Man?"

"I do. With all my Heart," Stephanie replied.

"And do you want to go with this Woman?"

"I do, with all my Heart," Shane replied.

"To the Moon and the Stars?" the Elder added.

"Yes! To the Moon, the Stars and a new home," Shane and Stephanie replied together.

The Elder draped a colorful blanket around their shoulders. "In the Eyes of the Creator you are joined. Go – walk a Sacred Path together."

"Be quick. There are cars parked at the fence." Diego and one of the Native people opened the barn door. The participants of the ceremony had not hid any of their cars, as they believed that the ship containing Shane and Stephanie could not be stopped or caught by any helicopter of plane presently on Earth.

Shane and Stephanie climbed into the cockpit and stowed the marriage blanket in a compartment behind the seats and fastened their seatbelts. His left hand poised over the crystals that powered and controlled the ship. One touch, and the ship raised on takeoff wheels, poised like a bird awaiting his command. Shane asked: "Where to? What is our first destination?" He had already guessed her response.

"To the Moon. Take us to the full Moon. Spirit told me that will be our first and only stop...and then to the Stars," she smiled confidently.

The men outside on the road, in the act of cutting the wire fence that denied them access to the cornfield, paused. They were witness to a sleek plane exiting from the open doors of the barn in the distance, and passing quickly overhead. The plane leveled out over the Grand River, climbed toward the full moon and in the blink of an eye disappeared from sight.

Enlightenment

As a Native of this Mother Earth,
I have Great Respect
for those who seek Enlightenment.
However my continuing goal is
to Walk the Path of Beauty
and Peace.
Like the Arrow
that is aimed at the Moon
I will be content
to "miss the mark"
and land among the Stars.
Then, one day
when the Sweet Wind
blows me Home,
Perhaps I will find
that I was already there.

...winterhawk

Enlightenment

ONE

At near the speed of light it did not take a minute or two to reach the moon. Shane and Stephanie did not have space suits; they were not needed as the journey to their final destination would not exceed the amount of highly compressed air that was stored in this futuristic ship. Shane recalled from his pilot training that the oxygen was refreshed from their surroundings when the ship was activated. The engineering was beyond him, but he did not question it, or his long-time dream of flying a ship like this one that brought them into a few miles of the moon's surface.

As they orbited the full moon, from the glowing sunlit side to the dark, he began to wonder. He glanced at Stephanie who was entranced, and seemed to be deep in thought. Was she remembering? "A penny for your thoughts," he said, as he wondered still: "Why are we here?"

She smiled serenely. "I am remembering," she confirmed. She sighed. "Beautiful honey-moon! I am ready to go home now." And she kissed him and settled back in her seat.

"Home?" he asked. "Your home or my home?" They had not planned for a home on Earth.

"Our home, silly. It is waiting for us out there among the stars."

"Of course." He pressed down on the third crystal that was one step from the speed of light, but still unimaginable back on Earth, and proceeded to orbit the moon, faster and faster from the light of the sun to the dark. And when it felt right, he poised the finger of his left hand over the fourth crystal and a finger of his right hand on the fifth crystal that would open the veil to their intended destination. His mind drifted to a healing ceremony in the forest to "remember" the sound that would take them home. His two hands, and his mind, and his heart operated in sync. And in a flash...they were no longer in the same time and space.

*   *   *

The planet below looked similar to Earth, with a different arrangement and shape of the continents. The planet that the ship orbited was a blue marble in space, like his home. "Why?" he said aloud, and realized that he was alone in the cabin. Stephanie was gone, but not from his memory. He eased the ship down toward the mysterious but familiar world, drawn like a moth to a flame. As he neared the largest land mass, he began to remember the way from his pilot training missions. Familiar mountains and cities appeared, until he found the glide path to the hanger outside a major metropolis. He touched down, and taxied to the opening door. It was like coming home.

One of the men in the hangar motioned Shane to bring the ship to rest on one side of the building, lined up with other similar ships, like he had done many times in his dream training. A familiar face approached the ship as he raised the cockpit dome.

"Should I still call you Dave?" Shane climbed down from the ship and offered his hand.

"Close enough of a translation." Dave shook his hand vigorously. "It is good to see you again, so to speak. Mind if I take a look inside?" And when Shane nodded, the other man climbed up to the open cockpit. He whistled. "Mighty impressive! We had heard that there might have been a prototype that Sam was working on before his daughter went to ashes. Sam is the one who we've been taught discovered how to use the crystals that we brought back from the moon. But between you and I and the Dreamers, another story has it that his daughter dreamed them. And she lived a very shortened life because of her exposure to the crystals. Another story — don't let the church hear you say anything about this if you want to be excommunicated— is that Sam's daughter disappeared along with the prototype. Either way, Sam lost interest when the scientists stepped in and moved the whole factory inside the boundaries of the Crystal City."

"So that is how the other crystals line up. Did you have any problems activating them?" Dave continued on, implying that his monologue was best forgotten.

"I just imagined the vibration of our shakers that we use in my Native ceremonies. I was able to remember a healing ceremony that I participated in, (for Kitt — I still want to call her by the name she gave me in our shared dream). This brings me to the main reason I am here. I will leave this ship open for you and your crew to see how it is put together. We can talk later – tomorrow. Meanwhile, I have a date by the nearest super-train track. The one that comes by when the sun is right overhead and the moon is just on the horizon. I remember that from my dream."

"Super-train?" Dave smiled. "That would be the express that passes through from one side of our country to the other every moon day. That train, as you would call it, does not stop anywhere in-between. There is a track just outside the city limits. You can make it if you hurry, but like I said, it will not stop for passengers."

"And by the way," Shane asked, "Can you tell me whose body I borrowed for the pilot training? I would like to thank him personally."

"Whose body? You got to be kidding?" Dave smiled wryly. "I guess you aren't really all back yet. The track for the super-train, is at on the border of the land that we Dreamers call home – just at the start of the city limits, in case you don't remember that too?"

"Can you point me in the right direction?" Shane requested. "And if you are OK examining this ship, I would appreciate if you didn't take it apart. I am hoping to take back a full complement of crystals in that ship when we have all the other ships up to speed."

The man Shane called Dave, who had been his personal flight trainer, accompanied him to the hangar door and pointed across a stretch of tarmac to the nearby city. "Take one of the flight jackets, the temperature will be a might colder than you are used to." At that point, Shane noted that this man was clothed in one of the green body suits that the woman who came to Earth had worn.

It was chilly for noon day by Earth standards. Shane zipped the jacket to his chin. The chill served to remind him that this world was warmed by a dying sun. But a more important thought surfaced in his mind. What could be more important than helping a dying world? The answer to that, he hoped, waited for him at the other side of the train track. He hurried, and then broke into a run, as the sound and vibration announced the coming express train. It was incredibly fast, like everything else on this world, powered by the crystals. The train blurred by faster than the eye could follow, like a western wind. Which way was west? And it was gone into the (Eastern?) raising moon.

Shane breathed a sigh of relief. Just like in the dream, there were three people waiting on the other side of the track – a man and a woman, and a younger woman in the center. Al three were clad in the now familiar green body suit. The older woman stepped forward and like part of a scripted play said:

"This is our daughter. Do you want to see more of her?"

"I do," Shane replied, and crossed over the track to meet the daughter, who the mother gave a playful push in his direction. "Stephanie? Is that really you?" She came easily into his waiting arms. The man and his wife stepped back. They were silent, embracing the moment.

"We are now married in the custom of my people." Stephanie hugged him. "Yes it is really me. There is a home waiting for us in the city. Are you ready to go home?" Her words tickled his neck and his mind.

Stephanie's father handed Shane a set of keys. Presumably to their new home. And Shane felt the need to say: "Miiguetch" – 'thank you' in his language, for the hand of their daughter. "I have brought you a pony that can take your people to the stars." The man and his wife exchanged puzzled looks.

"It is a custom for Shane's people to give the family of his intended bride a pony – it is an animal also called a horse," Stephanie explained.

Her mother laughed. "That is a strange custom! If we were to ask for these animals in return for our daughter, it would take more than one pony, no matter how valuable they are."

"I understand," her father smiled. "It is a token of your love. I think he really means that he brought the ship that will help our people travel to a safe world in the stars before our planet dies."

Shane nodded in agreement. He followed, hand in hand with Stephanie in the direction of the city. Her mother and father on this world went their way, and Stephanie led him to a door in a low-rise on a bright coble-stone street.

"This is our new home," she announced, and stood aside as Shane unlocked the door. "Well?" she smiled.

"Well what?" And then he realized what she was waiting for. He scooped her into his arms and carried his new bride over the threshold. "Who's customs are we following here?" he asked after setting her down in the place that was to be their home. He locked the door, and hugged and kissed her.

"We will follow the customs that our hearts decide." She replied. "I have memories of both worlds and two sets of parents now. Does that seem strange to you?"

"No stranger than finding the woman who I have dreamed about for most of my life. Even if it took me a while to recognize who she really is. I will admit to believing that Katherine was my soul mate for a long time and it messed with my mind. How can you be two women at the same time?"

"Let it be…for now," she smiled and led him to another room where a large bed awaited. "I am not trying to be coy—I am caught up in the mystery as much as you are." She wrapped her arms around his neck, and they kissed with deep emotions. "Can you please unzip me?" Her breath was warm on his neck.

His trembling hands found the zipper at the back of her green body suit. "Will you turn to ashes if I undress you?" He stared into her blue eyes.

"No, but you will find that I am on fire." And as his hands wandered down her pale back in the moonlit room, he was discovering that she was telling the truth. And soon he was thoroughly convinced that she was a living spark of the Creators Fire!

Shane woke in the early morning – or the middle of the night? It was still night. The moonlight streamed in the bedroom window and illuminated the face of an angel who slept in his arms.

"Are you ready for more?" Her sleepy eyes entranced him.

"Yes, but I am remembering something about the moonlight. How about if we go for a walk…after." And the minute he uttered the words another memory took hold.

"We can't go out after dark." She snuggled close. "I don't remember why, but then again I don't really want to. Do you?"

"No, I have other ideas and no plans. I agree, though, it is not safe to go out after dark. How do I know that?" He dismissed the subject for the moment, lost in her arms and the fire that she was.

Somehow the fire burned away the old memories that had repressed his dreams. He lay in the bed, alone now, aware that Stephanie (she had a new name now) was in the kitchen fixing breakfast. He heard her singing a song that triggered another memory – it came to surface like a bubble rising out of a calm pool of water. He settled back to embrace another truth.

He had been born almost the same moment as "Stephanie." As they grew up together, the families and friends joked that these two children must be soul mates. His distant memory of having the full green suit that he had worn since birth removed, and similar clothing given in its place. The memory was foggy.

"How could you remember something that happened when you were only two?" his father chided him when he told his parents: "I had a dream that I was ill in some way, and was taken to an old woman who cured me, by taking away something that was blocking my ability to know who I really am." His mother would not be silenced. "See, I told you. Your son was born to be a Dreamer."

And then something followed that made it harder to remember things that should be, rather than being a truer representative of reality. He was taken to some type of healing clinic by his parents, and his thoughts were suppressed, it seemed. And this bothered a young boy who was already dreaming of a different place and time.

"I must ask... Stephanie when I am fully awake," he promised himself, and lapsed into remembering his growing up years – years that were taken from him as a natural part of this world's way of coping with the knowledge that their sun was nearing the end of its life and the fire must be captured at all cost – including the primordial fire that animated their bodies. Life went by all too quickly as a boy became a man – a man who lived for his dreams to escape the very thing that was prolonging his life. If it had not been for her, he might not have made it to adulthood. She was his constant companion in his waking world and his dreams. Somehow, she was able to live and dream and for a while, find a balance that he was not able to on his own.

And then the time came for their destined union. He was trembling with anticipation. "Will I remember my lines?"

"There is only one thing you need to remember," his mother had told him. "When her parents offer their daughter to be your wife, they repeat the customary words: this is our daughter, would you want to see more of her?"

"That is about the craziest thing I have ever heard," he sputtered, "Why, after all this time, does this need to be said?" And his mind supplied "Of course, I want to see more of her! We have both waited for the sacred time that we could remove these silly green suits and...and."

"And you will step forward and say 'Yes I do-. And then you will be wed in the eyes of our people. Is this silly custom too much to bear for the reward of sharing the rest of your life with the one you were destined to be with?" His mother asked.

"No – nothing is too much to bear, no matter how silly or difficult to understand when he stood waiting at the symbolic division of their world – dividing the old from the new life that would someday spell the end of their sun. Sacrifice – and submission. His mind, as he waited at the tracks of the subsonic train, recalled words from a dream: "Today is a good day to die." And then when, the train thundered by, he was caught up in the wind and pulled out of his reality. And even when he saw his long-time friend and her parents waiting when the train passed, his step and his surrender culminated in all consuming blackness which literally sucked him in until he woke up ... this bright morning with new memories of the sharing of the fire that had ignited his mind and heart.

"Are you getting up sleepy head?"

"How did I get here?" he asked shaking his head.

She smiled and tears formed in her eyes. "What is my name?" Her question was not a trick. Nor was it a test. But he had to think for a minute.

"Lise." he replied while some part of his mind shouted another.

I was waking up. My eyes were open and it was like seeing daylight for the first time.

"Our deepest fear is not that we are inadequate. Our deepest fear is that we are powerful beyond measure." From the book *'A Return to Love'* (1992) by Marianne Williamson

#

"Lise? I asked again: "What happened? How did I get here?"

"There was an accident," she answered, joining me on the bed and enclosing me in her arms. "But everything is OK now, because you have finally woken up."

"Woken up?" I was confused. "Was I asleep? I don't understand.

"You have been in a coma for over a year," she explained. "On the day of our joining ceremony, you were swept up by the wind from the passing train and although the doctors could find nothing physically wrong; you went into a deep sleep and didn't wake until yesterday. I got a call from the man you call Dave. It was a short and strange call. He said that a ship came in and you were the pilot. He did not know where this ship came from, except that it was an advanced model that you had told him about before your accident. And when the ship docked, you were the pilot. And then I got another call back from Dave to tell me that you were going to the place that the accident had occurred. I have been living with my mother and father, who supported me for all this time, so we hurried to meet you. You did not seem to have fully recovered your memory, but now that is over – you have woken up."

We rolled together on the bed, and made love again. And after that experience of the fire, I remembered more. I was what Shane's people call a "two-spirited" person. I remembered being born on this world in a place on the other side of the tracks, outside the Crystal City. And I also remembered living a life on a distant planet called Earth.

"Lise? I do remember a lot more now. But there are so many memories—nothing really conflicting, but it is as though we had different names and we lived in different places. I know that you are the woman I have loved all my life, but you had a different name too. Does that make sense? Yesterday I thought you were called Stephanie."

"I was and still am." She kissed me. "That is one of my dreaming names."

"Dreaming names? I don't need to ask — I have different names in my dreams too. So you ARE Stephanie. That's so good to know. I thought I had lost her."

"So did I." Lise replied. But now you remember who I am, and that is all I have waited for. You know, a year on Terra is no longer measured in time like on Earth."

"Oh? My mother? Is she still...?"

"Yes she still lives, and has held on to the belief that you would wake up — even though the doctors told us there was no hope— no visible sign of life. But I am sad to say that your Father went to ashes shortly after your accident. I think he just gave up."

I kissed Lise again (and again) and leapt out of bed. "I need to see my mother—to tell her that everything is OK."

Lise and I visited my mother in another part of the city, and I was immediately smothered in hugs.

"Wait," my mother exclaimed with tears in her eyes. "You are a nice man, and you seem so much like my son, but I visited my son in the hospital just yesterday, and he was still there, sleeping. Did you really wake up — or what?"

I steeled myself for the truth. "How about if we go together to the hospital and see?" I suggested. The hospital was a quick ride away in one of the shuttle buses that were available free for everyone. I remembered that the buses could be called at any time of the day or night—especially if you need to go somewhere at night, when it was not safe to venture out – more about that later.

The three of us—Lise, and my mother and I—paused at the door to the room that had been my resting place for over ten years of "Earth time". I opened the door of a dimly lit room with one special bed—unit that was similar to a cryogenic sleep chamber. The soft hum told me that the life support was still operational and available to keep the occupant alive in a coma – almost indefinitely. But on closer inspection, the chamber and the bed was empty, except for a small pile of ashes. I should not have been surprised. And my mother took it all in stride.

"My son has risen from the ashes like the prophesies of old," she cried out and sobbed in my arms. What could I do? I just hugged her and Lise at the same time. It was like no feeling I have ever experienced. Being present at your own funeral, maybe?"

My mother gave over the ashes of her son to me. After all, despite her amazing ability understand, it was beyond logic. And logic should have been the basis of my mother's understanding. As I recalled more of his/my memories, I knew that my mother got her yearly induction—religiously. The induction was originally created to enable the people of our world to mentally control the inevitable escape of energy through the top of their head once the protective cap was removed a year after a child's birth. The induction was created, like Stephanie's helmet, to program a person's mind to follow suggestions for their own well-being. Our scientists have yet to discover if it is the death of our sun that caused the speed up of our people's metabolism or the continued use of the crystals. Perhaps the answer is that nothing stands alone. Our moon reflects the energy of our sun, and the moon is where we found and mined the crystals.

"Your mother is a marvel." Lise exclaimed. "She is the oldest surviving person in our city— possibly on our world. There is no logical reason for her ability to flourish. On another, but not unrelated subject, I know of the perfect place for her son's ashes."

"Everything is related," I replied. "I must get my genetic durability and non- logical thinking from my mother. My father's ancestors were originally Dreamers, but my mother gave me the imagination that enabled me to have a reason to Dream. It is like the system that you and I invented to power and pilot the ship.

The crystals provide access to the energy and our beliefs focus it in a good way."

We paid Dave a visit, to borrow one of the ships so that we could take "my" ashes to a place that Lise knew would be right for "him".

"I guess you don't need to ask in whose body you took the pilot training?" Dave gave me a wry smile.

"I agree." I replied, "But I have a lot of waking up to do yet."

Lise piloted the ship, and on the way, I asked her again.

"You are Stephanie, right?"

"I am," she replied.

"And you and I were in the garden together as little children?"

"Right again. But there is more to this than you have remembered yet. I think when we get to our destination it will become a bit clearer."

"But then— who is, or was Kathleen? I remember her there, too."

"Kathleen...is her own mystery. I hope it will all be explained as much as possible, but the Mystery will always be there." Stephanie went silent at this point.

We flew out over a large body of water at a casual pace for the ship that could travel at speeds equal and beyond imagination. Another continent appeared in what might be considered the North-East of this planet, a direction that remained almost constantly nearer to the sun.

"What a beautiful place! So green and lush." I exclaimed. "Why would our people not settle here instead of the cold Crystal City?"

"Ghosts," Lise replied. "Search your memory. Our people—on both sides of the tracks (on the city side more so) worship the crystals and all that they can do for us."

"But as I remember, the people who inhabit the Crystal City have a religion based on Sun Worship."

"That is true – I am speaking metaphorically. They are addicted to the power of the crystals, even though many still worship the Sun as though it were a living entity. They brought that belief over the land bridge from their former home on the third landmass in the West." As she brought the ship down in a small clearing in the woods, my mind became filled with memories.

I jumped out onto a familiar beach, and hugged Lise. "We came here when we were small children." I gasped.

"Yes, we played on this beach and swam in this pool. My father was one of the gardeners. We came here with him." She confirmed, and hugged me back. "I knew you would remember. What else do you remember?"

"Something – not very nice," I replied. "The ghosts are not all what they seem to be."

"Right," She replied, but now – with the passing of time, and the cooling of our planet, we are sure that only ghosts remain, and the real dangers will no longer fly this far North — or East — for that matter.

"What I remember was not a ghost. Or was it?"

"Maybe – maybe not," she replied. Mother Earth has her Mysteries too."

I sat on the beach to explore repressed memories.

"You and I were here together, contemplating our coming of age."

"That is one way of saying it." Lise replied. "We were about to make love —for the first time, and—is it too painful for you?"

"I need to know," I fought back the tears. "There was a large creature – an overgrown bee. We thought it was a ghost. But a ghost could not sting. It strung me, and I was paralyzed. And then...the rest is foggy."

"I called my father on the emergency phone that he gave me to use when we came here on our own. And he took us both back to the mainland."

"Is this when I went into the coma...? No. Sorry, I have a habit of sleeping away the most important parts of my life. My father took me to a woman who was using a form of induction therapy that was designed to remove blockages to our memory. The reasoning was based on sometimes we become immobilized by our fears or feelings of guilt. Apparently no one believed that the bee creature that stung me was real, since there was no mark anywhere on my body."

"So they thought it was all in your mind," Lise remarked as we reminisced on the grass by the stream. "When you walked out of the clinic you were eager to go back to work with Dave on the newest model of the ships that the dreamers were building to take us to another world before our sun dies. But you never did tell anyone what cured or inspired you to go on."

"I guess it is past time that I told you about what happened to me in the clinic. We should not have any secrets from each other especially now that we are married and committed to spending the rest of our lives together." I lay back on the grass and began to recall what I needed to tell Lise.

"You don't need to do this if it is painful in any way," Lise replied. "I love you but I don't own you."

"I want to. It might help me to come to grips with the reason my mind works. The woman who was treating me worked out of a small clinic using a modified version of the induction helmet to reprogram a person's mind. Kind of the reverse of the regular induction process that everyone on the planet is "strongly encouraged" to undergo at least once a year. And we all know who is in charge of the induction that is provided to help regular people meditate in a way that will slow down the loss of heat and energy from the top of their head while they are wearing the green suits."

"I am not thoroughly convinced that the Church of the Golden Sun is modifying the induction units," Lise responded. "Otherwise I would not be recommending the process to — any small babies." She became silent.

"I need to make a confession," I spoke after some moments of silence had passed.

"You do not need to," Lise replied. "And before you continue, you should be aware that although there are no secrets between us — and I most likely have shared your dreams in ways that are still a mystery to me, I will repeat that I do not own you, and I accept you as you are." She kissed me to confirm her statement.

"Point accepted and I agree to the Mystery, too." I nodded. "Still, in respect for our joining, I need to get this off my chest—and out of my mind. She smiled and I continued my story.

"I was paralyzed by a sting from an animal that, being a ghost or not, was very real to me. The Elder who ran the clinic employed the reverse induction treatment on me daily, through a helmet similar to the one you invented to pilot the ships using the crystals. It turned out to be slow process. She was amazed at how slow it went, and concluded that my mind was fighting the process."

"Be patient with yourself," She advised. "I notice that some healing has taken place because you are able to speak and no longer need to be fed through a tube. I will check in to see that you are OK, but otherwise it is mainly up to you to accept the truth of your ability to heal yourself. With the aid of my unit, it is similar to the process of forgiveness."

And so it went. Hours turned into days and I was a prisoner of my mind. Until one morning, the curtain was pushed aside and a woman in a wheel chair rolled up and stopped beside my bed. And when I saw her, and began to believe that I knew her, she said:

"Hello. I am, Kathy. Do you remember me?"

"Are you…?" I spoke the name that was a secret heart name.

"Yes—I do believe I am," she replied. "But I have forgotten so much that I am like you. My belief is now that I was born this way—never to walk because of my previous life of sin."

"Sin? I was aghast, and for the moment I forgot my own condition. "Who- ever would tell you a lie like that? I don't believe that the religion of the Golden Sun even believes in past lives, let alone that someone be born an invalid because of a past life's mistakes."

"They don't" Kathy moved closer to the bed and took my hand. "But in my case they made an exception, because there is no other answer. When our religion did not have the answer in their book, they judged that the problem must be due to a source outside their knowing – a demonic idea that was invented by feeble minds called reincarnation."

"Posh!" I was able to turn my head to look in her all too familiar eyes. "I am a dreamer. Do you know what that means?"

"You spoke a name that no one else could know, and I only remember from my dreams." Tears formed in her eyes. "Are you telling me that what they say about me is all lies?"

"Not exactly lies but accusations that are based on not being open to another truth except what is written in the Book of the Golden Sun. Their book was written by their Prophets after they migrated over the land bridge to our side of the ocean – so they tell us – and after they were given the vision to give up human sacrifice, and start a new religion called The Church of the Golden Sun."

"That is my religion, too." Kathy confirmed. "But I was always a bit reluctant on believing that God lived in the heart of our sun."

"And that the fate of all the people of our world depends on this deity's life in the sky. And when he dies, he will take us all with him to a better place in the sky? I am sorry – not! I believe in the free will that the Mystery who gave us our lives also granted the permission and the ability to follow our dreams. Why else would the Creator give us a Heart if we were not also granted the gift of Dreaming a better dream?"

"I—I remember those dreams," Kathy responded. Her hand trembled in mine. Somehow I found the strength to return the pressure of her squeezing. She let go. "I have to go now," she whispered. "I will be back when I can. I have a lot to think about."

Later that afternoon the Elder who was looking after me came by to check, and smiled to see that I could raise my right hand. "You are making great progress. Keep it up!" She squeezed my hand like Kathy had done. "Time for another treatment," She announced, flipping some switches that activated the helmet on my head. "If you would only not fight the process, those damaging memories would be erased, and I believe you will walk again," she smiled benignly.

I smiled back. The process of reverse induction had helped many people before me, so I knew she meant well. But now, I had another reason not to forget. When the process was complete for the night and the Elder prepared to leave, I was tempted to ask her about the woman in the wheel chair, but I let it go, for the time being. The healing process sometimes take a week or more on Terra time to complete. This was what the Elder informed me. She also told me that could depend on how much I resisted the process. I agreed quietly that my resistance to give up my guilty memories were playing a big part in my recovery.

The next day, Kathy visited me again, eager to continue our discussion about the "Fall".

"The fall?" I asked her. "What do you mean? Are we responsible for what religion calls the fall of man due to the temptation of woman and a strange creature who advised her? I have never believed in that story. It has always seemed to me that it was made up so that the men who wrote the story could appear blameless for what happened."

"My thoughts, too." Kathy held my hand. "But there is truth in every story if we are brave enough to look. I believe that we are part of the story – every man and woman since Creation."

"But I need to put aside the judgment of some men that are unable to face their fears. I am not 'some men', and you are not the temptress..."

"I would not dismiss the temptress part entirely." Kathy squeezed my hand tightly. "I was born like this due to another life in which I was an erotic dancer, who was tricked into selling her body. I have those dreams to deal with as you have yours."

"And that is what brings us together today." I sighed, and amazed myself by sitting up on the pillow. "I also dream, and in my dream I met and offered to help you heal, by reclaiming your Beauty. Do you remember that?"

"Yes," her face flushed. "You rescued me in a respectable but unique way."

"And you taught a young man the secrets of the Fire. I do not regret that at all."

"So why are you in this bed?"

"And why are you in that wheel chair still?"

"I have been in this chair since birth," she smiled. "But the time has come to face my truth. This was my dream – and is between the Creator and myself to judge me for my mistakes."

"About dreams? I recall someone—a sacred man—saying that "what we think is already done." That has distressed me for a long time. I dream a lot, and have shared love with many women…"

"Shared Love. You said. There is more than one dream! I found that out the hard way. We have dreams about Love and finding our soul mates, and guess what—our dreams come true. A lot to think about? Until tomorrow…" She rose out of the chair and stood unsteady to bend over and give me a kiss. And then Kathy and her wheel chair were gone.

Later, about noon-time, the Elder came in to give me a light lunch, and another process. "It is working." she smiled benignly. "You are able to sit up and feed yourself. I think you will be ready to go home by the week end."

Three days and I can go home? What home? Lise and I had been selecting a home that we would share after our joining ceremony. That night, Lise was on my mind and I had a fitful sleep — dreaming of a visitor who got into my bed and shared her fire with me, and departed before the break of dawn.

I was contemplating my condition – my inability to accept my part in the reality of life – that led to my feelings of guilt. "Who am I? Really? Am I the dreamer or the dreamed? If I am truly the dreamer, then I need to take responsibility for my actions in all the dreams that I co-created, even the casual ones. No dreams are unimportant, and every person in the dream is a sacred part of me to be respected." I was deep in these thoughts when a familiar voice…

"A penny for your thoughts." Kathy stood by my bedside, supported by a cane. She sat on the edge of the bed.

"And a million more for yours," I replied. "Look at you…walking without the chair! You are on your way to a complete healing."

"I am," she agreed. "I came to share a healing dream. And with that, hospital gown flowing out like an angels wings, she stretched out on the bed beside me.

"I don't know if I can dream like this…with you so close." I gulped.

"Oh c'mon, we both know better. You do this all the time."

And I have done just that. It was just that…and then the dream came, and another. Warm happy dreams of time spent on a lonely highway – hitching a ride, and then the forest – the garden. And hours may have past, or days? Kathy stood over me with her good-bye-for-now kiss.

"We do not know a word for good bye." She smiled and discretely wrapped the hospital gown about her as she took her leave.

"You are definitely ready to go home. A few more days will do it." The elder proclaimed later and I thanked her, only to ignore the reprogramming of my mind that followed.

And that night my secret visitor appeared, and stayed almost till dawn. I knew her, but was not sure if it were another dream.

"Who else is here, in this clinic right now?" I asked the Elder healer.

"Right now, besides you, there is only one other patient, down on the lower floor. We, uhh I, do not have the space for more than four people at a time on each floor, and that is just as well as I need to devote my time to each of you for a speedy recovery."

"Who is the other patient, if I may ask? Is there an elevator that someone could take up to this floor?"

The Elder frowned. "Yes, we have a freight elevator to bring up patients that cannot walk, like you were when you first came to me to be healed. But I cannot give out any information about our other patient, except to say that he was not in as severe a condition as you when he came in, and I sincerely doubt that he would violate your privacy. Who might you be concerned about anyways? Have you been bothered by any secret late night visitors?" She smiled knowingly.

I shrugged. "One of my problems has been that I dream. And sometimes it is difficult to separate reality from my dreams. Has this clinic been here long? Do you have any idea what was built on this site before?"

The Elder sighed. "Ghosts is it?" And her face brightened. "Most of my patients are dreamers, and as you are aware it is not unusual for dreamers to see ghosts. Before this clinic was built long ago, there was a factory and a test facility here. This was the building, long ago where Sam discovered the potential of the crystals that we almost take for granted today. And then the factory was re-located to the inner city. But I guess that you know all about that bit of history?"

"Did Sam have a child, a daughter?" I took a bold stab to discover another truth. "I heard that he had help in making his groundbreaking discovery."

"So the story goes," the Elder chuckled. "If you must know, Sam published a book, a journal actually, after his lab was moved, and after his daughter went to ashes. He claimed that it was her journal and that she was responsible for making most of the discoveries that were attributed to him. His daughter, Kathy was a dreamer. Sam's book was forced underground by the church. You see those were difficult times and the conflict between the Golden Sun and the dreamers was a tender topic for discussion."

"So how has that changed?" I ventured. "The difference is that the church is more diplomatic about their burning of books that don't support their religion."

"You ARE your old self again," The Healer exclaimed. "I might agree that we still have a way to go in the area of women and dreamers' rights, but we prefer to take a more respectful approach, and work together if any of us are going to get off this planet before the sun dies."

I shrugged again. "The last I heard, the Church of the Golden Sun is opposed to leaving this world. Their official doctrine is that the Sun will die, and his people will be taken to a higher world."

"True, but if we work together, even the most hard-lined beliefs can be changed. Hopefully before our sun goes Super Nova. The factory that is part of the hangar where the dreamers work toward that end may be our saving grace."

A Spark of the Fire

And that night my secret visitor appeared, and stayed almost till dawn. I knew her but was not sure if it were another dream

The next day I was ready to go home, but I was looking forward to another visit by my fellow patient, if that was what she was.

Later that morning Kathy pulled aside the curtain and walked without a cane to stand beside my bed. She still wore the hospital gown and I was tempted to ask why, since she was not and never had been a patient at this clinic, as far as anyone knew. Instead I asked:

"Are you real or are you a ghost?"

"I have laid beside you on the bed and shared dreams with you," she replied with a smile. "What do you think?"

"I would like to know if I am cheating on my future wife." I replied, "Is there any way I can know for sure about the guilt that paralyzed me?"

"There might be away," Her smile broadened. "But you might still think you are dreaming. The guilt you hold onto is based on a logical world's truth and not who you — or I really are."

"Show me." I volunteered.

"Don't say I didn't warn you." With that, she opened the hospital gown and let it fall to the floor. I stared unblinking at her nudity, and pulled aside the bed sheet so she could join me under the covers.

She was very real! All my senses confirmed that fact, and then sometime after our proving of that....

"Ooops, I have to go." Kathy jumped out of bed and slipped on the gown, not bothering to tie the back. "You have a visitor." She blew me a kiss and disappeared through the curtain as if she had never been there, but leaving behind, a memory of an angel with flowing wings.

"Are you decent?" The voice of the Elder healer called out to announce: "I brought you a visitor – she's come to take you home."

THREE

This "Are you decent?" the voice of the Elder healer called out to announce: "I brought you a visitor – she's come to take you home."

"Of course I am decent," I replied making sure that the covers were close around my hips to hide my otherwise nude body. Caught in the middle of my own guilty dream – if that is the truth? I am wondering again, what the truth really is? "Why wouldn't I be?"

"Well..." The Elder pulled aside the curtains, and I saw Lise waiting behind her. "Well I was beginning to wonder at some of the sounds I have heard. Were you carrying on...I mean speaking to yourself? And there is the matter of the midnight visitor." Lise smiled and her face flushed

"I've come to take you home." Lise announced.

We were back to the reality of the beach in the Forest.

"Lise! It was you that visited me every night in the clinic."

"Yes. How could you not know? Or maybe you didn't want to remember?

"And stayed until the break of dawn." I kissed her passionately as the memories returned. "What about the dragons? What about the conditioned warnings about not going out at night?"

"When someone you love is in need of you, not even dragons, real or falsely remembered will keep you from their side. "You did need me there, didn't you? Or was there another dream that helped you to heal?"

"Yes. You were a major part in my healing. I thought it time to confess. And there were dreams that helped me to face my guilt." Sometimes I wonder if it was a matter of re-living my guilty dreams that played a big part too." Now Lise knew about the dreams of Kathy.

She shrugged. "We are more than we seem to be." She lay back on the sand, with her head in the grass at the beginning of the beach. "And the Elder told me about the ghost visitations that her former patients had encountered. Kathy is one of those that people call ghosts. But we know different. Don't we?"

I sighed. "Yes, we do. Kathy has her own reality just as you are also Stephanie. And I am Shane as much as I am ..."

"We all need to face our ghosts." Lise exclaimed. And I could see that you were still dealing with yours when I took you home—to the home what we would be sharing when we were legally married—in the eyes of our families."

"And we hurried along the preparations for the ceremony that would make it all true." I continued the story for both of us.

"But when the day came for the commencement of our marriage at the tracks that divide Dreamers from the Crystal City something happened that I still do not understand." She shut her eyes as we both recalled that fateful day.

"I was still so immersed in my guilt of cheating on you, that when the train came, as part of the ceremony, I let myself be caught up in the wind that followed, and I was left in a coma."

"And here we are today." She opened her eyes and smiled at me reassuringly. "You have woken up – returned from the ashes of your former self and the ceremony went off just like we planned together. So who are you now?"

I smiled back and kissed her in response. "I am still Shane inside, and I am coping with being someone like his people might call a 'two-spirited' person. I am still sorting out his and my memories. I might be doing this until I pass into ashes again."

"Well you might need to learn to live with the reality that we are more than most people think we are – and in fact we sometimes live in multiple worlds at the same time. It comes with being a Dreamer. It comes with facing and learning to love yourself. Don't you think? Speaking of reality, how about if we go back home and get started at what we came here to do?" She rose to her feet, and I followed her back to our ship.

"When I was speaking of dragons, I was thinking that there had to be a reason that warning was originally placed in our minds?" I mused out loud as I piloted the ship in the direction of the Crystal City. "And there is the part of there being a no-fly zone when we come to the western most part of our land. One day, I will take that journey and see what is on the other side of the water."

"A conspiracy theorist to the end, and beyond." Lise's smile was strangely tight-lipped. "I agree that when the ships were built that had the capability with the aid of the crystals to cross the ocean, the old teaching might have been incorporated into our induction along with other teachings meant to keep us safe. But I hesitate that we are being manipulated by the Church of the Golden Sun. It was and still is for our own good."

"Oh? You do agree that the induction programs our minds with other things beyond enabling us to live in a meditative state so that we no longer need to wear the hood that would be part of the protective suit?"

"Yes," She hesitated. "When our people began to use the crystals in all of our daily devices from transportation to communication, our metabolism was speeded up as well, so that without the protective green suits, that the scientists that are part of the Order of the Golden Sun invented by the way, we had our life expectancy cut in half."

"So the first protective suits were meant to cover our head as well, to stop the loss of heat and life energy through the top of the head." I recalled reading this in the history books. "But they fail to mention that the controlling of the loss through the top of our head was first solved by a Dreamer, who was able to use meditation to live almost as long as was previously thought possible. And then the scientists took this over and made it part of a yearly induction process similar to the mind programming helmet that Stephanie created so that we could all fly the ships using the crystals."

"Yes that is true," Lise sighed in resignation. "And that meant that we could remove the protective hood from our children's head soon after birth and they would be as free as though they had learned to meditate in the normal way."

"And I agree to that temporary measure, as long as the other bits of mind- washing were not included," I replied. When Lise firmed her mouth and looked away, I said: "OK, we had this conversation before, when we were talking about having a baby. It does not need to be re-hashed. How about if we go home and start our new life together? In the morning we can go over to the hangar and see how Dave is coming along with installing the new crystals that will enable us to find a new home for our people out there among the stars?"

"That sounds like a good idea," Lise sniffled. "Tomorrow will be the start of a new life."

Later that night, Lise was back in good spirits again, and we made passionate love before drifting off to sleep in each other's arms.

I woke from another dream the next morning before sunrise. Lise was still sleeping soundly, with her back toward me. The dream that I woke from ended with seeing Kathy exit my hospital enclosure. Her gown untied, left me with a vision of a nude angels back, with wings unfurled. My face burned afresh with my former guilt. I felt unworthy of the love and trust that my new wife had shared with me. I slipped quietly out of bed and dressed for the cool temperatures that I would find outside the door of our home, on a planet whose sun was dying.

It was my intention to visit the hangar where Dave and his crew were working nonstop at outfitting the ships with the new crystals that they had harvested from the cave on the dark side of the moon. I walked through the quiet streets of a city where the inhabitants were told by mental programming that it was unsafe to venture out at night – in fear of being taken away by dragons that no longer existed. I wondered if this was a just another lie to keep the people on this planet under control of the church. In my musing, I halted at the train track that divided the lands of the Dreamers from the people who lived under the watchful eyes of a government that was a marriage of church and hard logical science. Soon, a wind would pick up that preceded the coming of the morning supersonic train. My guilt burned at my face and heart, like a replay of another time....

"Don't even think of it!" A voice interrupted my mental fog, and another kind of fog or smoke revealed a woman on the other side of the tracks.

"Who...?"

The smoke in the wind is not of my making," She replied. "Clear your mind! You and I have met before. I am a Jinn – a friend of Shane. And you are still Shane. I am a Being of Fire, and the magic I can do is to remind you of who you really are."

"Who am I?" I managed, as the wind began to swirl about us.

"You are a Dreamer who is caught up in his Dreams, and has forgotten to be accountable for his actions. We have very little time – the train is coming."

"But what can I do to make things right?" She was right; the wind that preceded the train was catching me, pulling at me.

"Remember why you came to this place. And be true to that dream, and be true to your new wife and your family."

"...and remember...we are all One..."

Her words were swept away as the train became a blur between us. And when the train had passed, the strangely familiar woman was gone, leaving me to step back lest I be caught in the powerful wind that followed in its wake.

When I returned to the home—my home that I shared with Lise—dawn was breaking.

"So, you decided to come back this time." She stretched and sat up in bed.

"Yes. For good this time." I replied.

"I should say I will believe that when I see it, but somehow I do believe you. I accept that you are a dreamer, but I am too remember?"

"Do you ever feel guilty about the other lives we lived?" I asked.

"It comes with the gift of insight. Yes I have, but a woman who dreams, and falls to Earth also accepts that it was her choice, and it is no longer a Fall, but a choice to know the purpose that the Creator created us - to be co-creator of our lives."

"Are you rapping my knuckles for playing where I should not?"

"Absolutely not – I am reminding you that it is your duty to be here and now – where I need you to be, for these people that we promised to help, and ...for your family..."

"Family?" I must be more asleep than I thought." I took her hand and looked into her eyes. There was a beginning of tears. "Lise? Are you telling me that you are pregnant?"

"I am not. No longer. But while you were asleep for so long a time, I was, and that came and passed. We...you have a son. He was conceived when I visited you in the hospital and he was born while you were in a coma."

"And when were you going to tell me?" I sighed and held her.

"If you did not come back this time, it would not be necessary. I reasoned that he would be better believing that his father had gone to ashes as all of our people will someday, than that he deserted his family." She sobbed in my arms.

What could I say? I held her until the trembling ceased. "I am here now, and I promise that I will not go on any dreaming until we go together."

"Silly!" Her eyes brightened and she wiped away the tears. "That is like saying that you will quit breathing. We are both dreamers. And the reason we are here, on this world where our child was born, is to fulfill the purpose we found by Dreaming. And we will act together now, to create or find a better world for our son and our grandchildren to come. Now, are you ready to meet your son? He has been staying with my father and mother until you were fully recovered."

"I am ready – I promise. What did you name him?" I could hardly get those words out.

"His name is Jak-Brin – the same as my father – and his true father Do you know who you are now? It is too late to turn back.

"Yes I know who I am. My father and mother named me Brin because that name came to him. My father was a dreamer too, sometimes much to my mother's distress. It is a gift that is easily abused." We let that conversation die – for the moment, as we were both eager to bring little Brin home. We decided it would be easier to shorten his name to Jak for short.

When I first held my son, my mind was not dwelling on whether he was really the child of the man who went to ashes in the hospital after being in a coma for so long a time. I am that man now, and have always been. I am Brin, and have been for as long as this Dream persists. The writer of the song had it partly wrong. "Dreams do not die – nor does the Dreamer." We start a new dream and nothing —; no one is lost — even when our guilt or troubled minds lead us to forget.

A child can be an amazing gift. He can help us to change the way we look at life…if our heart is open to compassion. And when Lise and I watched little Jak sleep with the contentment that only some children can, the realization comes so sweetly and completely. "Our children do not belong to us – they are a Spark of the Creator's Fire…given life through our expression of Love. But for this small, precious bit of time, on this dying world, he will be our son. And he becomes a beacon of the purpose that we came here for.

Speaking of our purpose for being here, for a couple of weeks it was the farthest from either of our minds as I spent as much waking time as I could manage just playing and enjoying our son. And then a dream interrupted and called me back. In the dream, we were in ships rising off the surface of our world, looking back at so many people huddled together – left behind! The morning after that dream, as if on cue, a friend of Lise from upper school connected her about getting together to reminisce. It occurred to me—both of us actually—that we had experienced little or no contact with any of our former friends or family since "returning" to Terra.

"I have been wondering, off and on what happened to my school friend Tris," Lise told me. "I have not seen her since our graduation gala dance. Tris asked me if we would like to go to a nightclub in the City of Lost Angels to talk about old times. She is married now, but they have no children. The nightclub is out in Vega at the far Eastern Point city."

Eastern Point Station is the end of the super-train tracks. At the other end, nearest the Crystal City is a short shuttle ride at South Point. The track that separates the land of the Dreamers from the rest of our continent begins at South Point and cuts a semi-circle to end at East Point, enclosing my people's land. A one time "my People's land" comprised all of the land mass including this part that the Dreamers call "the Smile of the Moon." Most of the animals are ghosts in our memories—killed and eaten by the ancestors of the invaders that came from another land far over the great ocean, so it is told in our stories and still dreamed by those who dare to keep the dreams alive.

"I have often wondered what happened to Tris," Lise repeated. "She disappeared like she was never real. Still I know she was real, and not a figment of my imagination or a random dream."

"Dreams are as real as our life together," I reminded Lise. "Dreams are as real as this child we love even if I am guilty of not remembering his creation." I gulped at the words that came from my mouth.

Lise smiled through her tears. "I agree." She kissed me tenderly. "I wonder what I should wear – that is if you agree to go?"

I nodded and replied that I would like to meet this friend from my wife's past, who I knew so little about. "What would you like to wear – from your vast collection of evening dresses?" I was kidding of course. Lise and I had a meager number of clothes, only which was what essential to our daily lives.

"I was thinking about wearing the dress that I almost wore from my graduation dance." She laughed at her private joke.

"What do you mean – almost wore?" I asked. "You are still the same slim woman you were then, even after the pregnancy and the birth of Jak."

"Let me show you, and you be the judge." She selected a long blue gown from her side of the closet, and hid it with her body. "Don't look. I want to surprise you." I waited while she went into the bathroom to change.

When Lise came out of the bathroom with the gown on, I was definitely surprised.

"Taa-daa!" She pirouetted to give me the full view. The dress fit her, as I knew it would. That was not a surprise to me. But as she turned, I saw the beauty of the woman I love – stunning in a gown that touched the floor, off one shoulder and across her chest to the waist. Her left breast was completely exposed!

"Wow!" I exclaimed. "And you almost wore that to your graduation dance? I wonder what your mother said. It is certainly inspiring – for me – to suggest that you might not make it out the door if you were still have thoughts of wearing it to the nightclub"

"And why might that be?" she smiled coyly. "My mother nixed it in the bud, by the way."

"Because I would be inclined to remove the dress and we would not show up at the night club," I replied, as she ducked out of my embrace and pretended to evade my reaching hands.

"It was Tris's Idea at first." She took my hand and moved it to the one strap on her right shoulder.

"And then?" I let my hand rest on the strap of the dress, resisting my initial impulse.

"We were young and reckless." Lise drew me into a kiss and a close embrace. "I was a bit of a renegade then, and I guess that attracted the young man who was to be my future husband." She whispered in my ear, as the dress slipped to the floor at our feet.

Afterward, I asked. "You are not really thinking about wearing that dress?"

"Of course not, silly." She got off the bed and went to the bathroom to retrieve the modest dress that she had worn earlier. "After all," her voice echoed from the behind the partly closed door. "I am a mother now, and much too mature to display myself in public like that."

I breathed a sigh of relief. I had not really believed that she would go out dressed like that, Even though I am her husband, I do not own her. I love her for being the dreamer and the mother of our child. It crossed my mind that Lise might "mature" more quickly than I will. There is a strange truth. I am Brin. I am Lise's husband, but I live in a body that made a trip in a ship from another planet. And I am also Shane, however that works out. I do not "posses" Shane's body. He is still inside me, and I get Ideas and memories that I know can only be from a previous life growing up on Earth.

FOUR

Lise's friend Tris and her partner met us on the platform of South Point Station. Tris was exactly as Lise described her, in fact Lise would tell me later that she did not seem to have aged at all. Tris wore a long blue evening dress with a shawl. And her partner a modest jacket and upscale suit to match.

"This is Brian;" Tris introduced him to Lise and I. "Brian is my partner in crime, so to speak." Did I detect a wince from Brian at her introduction? Either way, he must be used to her jovial manner by now, I would imagine, since Tris had told Lise that Brian and her had been living together for at least ten years.

Tris talked a mile a minute – literally, as the super-train covered the distance to East Point Station and the City of Lost Angels in a mere space of half an hour. I tried to catch a view of the level crossing where Lise and I had been married, but it went by as a blur. At some point I asked Tris (and Lise) why the city was called "Lost Angels."

"As the story goes," Tris jumped right into the change in the flow of conversation, and Lise just smiled. "As the story goes, the city was named a long time ago, before our ancestors came over and colonized this part of the world. The official name came to be as a result of a previous meeting by the original people and the people from the North, my ancestors. Three ships came over the ocean led by a man who was devious in nature but claimed that he and his men were both Kings and angels. Apparently the original people were not easily fooled, and caught on to this man's lies. The original people overcame the group of men and disarmed them. It's not known how, since the people from the ships had superior fire power – in fact the first rifles and the red-skinned people only had bows and arrows. Anyways, the fake Angels were disarmed and helped to build the city in the South that was subsequently named 'the City of Lost Angels'. It seems that the original people must have had a sense of humor, don't you think?"

I agreed, quietly thinking that my ancestors, the Dreamers, had a greater insight into the Mysteries than some of their descendants were afforded after the hordes of war-minded people arrived to take whatever they wanted, in the name of the God of Fire. Same God that my people knew, but it seems He had a much different face for these greedy people. Those thoughts went with the wind of the super train, as Brian announced that: "we are here."

The City of Lost Angels did not appear much different than the main Crystal City back near South Point. They had all of the electronic toys and devices advertised in their storefronts and the usual proliferation of cameras that taped anything and anybody on the streets and inside the clubs and restraints. "The main difference," Tris explained, "is that there are laws that enforce the actions of the people who live and vacation here. You must have heard that what happens to Angels stay in the city? Lost Angels that is," She laughed aloud as we entered the posh dining hall. "*Swing*, is one of the finer places to eat and have only high-class entertainment. Except for tonight – in *Swing* we are all amateurs. It is karaoke night tonight. It will be fun, you'll see."

I had done some reading up on this City at East Point. It wasn't without laws – in fact the laws were rumored to be twice as strict for offenders here. This made me wonder what happened to the offenders. I have never heard mention of jails anywhere in and around the Crystal City. Maybe the worst criminals were shipped overseas to be detained in prisons West of what my ancestor had affectionately called Turtle Island. But then the lands over the great Western Ocean were forbidden travel zones. Maybe this was part of the reason. I made a mental note to ask Lise or Tris, as my memory was sketchy about such things.

Tris, on the other hand, seemed a fountain of knowledge, which I mostly quietly filed away as negative judgment. She seemed to know all there was about the lands we lived, in relation to religion and spirituality, but it was not the view a Dreamer might possess, unless he or she was still anguishing in the pain of our ancestors.

"You can do almost anything you have in mind in this city." Tris informed us. "You can even hurt yourself, to some extent, but not terminally, since you would then be arrested as a pathological criminal who was likely to do harm to someone else. And by the way, children under the age of maturity are not allowed even to vacation in this city. There is another city over the tracks that is almost like back home, where you can take your children to enjoy themselves... but back to Lost Angels – the people who vacation and live here are on the edge of being just as the name implies 'Lost'. Our Patriarch and his advisers believe that a place like this will allow people to blow off steam and come back a more responsible citizen. But between you and I, a lot of people choose to remain engulfed in their addictions, blissfully ignorant of their wrong doings."

"Wow! Some heavy judgments!" I wondered what Tris and Brian were doing here? And then a whiff of smoke caught my attention. "So drugs and smoking are acceptable here?" I asked.

"Legal laws are bent to spiritual false truths," Tris laughed. "We are on the south side of the tracks. This land used to belong to the Dreamers" Weed and natural plants are considered sacred to the People of the Feather. This is overlooked as being a spiritual practice and as such is not deemed harmful — or to a limited extent helpful in our mental and physical state like the smoke of sage."

"Weed is considered healthy here?" I could not help to smile. "How about hard drugs?"

"No. Hard drugs, especially chemically manufactured are forbidden. The user could be put away for life." Tris suggested, "You are in the land of the dreamers now. Be your normal addicted self, if that's your thing. Live and let live. We are all self confessed sinners here."

I was about to object to her declaration – that this did not include me or Lise, but Tris looked me straight in the eye, like a dare, and shrugged out of the shawl. She was wearing an exact copy of the evening dress that Lise had auditioned for me in the privacy of our bedroom. It was cut away from one strap to reveal a well-shaped breast that drew my eyes like a magnet. I hastily returned my gaze to her face. She smiled a sly and sparkling smile, and provocatively flicked her tongue across her lips.

"Tris!" Lise exclaimed. 'You have not changed one bit."

I met Tris' eyes straight on. "It's a good thing to speak our truth." I smiled and resisted the urge that compelled my eyes to go elsewhere. "My truth at this moment is a memory that surfaced naturally when you took off your cape." She did not blink and neither did I.

"A memory?" she asked. "Tell me?"

"I remembered a young woman that I worked with who liked to wear a form-fitting shirt, with the words printed across her chest. "My eyes are so not down here."

"So?" Tris smiled. "Did you look?"

"Yes, she was well-endowed, and a feast for my eyes. At the same time I renewed eye contact, and said to her: "You might not want to flaunt the fashion if you don't own the passion."

"Meaning?"

"I was a single young man at the time, and it was my intention to make it plain to her that in no uncertain terms, I was unashamedly enjoying the view. And if she was open to more, I was interested in what she was offering."

"Brin? I don't remember you telling me this? Where did this take place?" Lise cupped my hand. "It was none of my business anyways, but where did you work?"

"I...I don't remember that," I replied.

"And what about now?" Tris did not let it pass unchallenged.

"What..."

"How do you feel about what I am offering?" she smiled seductively. "Would you like to touch?"

"Tris!" Brian interjected. "Do we need to continue this?"

"Well?" She ignored her partner's words as though he was not even present.

"Yes!" I was truthful. "But I respect my feelings, and I am not driven by them. We are adults here and both of us – and the young woman I mentioned was just doing what she felt a natural expression of her urge which some might call being an exhibitionist. Then, I would have, but now I have changed — I am more respectful for both of us." I sat back and accepted the menu that our server brought to our table.

Lise sighed, and Tris shrugged and eyed the menu, glancing up now and then to let me know that we were not done.

When the four of us had given our order the server brought us the wine that we had chosen. We clicked our glasses: "To Truth."

"I suspect that you are hiding your real truth. Even from your wife," Tris began again.

"I can vouch for Brin," Lise replied. "We are soul mates and destined from before birth." It was a bold statement, and she was one step from revealing our secret of our ancestors.

"Hummm?" Tris laughed playfully. "You were always a strange bird Lise. But Brin? Let me tell you something that I have known from birth. We are all filled with sin. We were born in sin, and our ancestors that came from the land over the North Ocean brought it with them. The God of Fire is not happy with us and when he returns, some of us will burn. But some of us who embrace our mistakes and own up to our sins can be saved."

"So that's what this is about?" I pondered in my mind. "I have heard that word. It comes up in my memory from the same source as the girl I worked with. But my ancestors did not know that word. It came over the great ocean with the white-bearded men in their ships. Yes...I am a Dreamer. If this is to be my secret, then let it out. I am proud of my heritage. My people's language has a word that sounds like this, but it means to eat — to share food. I have another memory of someone who ate an apple in the Garden and that amazes me to no end how our people could be so alike, but so different. What do you think about that?"

"The floor show is finished, but the food will be a little while yet. I think we could talk this into the ground and, I hope we agree to disagree." The floor show had attracted my attention since we sat down, and then I was distracted by the show at our table. The floor show had consisted of a man and woman clothed in form fitting body suits performing a sensuous dance – so close to being real that it entranced the audience, and brought a resounding show of appreciation. As the clapping died. Tris reminded us that:

"They are not professionals; they are like you and me – not afraid to show their feelings. Which reminds me—it is Karaoke night!" She rose from her chair and donned her evening cape.

"Oh Tris!" Brian complained – not too strongly but enough to voice his disapproval. "Must you?"

"Oh yes! I must." Her eyes sparkled as she left our table and marched brazenly to the platform where the two dancers had performed. She stopped by the dee jays table to tell him what music she wanted, and then up on the stage striking a daring pose while the music started up. She did not have a mic, I noticed.

"Is she going to sing?" A memory of a usual Karaoke night popped into my mind.

"I only wish," Brian shrugged and smiled.

And then the music began a deep drum beat that gathered in momentum and energy. It was unmistakable – a strip tease! And Tris was at one with the beat. She gyrated as the music built, and soon her shawl slid down her body to the floor, to reveal what we had been given a taste of at our table. I confessed (to myself) that I was entranced — waiting to see what would come next. How far would she go?

"Does she do this often?" Lise interrupted my train of thought. "Whenever she feels inspired," Brian flinched.

"And by inspired, do you mean that I am responsible in some way for bringing this on?" I found that hard to believe, as Tris was obviously enjoying her moment in the spotlight.

"Our – not hidden secret," Brian tore his gaze away from his partner as her dress joined the shawl at her feet. She kicked it away and let everyone know that she was not finished. The audience that had watched in wrapped silence at the previous performance, were clapping and encouraging her to "take it off", like any group of men that might gather in a seedy tavern, except this stylish restaurant was populated by an audience of an equal number of women who were cheering right along with their partners.

"Our secret", Brian spoke again, "is we, Tris and I are missionaries."

That stunned me. "Missionaries?" It was hardly my idea of religious followers who felt it was their purpose to convert the sinners. And "woops," she was teasing them—and me, her thumbs in the waistband of her panties. I tore my eyes away. "How long has Tris been like this?" I asked.

"As long as I have known her." Brian answered and the clapping and cheers indicated that she was up to the dare. "Tris is an orphan. She was raised by a religious step father and mother, but she has confided in me as feeling abandoned. And she has secrets that I can only guess about. I am not revealing anything that Tris will not openly tell you – probably when she comes down and returns to our table. She will tell you anything that is true for her, if it means the possibility of saving your soul. That is what we are all about."

On the stage, Tris was pirouetting, completely nude, in her moment.

"Are you married?" Lise asked: "You don't need to answer, but the Tris I knew, single and reckless – wild, is still the girl up there on the stage." Meanwhile the music had finished, and our dancing friend was gathering up her clothes.

"No problem," Brian smiled and blushed. "We are not married, but we sleep together. Crazy? Tris believes that it keeps us in touch with our sinful nature so that we are not living a lie when we tell people that we are the same as they are, except we have given our souls to the God of Fire. We are a team. Mostly I protect her." He certainly had the physique for the job. "I would like to get married, but Tris also has a secret that she has not revealed even to me. And that secret would end our marriage – she says."

"But what if...?" I felt a need to change the direction of our conversation as Tris was now fully clothed and thanking the dee jay. "What if I had accepted her invitation – to touch? Isn't that illegal here? Bare-skin to skin? Would I have been arrested?"

"It is illegal in public," Brian replied. "But there are much seedier places, dumps in the darker part of the city, and you might be inspired to share your sinful or evil thoughts with your partner later. Just remember, though, there is nowhere that you can hide from the cameras. If you had touched, even though she tempted you, you would receive a warning as a first-offender, and on the third offence, you would be taken away."

"Taken away?" There was that threat. But where?

"Hi!" She definitely was. Tris joined us at the table fully clothed, including her shawl. Perhaps a bit more demure? "Did you see anything you liked?" Tris smiled at me, and then Lise.

"I liked the dance," Lise answered. "I swear, Tris you have not changed a bit. In fact, if I didn't know better, I would think you are the same age as when we graduated together."

"That is a thought," Tris replied mysteriously. "How about you?" She reached out her hand. That wouldn't be illegal would it? Still I smiled and declined.

"Me? I saw everything – literally. And I have to admit I liked all that I saw. And if you still wonder if I was tempted, Yes I was, and still am. Are you thinking to save me from my evil thoughts?"

"May-be not evil, yet." She moved her hand back to make room for the plate that the server placed in front of her. "I am hungry – dancing really gives me an appetite. How about you?" She did not give up easily.

"Me too," I agreed and dove in to a perfectly prepared salmon steak. Lise and I ordered from the near-vegetarian items on the menu, while Tris and Brian devoured a healthy portion of an animal, fully cooked mind you, and garnished with a beautiful assortment of steamed vegetables. Meanwhile, my mind burned with the sight of the lithe nude nymph who believed she needed to save me and perhaps her high school friend as well. I felt my guilt, and was intimidated as well. I realized a need to respond.

"I liked – more than that, I really enjoyed your dance. It was primitive and beautiful and I admit openly that it awakened the primal urges in me – urges that if I pretended to ignore – I would not be a man who was true to his inner Fire. I don't want to be saved from those feelings and emotions. I cherish them when my mate shares herself with me alone, in the privacy of our bedroom, or in a quiet forest by a stream. I don't own Lise, and I have no right to try to deny her from doing what you did up there on the stage if she chose to."

"I don't," Lise replied, "but even not being a man I could enjoy the energy you shared. I am honored that you danced for us."

"Honored?" Tris exclaimed in near exasperation. "Lise honey. I am turned on by my dancing and exposing myself. But I don't feel honored. I feel ashamed of the sin that I have in me. I do this to help you – mostly men to feel the sinful thoughts that they were born with. And my purpose when they are burning with those emotions is to offer to help them accept our God of Fire who will take us with him when he dies to a better place in the sky."

"And what if, like I shared with you, I don't want to be saved?" I responded. "What happens if I am not saved from my sins. Where did you get that word anyways? I hope you don't feel we are ganging up on you?" Her eyes were beginning to fill with tears. "I want you to know that I agree with Lise that it is not an evil thing to feel the Fire of Life that the Creator gifted us with."

"If you are not saved," Tris wiped away the tears, "anyone who is not saved will die in the end with our planet and sun. They will be lost for evermore."

I waited for that moment to pass. "What about the people, even those who are not Dreamers, that remember past lives? There are those who believe that they have lived before and will live again, even though it will be a Circle of Karma. Those words and beliefs come to me from the same source as my knowing that I am another man in my dreams."

"Sad," she announced. "I thought I might be able to help you see the error of your ways. Those people, who are not saved, will die, and that is the end of them."

"Let us part tonight as friends," I suggested, raising the glass of wine that I have been sipping. "We will agree to disagree. Time will be our ultimate teacher, and revealer of Truth. I believe in the Greater Good that all four of us at this table are part of."

Later on, Lise and I said good bye to Tris and Brian and sped back to our home, we pondered the reason why all this had happened.

"There is no coincidence there," I whispered as Lise snuggled her head against my shoulder. "I think it might have been a set up."

"I'd like to think not, but my heart agrees with you. Tris is like one of our people, don't you think? You notice that she does not wear the green heart suit that delays our aging, but she appears to be as young as the last time I saw her."

"A dreamer?" I wondered. "Your friend at least has blood in her veins like that of the People of the Feather. Who can say? I will be watching my words and actions so that I am not arrested by someone in the higher order of the Church of the Golden Sun. Do you think they can or would do that?"

"I think there are the hardcore religious people who would do just that—if they can is another matter."

FIVE

Jak was growing, like my grandmother (and Shane's) liked to say "Like a bad weed." But whose judgment is it that most weed are not flowers or medicinal plants? Jak was a walking and talking example of his parents – his mother mostly. Lise, on the other hand, was maturing faster than I cared to admit. She wore the Green Heart suit, but surprised me by revealing a dream that the ships would not be ready in time for her.

"You just might need to come find me again – somewhere among the Stars." She did not seem disheartened by that. We found each other once before – how many times, I wondered. It is a Truth that Dreamers know, but knowing is one step. The Knowledge is little consolation if we don't transform it into Wisdom as we were doing by our sharing the mystery of love.

I shared as much time as I could with my family, Lise, Jak, and my mother, and helped to test out the new ships that would give the people of our planet the choice of a very human survival – for those who might not believe otherwise. One morning, on a whim, I flew out over the ocean to the West, to investigate the fears that became a law – that created a no fly zone.

The trip was almost instantaneous due to the refitted ship. The new ships are fast with the possibility of eight crystals. The first four that were powered by the Drum beat of our heart and made possible by the green crystal. It was my intention to test out the other four, the first of which seemed to make some sense, but the white crystal was a mystery that defied reasoning. I arrive on the shore of that abandoned land with the expectation of finding...? I didn't know what, but I had some guesses.

The land was a deserted paradise – untouched by the hand of man for centuries. I flew over the sleeping trees that were preparing for what might be the last winter. From the air I caught a glimpse of animals and birds that were unknown to our side of the ocean. The creatures were large and hairy but not as plentiful as I expected. I flew lower and skimmed over the mountain tops, and lower still, to land on a beach out of time. I was confident that any creature I might encounter, I could easily escape in a ship that could fly faster than Light.

Stepping out on a beach that was deserted, I began to wonder why? Why the people in the East didn't choose to colonize this land? And now it was too late. Deep in thought, a movement caused me to look up, I narrowly escaped being caught up by a winged creature that swooped to make me its breakfast. "What?" I ducked and climbed back into the safety of my ship, as the large bird like animal prepared for another try. I was in the air in a flash, surprising the creature that my hidden self recalled. "A terodactyl!" Actually a pterodactyl, if my memory of a history book was correct. I was treated to the living thing – a left over from the age of dinosaurs. Why had this creature survived the extinction that began with a comet or meteor striking the earth so many years ago? So the history books that I recalled surmised. Not the books that ware authorized by the Church of the Golden Sun—another version known—to perhaps only me? Perhaps the fear in the minds of the people who wrote their book helped to keep it alive. And as I wondered about this, I was alerted and swerved out of the way of its claws.

This pterodactyl, this creature out of someone's nightmare, could not possibly come close to matching my speed. But if I didn't pay attention it could have damaged my ship and I would be stuck here in this god-forsaken place. Even worse, if I did not disappear at a speed that it could not comprehend, it might follow me over the ocean to make itself known to a modern world that lived in fear of this very occurrence. It had happened. In the not so distant past, the history books recorded that something snatched little ones out of the street in the dark of night. A story meant to keep children and their parents in line, but based on a living fact no doubt.

I sped away so fast that I left the creature and its family, if it had any, hanging in the sky. I explored some more, but the creatures I found only served to confirm a growing suspicion that the reason for the no-fly zone was in some ways upheld for anyone who could not or refused to change their view of the world. My exit stage left was a quick and blinding light. Back to the hanger where the ships were being constructed and tested, and back to share my findings with Lise.

"And oh yes. I did some experimenting with the fifth and sixth crystal in a safe place where I could not be detected," I told Lise after our late supper and Jak had been tucked into bed.

"And? What did you discover?" she asked.

"What about the white crystal – the eighth?" Lise asked me.

"I just meditated a bit on the white crystal and found a contact, like it might contain the ability to access all seven that went before. And this inspired me to think that we could have made the journey here with the proper intention using the first four crystals only, since it is a destination that was known to us. Of course, this would require the outward stimulation – the vibration of the rattle. All in all, it seems that we have the abilities of the second four crystals present in the first four, if we are patient enough to find a corresponding activation point within us."

"Then, when the ships are ready, we will need to re-program the induction helmets so that the vibrations of the Drum and the Rattle can be accessed more easily by the pilots who will take us to our new home in the Stars," Lise suggested. She knew how I disliked the programming of the induction to "force feed" our children – since the old program included fears to keep the population under control of the Church. I had personally visited the land of the fears of these people's ancestors and almost came face to face with the object that put the fear of God in to the minds of an entire race.

"I agree. But the old programs will need updating to help give our sons and daughters the jumpstart they need. If it was only the Dreamers, and we had more time, we could teach Jak to meditate and the Green Heart suit might not be needed for future generations."

"But the reality is, since the integration of our races, many dreamers and the people they love are equal as they have ever been in the eyes of the Mystery and no one that chooses otherwise will be left behind. This is the code of Honor and Humility of the People of the Feather." Lise spoke my thoughts – almost word for word.

The next day I was helping Dave at the hangar and I asked him how things were going. "Are we going to be ready to take off on time?"

"At the pace we were making here and at the major factories in and near the Crystal City we will," he answered. "But in the last couple of weeks I have not heard from the others in the city. Nothing. I called but no one is answering. I am thinking I need to go over and check on them."

"How about if I do just that?" I offered. "I will take the shuttle on the other side of the tracks and pay a visit to the factory that is building the large ships to see how they are progressing."

As if on some kind of queue, an official-looking man appeared in the factory beside us. We do not lock the doors while we are working, and the work does not stop during twenty four hour shifts.

"This is an official warning," the man informed me. "You have been seen violating the no-fly laws of our country. These laws were not made frivolously and the penalty will be severe if you continue to disobey." With that, the man turned on his heel and left the building, leaving Dave and I in a moment of shock.

"Maybe it is not such a good idea?" Dave suggested.

"Who is he kidding?" I retorted. "We are in the free land of our ancestors. And this only makes me more committed to investigating the factory on the other side of the tracks. The laws in the Crystal City are just the same as ours – people have rights, they are no longer pawns of a Father State. Just the same I remembered the words of Brian, Tris' companion in the City of Lost Angels.

I got off the shuttle, some distance from the factory. It was quiet, and no sign of smoke or people about. The gate was closed but the latch was not locked. I hesitantly opened the gate and headed for the main doors. Still no sign of any workers or for that matter, the place appeared deserted. The main doors were locked down tight, but there was an employee entrance so I tried that. The door to the employee entrance was unlocked, so I let myself inside. This factory was huge! But the assembly line was silent. It was like a ghost factory where no one had worked for a time I could only guess. I walked down the line, observing the huge ships in various stages of completion, lost in my thoughts as to what had happened here.

"Stop right there!" a commanding voice assailed my ears. "Don't make a move."

I stood still as a statue, and was surprised by a couple of Guards. "Caught in the act!" one of them declared. "And who do we have here?"

I told them my name. "Can I put my arms down now?"

"Yes, you can." one of the guards said in a gruff voice while the other kept me covered with what I recognized as a stun gun. "You can hold your hands out for the hand cuffs."

"Oh come on!" I complained. "Why would you be cuffing me just for taking a look around? Just lead me back out the door and I will be on my way."

"Not a chance." The gruff speaking guard put the handcuffs on my outstretched hands. "We were told to be on the lookout for someone like you. And in case you pretend not to know the law, when someone commits their third offence, the punishment is severe. You will be taken away to a holding cell until the Church and the Law decides your fate."

"Taken away?" I protested. "Without as much as a chance to make a call, or to provide for a defense? That is not the law that I know."

"Maybe it is not the law that you might know on the other side of the tracks, but our law is strict and punishment will be quick and just." He and his companion laughed, and to my surprise, put a dark cloth bag over my head. "You are in our hands now, and we will be taking you to somewhere that your people will not find when and if you are allowed a phone call. So just cooperate and everything will go smoothly for you."

The blindfold was removed at the door to a modern building that resided on another landmass over the ocean. I could tell by the smell of the water. Once I got my bearings, I would be able to meditate and pinpoint the location of my temporary confinement.

"How about my phone call?" I asked as the two security agents led me down a long corridor that housed people many of whom I recognized from the factory that built the ships in and about the Crystal City.

"Don't hold your breath," the guard laughed as I was roughly shoved into a cell and the door locked behind me.

"How long have you been in here?" I asked the man in the cell next to me. "Were you allowed a phone call? It's the law you know."

"I've been here over a month, but some have been in here a lot longer. And no one that I know has been allowed a phone call. Our families must be wondering what happened to us. You might as well settle in for the long haul." He returned to his cot and his nap.

After a while, I found a comfortable seat on a pillow against one wall. I shut my eyes and let the room go away. I was in a previously unknown building north of the city that was my home – over the ocean, as I suspected before. Once I contacted Lise, she would be able to tell the proper authorities where I was unjustly held. But in the meantime, how could I let her know? I recalled a memory of "another me" who was able to contact his soul mate in the forest, and call her to him by a special name. I pictured Lise's face, and reached out to her. My mind brought up a recent conversation:

The blue fifth crystal as I had discovered before worked in conjunction with the sound of the rattle to go to a place that I knew about and opened a door at my bidding.

The dark blue – almost violet sixth crystal gave me a sense of far-seeing —I could see destinations that I had not traveled to, the possible outcome of going there.

The seventh violet crystal seemed to help me know that I belonged as part of the whole. But I did not feel ready to pursue a test with the ship using this crystal because it seemed a distant thing to me. My purpose was rooted in the now, and helping our people to escape a dying planet.

"Talking to yourself again?" Another voice popped into my head.

"Yeah, I guess I am," I replied. "So who are you?"

"Who do you think I am?" Laughter in my mind. "Maybe I should be the one asking that question. Who are you? Let me guess some names? Brin? Arbrin? How many more? How about Shane? Oops, that's me. Are you me or am I talking to myself, too?"

"You and I are part of the same collective soul or spirit," I sighed. I didn't possess your body, because I am you experiencing a different dream. Does that make sense?"

"Not logically, but I am getting use to that. Usually you ignore me like I am your inner child or something. I am not your inner child, but I might have been, at one time. Who is the teacher and who is the student? Don't answerer that. We need to contact Lise and tell her where we are."

"And how do you propose we do that?"

"Well, I am not confined to our shared body. Didn't you notice that? Let go of me and I will see if I can step out into the hall beyond the bars."

The next moment I was looking out though his eyes in the corridor outside our cell. A guard was approaching with a meal tray, but didn't appear to see me.

"Here is your breakfast." The guard chuckled sliding the tray underneath the cell door. "Eat well because you will be a guest here for a while – maybe till the end of days?" He went away laughing, as though he had made a great joke. All the while, he did not see me following him down the corridor.

"Wait here," Shane's voice echoed in my head. "I will go to let Lise know where we are."

"Wait? I can see everything that you can," I replied, watching as he stepped through the main door of the prison.

"Whatever," he said.

I was aware of lifting off – into the clouds. "Wow! I can fly! Now where is home? Lise's face appeared, and the ocean below became a blur. In the next moment my energetic self was standing in our kitchen. Lise was talking on the phone. Jak was sitting in a higher chair at the table. He turned and shouted "Daddy's home."

"Brin?" Lise exclaimed. She rushed to hug me, but her arms met with air. "Brin? What gives? Did you die or something?" Her eyes filled with tears.

"Daddy is a ghost," Jak did not seem bothered.

"I am a ghost of my former self." I agreed. "I am not dead. If I were gone to ashes – again you would be the first to know. It appears that you can see me alright. What you see is Shane, who is part of me – like I am part of him. Long story that I believe you know. Anyways – I was arrested and taken off to an island prison – I think located somewhere in the forest. Can you please contact the local law enforcement or if need be someone in the Church? I am pretty sure they are being kept in the dark about the disappearance of the people who were working on the ships. Or maybe they know, but are pretending not to."

Lise dropped off Jak (who was delighted that his daddy was a ghost) at my mother's and she proceeded straight to the local security office. I went along, but none of the people seemed to see me. The sergeant at the desk suggested that Lise fill out a form to report her husband missing, but she declined. "I know where he is," Lise insisted. "This is a breach of the laws of our country. It is not against the law for someone to question the Church. We have freedom of speech now."

"Perhaps that is true," the officer replied after she had listened to Lise's account of how I was arrested and taken away without council or a phone call. "But there are laws on the book that have never been removed. Laws that are used at the discretion of the Church to punish terrorists and renegades that threaten our right to religious freedom."

"Well, what about my rights to freedom to worship as I see fit, as long as I do not intend harm to anyone else," Lise sighed.

"The original laws were made to protect our citizens. Our church can decide that it would be in everyone's betterment that this "escape" from our world is against the wishes of the God of Fire. You might want to make an appointment to see the Patriarch. But I hear he is pretty busy these days."

Lise was fuming, as we left the precinct. As it turned out she had an in—someone who worked in the Patriarch's front office, who was a closet Dreamer. She got an appointment for the next day.

"Let me know how it goes," I suggested. "Better yet, send a message out to me and I will come back and go to see the Patriarch with you." I pulled Shane back and ate the food that the guard left for me. Then I napped and came to the realization that while I usually slept, Shane traveled in our shared dreams.

The next morning, Lise and I (and Shane) stood before the Patriarch in his office for a closed door private meeting.

"Please feel free to call me Joseph." He shook Lise's hand. "That was the name that my father passed down to me. Patriarch, sounds cold and distant. What can I help you with sister?"

I listened as Lise told Joseph the story that led up to my internment. All the while I had the impression that he could see me – or was aware of my presence in some way.

"Oh my!" the Patriarch exclaimed. "This is not good. Those old laws are not meant to be used indiscriminately. This is a breach of the treaties that were made in good will between the Church and the People of the Feather. You can be assured that I will see that this is made right, and your husband will be released and returned home by tomorrow at the latest."

"Thank you...Joseph," Lise bowed respectfully, and left the office in a much better mood than before. "I didn't pursue it anymore than necessary," she explained to me. "Our next step, when you are safely home, will be to petition the Patriarch for the release of other people who were not committing any crime other than working in the factories to build the ships that will take our people to a new home in the Stars."

* * *

"I feel like I already know you, and what you are about to ask," the Patriarch told me as he shook my physical hand this time. "Please call me Joseph." I stood across his desk in his office and shook his hand and began to tell him about the prison that I have been in for a short time at the hands of members of his Church. He listened intently and shook his head.

"Sometimes it is possible for the leaders of our society and Church to pretend not to know what our dedicated followers are doing in our name. Like the old saying, the left hand is not aware of what the right hand is up to. What are you asking of me? I represent the same church that my father did before me, so I cannot let down my parishioners. At the same time I cannot forget the promises we made in the name of God."

I found Joseph easy to talk to, almost like talking to myself. "I only ask that our people – all of the people, the dreamers' and the those who call themselves the Children of the God of Fire – the Church of the Golden Sun, I ask that everyone be given the choice to follow their hearts and chose to love as they see fit."

He sat back in his regal chair with a thoughtful expression on his face. "It will be done," he said at length. "You had only to ask."

SIX

"It will be done," The Patriarch of the Church of the Golden Sun told me. "You had only to ask."

And surprisingly enough, it was. In less than a week, Joseph, as he had instructed Lise and me to call him, issued a proclamation. "All people will be allowed to worship as they see fit, to follow their hearts if they choose to join the ships to the Stars, or to stay behind and embrace the beliefs that they had been following since childhood. I will be remaining true to my calling," he announced. "I will be here to the end of times, to support those who stay behind."

"How old is Joseph, you think?" I asked Lise.

"No one seems to know. Perhaps he is the latest in a long line of Patriarchs, or he is the Son of the Original. We have seen Mysteries before and this will not be the last."

The construction of the ships was cranked up. It looked like the only people to be left behind would be those who chose to. That didn't mean that the objection to the imminent departure would not go uncontested. As the days and months went by, and the climate grew colder, we were greeted at the gates to the factories by protestors carrying signs and dressed in the colors of the Golden Sun. "Blasphemy! Traitors to God!" they chanted as we passed by.

One day, I walked through the gates I spotted a familiar face in the crowd of protestors. He quickly turned away, and then a couple of weeks later, I encountered Brian, looking a bit more mature and graying at the temples in the lineup of men and women who were applying for training to be pilots. Everyone had the right – all men and women, dreamers or church members. It works both ways.

"How is Tris? I asked. He just scowled at me.

"It isn't fair," he looked at me in scorn.

"What isn't fair?" I asked.

"Look at you. So young and healthy, like my former partner. It is not fair. Tris betrayed me! She is like you. Her secret was that she does not get old like the rest of us. Like you!"

"I will get old," I replied. "But I come from a planet where my body was created under different physical laws. My DNA is different than yours. That is all. Otherwise, you and I are the same in spirit."

"That is such a lie that you Dreamers tell," he spat out. "You are in possession of another man's body and that is closer to the truth."

I shrugged. There was no denying his facts. Especially when in a logical way of thinking, he might be right. "So what are you doing in this line up?" I asked.

"I am claiming my rights, the same as you. Are you going to deny me that?"

"I cannot deny you the same choice as the rest of us," I replied and moved on to talk to Dave.

"You might want to watch that man I was talking to," I whispered to Dave. "One week he is out there with the protesters and the next he is signing up to receive pilot training."

"No problem," Dave replied. "A lot of the church members are coming over to join us. Some of them will be trained as co-pilots, just in case; in the end anyone might be called to step up. I will watch him just the same."

Life got busy for all of us, and I chose to spend as much of my time with my family as possible. Lise was slowing down though she pretended different, and Jak was maturing into a strong intelligent young man. My son would be one of the pilots that led our people to a new home.

"Do you remember that man called Brian?" Dave informed me one day. "Well he disappeared in one of the small ships and has not returned."

"How is that possible?" I asked. "Did he complete the training? I remember that everyone who goes through the training to be a pilot will do a solo with a veteran pilot."

"That is true," Dave affirmed. "He did complete the training to be a co pilot, and of course he had the latest induction that will enable him to visualize and be aware of what it means to use the crystals. We usually use the older four crystal ships for soloing, and he did that. But when he returned there was a slip up. He disappeared along with one of the newer models – alone I am told. And he didn't return. Do you think he would...?"

"Yes, I do think it more than possible he would use the crystals to time travel to Earth, I replied. "It was part of the Induction as a destination, and someone with burning intent could do it. In fact I am sure he will, now that I wake up to Shane's memories. And he will try to change the future by getting rid of an earlier me – or Lise. Confusing?"

"So, so." Dave shrugged. "Our experience is that no one can change the past. We can only change a probable future. That is the reason for the gift of far seeing. We will be here to make our journey to the Stars no matter if he succeeds to create another time line."

"You are a wise man." I slapped Dave on the back. He was one of the Dreamers who learned to "let go" and live a long life, like my mother. "But one day I will follow a promise that I made to Shane and Stephanie and I will take a ship back to Earth with a complete bank of crystals. I feel that is part of my duty to my former selves, to stop terrorism at home if I can."

"Terrorism?" Dave squinted. "I find that hard to understand. I don't think, believing as I do, I could intentionally harm anyone."

"My thoughts too," I replied, "but it is not my intention to do anything more than defend those I love with the truth that I have at my disposal."

"Truth?" Dave smiled. "Just be careful, old friend, that your truth does not get in the way of someone else's right to believe what they may. Even when it appears to be an expression of evil. Love is a mystery that we only can know by our freedom to choose."

Lise was slowing down. She appeared to be young in body, but she was embracing her expression of Love, as Dave so wisely put it. Instead of running as we had as part of our morning ritual, we walked, hand-in-hand along the track of the super-train, feeling the wind as it swept by, threatening to pull us into the future. Our future was the moment of now and the time we spent together. Then one day, after we swam in the pool in the forest, she turned to ashes before my eyes. "Come find me again – out there in the Stars." Her sweet voice echoed in my ears, and she was gone. But our promise to each other would not be forgotten.

I sat and collected my thoughts while tears streamed down my cheeks. After I got dressed, I made a phone call from the ship we came here together in.

"Your mother has gone to ashes,." I said to our son, gulping down the tears. "Please come to the pool in the forest, and bring that ship that you made when you were just a little boy."

My grown son and I made a fire to celebrate his mother's passing, and after prayers were added to the fire, we gathered up her ashes and placed them with the remaining fire in the small wooden sailing ship that he had made. Then together, we pushed the ship and the fire out into the pool, and watched as it burned. The ship itself caught fire, and was soon gone. Lise's ashes spread for a while on the surface of the pool and sank into the well of time.

It grew dark as we sat in contemplation. "I will not be going on the ships to our people's new home in the Stars." I said to my son.

"I know," he replied looking up at the sky. "I guess I have always known. Please wish my mother my love, when you find her again."

The ships are ready now, and the people from South Point — the city of Lost Angels, have joined us. No one will be left behind unless it is their choice. I said my goodbyes—not to my mother or Jak. Our people do not say good bye. We say 'see you later'—and mean it. "Look after your grandmother," I instructed my son in parting, "Our Grandmothers and Grandfathers have so much to teach us and it would be such a waste to let their wisdom go unshared."

I packed up the ship that Dave had kept aside for me, that had the built in security to be opened by a certain woman if she so chooses. In a compartment behind the seat, I wrapped a complete collection of all eight crystals to be used by those who found them to power another ship to the Stars and beyond — again, if they chose to do so. And I have a knowing, rooted in firsthand experience that they will, some day.

One other thing. I placed Lise's wedding ring in the curvature of the passenger seat. Then. I pressed my fingers to the crystals in succession, ending with the sixth and seventh and a heartfelt wish to be:

"Home!"

***Inspiration
and
The Smoking Mirror***

In the stories of the People
Before the First Breath
There was Inspiration
Before the First Out-Breath
A Dream of Inspiration

After the Mystery
Breathes the First Breath
The Dreamers
Remember themselves
As a Spark of the Fire

Some other people
Named a God
Outside – themselves
Who Created them
In His Image

The Story about the Other People
is about the Creation
of the Smoking Mirror

...winterhawk

Inspiration

ONE

While the concept of time within the Story of Creation is unclear, the rest of the Book of the Golden Sun is quite clear about how the People of the Sun became the most powerful creatures on Terra. It is written—was written many years later—perhaps eons, after these people learned to record their history. Much later, the ones called the Dreamers will recall some parts of the story in a different way, but what is written in The Book is the one and only version to be believed—it is the Law.

In a far western land on the planet that would eventually be named "Terra", the first known history would be remembered as a "Big Bang!" A large fiery object from the sky struck the "earth", and caused much of the life to be extinguished. The previous inhabitants of this continent were mostly huge fearsome creatures that fought and preyed upon one another along with a scattered group of two-legged animals that had just recently learned to walk erect. Many of the larger creatures were obliterated, as though by some "greater plan", to inspire the smaller two-legged who possessed a rudimentary intelligence. Shortly after this cataclysmic event, the two-legged would notice a remarkable increase in their ability to think – to reason. As time progressed, the two-legged began to communicate through verbal language and named themselves as "man". And then, with the help of the unknown source of inspiration, they began to believe in a greater power – outside themselves who was responsible for their survival.

The first experience of this greater power was almost immediate. A hunting party that witnessed the fiery object from the sky strike the Earth and were flung aside like children, woke to see the forest that remained around the great hole in the Earth ablaze. "What is this strange thing?" The leader of the hunters ventured closer and dared to touch a branch of the nearest tree.

"Aiiie!" He drew back his hand in pain. "This is like no other thing we have seen." It did not occur to him, or his fellow hunters, until later, that something equally as strange was happening inside his head. Soon, the leader began to reason, that if this were able to cause him injury, then it would be useful as a weapon against their enemies. This leader of the hunting party became the first Shaman. He tested, touching the tree branch near the fire and then found that he was able to use another broken limb to catch a bit of this fearful thing to take home to his tribe. Later, this Spirit man was able to reason that he, and the rest of the men who spent time near where the object from the sky fell to earth experienced a change – an acceleration in their ability to think. That may not have been his original thoughts, but the effect was the same none the less.

After a great amount of experimentation, this resulted in revisiting the crash site for more fire. The Chief of this hunting tribe was impressed by the Shaman's acquisition of this powerful tool that they named fire. The Shaman shared with his Chief that this fire was a gift from the God's.

"Who are the God's?" the Chief wanted to know, as he had not spent as much time near the site that brought the Original Fire.

"The Gods are the sky beings that created us." The Shaman groped for more knowledge to explain what was still much of a mystery even to him. "I believe that a God in the sky sent this fire to us so that we could grow in our knowledge of Him."

"If that is true, then we should go to the place where this gift fell from the sky to get more knowledge so that we can worship the Fire God in a good way," the Chief reasoned.

"I agree, but this would be very dangerous. I know enough that this gift is something that must be approached with Respect. I suggest that we wait until a sign appears, before returning to the Sacred Circle."

The Chief was frustrated. "This waiting is not our way. If we waited for a sign we would have died at the hands of our enemies.

We are great warriors and the Sky God would know this, or he would not have gifted us with this fire."

The Shaman reluctantly agreed. "Your word is law, Great Chief, but can we at least wait until the bride of the fire god is full in the sky. That would be a good time." He pointed up to the moon that was barely more than half complete. The chief agreed, but during the days that followed rain came in torrents and extinguished their campfires.

"We have lost the gift that the God of Fire gave us!" the Chief was fuming. "Why were you not able to protect our fire from this happening?"

"I am sorry Great Chief," the Shaman replied. "I could have protected our fire by having it burn in our cave, but I was not concerned, since I have learned how to start the fire again."

"You can start the fire?" The Chief was astounded. "This means that you —we have the ability to be like a God."

The Shaman simply smiled a sly, knowing smile.

The Chief watched as the Shaman used the spark from two rocks being struck together to call forth the fire. He became envious that this man had somehow gained knowledge that was beyond that of the leader of the tribe. He reasoned that this leap in the ability to think came from having spent a greater time closer to the valley where the fire had first been discovered. "It is not right that someone has a greater understanding of the God of Fire than the Chief." He decided then and there that he would overcome his fears and claim the knowledge that was meant for him, or die trying.

So the Chief stole away in the middle of the night with his sleeping blanket and his sword to sleep near the crater where the fire had fallen from the sky. A couple of mornings later, the Chief was granted with what he believed was a sign from the Fire God that he was to be gifted the wisdom he sought. As the day was breaking, the Chief saw a giant black wolf that he knew had been watching him as he slept. The wolf was many times larger than a man and black as the coals that were left after a fire has burned, so the Chief believed it to be a creature that came from the fire that fell from the sky. Even stranger, the wolf had intelligence in its burning eyes, and it did not appear to desire to attack him—if it had, it would have done so while he slept.

The Chief decided that he would bring some of the flesh of their daily kill to offer to the Fire Wolf the next night. Meanwhile, the Shaman seemed unaware of the Chief's coming and going.

"The bride of the Fire God will be full tonight," the Shaman spoke to the chief that morning. "It would be good time for us to visit the valley where the fire came down."

The Chief pondered his reply and eventually said: "I agree. I will go ahead and you will meet me in the morning at the edge of the valley." And that was how it was to be. A look from the Chief made it clear that his words were not to be questioned.

That evening, the moon was full as the Chief visited the valley and the great sloping impact crater where the fire had come to Terra, the Chief was now accepting as the name for this planet. The Chief had grown spiritually in his visits to the sacred site. He began to see his part in the "bigger picture."

In the light of the moon that was almost as bright as day; the Fire Wolf greeted the Chief in a friendly way, and accepted the gift of the flesh that the Chief brought with him. "What is your purpose?" The Chief asked aloud.

"The Wolf is the protector of the knowledge—the protector of the "Odin Stone," a voice replied. The Chief looked around, and gradually a man-like creature came into view. Except this "man" was a Living Fire in the Chief's new vision.

"I am Odin," the Chief replied at once with the knowledge on his Spirit name.

"Yes you are," the Creature of Fire replied. "There is a destiny that comes with this name and all it stands for."

"And who are you? You must be the God that gave us the Fire?"

"I am a Spark of the Fire. As are you. All that IS – is a spark of the fire of love!"

"Love?" This was a strange word to the ears of the man who was named Odin. His way and the ways of his people had been based on fighting for their lives – killing animals for food and making war on other two-legged tribes – taking what they had for their own. War was all that he knew. "How is it that you talk about this? Are you not a man like me? I have believed that our God must be like us – the more powerful man is the one who lives by his sword."

"Before I came to be known by you, I was neither man nor woman. I have known myself simply as a Spark of the Fire," the fire creature replied. "In my time with you and your people I have come to think like a man, so I will be known as a man by you. The question you have about love will be answered in time. For now let it be known that you are Odin and you are worthy of the gift of the Stone of Knowledge and Life – the Odin Stone."

The rising of the morning sun interrupted the conversation between Odin and the Being of Fire...and a voice from the edge of the crater:

"Who are you talking to?" and as the shaman made his presence known, the Fire Wolf advanced to meet him with snarling fangs.

"I am the Fire," was the answer to the Shaman's question. The Large Wolf stood its ground as the Shaman took a step backward. "And you are Loki." It was a statement and not another question. "I am aware of your part in this story, and so is the Wolf born of Fire. The Fire Wolf is a protector of the Odin Stone, and can sense that your intentions are not always for the good of ALL."

"I am Loki," The shaman replied. "I accept my Spirit name gracefully, but I disagree that this creature can see my true intentions. I am a Shaman for our people, and as such, I represent our people's good." He adjusted his eyesight and he could make out what appeared to be a man-shaped being bathed in the light of the morning sun.

"There is more than one people's good that is at stake here," was the reply. "Until you prove your true intentions, the Wolf will keep you at a safe distance from the Stone that is a gift of Knowledge of the Fire."

"I am at your disposal," Loki replied with a gesture of obedient worship. "And to you, too, Odin, my liege." He bowed low and the Wolf halted between him and the centre of the crater, where a large shining rock was embedded in the earth. "Is there a plan or a purpose that this Odin Stone was gifted to our world?"

"Yes." Odin replied. "There is a plan. I know this, but I have not been told what the future holds for our people and this knowledge."

"There is a reason that even the leader who is put in charge of this Stone of Knowledge has only a glimpse of its purpose." The Fire Being replied. "It will take a passage of time and patience so that this Knowledge will work at opening your hearts and the hearts of all people, until this Knowledge is transmuted into Wisdom for All sentient beings."

Loki pondered the words of the Being of Fire and returned his gaze to the large black Wolf and the stone in the center of the crater. The very moment his eyes rested on the stone, a burning desire was ignited in his mind, and the Wolf showed his teeth. Loki sighed and bowed low again.

"I will help you and your people to understand your destiny," the Fire Being spoke to Odin. "I am sensing a change in this world at this time. There will be a great winter and the Path will be revealed. That is all I can say at this time."

"Wait," Odin requested. "Do you have a name that we can call you and make an offering to you now that we know that you are a messenger of our God?"

"I have no name. Before I came to be with you, I was called Jinn, a creature who is a Spark of the Fire. I did not even know myself as a man or woman. In the presence of your people I am a man like you."

TWO

"I have no name." Before I came to be with you, I have been called Jinn, a creature who is a Spark of the Fire." The Creature of Living Fire spoke to the Chief called Odin.

"It is clear to me that you are a messenger sent by the Sun God – the God of Fire," Odin replied to the Jinn. "Therefore, you are a man, created in the image of our God, like we are."

"This must be so," the Fire Creature pondered. "I am a Spark of the Fire as you are, too," he repeated. "I have been sent to help you find your way and to claim your rightful place in this world."

"How can we make claim to the power that is rightfully ours?" Loki asked before Odin and the Fire creature could utter another word.

"It would seem that the Wolf was rightly placed here," The Jinn replied. "The power that is due to the two-legged race as custodians of this world will come in its time. This power must be earned, and it will be aided by the energy that is contained in stone. I must warn you. This Odin Stone contains knowledge and healing powers that mankind cannot assimilate without the passage of time. As you learn to come close to this knowledge, you will see that your life will be increased many years, but if you were to attempt to claim this power before you are ready, you and this world would die a quick death before your time."

"This land that we live in is a constant battle – against the elements and the great creatures that we must hunt for our survival." Odin spoke. "Are we to learn to fight against all odds, and each other, in order to gain supremacy? It seems to me that there must be a better way?"

"There is a better way," The Fire Creature replied. "The first step is realizing that this is possible. I have not been sent to make choices for you. That is not my purpose. I am to help you see the choices you have, but the final decision will be yours."

"I feel it is our right to claim the power that is rightfully ours," Loki repeated. "Can you at least show us how this might be accomplished?"

"I agree, at least in part, with Loki," Odin replied. "The first part of this has begun. Our people have met others like ourselves, and agreed to a truce. The gift of fire is uniting us in a common goal. We are searching for a better way to live. Can you help us with this?"

"I can. There is a better place waiting for you – a Promised Land, you might call it. The fire is the start of knowing your heritage. You and I come from a source that sustains and Inspires us. The power of the Odin Stone will help you heal with time, so you must prepare to take this source of knowledge with you on the journey to the new land."

"How can we take something with us that is so dangerous that we cannot even approach it?" Loki asked. "Even if the Wolf were to allow it?"

"A good question," the Jinn replied. "I will point out that this large crater is strewn with fragments of stones. These are parts of the same source as the Odin Stone. In fact the fragments are the same that make up the covering that protects you and your world from the true power that is within the stone. Your first job in preparation for moving the Odin Stone is to make a cover for the stone, a cloth that will be imbued with the stone fragments that you can gather."

"That seems like a great task," Odin replied. "And I am wondering how this might be done? Perhaps the Original Fire might be used in accomplishing this?"

"Right," the Jinn laughed. "You are already half way there when you can see a possibility. I can tell you no more except to gather the stone fragments and allow your newfound intelligence to help you find a way."

"A cloth?" Loki pondered aloud.

"A covering like that which you clothe yourself." Odin replied as they gathered the fragments of stone that had fallen from the sky at the time the Odin Stone fell to Terra. Indeed, Odin surmised that many of the pieces might have been part of the original stone before it struck the ground. "This cloth must be covered with the stones that fell and were cast to the winds at the edges of this great hole in the terra. Nay – the stone must become part of the cloth."

"First the cloth, then the stone becomes of the material," Loki muttered as he helped Odin to gather the fragments – all the while with one wary eye of the Wolf, as the Creature seemed intent on watching him. "Perhaps the women will be helpful with their newly acquired knowledge of weaving?"

After a good amount of time, a large heap of the stone pieces were gathered at the edge of the crater for the other men to haul back to their village. Neither Odin nor Loki wished to have the men or women of their growing village become exposed to the stone in the center of the crater any more than they need be. This was partly due to a warning of the Fire Being.

Back at the camp, Odin and Loki gathered the people together to tell them of their quest and the tasks ahead of them. Even at the distance from the crater that Odin's people gathered, the effects of the Stone was evident in an increased awareness and intelligence of these previously slow witted cave dwellers. The gift of fire kindled this to be sure, but they were already working on more sophisticated weaponry. Soon the sharpened sticks gave way to lances tipped with stone, and rudimentary swords took shape with the help of a forge and bellows to fan the fire.

"We have come a long way in such a short time," Odin told his people as he hefted the latest broadsword.

"But we are nowhere near ready to make the cloth and armor that will enable us get close to the Stone of Knowledge," Loki replied.

"Armor that is like cloth?" one of the women who had been working with the black-smith asked. "How could this be? And why do we need to weave this? To protect our warriors in battle, I can understand, but why do we need to get closer to this Stone of Odin anyway?"

"Hush woman," Loki replied. "This is not for a weak woman to know. Just do as you are told and weave the cloth. We will tell you how to combine the fragments of rock into armor when the time is right."

When the rest of the tribe was about their tasks as ordered, and Odin and Loki stood alone at the edge of their camp, the Chief spoke to Loki in a low voice:

"And how will we instruct the people to do something we have not envisioned ourselves?"

"That word you used, envisioned," Loki looked back in the direction of the crater as he spoke. "Can you recall when a thought like this occurred to you in recent times? Being near this Stone of Knowledge has already changed us beyond belief. We will know when the knowledge is required."

Perhaps the Shaman Loki would be correct, if his patience were to match his urge to know more. He was soon fretting and pushing the weavers and blacksmith to complete something that he, himself could not conceive.

"We believe that we have accomplished the task that you requested," one of the men at the forge replied one day to the insistent prodding by Loki. He showed the Shaman a metallic cloth-like creation that he and his fellow blacksmiths had made. "We are calling this 'chain mail'. It can be used to form a body suit of armor that will protect the user from attack by swords and arrows." The "cloth" was composed of miniature circular links of metal made from melted down fragments of the stones that they had brought back from the site where the Odin Stone had come to Terra.

Loki and Odin brought the section of metallic cloth to the crater and presented it for inspection to the Fire Creature, the Jinn that appeared whenever they visited the area. The Jinn had transformed, too, over the time spent in the presence of the Odin's tribe. He seemed to be taking on a familiarity of the people and in some unusual way, close yet aloof — a true messenger of the Fire God. Odin noted that the Fire Being was behaving as though he might be an image of the God of Fire himself.

"Remarkable," the Jinn commented. "This shows real promise as an addition to your personal armor. It will undoubtedly protect you from assault from physical projectiles, but will not be suitable for the task that I put before you."

"What is the problem?" Odin asked, holding up the chain mail for scrutiny.

"Hold it higher," the Jinn requested. "Tell me what you see."

"I can see the sun's light shining through," Odin replied.

"Exactly. This will protect you from the physical, as I pointed out, but will not serve as a shield from the unphysical effects of the Sun, that is similar, if not the same, as the unseen energy that emanates from the Stone that fell from the sky."

"What is it that the Odin Stone emanates as you describe?" Loki held the metallic cloth before his eyes. "Is this emanation something that might hurt our bodies in some way? I cannot believe that the Sun God would give us a gift that would endanger his people."

"Good and correct thinking," the Jinn replied. "I would not give my people something that would cause them harm – indirectly, at least. Let me explain. The Spirit People and your God want to help you evolve to be like them. In fact, you were created in His image. But you are still so much like small children, in the way you think, as well as the makeup of your bodies. You were created with a seed if, if you will, a Spark of the Fire in you. This seed will grow over time, and you will become like your Creator."

"Time?" Odin mused. "I have a small understanding of this word. I believe you mean to say Life?"

"Very perceptive," the Jinn congratulated the Chief. "You have been blessed with a very long life, due in great part to your exposure of the gift from your God. With patience, over the time that you are given, you will transform to the next step in your evolution. In reply to your previous question of harm, I can tell you that this evolution of your body and minds will not harm you, unless you try to run before you learn to walk. You are children of God. Now, back to the reason this metallic armor will not protect you from spiritual energy – I think you can see this as true. I foresee you and the Odin Stone moving to a safer and better place that your God has prepared. The cloth that you will need to create is to protect you, and your people from overexposure to the transforming energy of the Odin Stone, during your moving and in the projected future. Go now. Go back and create the cloth of metal and stone. I am beyond age and time. I will wait here for you to do as I requested."

Odin and Loki returned to their camp a safe distance from the crater and the Odin Stone. Odin assigned one group of blacksmiths to continue working on the task of creating a cloth that would be part metallic that could be use to block or filter the emanations so the stone could be moved to another land, a land promised by their God. Another group of blacksmiths were requested to work with the women, the weavers, in creating armor of chain mail from local stones for the people's army. Meanwhile, these people with their increased intelligence and weapons conquered any and all other human and other creatures and formed a community that surrounded the crater so that no other tribes could gain the knowledge. Soon, the other tribes were given the ultimatum: either submit, to be part of the People of the Fire or die. The only creatures that seemed to be unaffected were the great original animals and flying creature that had survived the impact of the stone on Terra. Although many of these creatures were rendered extinct, there remained enough to force Odin's people to be on a constant vigil. Other new large creatures like the Fire Wolf were appearing to make the two-leggeds' lives a difficult venture.

"The great hairy mammoths provide us with a source of food that we did not have in times past," Odin remarked to Loki. "But our survival is a constant struggle when you add the changes in the weather. You cannot help but notice that the air is becoming more frigid, almost day-by-day. We will have great difficulty to

A Spark of the Fire

survive this approaching winter. Have you news on the creation of the cloth?"

"I do not," Loki answered. "Our people who man the forges are at wits ends to find a solution that the Messenger of Fire will approve."

"And what about the other group that includes the women weavers?" Odin asked.

"Paah!" Loki spit. "Women are only fit to weave, not to create armor – without the constant supervision of our blacksmiths. These women are constantly straying from their assigned tasks."

"Straying?" Odin puzzled. "In which way? To what ends?"

"Some of the women believe they can do what the men cannot," Loki laughed.

"And can they?" Odin asked. "Have you given their ideas a chance?"

"My Lord, can you be serious? Our men have been fighting and making weapons for as long as we have been alive."

"But we are now newly alive." Odin reminded the Shaman. "We must not refuse a new way of thinking, when the old has failed. Besides, if you recall the words of the Fire Messenger, this cloth is not weaponry in the usual meaning of the word. It is like a combination of Fire, Stone and Water. What better ideas could we seek than from women who are the carriers of water? Go – be humble, enough to see what ideas the women can provide."

Despite his inborn reluctance and with much grumbling, Loki agreed to request the women weavers for assistance. And he was surprised.

"Yes, we do have an idea that might work." The woman who was in charge of the weavers replied to Loki. "It is a woman's task to clean and prepare the food that the hunters provide. We are faced with the task of cleaning this food – including the fishes. This is where the idea sprung. A fish is covered with scales, as you know, so what if we were to make this cloth from thin pieces of overlapping fragments of the protective stone – like the scales of a fish?"

For once – perhaps for the first time in his life, Loki swallowed his pride and told the weavers and the blacksmiths to work together to make a flexible cloth-like creation that he and Odin would submit for the Fire Being's approval.

THREE

"This is not what I expected, however it is acceptable," the Creature of Living Fire spoke to the Chief called Odin and to the Shaman Loki upon examining the cloth constructed of scales of tiny overlapping metallic pieces similar to the fish that the women of the tribe would clean. "It is more acceptable because of the way that you enlisted the help of the women. This journey to wholeness will be accomplished by the combination of male and female cooperation. I am pleased with the progress that you have made and I will help guide you to your new home on the other side of the bridge of Ice."

"A bridge of ice?" Odin puzzled.

"Yes. Due to the increasing frigid conditions of your world – due to the Winter that is upon this land, a Bifrost Bridge has been created that will enable you and your people to journey to your new home – the land that I promised you."

"The land that you promised?" Loki was somehow suspicious. "Is not our new home a gift from the Sun God?"

"That is true. But I am the Living Fire – a Spark of the Fire of your God. I speak for Him."

"Be that as it may," Odin agreed. "We do have need of a better home where we can prosper and learn to become all that our God desires. What is the next step in this journey over the bridge?"

"You will construct a wagon of wood that will be used to transport the stone. You will be able to move the Odin Stone safe from overexposure of its energy, by using the covering that your created. I have foreseen that one of the purposes of the Fire Wolf will be to pull this wagon across the Ice Bridge to the land that I have prepared."

"I hope that the Wolf is aware of this?" Loki remarked eyeing the large black creature as it watched him and maintained its place between the humans and the Stone.

"He is aware of his purpose, as I am," the Jinn replied.

Odin noted again that the Fire Creature — the Jinn was speaking as though he was the God. He let that go, for the present.

"If you lead us to this new land over the Bridge of Ice, won't your fire cause the bridge to melt?" Loki enquired.

"A good question. But as your knowledge of the fire that I am increases, you will understand that the same Spark of Fire that is within you is a spiritual fire. True, this Fire can melt or burn away and eventually change you and your people but a greater understanding of this fire will come with time and patience. Eventually the fire will bring about a new season over all this land. One step at a time." The word, and the concept of the "wagon," was somewhat foreign to Odin's people, but it was not a great leap of understanding – that came more frequently now as they worked in harmony with the wishes of their God. They were already using sleds that moved over the snow, and when the idea of a wheel was presented to them they easily envisioned and created it. At first it seemed that the sled would be a better mode of travel in the winter conditions but who is to question a God. The people were still not able to see the Jinn as Odin and Loki were, but considered it not a good idea to doubt that their leader was not talking to the wind as they sometimes observed. To these people, the fire was a gift from an invisible God who sometimes appeared in the heated air above their community fire. Perhaps, as Odin suspected, this Fire Creature was somehow aware of the primitive feelings of the people who worshiped him? If so it might mean trouble in the future, if this Jinn continued to bask in their awe?

"The wagon that you requested is ready," one of the men who worked with the blacksmiths addressed Odin. "The wheels were a bit of a problem but we learned to keep them together strengthened with metal strips. We have also built smaller sleds that will carry our belongings to the new land. We can pull these and some will be pulled by our oxen, but in the event the journey is longer than we know, the sleds are small enough to be pulled by our people if we need to eat the animals.

Loki noted the creative inspired inscriptions decorating the sides of the wagon. It was indeed a ceremonial masterpiece to be sure. "Who is responsible for this?" he asked the man who showed off the wagon that had high sides with wheels – circles inscribed with runic symbols.

"I am," the man replied with pride. "At least I think I am. I felt guided, as though someone or something was doing the work through me. Perhaps our God of Fire?"

"Perhaps." Loki replied, and he knew that this perhaps was true. When they delivered the ceremonial wagon to the crater, Loki spoke to the Fire Being. "Somehow, I suspect that you had something to do with this. Our newly discovered magical writing is being used to decorate this vehicle, but the circle and the wheel is a new Teaching."

"Yes," the Jinn smiled mysteriously. "This is one of the reasons for using the wheel instead of a sled. This is a Teaching through the use and creation. The sled and your written language is an example of your life as you see it. Certain people of your tribe have been inspired to record your journey as a beginning to an end. Thus the runes are all written in straight lines. But here is something that is not new perhaps to a man of mystery like Loki, even though there is a truth that the common man will be opened to. The line that you call time is more than a small stroke of fire. One day you will see that this time line is a Circle, and more."

"And more? A circle is beginning to be real to me. But where does it go after that?"

"If you are patient, this will be answered for you – you might one day see time as I do."

Loki had a feeling that beyond this Beings desire to teach, there was smugness – an attitude of growing superiority. But he let that go, for the moment. "We will see," Loki smiled. His new mind was busy working on his own plans.

With the Jinn's advice also at a distance, Odin and Loki placed the newly created cloth over the object from the sky. The first time they attempted this, they both staggered back, and had to wait for a suit that covered their bodies made of the same material – the fragments gathered at the crater. The body suit of armor was luminous green. The stone fragments when melted and made into a thin but protective cloth of scales, reflected the green light that the Jinn, who would not tell them where the stone originated, told them that this was the true color of Terra. This did not surprise them except that it came from the sky.

"Try not to look directly at the stone," the Fire creature said, as Loki and Odin began to dig around the base of the Standing Stone. It turned out, as they dug; that the base was embedded in the earth. It sloped into an oval, giving the revealed stone the rough shape of an egg. The ropes they wrapped around the stone were not affected. It would appear that the Odin Stone's transforming power acted only on animate objects. At a great distance, the ropes attached to teams of oxen were used to carefully pull the stone up a ramp, inch-by- inch and into the wagon, where the stone was secured for the journey. Although the wooden box that enclosed the Stone would not stop its energy by any stretch of the imagination, perhaps it did in some way. Out of sight, out of mind, seemed to apply.

The journey began with the Jinn in the lead, followed by the Great Wolf who was immediately aware of his purpose, allowing himself to be attached by a harness by Odin. Loki, stayed a safe distance away and followed the wagon, and at a greater distance, the men and women of the tribe strung out with their oxen and sleds. The first part of this journey was not without danger, as the land that the people hope to leave behind had large creatures like the Fire Wolf – great toothed felines that were drawn by the scent of the humans – seeming to be easy prey, now away from their protective campfires. An occasional battle erupted that resulted in proving the superior weapons of these people who had now learned to temper the steel of their broad swords with fire and water, and also invented crossbows. The intelligence of the people close to the "Fire from the Sky" was increasing by leaps and bounds.

As the journey progressed, Loki, looking back on the procession of changed people began to wonder why the power of this stone could be something that was not embraced and began to doubt the words of the Jinn. "Maybe he wants this power for himself?" Loki pondered, but the moment he quickened his step and approached the rear of the wagon, a fear caught hold of his heart that sent him back to his place between the tribe and the stone.

"There!" the Fire Being called out to Odin. They had traveled four days with the exodus of people trailing out behind like the tail of comets that sometimes passed overhead in the clear night sky. "There is the Ice Bridge as I promised, and the new land lies beyond. The new land, the Promised Land appeared on the near horizon. All they had to do was cross the bridge of frozen water. The people surged forward, anxious to cross to a better land and leave the dangers and hardships behind. "Hold your people back," the Jinn urged Odin. "It would not be safe to cross that open ice at night. Don't forget why you have sought the safety of your caves and your campfires before when the night came." The fear was still strong in the minds and hearts of a primitive people despite their newly acquired mental abilities, and the Jinn seemed to sense the surge and the desire to leave it behind.

The People of Odin gathered in a large circle around the wagon with their campfires at the parameters, like they had each night since the beginning of the journey, and for what seemed years before that, and before that. One more night! And they would be free! No one slept except the children. The mothers and fathers, weavers and blacksmiths and warriors, passed yet another night on guard from the dangers that lurked in the dark – in the surrounding forest and the night sky. The last night passed uneventful. With the morning sun came hope and then other fears in the minds that told the thinker that "this is not logical". "What if the ice is not strong enough? There is a great mass of people, and that wagon must weigh a ton." In the far distance, on both sides of the frozen ice the sea water sparkled in the new morning sun.

"How do we know this is safe?" Loki echoed the fears of the people behind them.

"In this part, where the two lands are close, the water is not as deep," the Fire Being explained. "Once these two land masses were joined, and due to the upheaval of volcanic action and the shifting that is still happening, they were split apart and the water, although it is deeper than we could cross during summer, is now a strong Bifrost Bridge. You must come to believe that there is no coincidence that you were given the Gift of Knowledge at this time, and your God has prepared a way for you. The time is right. The season is right, and so are you. Can you not see this truth?"

"It all comes together for us now," Odin agreed. He was compelled to stand on the top of the wagon, and raise his sword. He pointed to the bridge of Ice, and the land beyond. "We will move on now. We will claim the gift of freedom that our God has given us." At that proclamation, the Great Wolf moved, pulling the wagon and Odin out onto the ice. The Fire creature moved, too, but he seemed, for those few that could see him, to float over the ice without the danger that might befall a mortal man.

The snow on the ice crackled under the wheels of the ceremonial wagon, but other than that, the Wolf pulled onward, undaunted, and the procession of people with Loki in the lead, followed at a safe distance. No one spoke, not even when the wagon reached the other side, and rolled up on the shore, not until the last man set foot on the new land – the promised land, and then...

"HO!" came a great shout from a thousand throats as one. "HO! To Great Odin, our leader! And to our God of Fire that brought us safely to our new home. Ho! We give thanks!"

"You knew that this would come to pass," Loki stood aside by the Jinn."

"Yes I did," the Fire creature smiled smugly. "If you could only see what I see," he said again.

A Spark of the Fire

The new land, at first examination and discovery, was a dense forest, teaming with game – animals and birds that defied description and names. The animals here, however were smaller and more easily preyed on than the creatures that these people had encountered beyond the Ice Bridge. Using new and sharp axes, the travelers created a clearing that would be their future homes. And the prospect of hunting and providing food gave the people hope on that first night. They cheered and drank wine around the campfires, toasting Odin and the God who had led them to this new land.

"We will be like KINGS in this new land," they shouted and sang.

"And what of us?" the women cheered. "Will we not be Queens?"

"Woman! Know your place." Loki stepped forward into the light of the campfire. "We men are Kings. It is a woman's place to be our companions and see to our comfort when the Men come home from the wars." This from a man wearing the green body armor that was created mostly due to the weavers (who are women) insight.

"You have much to learn," the Jinn informed Loki from within the fire. And Loki stomped away with plans to deal with this creature who believed himself to be like a God.

Later that night, when clouds hid the moon, a familiar cry sounded. A scream in the night: "My child! My child has been taken!"

The camp arose as one as the fires were rekindled. The night clouds parted to reveal a large flying creature with a child in its claws – a creature familiar in the minds and fears of these people.

"They followed us," the people cried out. This was plain to see, but quicker minds and hands leapt to enact a solution to this ongoing war that they had hoped to leave behind. Catapults were bought into play and they began to fling large boulders in the direction of the group of leathery-winged creatures that had followed the people from their former land. With luck, or the hand of God, the creature holding the child was struck, causing it to drop its prey and fly off to join its comrades amid the brief hail of boulders.

As the last of the winged creatures disappeared into the western sky, the people with the aid of torches retrieved the lifeless body of the child. It was a sad and heart breaking reminder that they had not left the objects of their fears completely behind.

"You promised us a safer place to live." Loki reminded the Jinn.

"Look around you," the Fire Creature responded. "This is a safer place. And it is a Garden of Plenty. Plenty of animals that are more easily hunted and domesticated for your use, and a forest of trees to build safer and more comfortable homes. More safety will come, in time, as I promised and as your intelligence improves to invent greater weapons and things that you have yet to imagine."

"There is that part again, about 'be patient, and one day you will see what I see.'" Loki replied abruptly. "A child died because we were not let in on the finer bits of knowledge that could have prevented this from happening. How much more is there that we should know to become a people worthy of Gods help."

"If you are patient," the Jinn replied as though he had heard little of Loki's argument, "one day you will be more than KINGS – you will be like Gods."

"Like you, you mean?" Loki muttered under his breath.

In the morning, a ceremonial burial was attended for the mutilated body of the child who was the first casualty of this people's new home. It may be a promised land – a Garden of Paradise even, but this did not come without a cost.

"We will need to post a guard," Odin stated. "Even as we move from this spot and expand into the forest, we will need to guard against other creatures that might follow us across the Frost Bridge. I need four of our strongest and sharp sighted warriors who will take turns watching the bridge – day and night."

That being done, the task at hand was to build homes and a suitable place of residence – a palace of wood, to house the Odin Stone, and the King of KINGS who would be set on a throne as the rightful ruler of the new world. Time, and busy minds and hands will heal most things, but to make sure that the lesson of the child that sacrificed his life for this knowledge was not forgotten, a monument in the courtyard of the palace was erected. This monument was a form of a child, holding up a Solar Cross – also in reminder of their Sun God of Fire. When Odin and his people passed this monument each day, they were reminded that although their life time was now greatly increased, one day they would all be taken to live in the sky.

"We are KINGS – but we are not Gods, Loki," Odin often reminded his Shaman. To which Loki replied, after Odin walked on, "You might be just a King, but we possess the potential within us to be like a God." He had heard this spoken by the Fire Creature one day, perhaps that first day he discovered the Fire that was at the same time ignited within. "Fire?" Loki pondered. "Is it the same for all of us? Or are some of us destined to burn greater in the eyes of God?" Meanwhile, as the great palace and homes grew seemingly out of the ground around him, Loki had plenty of time to imagine, and make steps in furthering his plans. With this in mind, he searched through the remaining fragments of the stone that fell from the sky, and having found a suitable stone, enlisted the help of the blacksmiths to create a formidable weapon of mystery, knowing all the time that little escaped his leader's new-found vision.

"What are you creating?" Odin questioned Loki one evening as they gathered at the door to the room at the back of the throne. In a room behind the king's throne, was the stone. The stone was kept covered and then the green cloth of star metal was ceremoniously pulled off so that the healing energy could be released into the throne room, and the surrounding encampment for one hour. During this time every morning, Odin would sit in meditation on his throne, and Loki would gladly sit facing the throne and soak up his daily portion of wisdom. The Fire Wolf was always present at Odin's right hand watching and ready for anyone who might disturb the King. At these times, Loki often believed that the Wolf was watching him alone, but the price of knowledge was giving into his personal fears.

"What are you creating?" Odin asked again.

"I am creating something worthy of a King. It will be a gift of great significance and power. You will see."

Odin simply smiled and bade the Shaman to go to his place at the center of the throne room. The King knew his Shaman all too well and both distrusted and respected the working of Loki's mind. Loki was the epitome of what was right and sometimes wrong in the common tribesman. He was curious beyond control when something appeared to be in his best interest, and had the unnerving fault of blurting out his ideas. Many of the Shaman's ideas brought inventions and insights that the common man and woman would benefit from. And then, isn't that the job of a Shaman after all?

The Jinn, the messenger from the Fire God was similar to Loki in Odin's eyes. Odin's daily ritual involving the Stone was instigated by the Jinn who preferred not to be named. "Seven days – each morning will you release the energy of the Stone," the Jinn instructed. "For one hour, and no more. This was one of the reasons that we needed to move the stone – to control our people's exposure. Seven, is after all, a sacred number. When you have completed this task seven times seven, you will double the exposure Thirteen times until the cloth can be left off completely."

"I guess thirteen is a Sacred number too?" Odin asked as Loki listened intently.

"Yes, thirteen is the tracking of the Moon and Her influence on the people and creatures of Terra."

"And then...?" Loki enquired. "What happens after the covering is completely off the stone?"

"Then you and your people will be in cycle as when the Stone first fell to Earth. You were not ready for it then, but you will be after the cycle is complete."

"Hocus pocus." Loki complained aloud. "These numbers are just ways to control and confuse us. To what end?"

"One day you will understand," the Jinn replied.

"Oh yes, let me guess," Loki turned away in disgust. "On that day we will be like Gods – like you?"

"How perceptive." The Fire Creature smiled and disappeared as he sometimes did for no reason that Odin could fathom at all.

"I can see that there is method in your wily madness," the Jinn said finding Loki in the company of a blacksmith who was working intently at the forge. The blacksmith, as intuitive and creative as he was, could not see nor hear the Fire Being, as was the case with all of Odin's people, except for Loki.

"We need a much hotter fire, to do what you are asking," the blacksmith was saying to Loki. "I would fathom that we almost need the Fire that only the God of our people could provide. Or else this will not be a creation fit for the King."

"I agree," Loki smiled. "I will petition the Fire God for his aid." He gazed intently at the Jinn as he spoke.

"Don't be looking for help from me." The Jinn folded his arms against his fiery chest. "Why would I think of adding my magic fire to this insane idea of yours – just to please the King?"

"I hear you asking 'what is in it for me'?" Loki responded. "I would guess that Odin would be interested in knowing where and what you do when you disappear. It seems to me that you have developed an appetite of a God – a God who desires more and more from his earthly subjects. Or am I mistaken?"

"So you would have me be part of your sly plans? I have the gift of far sight and I am not fooled by a man who is driven by curiosity and addiction to Knowledge. There is a very old and wise saying: If you play with fire, you can expect to be burned."

"And there is another that goes something like: hunger for power makes for strange bedfellows." Loki muttered.

"Who are you talking to?" The blacksmith paused to wipe the sweat from his brow."

"I am petitioning the God of Fire as you suggested." Loki replied, and as he spoke, the fire grew so noticeably hotter making the blacksmith return to his work once more.

"Yes!" the blacksmith shouted. "This will be done! You must surely be in favor with our God of Fire."

"Hush," Loki smiled. "Remember this is to be a surprise gift for our King. Into the water with this so that it will be a thing of power and beauty – tempered like our new broadswords."

"This is the product of Fire from the Gods and water of moonlight." The blacksmith held the completed object up to the full moon. There will never be a weapon like this unless it is created in the forge of the Dwarves that our old stories tell of."

"A hammer!" Odin hefted the object that Loki presented him with. "Short in the handle, but finely balanced. A mighty weapon indeed! What might have possessed you to create such as this?" He swung the Hammer about with obvious pleasure.

"It came from an inspiration." At least Loki was truthful in this statement. "It occurred to me that even with your long life you might one day, wanting for a symbol of the power that you hold. And one day you might desire to pass this on to someone who will be a worthy successor to your throne."

"Well thought!" Odin continued to swing the Hammer about. "My wife and I have considered that very idea. Well thought and inspired! The idea of a son has appealed to me for some time. I would never have thought this of you. To be truthful. I have experienced doubts about you being satisfied with your position as the Shaman of our tribe. You have greatly and pleasantly surprised me this day"

"Sometimes I surprise myself." Loki lowered his head, and retreated from the throne room.

"Didn't go as you expected, or did it?" the Jinn greeted Loki at the door.

"We shall see." Loki retorted.

FOUR

Odin was pleased with the gift of the Hammer which he kept within reach by his throne, vowing to name it and present it to his son. He and his wife planned and found pleasure in the conception of a son which they believed would be soon. The conception and birth did not happen overnight – but that did not stop his infatuation with the inevitable outcome. Odin turned a blind eye to the events within his kingdom much to the dismay of those close to him.

"You really started something." The Fire Being, the Jinn, remarked to Loki. "Your King is obsessed with the idea of a worthy successor to his throne. Perhaps this was not what you had in mind? Don't you wish you had my far seeing ability to see how this will all play out?"

"You just go about your nightly forages into the minds and hearts of the lesser mortals," Loki responded. "I am guessing that you see yourself in the role of King one day, as well – of maybe a God?"

"An inspiring thought! Isn't that what Odin said to you? I am doing my bit of inspiring, as well. Although the people are not yet able to see me, I believe this will come to be one day as well, and they will know how I feel as they do and will realize who I am."

"If the King was not so infatuated with creating a future son, perhaps he would see how much unrest is brewing in the minds of his subjects. And we know who is to blame for much of that," Loki observed.

"I am only helping them to become what is in their hearts. Patience my friend, Loki, one day…"

"Yes, one day..." Loki walked away in disgust that his plans seemed to have stalled, and resolved to do something to help put things in motion. The next day he spoke to Odin about the wild sexual behavior and the infighting that was becoming so prominent.

"Our people need a way to release their tensions now that we are not doing battle with other tribes and the animals," Odin replied.

"It seems that your people are reverting back to animals themselves." Loki spoke carefully as he desired to keep on his Leader's good side as much as possible – his plans depended on that. "Is there anything that I could do that would help the problem of our people's lives being one great drunken party after another?"

"You wish to help? Perhaps you could lead a group of our men on a mission – to explore the lands to our south – beyond the great ocean. The waters of the ocean run deep, and are not for the most part, frozen over. Yes. If you really wish the help, this is a mission that would suit the purpose. I will ask the men of our tribe to begin to build great wooden ships that can cross the ocean. And if this land is like our new home, perhaps we will find more riches and people to conquer."

The idea of being in charge of the men who would conquer the land beyond the ocean, easily overcome Loki's better judgment of the perilous voyage. So he and a group of highly trained and ferocious fighters set sail to explore the new land to the south – and returned bedraggled like dogs with their tails between their legs.

"You did not stay long in the new world," Odin said to Loki and his fellow travelers. "You could scarcely have had time to set up camp. Was this land and its people so difficult to conquer for men who would call themselves Kings?"

Loki and his trusted men looked back and forth, before talking almost all at once. "There are Ghosts in that land. It is desolate and foreboding and home to Ghosts. Yes, there are great forests, and many animals that would have kept us from being hungry for as long as we wished, and there are minerals and stones that a man could use. But the land and the forests are the home of Ghosts."

When the bedraggled group of travelers had left, Loki remained as Odin wished to know more about what had happened in this strange place.

"Ghosts?" The Jinn appeared and joined in the conversation. "The great Winter is upon that land, as it is all over our world. The Ghosts that Loki and his men encountered are the spirits of the people who have not woken up to the land. They are not Ghosts as your people would think – they are Dreamers that have yet to wake."

"Spirits or Ghosts – they are the same," Loki spat out. "If they are Dreamers, as you say, then they are also fearsome Spirits that defied our ability to communicate or to conquer. These apparitions protect that land by attacking the minds of our strongest and fiercest warriors. We cannot fight Ghosts. We had no recourse than to break camp and leave as soon as possible."

"Dreamers?" Odin asked the Jinn. "If they wake, then what?"

"They will awaken one day, as your people are now – in their own way. One day they will awaken and become as mortal as you. They will however have one advantage – that might not seem so to you. These Dreamers will know that they are part of the Land and the creatures. They will remember that they are Sparks of the Fire."

"A lot of good that will be," Loki retorted. "Perhaps we will visit those Dreamers when they are men like us. And the outcome of this meeting will be much different then."

Loki's plans were taking shape. As the Jinn had strongly suggested, it would take patience. Everything must be in place and timing had to be right down to the moment. He wondered if the Jinn was in fact aware of what he had in mind, and at times he also wondered if this was not somehow to the Jinn's advantage, but Loki's curiosity and thirst for power and knowledge would not be quenched. And the presence of the Fire Being was all part and parcel. He watched and charted the movements of all three involved—Odin, the Great Black Wolf, and the Jinn.

Loki appointed himself the duty of checking the Kings daily meals that were delivered while he sat on the throne. Each morning and noon, a trusted servant would deliver a flagon of mead and a serving of food that Odin would pick at his convince. Loki met the servant and made an elaborate gesture of checking that the food and the drink was safe and appropriate for the King. He noted that Odin consumed the beer even if the food went relatively untouched. And then the King would doze for the morning on the throne, keeping watch when the Wolf would go out for its walk in the woods. The Wolf also was provided with food, but it also went hunting. And on the mornings that the Wolf was out in the forest, the people stayed inside their huts. And when the people were inside their homes, the Jinn disappeared – to find his way into their minds. Loki was not fooled by the Fire Being's addiction to the sensory and emotional energy of the people as they interacted. The timing of these events had to be just right for Loki's plan to work. And then one morning it all came together.

That morning, Loki checked the King's food as usual. And he waited at the gate of the King's compound until the Wolf appeared to disappear into the forest. The Gateman had stepped to one side in preparation. It was his duty to make sure no one entered that might want to harm the King or his wife who busied herself in their cottage while the King guarded the throne and the Stone. The Gatekeeper would not question Loki about entering and would not dare to be in the way of the Wolf. It all went like clockwork.

Loki entered the main gate, and proceeded to the throne room. It was deathly quiet except for the snoring by the King on his throne. Loki had slipped a mild sleeping potion in Odin's mead, and with the combination of the tired man's body, would mean that the King would be out for an hour or more – until the Wolf returned. The Jinn was absent and this was no surprise. Loki carefully approached the throne and was relieved to see that the goblet of beer had been consumed. The King snored on. Loki took a deep breath, and saw the hammer leaning in its usual position by the throne. He carefully reached and picked up the hammer. And breathed another sigh of accomplishment.

Hastily, Loki proceeded to the room at the back of the throne and pulled the cover off the large egg shaped stone. He was immediately thankful that he wore his green protective armor as the energy of the Stone seemed to reach out and touch him. Just for a moment, he faltered, in fear of what would happen next. But his urge to possess the knowledge was too great. Without another thought, Loki raised the Hammer over his head and struck the Stone with a blow at the apex. A cracking sound followed and the Stone fell apart like the egg it resembled, the two halves rocking and spewing forth a light that momentarily blinded Loki as he fell back into darkness.

Much later, time having passed, Loki woke to a changed world. It was all different—changed in some unfathomable way to a groggy mind that was rapidly becoming filled with mind blowing Knowledge. Loki shook his head as he staggered to his feet. He recalled what he had done and a deep sense of guilt seized him, with a feeling that he must somehow hide the evidence of his act. He looked away from the stone as he managed to pull the broken half up and over the side that spewed forth a near rainbow of Light up to the heavens – through the ceiling, and out in all directions to a new unknown world and through Loki himself. With the "egg" now temporarily resealed, Loki covered his dirty work with the protective cloth, as thought this would call back the act that could not be undone. In his haste to be gone and to hide, he bent to pick up the Hammer to take it back to its place by the Kings throne, but…

…Loki was no longer able to lift the Hammer no matter how much he tried. He shook like a leaf in a storm and crept out of the room to find the King waking up. Loki quickly walked to the door, out the main gate where the Gate keeper was also waking up and he ran.

Odin was aware of waking from a long sleep. He shook his head, and saw someone, a shadow exiting from the throne room.

No matter. What did matter was a feeling that he and the world had undergone a change. The temperature was the first clue to a foggy mind. It was so much warmer! The King was aware that he had slept though the winter, and spring, and summer had come upon the world. His mind gasped things in a different way – sensing more than he had before. Understanding but not knowing why.

Odin took in the throne room at a glance. The Wolf was not at his side – perhaps had not returned from its morning forage. And the Hammer was not at its usual place. A knowing dawned. He staggered to his feet and quickly found his way to the room behind the throne, all the while "guessing" what he would find there. Everything looked normal, almost, although he knew it was not. He lifted the covering from the Stone to find it on its side and a small but powerful Light emanating from a long split. He hastily covered the Stone, all the while knowing it would be too little and too late. The damage was done, and the world outside – perhaps the whole world as he knew it was changed, including himself. But to what end? He bent and hefted the Hammer. At least this much was right.

"Loki has gone into hiding," the Jinn greeted the King when he exited the room behind the throne. The Creature of Fire was reclining on the King's throne.

"What do you think you are doing?" Odin asked, raising the Hammer as he spoke. The Hammer came alive in his hand crackling with energy like fire or lightening. The Jinn hastily relinquished the throne.

"I was trying out what it feels like to be a King – or better yet a God. That is what the people will think now that they will be able to see me as their true benefactor – for the first time. And don't be waving your magic hammer at me. I am above such earthly weapons." Still, the Jinn kept a safe distance.

"Do you believe for one moment that I will give up my throne to you?" Odin raged. The business of Loki and the world was momentarily dismissed,

"Perhaps it will not be your choice," the Jinn replied. The people are mine now. Have been for some time, while you slept. The winter is over and summer is here. The time to put Dreams into action is upon us. You and your old ways have been left behind. The people will bow down to me now. And it you don't agree, you will see how I can manipulate their minds. I could ask them all to sacrifice themselves to my name if I so desired. Then you would be a King of nothing. Think about it, I will return when I have finished playing with my subjects emotions." The Jinn disappeared, but not in a flash as he had before He slowly faded from sight.

Odin regained the comfort of his throne, and pondered the situation at hand. Loki and the people were changed – perhaps beyond his ability to repair the damage, if that were the truth. Loki and the Jinn, as well. And perhaps the entire world? And it had begun as he slept. Only the Hammer remained true to itself, but no – the Hammer had changed, as well, becoming filled with power that he had yet to understand, if at all. There was only one thing he could do, sparked by the Jinn's word about sacrifice. Odin came to an epiphany that this Jinn was simply a messenger of some type, and neither the Creature of Fire nor Odin nor Loki were Gods. "We are all Sparks of the Fire," Odin concluded. He hastily returned to the room behind the throne, and prepared to sacrifice himself to the greater good.

Odin removed his protective green armor, and pulled the protective cover from the Stone. Next, he slid the top half from the broken egg, and stood strong in wonder as the Light rose through the ceiling to seek contact with some unknown destination or object in the sky. He breathed a deep breath and bent over to stare directly into the Light that emanated from the Stone. He was momentarily blinded, and when he pulled back, in his mind was burned an image of...four crystals – one red, one orange, one yellow, and the most important, he sensed, was green. And then this field of vision blurred as if both his eyes were fighting for control.

Odin paused and shut his eyes, to open each to an individual view of the world. To his left eye the room looked normal—nothing had changed. But when he shut his left and opened his right eye, the walls of the room were not there, even though his logical mind knew better. Or did it? The sight of his Right eye was not blocked by physical objects nor impeded by distance. He "saw" a scene – a far-away land where a Red-skinned people were going about their lives. "Who were these people?" he wondered. "And what do their lives mean to me?" It was all too much to take in at one time. Odin closed his right eye and opened his left to be able to see the world as he was used to.

Odin put on the green suit one more time and returned to his cottage where he intended to don the gold armor of a King. Going through his mind as he chose to visit the room behind his throne, and do what he deemed necessary, was a fear for the safety of his wife. The woman who greeted him had not been privy to a protective green suit. It had not seemed necessary because only the King and his Shaman would have been exposed to the energy of the Stone. At least that was the original thinking. Now, the changing of the world was catching up to the woman who greeted Odin at the door to their cottage. There would be no son in the foreseeable future and more devastating than that, his wife's years might be numbered to the fingers on Odin's hand. Odin spent time with his aging wife before facing the prospects of the world outside their door and outside the compound and his village. His people would be at the mercy of a creature who proclaimed himself the new King and God. This creature could move as he pleased through the minds and emotions, possessing anyone and everyone who was not as strong-minded as Odin or Loki. Loki was hidden away for the moment and out of sight and out of mind.

"If you promise to treat the people fairly, you can set on the throne," Odin told the Jinn. He spoke in a tone of resignation, but his mind was working fiendishly on a plan to overcome a creature he might not be able to, much less touch – even with the mighty Hammer. "How is it that most people have changed, but not all for the better?" he asked the Jinn.

"To benefit from the knowledge and power one must have earned it or be worthy of it in some way. This is what my continual urge for patience was about. And to answer this in reference to your wife and other people who were changed as our winter ended," the Jinn continued, settling himself on the King's throne, "winter, followed by spring and summer and fall is a natural occurrence even if this holds a greater meaning than your people have of time. And if you doubt the validity of my statement you should look at the world and the people about you.

The Dreamers that your people once visited will have now woken up and are living in harmony with their land and the animals. And the Hammer cannot be held – cannot be picked up, by anyone who is not worthy of its power. And if you are thinking otherwise, I do not require the Hammer to verify my right as the new King – and God."

Odin spent as much of his time with his wife as was possible, and as the days went on he began to realize how it was important for him to solve the problem of the Jinn. Loki was the furthest from his mind. He was sad at the turn of events that resulted in his wife accelerated aging, and the totally unaccountable behavior of his people. The jump in their consciousness, brought to the surface their base nature, with a belief that they were beyond mortal law, and answerable only to the God now living in their midst. Not all were affected like this however; a small number remained seemingly unchanged, and accepted the fate of their shortened life span with a sense of grace. The Jinn became more human like with the passing of time, but Odin was reluctant to challenge him, as the King's far-seeing eye was able obtain information about the powers of other Jinn's on other-worlds and times.

Odin forsook the green protective suit he had worn as King, for a simple gold suit of armor, and had one of the blacksmiths make him a patch for his right eye from a piece of the stones that were brought along from the crater. Now he could concentrate on the "real" world at hand using his other eye only when he saw the need to. "How much of the fragments are left?" he asked the blacksmith. "Is there enough to construct something for me?" He gave the specifics to the man.

"I believe that I can do this," said the blacksmith, "but it will use up the remaining pieces."

"How long will it take?"

"A couple of days," the man promised.

Then time went by and one day the Jinn was on the throne, freshly back from basking in the adulation of his followers. He was now remarkably like a human, but Odin was aware that looks can be deceiving. "I do suit this throne, don't you think?" the Jinn taunted Odin as the man entered the throne room. Odin locked the door behind him.

"That is a feeble gesture," the Jinn smiled smugly. "Was that meant to keep me in?" He waved his hand and the door swung open.

"You misinterpret my actions and my thoughts." Odin gently closed the door once more. "I bear you no malice or thoughts of revenge. The Stone changed me in a positive way. I learned that to evolve, we need to embrace change and let go of the past. I come as a simple man bearing gifts."

"What could you give me that I don't already have, or could take any time I wish?" the Jinn smirked. "And what simple man walks about dressed in the golden armor due a King?"

"This is the armor that I wore to lead the people into battle," Odin replied, and to court my wife."

"And how's that going for you?" the Jinn retorted.

"Life has changed, as the relationship with my wife has. One day soon she will pass into ashes, but you and I know that this is not the end. We will all die one day, some sooner than others, but I will be reunited with the woman I love in another world. And that is not why I came before you today. I am here to tell you that I accept you as the King, and I have a gift. I bring you the special green amour that was made for me when I saw myself as a King – a man like a God. Will you accept my gift?"

The Jinn scoffed. "I do not need your Hammer or your amour to know that I am now King and God to the people of this world." Just the same, he took the amour as Odin suspected he might due to his loud prideful nature. Odin turned and placed his hand on the door.

"Oh don't turn away now. Don't sulk away. Don't want to see how your King looks in his Godly amour."

The prideful Jinn put on the green armor, and flaunted it before Odin. Odin stepped forward and made as though to bow, but instead, he grasped the Jinn, holding on to the armor. A struggle ensued and the two combatants rolled on the floor of the throne room. Odin held tight, calling up all his strength, until the other became immobile.

"How long do you think you can hold me?" the Jinn exclaimed. "I am Fire, I will burn eternally and my strength will remain undiminished."

"You have begun to believe your own lies," Odin replied. "You have already allowed yourself to be weakened by giving in to mortal desires. I have gained the knowledge of your kind. You are not a God, and you are not the only Jinn to be created by the true God. We are all the Children of God, and in various stages learning to be like our Creator. We are all Sparks of the Fire. We were created in God's image – but our small thinking and prideful ways have lead us to believe that God is like us. I am aware of my limitations, and this struggle will not end in letting you go again to play with the minds of my people."

"Then what is your plan to deal with a force that you cannot control?" the Jinn relaxed and smiled.

"I have acquired knowledge of another Jinn who interacted with mankind." Odin's grasp tightened. "I have had a box, an enclosure built of the Stone that followed you to earth. It is my plan to imprison you in this box until the end of time, if necessary – unless you grant me a wish."

The Jinn appeared thoughtful. "Oh it has gotten down to the old 'grant me a wish' game, has it? I would not have thought that of a man who pretends to want the best for the world and his people."

"I do not want a greedy wish," Odin replied. "My wish will be for the best of all people and creatures at this time – including you. But if you do not agree to grant me this wish, I will not think twice about doing what is the second best – for all the people of this world. You will be imprisoned for all time – at least until my race has learned how to deal with the likes of you. The box is there against the wall. Make a choice and make it quick."

The Jinn sighed. "It was an enjoyable ride," he conceded. "A creature like me only gets the chance to be like a human and feel like them once in a million of your years. You don't know how fortunate you are to have been created with the Grace of God available to you for the asking. OK, I agree. What is your wish?"

"My wish is for you to return to where you came from – to the source of your creation and to forget about this world and the people on it."

"What? Is that all? I could grant three wishes. Perhaps you would like the life of your wife restored and she be young enough to give you the son you so desperately wanted?"

"I gave that great thought," Odin confessed. "But no. That would not be fair to the woman I love. She has a right to live her life to the end. Who am I to question God? Perhaps there was a plan. Why else were we brought together at that moment in time?"

"If I may offer a parting bit of wisdom?, "the Jinn replied. "The truth that you have chosen to follow is based on a lie called time. I can say no more. Now release me and your wish will be granted."

Odin released the Jinn, with the knowledge that such a being was bound by his agreement.

The Jinn stood up and stepped out of the green armor, and proceeded to disappear. His smile went last, and his voice echoed in the room. "See you around – at the end of time."

Odin spent some time with his wife before venturing out to mingle with his people. The Great Black Wolf had not returned. Perhaps when his purpose had been fulfilled, he too would be free. Odin inquired as to where Loki could be found.

"I thought you knew," the Gatekeeper answered. "Another ship went out to the new world across the ocean and returned, reporting that there was a red- skinned people living there now. Loki gathered some of his loyal friends together to pay another visit to the world across the great ocean."

"Hmmm?" Odin was somehow not surprised, but he guessed that the conniving Shaman and his crew were in for a surprise of their own. "Let it go," he shrugged. "It was far time that Loki got his comeuppance – and became accountable for his previous behavior."

In moving and spending time with the people, Odin could see the change in them. They were in varying degrees of waking up intellectually, but most were stuck in a spiritual dawn. Sudden access to knowledge does not make someone wise. Some were able to accept their new intelligence more easily than others, and for some it caused their base nature to come to the surface. There was a general sense of not being accountable for their part in the state of their changed world – a pervading atmosphere of blame existed. The average person sought blame outside themselves – particularly in their female companions. The seed of an idea had been watered by the Jinn that women were the tempters – and the reason the men could not control their own emotions.

"Your messenger – the Fire Being is gone!" Odin spoke to an assembly. They muttered and complained aloud. "Hush," he held his Hammer high. Lightning flashed from the Hammer into a dark cloud high above, and they stood in a short downpour. When the rain had cleared the air and the sun came out once more, Odin spoke again.

"This Hammer is an example of the power available to someone who is worthy – someone who takes accountability for their mistakes and surrenders to the fire that is a spark within. This Creature of Fire was not a God, any more than I am and each of you are. WE are all Sparks of the Fire. The Fire Being was a messenger sent from our God – no more and no less. I, as your King, have accepted my humanity as a gift from God. One day, I will pass on and you will need to choose a new King, or form a society of your making. In the interim, I will set a challenge. Anyone who can lift this Hammer will be my temporary successor to the Crown."

There rose again a great clamoring as Odin set the Hammer down in the centre of the compound and bid his people to form a line. Each man would be given a chance to lift the Hammer. He was about to offer the same chance to the women but they shied away and left. "Perhaps one day?" Odin pondered. "They all need to grow at their own pace." A long line of men tried, one by one, each struggling until they were forced to give up. Not all the men tried, as well. So Odin was gratified that there might be leaders among them that did doubt their worth.

"Humility is the seed of a King or statesman," Odin announced, as the last man failed to budge the Hammer. "I will remain as your King until my time is come, and then you will agree among yourselves to select a worthy leader." Afterwards, the discouraged crowd dispersed. Odin thought it best to leave them all to lick their wounds. "My Gate will be open to anyone – man or woman who wishes council with me." Odin told the departing crowd. His gateman remained loyal and Odin was also of the belief that the display of the power of the Hammer would make anyone think twice about claiming the throne by force.

Odin was present when his wife turned to ashes before his eyes. He sat in silent contemplation on the small pile of ashes on the wooden floor of their cottage. One moment she was a vibrant woman who loved life and her husband, and the next...with reverence, placing the ashes of his wife in a small boat, he launched it into the water where there had once been a bridge of ice. The boat circled as thought seeking a direction and was caught up in a current that took it North.

"Good! I thank the spirits and God for the gift of her life. He watched as the boot disappeared on the northern horizon. "Good!" he exclaimed again. She will dream again and we will meet in that dream of another winter."

It occurred to him to see more. Not more of his wife's journey, because that was right in his heart, but more of the fate of the people of his tribe. Odin removed the patch from his right eye and his gaze was drawn to a large black hole at the center of the galaxy. This black hole was spinning and devouring all light. "Is this the destiny of my people?" he asked aloud. And then his far-seeing revealed a vision of the sun that was in the sky overhead. In his vision the sun went cold and exploded – and died. "Or is this to be the fate of our world?" Was this the only choice that the God who created them promised? He sighed, and placed the patch back over his eye and looked within and out from this world as he knew it.

"How is it that some people are able to go about their devious and evil ways while others realize their potential in being a light in the darkness?" he pondered. "It must be that the gift of life is freely given – without conditions? I will speak of this to the people in the time I have left."

In a moment of inspiration, the King removed his eye patch once more and swung the great Hammer above his head – faster and faster. "This is for my son who will be worthy." He let go of the Hammer, sending it into the black hole at the center of the universe – into the well of time.

The Mystery

Another Face of God?

In the stories of the People
Before the First Breath
There was Inspiration
Before the First Out-Breath
A Dream of Inspiration

The Dreamers were born from a dream – their personal dream – a Gift of life from the Mystery. They were aware of their part in the world and the southern continent that was shaped like a giant turtle. They lived in harmony with all creatures at first, until the world changed. After the world changed an awakening occurred that made the Dreamers question their existence and place in their purpose. Knowledge flowed into their minds – knowledge without wisdom that caused the people to wonder at the validity of their dreams. Unrest caused the Dreamers to experience fear, for the first time in the memory of these people. Some felt a prisoner of this fear, and turned to their Chiefs and Shamans for answers.

A great Shaman and Chief called Soma, named this way because of his strong connection to the Dream worlds, went to the top of the highest mountain in the land for a Vision Quest – to ask the Mystery for answers to the fear and unknown troubling that had possessed the minds of his people. "Help me to understand," he prayed by his fire. "Help me set my people free."

As Soma meditated the smoke from his fire caused him to look up to the sky, where he saw a great-winged creature. This creature was also drawn to Soma by the smoke and began to descend on the wind – swooping down to devour the Shaman. Out of a cloudless sky, a great Eagle came to the aid of the man on the mountain top. A brief battle ensued. The Eagle was no match for this creature that was from a land that time had forgotten. The man below, Soma was showered by feathers that resulted in the Eagle's sacrifice. It seemed to Soma that he was to be next, so he surrendered to his fate – he surrendered to the Mystery, and Greater Good.

A fire appeared in the sky above the mountain and a Creature of Fire intervened, much like the Eagle, except this Fire Being was more than a match for the large winged bird. The Living Fire drove the prehistoric bird back – over the ocean to the West.

Soma watched in awe as the Living Fire and the great predator disappeared over the horizon, and then with great thanks, gathered up the Eagle feathers that had rained down around him, and returned down the mountain to share the message of Love with his people.

"We are to be called: 'the People of the Feather.'" Soma announced. "The Eagle is our totem. I witnessed a battle in the sky above us, and I am sure it was our God that I saw, who was foretold by the ancients in our Dreams. We have nothing to fear. Our God will protect us." As time passed, however, the men, the warriors and the hunters did not stop having dreams that told them that they should make ready for the coming of dark forces. They increased their skills to defend their tribe and added feathers to their arrows so that they would fly straight and true.

When the troubling began to grow, another Shaman, a female Elder called Terra, decided it was necessary to seek out this God that had appeared to Soma. She also went to the mountain and built a fire and prayed for guidance. After four days and nights of fasting, her campfire burst into a mighty flame, and a creature appeared before her.

"Who are you?" Terra spoke with her head bowed. "Are you the God that our dreams spoke of? Are you Quetzalcoatl, the Feathered Serpent, the God of our dreams and legends?" All that had preciously occurred in the sky above the mountain seemed to indicate this.

"I Am!" The Fire Being replied in a gentle female voice. "But I am not the One you call the Mystery. I am not a God – I am a messenger. I am a Spark of the Fire. Before I came to this place, I had neither a name nor did I know myself as a female or a male. In the presence of you and the Heart of the People that you represent, I know that I am a Female, and that I was sent as an answer to your prayers. I am now called Quetzalcoatl. How may I serve you?"

The Shaman Terra was in awe. Here was a Living Fire that came in answer to her prayers from the Mystery of Life. "Our

People are troubled," Terra began, "They are losing faith in the dreams. They have lost faith…"

"In Love," the Fire Being finished Terra's sentence. "I am to be the answer to that problem. You can tell the men who prepare for war, that the Mystery has sent me to rekindle the belief in Love. I will spend some time with you and your people, to help you believe once more in your Dreams, and then I must leave. That is my purpose. The Mystery gives life and love but does not tell you how to live. Life is a gift for you to do as you see fit."

"Wait," Terra requested. "This sense of foreboding among my People? Will great birds return from over the water? We lose our faith in our dreams. We have dreamt that an evil will come to this Turtle Island and cause terrible things – perhaps an end to all of the Red-skinned People. Should we believe such a dark dream?"

"I come from the Mystery," the Fire Creature replied. "Before I was sent here, I was fire – a creature some called a Jinn. In the moment I appeared here, there was a purpose. Part of this is about believing in dreams. There is a Great Promise of the Mystery that nothing will be lost. And your Dreams will go on even if you do not. And like me, you will change and live a life of purpose in another time and place."

"You sound like a puzzle that has no solution," Terra sighed. "Will it always be a mystery for us? Should we believe in these dark dreams?"

"These Dreams can be true," Quetzalcoatl replied. "Am I not a living example? But the truth is in the teller of the dreams. The great birds are not the fear. The fear is based in the hearts of men who have no respect for the sacredness of life. I can only tell you this: the objects of your fear will come—one day from the North, over the ocean in wooden ships. They will pretend to be friendly and express a desire to share with you. But these people are not to be trusted. They speak with a forked tongue like a great snake that pretends to circle you in a friendly embrace. This is all that I can tell you, as the challenge will be to live your truth and believe in your dreams."

"Then it is True!" Terra sighed once more. "I have seen the white faces in my dreams. White faces covered with hair. We are not a war-minded people, so we will offer the hand of friendship and sharing but we will be weary of deceit. This is truly a challenge of our faith - and the Mystery that tells us that all creatures are from the same Dream."

Quetzalcoatl lived among the People of the Feather and observed that most of them could see her. Those that could see the Messenger of Fire began to worship her as a God, and the others spent most of their time preparing for war. Quetzalcoatl was troubled both by the adulation heaped on her and the warlike intentions. "I am being swayed." She spoke to an aging Terra. "I am not a God. I am simply a Messenger of Love. Perhaps I have done too much. Perhaps I have outstayed my purpose. I will leave you now, but I will return one day when you have need of me."

Quetzalcoatl disappeared back to the Source of the Fire. And one day. the object of the dark dreams appeared on the horizon to the North – in the form of three large ships. The People of the Feather, who had dreamed this day, were on alert.

The Elder Shaman called Terra met with the leader of the white-skinned bearded men as they stepped ashore from a small boat. The leader wore bright green armor, the color of the Earth and Love. This surprised Terra and her people, but they had been warned not to be fooled.

'I am Loki," the man in the green armor proclaimed. "We are Kings and Angels of a high order. We come in peace to ask to share and trade with your people. And if this is good in your eyes we ask to stay and live among your people."

Terra and her people could see that this man and his fellow travelers had large knives that hang from their belts, which they cautiously touched as they spoke.

"They come with the open hand of friendship, but the other hand seeks their weapons." Terra whispered to her party that greeted the people from over the ocean.

"We are the People of the Feather – the Eagle tribe," Terra grasped the hand of the man called Loki. "We are sworn to share all that we have with all creatures on this land we call Turtle Island. You may stay and live among us as long as both sides see that this is Good."

The sharing was mostly one-sided. The men who came ashore from the three ships seemed to have brought nothing but weapons with them, and they were unwilling to trade these. And then one evening a woman from Terra's people noted that these men had metal pots and other cooking utensils that they used to prepare the meat and vegetables that were offered freely to them. So a trading and sharing that seemed good was begun.

The sharing was good and some of the white men even joined in marriage with women of the People of the Feather. With the passage of time, the men from the North began to build their own homes, like they had in the land of their birth. It started small, with a handful of wooden huts, and then almost overnight, a high wall was built around the homes of Loki's people. When the Red-skinned People asked about the wall which seemed to be a fortress, Loki sent out a message, delivered by one of the men's wives, that they were declaring themselves Kings of this part of the land, as was the right given by them by their Fire God.

"Is there not just One God of Fire?" Terra sent back the message. There was no answer, at first, and then one morning, a deer appeared out of the forest near the fortress, and a loud noise and a flash of fire struck down the animal dead where it stood.

"These men have a terrible power," one of the men reported. "Their God has given them a stick that speaks death with fire! This is a power that disrespects life. The deer was left to die where it stood, without a reason."

Terra and the council of Elders were shaken. "What happened here is the foreboding dreams come true. It is the dark prophesy that Quetzalcoatl gave warning about. Can our God of Fire and Love not help us?"

"I will ask. We will pray for help." Terra replied. "When the messenger departed she promised to help us in our time of need."

In the council hut, Terra and the other Elders prayed, but although their fire burned comfortably, no answer was received. "She said that we should trust our dreams." Terra spoke. "It is late in the evening. We must trust that the Mystery will provide an answer to this. Perhaps one of us will be granted a Dream."

The council of Elders went, tired and dejected to their huts. Terra slept soundly, and at the morning light, she woke as if in a dream. She was standing on the mountain top and the Being called Quetzalcoatl stepped out of the Fire to speak to her.

"I cannot do anything that will cause harm to any of the creatures that are children of the Mystery," Quetzalcoatl sighed. "All creatures, two-legged and winged, and crawlers are Sparks of the Fire. The only action that is allowed is to defend yourself from those who intend harm – this is the code of Life that the creatures of the forest are granted—so it is for the two legged. You are all brothers and sisters."

Terra pondered. "Then is there some way that you can help us to defend our people against the harm that these people bring to our land. Can you perhaps disarm them – and take away their weapons? This stick that speaks fire is something that we have no defense against."

"I cannot. But perhaps I can make it possible for someone who has no thoughts of harm in their hearts. Someone who wears the Eagle feathers could do this while those who intend harm are asleep. I can help do this if you trust in the Mystery of Love and Life."

Terra woke full from the dream, if that was the truth of what transpired, and met later that morning with the Council when an expanded vision filled her heart and mind. She spoke about her dream vision in which she met with the Messenger of Fire, and then the plan that was revealed to her as the morning sun crept into her hut. The other members of the council had similar dreams, but not in such detail.

"This will require a great amount of faith in our dreams and our God of Fire," one of the other Elders spoke. Can we do this?"

"If we do not do this with complete faith and belief in the Mystery and her messenger, then we will die," Terra replied. "The men and women who approach the stranger's walls in the bright light of the full moon will surely die at the hands of the men and their terrible fire sticks. It is four days until the moon is full, we will agree to fast during this time, and a message of confirmation will come."

The first sign came when two men with the Sacred Eagle feathers went out bare-chested, so that it could be seen that they had no weapons, in order to gather the remains of the deer that had been put to death and left to rot outside the bearded one's stronghold. The two men approached the high wooden wall to see two sentries standing guard at the gate. The men of the Eagle Feather kept their heads bowed as they gathered up the remains of the deer.

One of the guards pointed his fire stick at the men and shouted: "Bang!" and then both of the sentries laughed as though they had made a great joke.

There was no other incident or move from the men outside or inside the fort, as the Men of the Feather took away the fallen deer's remains to be given to a ceremonial fire and returned to the Earth.

The second sign arrived the next day in the form of the young woman who had been married to one of the men within the walls. She came out half-way and was met by Terra and one of the other elders. She brought news of a list of demands from the men beyond the walls.

"These are not my words," the woman relayed, with tears in her eyes. "The leader of the men who is called Loki asked me to tell our people this: The men who are Kings wish to be treated as such before the God of Fire demands. They will be bowed down to and treated like the Kings of this land that they were given by their God. The Red-skinned People who are like the animals will put away all weapons and promise to serve the God of the white men. If these demands are not met in three days, the Red Men will be struck dead at a distance by the fire sticks that the God of Fire has given to these Kings."

Terra and the other Elder listened intently before replying in a low voice, with heads bowed, so that their words might not be known by anyone watching with their far-seeing eyes from within the walls.

"Are you allowed to wear your Feather within the white man's fortress?" Terra asked. The woman had indeed worn a white feather when she was sent out from the fort.

"I am allowed, but my husband prefers that I become like one of his people. It is not a sign of respect in the ways of their God."

"Then this is what we require of you. On the eve of the full moon be sure to wear this Feather, and when everyone else within the walls has fallen into a deep sleep, you will be still awake. We will send a group of sacred warriors to the gate that you will open. These warriors of the Feather will take away all of the weapons that the men would use to bring harm to our people. Is this clear?"

"It is, but…" the woman's tear-filled eyes grew wide. "I ask that none of the men are hurt as a result of my actions. I have grown to love my husband, and although these men are war-like, not all of them are as misguided as their leader."

"I will promise – no harm will come to any of the men within these walls." Terra answered. "After all, even though these men do not see it the same as our people, we all love the same God of Fire and Mystery. Go now and tell this man, Loki, that he will have the answer to his demands on the morning following the full moon."

Terra and the other Elder returned to the Council in their camp. After conferring, they gathered the people together and told them the beginning of their plan, and asked in humility and respect for those who wore the Sacred Eagle Feather to join in putting this plan into operation.

"Would it not be simpler for us to gather all the people and attack and set fire to this wooden fortress, and burn them all alive?" one warrior asked. "I have seen this fire stick in use one time before even though they hesitate to make it known. I watched them attempt take down another deer at a great distance but the deer escaped unharmed. I do not believe they can harm us at the distance they say."

"I would agree that they are boastful and tell great lies, but the weapons that they have are far superior to ours, and there will be a great loss of life on both sides. This is not the way of our people," one of the Elders replied.

"Anyone with the intent in their heart to do harm will not be asked to be with the men and women of the Sacred Feather as part of this," Terra spoke firmly. "And as I have been told by our messenger from the Mystery, this undertaking will fail if the intent is not peaceful. These men may wake up and kill our warriors who will go there with no weapons to protect themselves except the Feather of the Eagle in their hair."

There was no further exchange of communication between the People of the Feather and the men within the fort. Plans were completed by the Red- skinned People to ensure that no evidence of their "raid" was leaked and to respect the Mystery, the people resolved to use only their sign language, replacing any spoken word until after the morning after the full moon. As the sun went down that day, and the moon rose in a cloudless sky Terra and the other elders met around the fire and dreamed together - an awaken dream. In that dream, they saw a great feathered Bird of Fire swoop down from the moon, over the huts of the People of the Feather, and out over the wooden walls of the fortress, and out to the ships that were anchored on the north side of Turtle Island. And there was a deathly silence as sleep descended on all two-leggeds who did not wear the Sacred Eagle Feather. "It is done." A member of the Council signed to a waiting warrior.

The events of the moonlit night flowed like a dream. In respectful silence, the men and women wearing the Sacred Feathers, approached the fort in moonlight as bright as day, to find the two men on guard duty peacefully asleep at their post.

Silently and carefully, the weapons were removed from the hands of the sleeping guards. A soft knock at the gate, and a woman wearing a feather opened the latch. She started to whisper: "It is a mystery…I…" but the people who slipped inside signed to her to be silent—to speak in another way.

Every room, every bedroom where the white men slept peacefully, was searched and all weapons—including the dreaded fire sticks—anything that might be used to harm, were gathered up and taken out to a hiding place in the nearby forest. It was a long and time-consuming process that ended almost at the break of dawn, with the woman who had opened the gate, locking it and returning to the bed room of her husband. As this was going on, a group of men had paddled out to find the men in the ships asleep at their posts. All weapons were taken ashore, and anything that could not be carried away in canoes was dumped in the ocean. The sun peeped over the eastern horizon to find a land called Turtle Island without weapons waking up to a peaceful morning.

The People of the Feather watched and waited. A day passed uneventfully, with not a sign of life from high wooden walls, and on the morning following, the seemingly unguarded gate opened, and a group of men bearing a white flag filed out. A similar, weaponless group of warriors and an Elder met the men from the fort half-way.

"We do not know how you did it," the appointed leader of the bearded men began, "but we believe that somehow you are responsible for the disappearance of most of our guns and swords?"

"Our messenger for the Mystery – the God of Fire helped us," the Elder replied. "Now we have a suggestion for you on how this might end. It is not a demand, but we believe you will find it in your best interest to consider our offer. Tell your leader that we will allow you to return to where you came from in your ships. You will go in peace taking nothing but food that you will need for the journey back home over the great waters. You will deliver a Message of Peace to your people saying that we are the People of the Feather who offer the hand of friendship in the name of the Mystery – our God of Fire who will protect his people."

"Our leader will ask for a meeting with your Shaman called Terra," the man replied.

"This is a good thing." And both parties returned to their camps.

"How is it possible that your God of Fire could be the same as our God?" Loki asked Terra when they met face-to-face.

"It is a mystery," she smiled serenely. "I am not speaking in riddles to fool with you. Our God of Fire is truly a mystery for us, but she is also the One God of all people."

Loki was thoughtful for a moment. "Perhaps that may be, but there is a problem with what you are offering to us. A problem of truth. We have not been entirely truthful with you. We cannot return to our homeland across the ocean, as you suggested. We are outcasts from our people. We cannot go back. We offer a request to you that we are allowed to stay on this land that you call Turtle Island and call it home."

Terra looked around for support from her fellow tribesmen. "This seems a good thing that will need discussing further with all of our people. The problem as you suggest, will be a matter of trust. Our people no longer trust you to live freely among us. You are too warlike in your thinking." She did not say greedy though it was in her mind. "You need a place to freely live and worship God as you see fit. This will be my recommendation to our people."

After conferring with her tribe and the other Elders, Terra presented Loki and his men with a plan that included helping to build them a new home on the far Eastern shore of Turtle Island. Your weapons are gone," she informed them. "But we will help you make bows and arrows like we use, and teach you to hunt in a good way. How you live will be up to you and your Creator. But remember, we will be watching."

The ships moved south to the new homes of the men from over the waters. For some time, the two races lived in peace, helping each other from a distance, until, one day after Terra had passed into spirit, and a new Shaman was appointed, a new ship appeared on the horizon.

The people and their new Shaman watched with trepidation as the small wooden craft brought men ashore for the large ship.

"We are searching for someone," a man requested when he got over his initial surprise that these Red-skinned savages were fluent in his language. "We are looking for a man called Loki, who might have come among you dressed in green clothing? He was the leader of three ships that never returned home."

"We know of such a man," the Shaman spoke truthfully. If he had not, these people would search on their own, and eventually discover the truth. And if they were to somehow capture this ship and its crew, more ships would come as the dreams of his people had foretold. It would be best to be truthful and offer the hand of friendship that he had extended to these peoples relatives who lived quietly to the south.

The man returned to his ship and sailed to the south. And the people of the Feather watched with bated breath. Time passed, and one day, four ships sailed away to the northern horizon.

"They have returned home," one of the people left behind reported. A man and a woman of a small group of people who stayed behind were welcomed to live once more among the People of the Feather. "The man from our home land over the ocean delivered a message to Loki. The message was that our King known as Odin has passed into ashes, and a new ruler has been appointed. The newly, elected ruler offered forgiveness to Loki and his followers in the hopes of creating a strong new way of life for our people."

Life returned to normal for the Red-skinned People of Turtle Island, and with it a new dream that surfaced from their hearts to their minds. This new dream was about the great water filled with ships and hordes of white people who would overrun the land and steal the dreams that the Mystery gave to the People of the Eagle Feather.

Time and Beauty:

Time is such a Fragile thing
A Butterfly on Gossamer Wing
Love and Passion, Joy and Sorrow
Beauty that is missed today
Just flits away,
lost in the 'morrow

...winterhawk

Time

ONE

The Dreamers were born from a Dream. Their personal dream from The Mystery gave them a tribal name of The People of the Feather – the Eagle Feather and a Messenger of Fire called Quetzalcoatl. This messenger promised that she would return when they were in need of her. Unrest and uncertainty caused the Dreamers to experience fear. The fear took the shape of something that had occurred before and the circle was about to begin again.

A fleet of ships appeared on the northern horizon - the answer of a dark dream. This time, there were many ships all converging on the shore that had been the point of contact for three ships that had come, and gone before. The Shaman called Wovoka watched from the shore with his people. Wovoka wore his feather down – pointed to the earth, to announce that as a shaman he was aware of the trickster that most shamans followed as part of their two-spirited make up. His body was scarred with the evidence of his physical and spiritual quests. Wovoka was prepared for this day. It lived in his dreams and visions and came to life as a dance. This Shaman had experienced visions related to a man who had sacrificed himself on the Sundance tree – gave up his life for his people. Wovoka saw himself in that vision of the other sacred man, through the ways and eyes of his people's traditions. He envisioned that a Sacred Dance would drive these white, bearded people away and the Red-skinned would be free of them forever. When the people saw the ships, it was a sign to Wovoka that they must dance the dance that would set them free. This had worked before, these men had left Turtle Island, but now they had returned.

The people were dancing the Sacred Dance, like a celebration. as the first white faces came ashore. These strange visitors spoke no words at first, until more and more ships arrived, and the shores were filled. They advanced, and the People of the Feather drew back, waiting to see what their intentions might be. When a great group of the white people covered the shore, like ants about to make a new hill and new home, a raft came out from one of the ships carrying a large wooden wagon to be pulled ashore by an animal that was large and bulky like a buffalo. It was impressive to see, but even more, as the wagon advanced, it brought a feeling of power that touched the people's hearts. They shrank back in alarm and their Shaman stepped forward to speak with the man in a green armor who walked before the strange procession.

"Where is the old woman called Terra?" The man in green addressed Wovoka. "I wish to speak to the woman in charge."

"The Shaman you speak of has passed into the other world," Wovoka replied. "I am the Shaman who you will speak to."

"That is just too bad!" the man in green replied. "I am Loki, and I would have enjoyed telling this old woman that she and her people have four days to surrender to me and my God. But you will do. You have four days to bow down to me and admit that this land belongs to the KINGS from the North. When I lived here before, the drumming and dancing were driving me crazy and it followed me home. I demand that this be stopped. There is to be no more dancing and drumming or there will be the penalty of death. And by the way, that war dance you have been doing will be of no avail. You will still die and my people will claim the land that was promised to us by our God of Fire."

Wovoka assured the leader of the white bearded men that no one was dancing or drumming at the moment. "The sound that you are hearing must be the heart-beat of Mother Earth."

Wovoka returned to his village to join his people in dancing a forbidden dance. His vision told him that if they drummed and shook their sacred rattles in a certain way, and danced the Sacred Dance; the ghosts of their ancestors would come to their aid and defeat the men who appeared in their dreams. The Dreamers had discovered our dreams can sometimes be dependent on the

A Spark of the Fire

personal beliefs of the one who is dreaming. Wovoka was soon to discover that very truth.

Four days passed, and when Wovoka did not show up to surrender to him, the army of the men from across the ocean marched across the land, following the sound of the drum. They met with little resistance, but got little or no help. The people would tell Loki that "he is dancing over there – he is dancing here – just over that ridge." Wovoka was not hiding – he and his people were dancing the Ghost Dance. One day however, Loki and his men rode in to the camp where Wovoka was dancing and demanded: "why did you not answer to my demands?"

"This is my answer." Wovoka replied as he danced. "We were asked by the Spirit of our Ancestors to show you that we are not savages. We live on this land, but we do not own it. We cannot give you something we do not own."

"If that is so, then here is MY answer." Loki took out one of the newly created rifles and shot the Shaman dead. A strange thing happened. Wovoka should have fallen over, but he simply turned to ashes before the eyes of Loki and his men. Loki's men had surrounded the camp where Wovoka and his people had been dancing and the angry leader ordered his men to kill every last one of the people – men, women and child. And all of the dancers turned to ashes.

The place where Loki and his men found Wovoka dancing was a valley, and when the smoke cleared, a great number of People of the Feather who had been gathering along his trail, appeared over the edge of the canyon and rushed upon the man in the green and his men. They carried the outdated weapons that they had taken from Loki during his previous stay on their land. Although their arrows and the older fire sticks were outdated by comparison to Loki's new weapons of Loki the sheer number of people would not be stopped. The inevitable outcome was never in doubt.

There was a smoke that arose from the site of the battle that day. Perhaps from the weapons of the white-faced men. Who could know? But when the terrible battle was over, and the smoke cleared, the valley was littered by the bodies of the men from over the water. As many of the white men were dead, many more of the People of the Feather were missing, having turned to ashes when they were killed. The Chiefs and Shaman of the Red-skinned People were in grief for the people on both sides. The dark and terrible dreams came true. They buried the dead on that spot with a ceremony that asked for their spirits to be released to find their way back to the land of their ancestors. One body remained—Loki's. They took his body with them back to the shore where his people waited.

A man called Geronimo led a group of Chiefs back to the shore with Loki's body on a spotted pony. The people who came with Geronimo had left their weapons behind. Although Geronimo was truly a war chief, it would not been evident to the strangers from a far off land. For his people, however, he was a proud example of a warrior of the spirit. He wore his one feather up, pointing to the sky, and this was his singular announcement of his position. His body was predominantly unadorned and might be taken for any other middle aged red skinned man who had survived hard times in battle and living off the land. The feather and his air of pride spoke of a different story. Those chiefs that came back with Geronimo were the ones that had led their people in the massacre of Loki and his men. The rest of the people who had followed the Chiefs into battle had scattered to the four winds.

"This man was the cause of a terrible battle that could have been a war between your people and mine. I am called Geronimo. I am claiming responsibility for his death and the death of the men who followed him. Do with me as you see fit. I am surrendering to the Greater Good."

The men stood open mouthed at the news. One of the Chiefs who was also a Shaman spoke: "We have experienced terrible and foreboding dreams about a war between our people in which many would leave their lives. This war would go on for years and end with the battle that you will learn about. Today. We do not lie. We knew that we could not win this war due to your superior weapons. Our

A Spark of the Fire

people were as surprised at this as you. We drummed and prayed, and danced for a better outcome. Our prayers were answered in a way we did not expect. It was our intent to share this land with your people as the Mystery informed us through the one we call Quetzalcoatl who is the messenger from our God of Fire. Now we know that there is only one God for all people. She has helped bring about this. We surrender to that God and ask that your people give us another chance for peace."

The great army of white people on the shores of Turtle Island muttered and spoke amongst themselves, until a man stepped forward. "There was no one in charge except for this man who called himself King. Somehow he inspired us when our King died. He arrived and the people felt hope. I am now the second in charge. I will order this man called Geronimo and those who follow him to be seized and stand trial for their crimes. I will send a ship back to our land in the north to ask the man who was the previous leader, to come here and help us find a way to sort this out."

Geronimo was put in a prison that was hastily constructed to hold him and the other Chiefs that had led the people into battle against Loki and his men. Years passed outside the prison, as the world changed. One day the guards who kept watch on the prisoners, found Geronimo's cell empty except for a small mound of ashes.

The new leader of the "KINGS" from across the great water turned out to be the head of an organized religion called the Church of the Golden Sun. He stepped foot on the promised land to claim it in the name of the God of Fire — a certified God of Fire that burned in the sky who would someday return to take them with him to a new home in the sky beyond the darkness that was about to swallow up their world.

"You will all be forgiven," he proclaimed. "Even the evil one who corrupted our minds and hearts. We do not know the purpose of the emerald armor that this evil man wore, except that it prolonged his natural life. This same armor was worn by our former King, but it did not save either of them from their destiny. There will no longer be a King – except for the One who lives in the sky. I am appointed to be the representative of this God of Fire.

"We know that mankind's nature is inherently evil. This has been proven by the power of the Stone that came down from the sky, which brings out your true intentions. You will all be forgiven, but first you must be judged accountable for your mistakes. Anyone that fails to bow down to the laws of the God of Fire will be punished accordingly, and all people that follow a personal dream and worship the green color of the Earth will be also be severely dealt with – in His Name."

The Lie
Is an Arrow without Respect

Between you and I
It's not just the telling
That hurts
It's the believing
That is passed along
With the whisper
Of the Lie.

We all Dream
Our Visions and Dreams
are Arrows of Truth
from Birth on thru Youth
But Between you and I
A lack of Respect
can create a Lie.

First there is a Vision
given to all Men
Then the Arrow misses
it's Mark - it's sad in the end
when the Dreams of Some men
Become the Law
for our Children!

...without Respect
the Arrow of Truth
may become a Lie
Between you and I

...winterhawk

TWO

"Am I bad?" the little girl asked her grandmother one evening after school.

"Of course not, lovely one," her grandmother replied. "Where did you get such an idea?"

"At school today, in religion class and at our morning prayer. Our morning prayer was to have the God of Fire save us from our sinful ways. Am I full of sin? I don't think I could be if I don't even know what this word is about."

"We do not have a word like sin," her grandmother said. "Our language comes from our ancestors – the Dreamers, who lived in Harmony and Love with all creatures."

"I am a Dreamer," the small girl repeated the word. "But I must not tell anyone who I really am. Why should this be? I am proud of my In...her?"

"Inheritance," the grandmother smiled. "It almost tells us that it came from Her – In Her we trust and believe. Words are strange like that, especially the words we use to hide the truth that is in our heart. One day you will not need to hide who you are. It will become known that our people were created to help everyone to see the truth. It will become known that we have been given a choice by the Mystery – the true Source of the Fire that lives in our hearts."

"But why must I pretend to be something I am not? My friend over the tracks, in the land of the Dreamers does not pretend. He knows – we know that one day we will grow up and be like the One in Love," she blushed.

"Hush child. You are dreaming dreams that might have another way of turning out before the end of our time. Sometimes we will need to learn to sacrifice for the Greater Good."

A Spark of the Fire

The small girl continued to pretend that she did not know a better truth and enjoyed the time with her grandmother and playing with her friend on the other side of the tracks. The tracks were built to be a division between the lands reserved for the Dreamers who still wanted to follow the ways of their ancestors, and the land that the People of the Sun had claimed. The original train tracks were laid down so that anyone could travel the length of the New World curving like a crescent moon from South Point to East Point and the city of Lost Angels, where the man Loki was rumored to have lived during his first stay with the People of the Feather.

Meanwhile, the girl's father dealt with this truth in another way. His wife had died in childbirth, and he devoted his time to the study of better ways of keeping women alive – investing his time in running a clinic that promoted mental and physical health. Sam, as he was known, had forsaken his heritage as a Dreamer. Or had it forsaken him? Sometimes the gift is not passed down until the second generation. Either way, Sam's mind did not sleep. His creative urge propelled him into other sciences, at a time when science was taking over the minds of the people and religion was being pushed aside to satisfy curiosity. Even so, the men at the head of the Church of the Golden Sun refused to give up what they believed to be the most important. The man elected to run the government of a progressive world was also a religious cleric.

One day as the young girl approached puberty, she came home from school to find her grandmother resting by the fire place with a grim announcement. Still her grandmother smiled in her usual way as she told her granddaughter:

"My time has come. The purpose that the Mystery set for me has been accomplished. HO! Don't cry. One day we will meet again." And as the tears streamed down the young girls face, her grandmother turned to ashes. The girl who was becoming a woman was devastated, she cried until Sam came home later that evening. He was also thunderstruck as it brought home a truth for him that he had denied.

Sam arranged a funeral and with the powers that his office provided, his mother was given a closed coffin ceremony, explaining that cremation had already been performed. Sam's daughter, Cathy, attended but refused to speak to anyone for some days after. Her dreaming mind and heart was closed down. And it was not until weeks later that she spoke again and asked her father if she could enroll in a school to become a lab assistant. Cathy, being a female could not in this society ruled by men become a full scientist like her father but she could pursue a career as his assistant. Her creative mind was channeled in ways that helped Sam invent breakthrough devices using crystals.

Electronic devices in every shape and form ran the cities and the world where Sam and Cathy lived and worked — sometimes into the night to satisfy the craving of their people for more and more. It was never enough. More power and more knowledge, until the scientific community began to ask to examine the Crystals in the Egg of Stone that had fallen from the sky. The cry for power would not be denied, so in order to appease the appetite of a dwindling congregation, the leader of the Church of the Golden Sun gave up its most holy possession. Under the cover of darkness, the object that was once known as the Odin Stone was moved to a secret facility on the other side of the tracks, for study by the top scientific minds of the day.

Sam informed his daughter one evening. "This must remain between you and me. I have been named the head scientist at a research facility in the lands of the Dreamers."

"Good luck with that," Cathy replied with a closed and firm mouth. "I will continue to do my job in a lab here." Her mind was mostly disconnected from the right hemisphere, with the creative side providing flashes during a dreamless sleep. She was incredibly intelligent but she was like a person who could not walk without claiming the aid of logical assistance. And Sam could not persuade his daughter that there was another way – in fact he had learned that any argument only served to further close her down. She was a reminder of his way of closing down when it came to dealing with grief.

A Spark of the Fire

The Stone of Odin – according to the religious minded, the gift of the God of Fire was moved to the new facility and the best scientific mind examined it inside a lead lined room with little results — except that the energy seemed to be similar to the crystals that they already used, but beyond the scope of their measuring devices. After a time, and a process of reverse engineering, they were able to learn to increase the output of the crystals that were already in use to many times their potential. And the hunger of the people was temporarily satisfied.

"Your former clinic was able to help with the fertilization of a woman, was it not? I believe that this was one of your reasons for applying for the money to study the beginning and end of life." Sam was requested to a private audience with the now aging leader of the Church of the Golden Sun.

"I did," Sam replied in a puzzled voice. "I did fulfill my grant in many ways – including making it easier and safer for a woman to become pregnant and to give birth."

"I heard that there was more – a breakthrough in manipulating something called DNA? Of course this is between you and me, because if someone could alter the way we are created, it would be blasphemy – punishable in the past by death. At best today it might mean losing one's license to practice in the sciences of man."

Sam gulped. "Yes I am aware of the grievous nature of the subject and any conversation between you and I will go no further than this office. Why do you ask?"

"I have a rhetorical question. If I were to tell you that the religion of truth might die with me one day, since I do not have a son to keep it alive, how would your response be?"

"I would honestly say that the truth cannot die, and another will be born to keep it alive." And as the words left his mouth, Sam was keenly aware that this was not the answer that this man wished to hear. He gulped again and said rather hastily: "But then, when a man has the Truth, he might not want to trust this to chance."

"You are truly the man I believed you to be," the man in the golden robes replied. "Is it possible, theoretically, to fertilize a woman past her time so that she might bear a child that would carry on the truth and live a life longer than the normal man? I have heard that the evil one, Loki, lived longer than three normal life times. Is that remotely possible to attain given the miracles of our scientific times?"

"Yes," Sam squirmed. "I confess to your ears only that I was near accomplishing this before I was ordered to halt that part of my work. It might involve fertilizing a healthy egg in another younger woman, and while transferring this fertilized egg to another woman to change the DNA – to turn off a switch that controls how long a man would live. Hypothetically, this boy child might live until the End of Times."

"The End of Times?" The man in the golden robe gasped in wonder. "How could anyone know when this might come about, much less say that a man would live to see it, is beyond my knowing — it would be supreme heresy?"

Sam sighed. "In for a penny — in for a pound."

"What does that mean?"

"If we are to talk about things that would change the life of a child, then there are other things that might need to be revealed." Sam looked the other man straight in the eye.

"Like? Go on."

"In our recent exploration by telescope we have been able to see into the centre of our Galaxy and what we saw shook our scientific minds and hearts. There is a massive black hole that is growing larger and larger devouring all matter and light. But wait – that is not all. Our scientific equipment and measuring devices have calculated that our sun, having reached its peak of power by some unnatural means is now growing colder as we speak and will soon go Nova – it will explode and die. We do not know which event will occur first, but either way, it will also mean the death of our world."

"So?" the leader in the golden robe replied. "I can answer the last question. Our God promised to return. When our sun dies, it will mean the death of our Sun God – and as prophesized, He will take us with Him to Paradise."

Sam did not reply. His scientific and perhaps spiritual mind had led him and his fellow scientists to believe that there was a choice. Perhaps a man was given this unique and creative mind because he had a choice in the events that would make up his future. When he did reply, he said: "I will seek out a volunteer for this theoretical question that you asked."

"Just remember that this will be a onetime endeavor, and should we attempt it, the instruments and any memory of this will be lost forever until the End of Time!"

When Sam came home late after spending some time thinking at his lab, Cathy was still up reading a book she found on her father's desk. The book was a one-sided account of history since the people had come from the land across the ocean. She set the book down and greeted her father.

"How come you are still up?" he asked.

"How come you are so late?" she replied, and kissed her father.

It occurred to Sam that he needed to share his dilemma with someone who would not divulge the secret of what he was thinking of doing. She listened intently as he told her what he had seen through the telescope and the truth of what he had found about the nature and life of their Sun. She took it all in but had a surprise for him when he told her what he was intending to do for the leader of the church and his strange request. "I believe it can be done. We have done many such projects in my lab for women who had trouble getting pregnant. Of course the change in the DNA of a fertilized egg will be something that no one has tried before except in mice. And then I will need to find a volunteer – a young woman willing to sacrifice a couple of her eggs. He had thought it over to the extent that his words might seem cold and scientific - analytical. And maybe it was the word "sacrifice"?

"How could you?!" Cathy rose from her chair with tears in her eyes. "How dare you ask such a thing!" and she ran to her bedroom and slammed the door behind her.

Sam followed his daughter to her room and listened to the sobbing. Cathy had not reacted this way or for that matter had shown little emotion since her grandmother's passing. "Go away," she sobbed when he tapped lightly on the door. He hesitated, oblivious to what he might have said to cause this, and decided to let it be until the morning.

Cathy cried herself to sleep and for the first time since her grandmother's passing, was opened to Dream. The book that she had been reading the previous night played through her mind and into the dream, where a different and expanded version came alive. This new truth explored a long and terrible war between the People of the Feather and the men who came across the great water. And then when the Red-skinned People were slaughtered almost to extinction, Geronimo came forward to surrender to the Greater Good. The years that followed showed flashes of oppression of those Dreamers that still lived among the white people to the extent that any woman who was found to practice her healing and dreaming was burned at a stake by the Church of the Golden Sun.

Cathy woke exhausted, but with a sense of purpose and a belief that her grandmother's teaching had not been in vain.

"Morning," Sam whispered and kissed his daughter on the cheek.

"Morning," Cathy replied. "Yes I will do the right thing and volunteer to be part of the sacrifice for our people."

"What? I didn't mean..." Her father sat down at the kitchen table across from her. "I was sharing my day with you. I should not have dumped on you. I am sorry. Please forgive me?"

"Maybe you didn't mean to say what I heard, but it was my ears that heard what I needed to hear," Cathy replied. "If all that I have to give is some of my eggs so that our people will have a baby born that might someday find it in his heart to do the right thing when the world needs it, then I am ready to step up and do my part."

"But what is the right thing?" her father pondered.

"The right thing is to use the gift of choice – and to find a way to leave this world as her time to die comes to be. After all, this is a dream that we are sharing with the mystery of love.

"Don't say that too loud," her father cautioned. "Especially when any of the religious fanatics are in ear shot. It is still not too remote of an idea that a woman who admits to dreaming could be put away for plotting against God. And besides, your body and your eggs are yours to share with a future husband in a loving marriage."

"I have no thoughts about that...anymore," Cathy sighed. "Once there was a boy that I knew when my grandmother took me to the land of the Dreamers, but he was lost to me when my grandmother passed into ashes. I tried to find him, but it is like that time we shared is just part of a dream that died with my grandmother." Her eyes attempted to fill again, but she fought back the tears. "I am ready to do my part. My time is the time leading up to the new moon that will be soon in the sky."

Cathy accompanied her father to the temporary clinic that was set up in one wing of the facility that studied the crystals over the track in the land reserved for the Dreamers. Once checked in, she learned that the nurses – the scientific assistants that had worked with her father in his former clinic could not be there to do the procedure until the next morning. "I will stay overnight," She told her father, "to meditate on what I am volunteering for."

"As you wish," he replied. "There will be some staff on duty and you can call me anytime if you change your mind either way."

One of the reasons that Cathy chose to stay was a strong sense that something was pulling her, and it was easy for her to guess that the Stone and the crystals that were in a closed, protected room of the same building might have something to do with this. The room that the crystals were housed in was lead-lined, but she intuited that this would not stop the emanations. Later in the evening, dressed in her hospital gown and laying in a comfortable bed, she was rewarded with a dream that confirmed her thoughts.

Cathy stood in the room that held the crystals and saw a bright, green light rise out of the "egg" and stream skyward. She followed the light and was somehow not surprised to see it connect with a source in the sky. It dawned on her that the source was not the sun, as many of the believers of the church insisted. Yes, there was a connection there too, but that was not the source. And then she was drawn back to her hospital bed.

The ward was silent, not surprisingly, because the process she was to undertake was to be kept a secret. Still there should be someone there—a nurse on duty as her father promised. She did not feel uneasy, rather she felt protected, and drawn to it, as before. She began to think back on the times her grandmother had brought her here – or somewhere in the land for the Dreamers, to play with her friend. They grew up together until one day...? Then she remembered that he had told her his name, and that he could be called in a magical way. She mentally concentrated on his name and...nothing happened, except a sense of belonging—as though she was where she needed to be. Maybe that was the extent of this magic—a feeling in her heart.

"I would like a drink," She looked around – peered out of the temporary "room" that was created by curtains drawn around her bed. The hallway was bright – brighter than she remembered, but there was no nurse to be seen. Just in case, she boarded a nearby wheel chair and rolled off down the hall in search of the nurse. "No one." The hall way went on and on – into a corridor that appeared to lead to another wing of the hospital. At the far end, there was another curtained room by a window. A light was on in cubicle. Feeling very safe and that she was where she needed to be, she followed her curious nature and said: "Anyone home?" while gently pulling aside the curtain.

"Oh! I am sorry," she exclaimed. And then: "How did you get here?"

"I believe you called me," Her friend exclaimed. "Or did I call you?" He was like she remembered, but he had also matured like her. She rushed into his waiting arms. "I was a long ways away, somewhere in another place," he began. "I was with you. Wasn't I?"

"How could you be?" she whispered in his ear. "I am here – I have always been here. I thought I had lost you."

"I seem to remember that I was with you in the garden, and then a bee stung me and I was paralyzed." He drew her close under the sheet and pressed her to him.

She returned the hug—a deep embrace, as she rolled over on her back on the small hospital bed and then—she gasped. "You don't seem paralyzed to me?"

Later, much later, he spoke in her ear. "I was dreaming about the crystals."

"Me, too." And a moment passed in silence. "What do you know about the crystals?"

"Most of it is what you told me, and the rest I kind of figured out on my own. The green crystal is our heart. I used it to...to..?" He lost track of the thought. "You told me how the crystals could be used in a ship that could take our people to the Stars and beyond — to a new home."

They talked most of the night, helping each other to remember, pausing to enjoy another gift of Love that the Creator had given.

"I hope this doesn't make you feel guilty," he whispered breathlessly.

"And why should it? We are destined to be together—married in the eyes of God in the Garden. What men think with their small minds doesn't bother me a bit. Men judge and the Mystery is not offended."

"I think I heard you say that we are together in the place where you came from?" she asked. "Is that here in our time and space—or where did you come from...?" Her mind did a double take, and the room faded away. She was back in her cubicle behind the curtains. "Was that only a dream? Only a dream?" The flush of her body told her the truth. She got out of bed and found a washroom with a shower just a few feet down the hall.

The nurse smiled from her station as she passed. "Are you OK?"

"I could not be more OK," Cathy replied. She showered and returned to the cubicle in a fresh gown.

That morning, Cathy's father paid her a visit on his way to his continuing scientific investigations with the crystals.: "How are you holding up?" he asked. "Have you changed your mind about the process? If you have, then the Patriarch or Father of the Church, whatever title he likes to bestow on himself, can go hang. And if need be I will find another woman to donate her eggs so that he can have his son to carry on his name. I am beginning to believe it's really about that — his name — more than seeing the teaching of the God of Fire being sustained until the 'End of Time.'"

"I am sure this is the right thing to do – now more than ever," she replied. "I have a question. Are there any other patients in the hospital wing of the lab?"

"No," He answered. "This is a makeshift clinic set up for this one procedure. Besides, it will remain a secret that will not be done again, and that part of the lab and the equipment will be dismantled when and if the procedure is successful. Why do you ask?"

"I had a dream," she blushed and then continued. "About the crystals. I know where the Stone that brought the crystals to Earth came from. You can check with your telescopes and devices to verify my belief. The crystals did not come from the sun, although the energy of the sun plays a part. The rock that fell to earth must have been part of a passing asteroid or comet that struck the moon a glancing blow."

"Of course! Why didn't that occur to us before?" In the same breath he knew the answer to that, and in his excitement he let it pass that Cathy's inspiration had come from a Dream. "What else do you think about the crystals? Is that a possibility that we might be able to get more, if we were able to build a ship to take us to the moon?" Already his creative intuition was kicking in.

"Yes, we can do that," she reaffirmed, "and the crystals can be used to power that ship and others like it – to take our people to another world before our sun dies."

"Beautiful! Beautiful!" Sam exclaimed kissing and hugging his daughter. "I will get right on the observations to…to. And if you're still open to it, giving the Father of the Church a son might help in his agreeing to a different way of saving our people. At least when his son takes over, there might be a chance for us to make a better choice."

THREE

Cathy's mind was operating at a blurring speed when the nurse showed up to wheel her down to the room where the procedure for artificial insemination would take place. She had many questions about the events of the previous night, which were occupying much of her focus of thoughts, until the nurse began the preliminary examination.

"This is highly unorthodox," the nurse whispered so that no one else might hear, although the lab and the hospital were vacant except for her and her patient. "Are you sure about this?"

"Yes, I am," Cathy replied. "And I am of the age of consent – apart from that, both myself and my father signed the forms."

"Your father?" the nurse sighed. "I recognize you even though this is supposed to be hush hush. You are Sam's daughter."

Cathy nodded.

"It's just that we do see all too many young girls in our clinic over this side of the tracks, that come in to get the results of a mistake removed."

"Isn't that illegal?" Cathy asked.

"It is, according to the Church, but we screen the patients really good, and over here, the belief is that women have the right to decide what happens to their bodies. And then, our main clientele is made up of women who want this procedure that you are about to undergo or a similar one that will enable them to have a baby when all else has failed. If you are sure, then I will proceed.

"I am sure," Cathy responded, and her mind went away during the initial embarrassment.

"Done," The nurse reported at length. "You will have to remain as you are for a while." The nurse sat down and picked up a book from a nearby table, and busied herself reading, and then announced that she would check in on Cathy in a while. "Meanwhile, you might want to read this. It is something we have available for the young women who are going through difficult times."

Cathy started to reply that she was not in the same category. But she accepted the book, as the nurse went her way. It was a book with a white cover that Cathy could not recall ever seeing before. She leafed through the book, and read:

"And they heard the sound of the Lord God walking in the garden in the cool of the day, and Adam and his wife hid themselves from the presence of the Lord God among the trees of the garden. Then the Lord God called to Adam and said to him, "Where are you?" So he said, I heard Your voice in the garden, and I was afraid because I was naked; and I hid myself."

Cathy read on, mystified that she had never seen this book before, but when she continued she saw that many of the stories were similar to the Book of the Golden Sun that she had been reading at home — stories that seem to go off on a tangent from the initial chapter. Many of the stories were about wars and "commandments" that were broken by people who worshiped a judgemental and angry God, not like the first chapter that began with a God who was loving and forgiving.

"Why would the nurses give a young woman in trouble this book to read?" And when she was closing the book she saw that there was a bookmark. She opened to that page, and read a few lines that were highlighted. It began with:

The angel said to her, "Do not be afraid, Mary; for you have found favour with God."

"I will take you back to your room now," another nurse stood smiling at Cathy.

"Where is my regular nurse?" Cathy experienced a momentary lack of focus.

"She had other duties – other patients to see to." The smiling nurse retrieved the book from Cathy's hands, and placed it back on the nearby table. Then she helped Cathy down from her perch and into a waiting wheelchair.

"Other duties? Other patients?" Cathy pondered this mystery back in her familiar cubicle. In a while the first nurse opened the curtain.

"How did you get back to your bed?" the nurse asked. "I came to tell you that the time of waiting for the procedure was over, but you were not there."

"Another nurse came and brought me back." Cathy replied, still in a bit of a daze.

"What other nurse?" I am the only nurse on duty here, except for the nurse who checked you in, and she is not part of the procedure. I will need to have a word with her. Are you OK? I am sure everything went right regardless."

"I feel OK," Cathy replied. "Except for being a bit lightheaded. Can I have that book that you gave me to read again?"

"What book is that? The only book I remember anywhere in the lab, is the Book of the Golden Sun which we are strongly asked to read and make available to any guests. But I am sure you must have read that more than once?"

"I have read it," Cathy confirmed. "My father keeps a copy on his desk at home. Never mind, I will take a nap and be up and about this afternoon."

"Our suggestion for this procedure is that you rest in bed for the rest of the day," The nurse replied. "You are requested to stay with us for four days to a week until," she whispered, "until it is confirmed that you are pregnant. And then another nurse will come in to do the final part of the procedure – and transfer the fertilized eggs."

"I hope this doesn't make you feel guilty" This was another thought that peeped into her mind – a shared memory? "Why should it? If anything, I feel..."

Later that day, after sleeping more than she might be used to, Cathy decided it was time to check out the reality of her dreams. She used her trusty wheel chair to explore the hallway outside her curtains. At the end of the hallway was a wall. No other corridor or door to another wing of a clinic that may or may not exist in this time frame. She sat in her chair staring at the wall, and called out in exasperation – whispered in her mind, for the one who had been there for so much of her growing up – who helped her find the answers when no one else had even a clue.

"Grandmother!" she stood on a path in a secluded forest – the wheel chair left behind. She ran with tears in her eyes to hug and be hugged – comforted by the Elder who seemingly sprung alive from her dreams. "Grandmother!" She sobbed and eventually accepted her Grandmother's hand to walk and sit by the pool where they had enjoyed each other's company. "Grandmother? Why don't you look different? You should have wings – or something – yet you look and sound exactly as I remember."

Her Grandmother smiled, and then laughed aloud. "Don't be fooled. I have changed, but you need to know that dying doesn't make someone wiser or "more advanced". Sure, we can see more of the greater picture, but that doesn't make anyone smarter unless they grow in compassion and love."

"But Grandmother, you always had the answerer that I needed. And I need your help more than ever."

"Think back – remember our time together. I never gave you the answers. I helped you to discover them for yourself. There are many spirits without form – that will freely admit that they have never incarnated yet they pretend to know all the answers about living on Mother Earth. How could it be possible for anyone to understand your questions and challenges if they have not walked awhile in your moccasins?"

Cathy pondered that bit of sagely advice. "I still need you to help me to understand. I have begun to dream again. And one of my dreams that haunt me is the same that I have had since being a little girl."

"I will listen," her Grandmother replied. "But that may be all I can promise."

"This dream that I am confined to a wheel chair has returned," Cathy firmed her lips. I believed that we solved that – with the help of my...my..." she blushed. "My friend."

"I hear and see the boy problem has grown into a man and woman relationship? But that is only part of what you are facing. Am I correct?"

"As usual you see more than I admit to." Cathy replied. "When I think about him, I realize that his feelings are shared but not entirely mine. It is confusing the rest of the picture. I called out to him, but he is more than I remember."

"And so are you – more than you will admit to. When I was sharing my Dreaming truth with you – something you might not recall, to be a Dreamer, is to accept that you will experience other worlds in which you are someone who is called by another name – yet it is still you. Do you remember that?"

"No – but I was only interested in playing. And now I am living that Dream." Cathy sat back clutching her knee to her chest.

"Playing is good. We should not take ourselves too seriously. That is part of the gift of Life. We learn to play act and then it sets the stage for playing with respect for the consequences of our actions. You have already answered that question. It involves respecting him but not trying to take responsibility for what is his. There is more."

"Yes. In my waking life, I am back in the wheel chair and facing something that I do not feel worthy of. It all fits together."

"Yes, it does. And it becomes clearer when you have someone to share your thoughts with. Being bound and limited to a wheel or a circle might be something that all two-legged accept until they are ready to walk or run free. Don't you think?"

"Yes. I am beginning to see that now. "I was reading a Sacred White book about a woman who might be like me, and about to give herself to a mystery of Virgin Birth. Is that possible? And am I worthy?"

"If you can Dream it, then it is more than possible. And is not love and the creation of life a gift that the Mystery has found you worthy?"

Cathy shut her eyes, as a warm feeling washed over her like a wave. When she opened them again, she was standing at a door that led to a long corridor to a wing of the clinic that logically should not exist.

She followed the corridor to a cubicle in the other healing clinic and sat on the edge of his bed. "I think you will be fully healed when you can accept who you are." She held his hand. "Have you thought about the guilt that you spoke about when we shared before?"

"I was and it is my truth. It does not belong to you." He pulled away. "I am not even sure if I am the man that you called."

"I called the sharing name of a boy that I met in a forest," she replied. "That sacred sharing cannot be wrong. You must be the one who came as an answer to my Dream."

"I am," he answered with tears in his eyes. "But that boy has grown, and gave his life so that I could live. He is the part of me Dreaming that came to help our people know that they have a choice to live. I am the one who received a name that tells of my purpose."

"And is that the name that you told to me in the Garden?" She drew him close.

"Yes. I am Wolf Dreaming Fire. He kissed her tenderly and respectfully.

"And whose fire are you dreaming?"

Cathy returned to share with him the four days she had to wait for the procedure to be completed. They talked and shared without guilt. One evening, she told him about the continuing dreams that she had about the crystals. "There are more crystals. My father and his engineers are working on a ship that will take them to the moon to harvest them and more of the green stone."

"There ARE four more crystals," he confirmed. "There is a blue, indigo and a violet and a white Crystal. I meditated and learned a bit about the use of the first three new colours, and that helped me to come to this world that is beyond the time that I could previously understand. But the white crystal is beyond my understanding. It is a mystery."

"I agree," she smiled. "The white crystal is not to be understood. It is like the blue but somehow the combination of all. I dreamed how we can use those crystals to give our people a choice – and to journey to the Stars and beyond." They talked and shared until one morning she woke in his arms in the light of day.

"Oh!" she exclaimed, while hastily donning the hospital gown, neglecting to fasten the back. "You have company. Someone is coming to take you home."

"You are pregnant." The nurse came into Cathy's cubicle to inform her that the next part of the procedure could be completed.

As part of the procedure that involved transferring the fertilized eggs, Cathy's father remained behind an adjoining cubicle where he had set up his equipment to make a change to the DNA. This involved altering a switch that decided how long the life span of the child would be. Two eggs were then given to a waiting nurse in another cubicle who inserted them into the womb of the woman who was the wife of the Leader of the Church of the Golden Fire.

A few days later, Cathy's father informed her that the procedure had been successful. "Our religious leader will have his son – perhaps two sons. We will know very soon. As the eggs became babies, Sam informed the man of the good news. "Congratulations – your wife will have twins."

"Two boys? That will be a difficult choice to decide for a new man who will carry on after I am gone."

"Well, no." Sam replied. "The twin babies are a boy and a girl."

"Then that makes my decision easier," the man shrugged. "Before they are born, you have my permission to dispose of the girl child and keep my son. Is that within your power to do?"

"It might be dangerous at this point." Sam told a small but not complete lie. "It would be safer to have the babies born and then you can choose."

"I have already made my choice." The religious man turned away. "Dispose of the girl as you see fit."

When two healthy babies were born to the wife of the patriarch, Sam delivered the baby boy into the mother's hands, and hid away the girl. He told the woman and later her husband that only one baby had survived. Later, Sam arranged to anonymously drop the girl off at an orphanage. The patriarch leader of the Church of the Golden Sun named the baby boy Joseph, after himself. Before giving the two children to their fates, Sam conducted a secret DNA test that provided him with a surprise that he would reveal to no one, not even his daughter. The good thing was that the DNA switch was turned off and both children would have lives that defied the ravages of normal time. The other thing, the real surprise, was although the girl child tested positive for having the patriarch's DNA, the boy, his son, had a DNA male match that could not be found.

Cathy devoted herself to the project of building the ships that would take the people to a safe new home out among the stars. She helped her father to create a new cloth that was partly made of the stone that was brought back from the moon. Soon, everyone, except the most die-hard followers of the church, was enjoying the benefits of the crystals and wearing the green body suits that would help prolong their lives. Cathy wore the suit herself, though she admitted that prolonged exposure was a bit late to stop her accelerated mental and physical process. Instead, she embraced her destiny and stepped out into the public eye as a Dreamer. Perhaps as a result of his daughter's journal and thus her personal statement, Sam was rewarded by having the production facility for the ships and the further exploration for the uses of the crystals taken away from his control, and moved to the other side of the tracks at the edge of the new Crystal City.

When she had, in her eyes, done all that she could to prepare her people to make the ships ready to go to the stars, a maturing Cathy disappeared. Some rumours said that she reached her time and simply went to ashes. That would not however, explain the missing prototype of the ship that was the first to be fitted with all eight crystals. Gossip circulated after Cathy's disappearance that she went to search for a secret lover. As there was no one to deny or confirm it the fanciful rumour quickly went to ashes along with the credit for her accomplishments which were being officially expunged from the Book of the Golden Sun.

FOUR

Joseph:

I will try to be brief as possible, as so much has happened that is already written. It was told first in the chronicle of our history, the *Book of the Golden Sun,* and then in what I have grown to call real time. Real time, as I understand it, began for me when I was awoken from my dreamless sleep by my first father. Until that moment it was not real as I understand it now. All it took was my first father to ask and I was compelled to obey. That, I believe was encoded in my DNA – either by chance or purpose, or as part of a plan of the Mystery. And when I woke I remembered my first mother and then, my sister who I had not even known to exist.

That must sound complicated, but if you have read my accounts of the dreamless sleep before I accepted my true reality as a Dreamer, you will have a glimpse of the truth. This might be only my truth, as this is my story but I believe all of us live in a state of being that we are part of a story that is more than incomplete— it is a wheel of time. We become trapped in that wheel compelled to repeat it until we begin to take responsibility for our actions. Then, as happened to me, when asked a simple question— a request from my first father, we accept that we have been asleep at the wheel.

I am not my father's son, nor am I my mother's, although I thank them for bringing me into the world. The story that I believed to be true was passed down to me, and I was obligated to continue "in his footsteps," to teach a truth that was only partly true. The truth that I lived and taught was an "Arrow of Truth", in that it led me to find the truth that is a mystery we have come to call

Love. And then it is still a mystery, but it is also no longer someone else's story. Now it is my story about how I am co-creating as I go along, with all of the other creatures that the Creator dreamed from the beginning of time.

I woke up to the knowing that we did not have a lot of time remaining before our sun went cold, and then supernova, and the ashes to be drawn into the Great Wheel at the center of our galaxy. There were a number of people who refused to accept this, who continued to cling to the Religion of the Golden Sun. These people are the ones that requested to be left behind after the ships set out on their journey to the stars and beyond. I remained behind to do whatever I could, like I promised my earth father and mother. I promised to console them and tell them that at the end of times. the God of Fire would return and take them to a safe haven that He had prepared for them. It was my choice to remain, and continue a story that I knew was, at best, faulty.

As the last ships were loading, the people from the City of Lost Angels were given the opportunity to board. No one was left behind that did not choose to be. It was then, when those people came from East Point Station— the City at the far end of the track – East Point Station arrived, I discovered my twin sister among those who would stay. We knew each other at once as if that was all part of the plan, and she remembered our first mother.

There was a joyful reunion, followed by a realization of the fate that we had chosen. My sister and I returned to the Church in the center of the Crystal City, and renewed the teaching for anyone who would listen. At first, we kept strictly to the Book of the Golden Sun, and as the world grew cold, we deviated just enough to bring them to an understanding that although this was true, there was a further truth that they would be given a second chance and their lives and mistakes would not be in vain. This may not have been such a good idea, as one by one, the people deserted the church claiming that this was not what they needed to hear, and that we, and the church had let them down.

"We do not want this second chance." One man vehemently declared: "We chose to stay behind and be saved by our God. The End of Times is upon us – rejoice and make ready!"

The End of Time, as we knew, it was close, and as the world prepared for her death knell, there was rioting and looting in the streets. Hardly the actions of people who were making ready to meet their God. My sister and I found lodging in separate homes near the church, lodgings which had been vacated by the mass exodus to the stars. We kept the church open to console those who might need it as the end approached. One or two visited us at the church and a couple warned us to be cautious as anything burnable was set on fire in a city made of crystal.

One night, I was awakened, and roughly dragged outside by a group of the rioters. "Look what you have done!" One man shook me. "This is your doing. Our world is burning with your lies!"

I tried to reason with them as they dragged me to the church across the street. "This is not my, our, doing. Our scientists warned us all that it would come to this. But we remained behind to fulfill the wishes of our God."

"Pahh!" One of my captors spit in my face. "Do you see the fire? Where is the God that promised to save us? He has abandoned us. And you and the whore that is your sister are responsible for deceiving us. Well, you and the whore will meet your fate tonight – the fate that is the promise of your church."

I was dragged through the doors of the church to find my sister, battered and bloody, hanging from the rafters over the altar. She moved her head to look at me as I was hoisted up beside her.

"Is this to be our end?" She bowed her head in resignation. "I was promised more in my dreams. Were our dreams at fault as well?"

"Our dreams were good." I attempted to believe as the rioters began to light the church on fire. "They were right! Don't give up – surrender to the Greater Good."

"How can I?" She showed a brief glimpse of hope. "I cannot die. I have lived so long and now it is my curse."

A Spark of the Fire

"The gift of a long life was not a curse." I clutched at straws. "I remember a Dream of our first mother that she told me, when you have fulfilled your purpose you will know in your heart that it is time to let go and let the mystery be."

"I will try," she winced in pain. "I am surrendering – I am a sacrifice to the Greater Good!" and in a blink of an eye, she turned to ashes.

The men that were setting the church on fire stopped in their tracks as, a Creature of Light and Fire arose from the ashes – a Phoenix reborn.

"I have returned!" The Being of Living Fire cried out, and the men dropped their torches and bowed.

"I promised that I would return when you needed me," the Woman of Fire said, as I struggled to remove myself from the ropes that held me suspended in the rafters of the church. "Release him," she demanded of the men. "Listen to me, I am the messenger of your God."

Released, I followed the men and the Being of Fire out into the street where the rioting halted and the men and women thronged, gathering in growing numbers.

"Listen to me!" she cried out. "I am a messenger from your God. I have returned as I promised, and I will remain with you until the End. You will return to ashes as your sister did. She was sent to be proof for you to see with your own eyes. And from your ashes, you will emerge new as I am — with the choice to continue or go to a higher place beyond the Stars."

"How much of this is true?" I asked the Being of Fire when the moment presented itself. "I do believe, but for these people it will be a stretch to give up all of their past conditioning."

"It is all part of the evolution of the soul," she whispered. "I am a Jinn. I will return to the Sky like all other forms that are Sparks of the Fire. My kind was created at the beginning of time with Angels and Humans and other creatures that were part of the Dream. "I do not have the final Truth any more than you or any of these worshipers of the God of Fire, but I have faith in the mystery of love and life."

Epilogue

Another Spark?

To have a new beginning we need to have an end. Even if this beginning is part of the Great Circle of Time that devours all that is, even Light. When this is complete we will experience what some will refer to as "the Big Bang," and life will begin again. For some that could not or are not able to let go, the circle, the Wheel of Life will pick up where they left off, except most will not remember this as true.

As I imagined it, the Dreamers began a new life on a planet among the Stars and some of the others that refused to dream joined them, as the Mystery of Love does not judge. Some others went on to a place in the Sky as they were promised and enjoyed a life that refreshed their souls, until they might choose to join their kin. The Jinn chose to be with the Sky People and for a time she was content. One day, however, the Jinn leaned over the Edge of Space and Time, the Event Horizon, and a small blue planet caught her attention.

"Those are My People down there!" the Jinn exclaimed to no one in particular, and when she leaned over to see better, she fell to Earth!

This is an account, as I stated above, that I imagined must have happened since it appeared in my mind like a vision or a waking dream. And then, who would know if it is true – like the rest of the dreams and stories that I tell. I only know that it seemed unquestionably right to me until a voice echoed in my ear as I completed this telling of a new beginning.

"PREPOSTEROUS!"

Home

"Home!"

This wish, this intention, as I have grown to understand, will take me to the time and place and the person I love. It will take me to where my soul needs to be. And then there is the part of surrendering to the Greater Good.

I woke out of my dream just a bit confused. I was in space, looking down at a beautiful blue planet wondering just for a moment what I was doing alone up here. Hadn't I just left? No—it began to come back. There was a safe place where this ship had been stored for the right person to find. I followed the calling back to that shack on the reservation flying low that I should not be spotted by radar. The door was open like I was expected. I flew in to the resting place and paused in the cockpit wonder, what next?

I climbed down and vaguely remembered something about a password or a key that would prevent the ship from being opened again except by a certain young woman's hand. I smiled and agreed that this was the right thing to do after closing the cockpit dome. I went out into the night that was quickly becoming morning, and latched the door of the shack behind me. My intended destination was the fence at the side of the road across a corn field, but as I stepped away from the influence of the ship and its cargo, I was pulled to another place, and woke again on a small cot in what I recognized as a hospital ward.

"Are you OK, Mr. Champion?"

I shook my head to clear the cobwebs. "Yes I am now. How long have I been here? How did I get here?"

"About a year ago you checked yourself in," a pleasant nurse replied.

"I feel that more time passed than that. Are you sure? What year is this?"

"1964," the nurse replied.

"And what month?"

"August. Are you sure you are OK?"

"Yes, I am now. Then I am not too late. How can I get out of here?"

"Why, you are not a prisoner. You can check yourself out anytime you want. You checked yourself in, remember?"

Now I knew what Scrooge must have felt when he woke up and it was still Christmas. I asked for the papers and signed myself out, and then was given the articles that were in my pocket at check-in. I had some money and, better yet, a driver's license and a credit card—and a sense that whatever forces deposited me here, I would not be too late.

I called at the front desk to order a rental car as I have a foggy memory of having parked on some quiet street by the U of T – University of Toronto. That car was either in pound by the police or had been collected by the organization that had previously hired me, neither of which I was ready to face right now.

My destination was a small town south west of Toronto called Hagersville. I knew it well – grew up there – went to high school there. Hold on! Don't; go off the deep end again. Those are not your memories. They belong to the Native boy. But I am he – in another space time – in another dream. Get a hold of yourself. You can sort this out when you do what you came here for.

My mind tried to rationalize it all—to sort it into some sort of sequence that was understandable but I had to abandon that to trust that whoever or whatever had possessed my mind, it was all for a greater good. I arrived at my destination and parked on a side street. Then I stood at the junction of the streets I remembered as leading to the high school. I waited all day and when the evening came, I found a motel and rented a room for the night—or a couple of days, as long as it would take.

Before I went to sleep, I made a phone call and charged it to my credit card. I phoned the University of Toronto and left a message on the night line, informing the secretary that I was back, and to

A Spark of the Fire

please ask someone who knows Joseph Champion to call me back. I left the number of the motel desk.

In the morning, there was a call for me that I accepted. "Are you ready to come back to work on the project? We hired a replacement to stand in for you in the event you might never be healthy to return."

I answered in the affirmative, that I was out of town but I would be back to talk to the leader of the project in a week – next Monday." So, I still had a job as an instructor for a class of young people who were creating a program—computer software to power a ship to the Moon, and beyond. And now I had a better understanding of the crystals that were found on the ship that crashed and was in the hands of NASA.

The next morning after breakfast, I stood at the aforementioned junction that I remembered so well, and lo and behold, my wait was rewarded. A young Native boy came up the street, hesitant and curious; he stopped and looked up and down the street. I walked out across the street to meet him. I waved. "Don't go!" I called out. "I know that you are expecting to meet someone here."

He hesitated, and decided that in the bright of day, I did not present much of a risk. "What do you want?"

I sat on a nearby bench and asked for him to join me.

"Why should I?"

"Well, I might be able tell you something about the dreams that you have been experiencing."

"Go on." He sat on the farthest edge of the bench lake a spooked animal about to bolt at the first sign of danger.

"I know about your dreams," I began, "because I have had the same kind of dreams, too, and I am looking for young people who are inspired to join a class that we have in Toronto. We will help you get a job and place to live if you will agree to attend our class."

"And what's in it for you?" He asked.

"It's more about what is in it for all of us – all humanity. Have you ever wondered what is out there?" I pointed to the sky. "If there is any intelligent life somewhere out there beyond the Stars?"

"I cut my teeth on Sci Fi books." My mother taught me to read before I started school – mostly comics and far-out ideas. And I have read enough to know that travel to the Stars is not possible. We could not reach the Stars because the distance is measured by the speed of light. Haven't you read about Einstein's Theory of Relativity?"

I nodded. "But what if there was away to travel beyond the normal logical speed of light? How much time does it take in your dreams?"

"So what are you doing here?" he countered. "Except recruiting for a fairy tale? Why should I trust you?"

"Aha! Don't trust me – trust your dreams. You do dream don't you?"

"Everyone dreams." He made to go, to stand up.

"But not like you and I." I ventured. "I will bet that you have dreams like me —and those dreams are why you are here today, expecting to meet someone."

"Maybe," he shrugged. "And are you saying that you are the one I am to meet? If you are—you would be wrong."

"No, I am not saying that. I am betting that you are here to meet the girl in your dreams. Right?"

Now he was running away in his eyes. "So what if I am. All boys have that kind of fantasy."

"But not all boys have that same dream in which your respect for her is stronger than your natural urges. I had that dream when I was your age, and I will bet that I might be able to guess her name." That was bold, I admit, but it was my last resort.

"You are crazy," he answered. "OK make a guess."

"She might be called..."

"No, wrong, try Rumpelstiltskin. No forget it." His eyes told me he might be lying. "How could you ever know, anyways?"

"I am sorry." I really was. I had pushed him too far. "Please take my business card if you change your mind to follow those dreams. I am legit. This is not a scam. Keep on looking for her and you will find her like I did." I left my card on the bench and went back to my hotel room. Maybe I was being crazy to think that a boy this age might be able to understand a truth that men of all the great religions could not grasp.

The next day, I arrived early, thinking that the boy might have been scared off. But when that was me – nothing could stop me from following those dreams. And then someone did show up. I watched her get out of a bus and stand at the same junction as I had the day before – strong and proud in her emerald green business suit.

"Kathleen?" I stepped out of the doorway. Yes, I was crazy.

"Joseph?" she smiled and hugged me. "Whatever are you doing here?"

I hugged her back. "Most likely the same reason you are here and then something— someone I did not expect."

"I had a dream." She smiled the way that melted my heart. "And it was too crazy to ignore. I am healed by the way—all the cancer is gone. So I am here to pay back. I could not let the boy down—you know that."

"He showed up yesterday, and I might have scared him away." I told her about my conversation with him.

"Then that is just as well," she replied. "We both came to make sure that he was safe and able to follow his dreams. And from what you tell me, he will not be stepping out to be rundown by a man from the future and neither will I, you can bet on that."

We waited together until about noon time. Students came up the street from the high school, and then the boy appeared. I stepped back into a nearby doorway. His eyes lit up and he quickened his pace as he caught sight of Kathleen. He reached the sidewalk and looked carefully both ways, and waved. Kathleen returned his wave, and motioned for him to wait. Their caution was rewarded as a white van rushed through the red light, followed closely by a police car with its siren wailing. The van and the police car crossed the tracks and were lost – out of sight into the Native Reservation.

Kathleen crossed the street and joined the boy on the same bench where he and I sat the day before.

"So what happens now, Mr. Champion—if that is really your name?" A man came out of the door-way of the store that I had been hiding in.

"What do you mean?" I asked, temporarily taken aback.

"Well, I followed you from Toronto. I have been interested in your story since before you had that breakdown last year. That really threw me for a loop. But I left a message with the promise of some good cash for the asylum to call me if you ever regained your senses. And it looks like it paid off. So what is with the woman in green and the Native boy?"

"Both good friends of mine from the past," I answered. "I know the boy's family and his school advised me that he might be a likely candidate for a computer course I am running in Toronto." It was pretty close to the truth.

"Oh, come on. You can come clean with me." The man squinted into the noonday sun, and then in the direction taken by the van and the black and white. "You don't recognize me, but I know all about you and your escapades. What do you think will happen when the police catch that van? Maybe it will blow up like the pretend terrorists that we hear in the news. I know about the alien plot to take over Canada and the USA."

"You do? Then you know more than I do. Where did you get these crazy ideas?"

"I have a mole in the FBI who sells me information," he replied. "I wrote a book to expose the JFK assignation. And while I was scouting out Area 51 your name came up. NASA has the real deal. An alien ship and the Feds have been following that man in the green suit. No coincidence there. He left it in an apartment that he rented in Hamilton and they followed his van to Hagersville. And here you are, and your lady friend in green no less. Is that green the latest secret color of the Illuminati?"

"Wow!" You have a bigger imagination than me," I laughed. "And do you suppose that I am recruiting young people to take over the world?"

"I haven't figured that one out yet, but when I do—man will I be there to expose you and your sinister plot."

"Have a good day," I replied. "See you around?"

"I will be around." he smiled slyly. "In fact, I will be watching you."

"OK? Now what did I do to deserve this entertainment?" I asked myself when the conspiracy theorist went his way. I had been watching Kathleen and the boy talking. She smiled and hugged him and sent him on his way.

"How did that go?" I asked, after the boy had left and I joined Kathleen on the bench.

"Good as could be expected. He was a bit down to learn that I was not his Soul mate. Heck, I am nearly old enough to be his mother. As a matter of fact, I have a son almost his age."

"A son?" I was surprised again. "What about your three daughters—the three sisters of Native folk lore?"

"Joseph Brin, you old fox, or should I say Wolf? I know who you are. We really need to talk. How about a lift back to Toronto? I came here on the bus. I assume that you have the use of a car? Or am I being too bold?"

I cancelled my room and Kathleen and I took Highway 6 North and the QEW back towards Toronto. "So who are you, and what happened to the Kathleen I knew with the three daughters," I asked.

"She has gone on with her life after being healed like me. No one is lost, remember? You cannot change the past, even the man with a burning desire to stop a boy from living his dreams. And as if you didn't know, there were two Cathys too, that I know about."

"Joseph?" Kathleen said in a soft voice. "You need to learn to let go, like I am now, or you will go insane."

"Been there, done that," I replied. "So you have a son? What is his name?"

"Jack...when I met his father, I knew immediately that this was the man to share my son. Past life connection, don't you think?"

"Or a dream?"

"However you see it, it is Grace in action. Like Kahlil Gibran wrote:"

"Your children are not your children. They are the sons and daughters of Life's longing for itself."

"Beautiful and true. And now? Where is his father?"

"We completed our purpose together, and both moved on. We had an amicable divorce and my purpose now is to be the best mother I can be for my teenage son."

The miles swept by. "So, you are forgetting? Letting it go? So what about the dreams? What about the people in that far future. Who will help them build the ships to take them to the Stars?"

"It's already been done. Don't you think?" Kathleen smiled. "And now it is up to the boy to follow his dreams. His name is Steven by the way. It will be his choice to look for the girl in his dreams, and if his heart is strong he will not give up."

"And Stephanie?" I asked. "If he joins my course to discover the use of the crystals with her, then love would be the answer that he seeks."

"Doesn't seem to be in the cards," she replied. "That is one of the reasons I showed up today instead of Stephanie. She called your office while you were out of action, and the call was directed to me. Little ol' dreamer me. She told me that she had discovered who her sister is and was going to France with her parents."

"So they might never meet—at least not in this dream?"

"If he is inspired, love will find a way."

"And you are forgetting?" I asked. Kathleen was silent the rest of the trip home, until I stopped the car on the side of Lakeshore Boulevard across from her apartment.

"What?" she asked.

"I said you are forgetting." I was preoccupied—looking in the rear view mirror

"And that means?"

"I thought maybe that we could have a coffee together some evening and talk about old times?"

"Old times? The past you mean? I cannot remember the past. I live for the future. I am a Dreamer, you know."

"So a coffee is out of the question?"

"I said that I am letting go of the past. I didn't say that I was not into making new friends."

"See you later then?"

"Yes, a definite maybe. After all, our people do not have a word for good bye." She had one of those Mona Lisa smiles that some women share when they just seem to know more than they are going to tell you at this moment. Kathleen gave me one of those European kisses – one for each cheek and got out of the car. My eyes were drawn to the mirror again.

"Preposterous!" came a voice from the back seat.

"How long have you been there?" I asked.

"Long enough..."

"To see or hear what? Do you have a problem with my story?"

"I like your stories – all of them. But this part about the Jinn – the Fire Creature falling from the sky? You and I both know that Cathy or Kathleen as you know her is the Star Woman Who Fell to Earth."

"And what about the bit of spiritual wisdom that you bestow on me almost every time we meet: *We are All One?* My take on that is *we are All a Spark of the Original Fire.*"

I turned my head to see Kathleen standing on her doorstep with a puzzled look on her face. I waved and she waved back and went inside. And when I turned back, the strange woman had left the car, chuckling to herself. Further down the street, for those who might see, she disappeared in a puff of smokeless Fire.

I did a "U" turn there on Lakeshore Boulevard, and when I passed the Mimico Roller Skating Arena, I was feeling that I was finally home.

You and Beauty - Essentially Intertwined!

If a tree were to fall in the forest
and You were not there to hear...
If you were not there to Wake up
and smell the Roses
Would the Roses still be there?
Test this out
Be still for a moment
And imagine waking up
with Your eyes shut tight
and You will find
...that the Roses were
waiting for You!

...winterhawk

During the Month of October 2014, I was meditating on and contemplating the ideas of the Native American meaning of Beauty. What you focus on comes to you, if you are open to receive it, in the way that the Universe or God speaks to you. I get my inspirations through my dreams. The following is a dream I had that has blossomed into a story.

Hot to Trot (an experience of Beauty in Space-Time)

In this dream, I am a young, single man, part of a team working on a planet on the edge of our solar system. Our objective is to discover a new type of Hyper Drive—a new method, a new rocket engine that will enable us to go to the stars.

I think best on my feet. Back on Terra (Earth) I liked to go for a walk in the forest or along a beach for inspiration, and then, if I am fortunate, the answer would appear later that night in a dream. Instead of taking the shuttle back to our sleeping quarters I asked my supervisor if it was safe to walk — about a half hour in Terra time. He replied that it was indeed safe, as the planet we were on was barren of life, but otherwise hospitable for humans.

"You will be completely safe," he smiled, "unless you are bothered by ghosts?"

"What did that mean Ghosts?" I wondered.

"Nothing," he replied. "Have a good walk. The rest of us will be happy in the shuttle."

The atmosphere was breathable, and as my supervisor suggested, suitable for human life. I wore a light jacket and soon wrapped it around my waist. The early evening found me walking through long shadows created by a sun not unlike our sol back on Terra. For part of my walk, I experienced being homesick, and wished that I had asked for company on my walk. But that was not to be, since my fellow workers were mostly made up of men and women who lived for the logical benefits that the ever-growing electronic "age" provided. They would be more happy plugged into a music device than in the company of a young man of Native ancestry. When I reached our sleeping quarters, I was refreshed, rejuvenated, and felt that I had company on my walk, in the form of the ghosts that my supervisor mentioned. I felt that I was "watched over." To tell the truth, I have always been happy in the company of spirits.

The next day, and the evening after that, I enjoyed my walk home along the path that we had laid down in the Terra-like soil. Sadly, there was no vegetation of any kind - no evidence that Life had ever been present on this planet in any form. I was happy with my walk except for that sense of being watched. On this particular evening I felt an urge to jog, and the next thing I knew, I was running at a good pace, and when I reached a certain speed, my outer senses, my eyes, ears and hearing began to come alive - that is, the world around me began to take on a different focus. I imagined tall buildings, skyscrapers, along the path that I was running. And did I hear voices?

I picked up my pace a bit, and a park-like setting came into view, and three people clothed in soft, gossamer material came into view, standing beside the path. I slowed down, and stopped as a young woman stepped forward and smiled. And then, the effect of my running, my speed, appeared to "catch up" with me, and the park, and the buildings and the three people by the side of the road faded away. And I was left with an eerie feeling that these were the people, the ghosts who had been watching me each day that week during my walk. That night, I mentioned nothing of my ghostly encounter to my fellow workers, as they were lost in their private digital worlds, anyways. But in my dreams that night, were the three people. The older woman spoke to me.

"This is our daughter," she said with a friendly smile "Perhaps you would see more of her?"

And the young, pretty woman stepped toward me, with a similar but inviting smile...and disappeared as before.

I woke up with the intent of discussing the encounters of the ghost people with my supervisor, but an inspiring thought about our project pushed it out of my mind.

A Spark of the Fire

During a day of rewarding work, I was visited by the reminder of the woman and her daughter that appeared during my run and in my dream the night before. I mused over "perhaps you would see more of her?" In the earlier days on Earth, my Native ancestors would have arranged marriages that were beneficial to bringing two tribes together. Although that custom was long gone and left behind on Terra, I was not distressed by the remembering, since it was not the intention of my ancestors that this be anything like the trade in human lives by the people who conquered the Native people, and pretended to be a superior culture. But one thing did concern me—this was the question about this being this woman's choice to be my wife, if I understood the offer correctly.

I laughed at myself, leaving work later that day, about thinking I could be wed to a ghost. Nevertheless, I repeated over and over in my mind as I set off at a brisk jog. "Yes! Yes, I would like to see more of you—if that is your choice."

I was repeating my mantra about choice, when I reached the right speed in my run, and the skyscrapers and the park began to come into focus around me, but the spot that I met the three people the day before was empty. I shrugged and continued on, until the young woman from the day before appeared at my side, matching me, stride for stride. She wore the gossamer body suit that I had observed on her family. It was perfectly suited for running. She smiled pleasantly and invitingly. There was no language barrier between us.

I returned her smile and said aloud: "Yes, I would like to see more of you —but only if that is what you choose, too?" My reply was the pleasant, knowing smile which I understood as "yes, it is my choice, too."

As we ran on together at a quick fluid pace, we became in a synchronized state which felt out of time—in fact, at this speed, I should have reached the destination of the sleeping quarters by now. We exchanged encouraging smiles as we ran, and I noticed that her face was becoming flushed. I wondered that maybe we should slow down and rest, but I knew at the same time, that when that happened she would surely disappear. And then I realized a sensation in my own body, a warm feeling that spread out from my heart and I knew the flushed face that I must have, too, was due to a sense of shared intimacy that was similar but beyond the physical sharing of sex. Time was suspended for me and my companion until I began to come back to the reality of the path through the park and it occurred to me to stop and hold her in my arms. As I was kissing her, the tempo of the run caught up to us, and she faded away in my arms.

That night, my "running" companion was in my dreams and so was her family. I woke the next morning determined to tell my supervisor about my encounter with the ghost woman and her people.

"Holy crap Engine Man!" My supervisor sat on the edge of my desk, shaking his head in disbelief, "Other members of our team have reported seeing ghosts, and had more than a few close encounters in their dreams. We sent them straight to the resident shrink when the sexual dreams took over their minds and got in the way of being able to concentrate on the job we came here to do. But you seem to be taking this to the next step—whatever that is. You seem to be able to make the dreams come real. Then, that is what I hired you for."

"That is what I am about," I agreed, ignoring his continued obvious ethnic slur.

Our supervisor had a similar nick name for most of his workers. I am an Indian man from birth, and I was hired at the last minute, to work on the software for the Quantum Engine when the person who began the project went quietly insane. "I live my dreams," I replied.

"Well, just be careful not to go off the track on me," he warned. "I don't have anyone else to take your place." Which was partially true — but I frequently discussed what I was working on with the other logically minded members of our crew. "Now, the ghost woman that you run with sounds like someone I might like to meet. She sounds really hot-to-trot."

"She is," I agreed. It was definitely a man thing. "But there is more to this than acting out my sexual fantasies."

"How so?"

"Well there is something happening on this world that seems to be devoid of life. My people believe in spirits — ghosts to you. But we also believe in a sharing of knowledge, and this is the amazing thing about this relationship with this woman and her people. Let me tell you about what I learned about the time- synchronizing effect. I mean, how I can only see this woman and her ghost world when I run at a certain speed. I am sure this applies to trying to break through the "Speed of Light" barrier."

The Theory of Relativity is based on Einstein's law, having to do with anyone or anything being unable to go faster than the speed of light. Without inventing or discovering a way to go beyond that limit, travel to the stars and beyond is impossible.

That grabbed his interest immediately, and we spent the rest of the morning discussing the possibilities this might have for our Quantum Drive. And for the moment the woman who was "hot-to-trot" was forgotten, until later that afternoon, when he dropped back to my desk to urge me to "keep doing what you are doing—with the ghosts, I mean. Just don't go off the track."

"This woman and our relationship is about more than sex," I reaffirmed in my mind when I left work that evening. "But the experience of intimacy is out of this world!" With that in mind, I jogged along the path in the direction of our sleeping quarters, and quickened my pace until I found her running at my side. "Here we go again!" And that evening, I dreamed and came back for more the next day, until near the end of our Terra-based week, she just did not show up - for reasons that baffled me at that moment in time.

I immersed myself in my work, trying not to think about her. And a couple of days later, she was back, but something had changed. She ran with me with both hands holding her protruding stomach. She breathed a bit harder but beamed when I noticed that she was pregnant! How in Spirit's name could that be possible? How can a man get a ghost-woman pregnant? I was almost at the point of "going off the track," like my supervisor warned.

I slowed just a bit to make it easier for her to keep up, and at the end, I hugged her, feeling her baby bump pressed against me and her smile being the last to go like the Cheshire cat in Alice in Wonderland. This is not Wonderland, Dorothy!

The next couple of days went by and she was absent again—I can only guess why. And then she was back, slim and in top running condition, cradling a baby. My baby? Good grief, how is that possible? We ran in perfect synchronicity together like before, and at one point she passed me the baby to hold. Then, at the end of our run, I stood hugging mother and baby while they faded away.

This was when I went off the track. Can I be blamed? I would happily be a doting father and husband to a family that I could hold in my arms—not just when I am running a cross-country race on some desolate planet at the edge of our solar system. I checked myself in to see the shrink complaining of "mental fatigue", and she told me to take a few days off, prescribing a sleeping pill that should stop me from dreaming—she'd been there before and seen it all, so she claimed. I didn't tell her all, though. Just about dreaming about sex with a ghost—not about the baby.

Back on track. I put in a fruitful day at work, and exited the door, prepared to be a good father and husband. I ran the course with expectations for someone that did not show. And the next day I ran alone too. That night, she was in my dreams, but not the baby. I feared the worst. And the next, and the next until one day about a week later, I was running my heart out, and a young man about my age appeared beside me—keeping up and looking like he belonged. After a while of keeping pace, he smiled and spoke:

"My mother is becoming an Elder." He said matter-of-factly. "She can no longer keep up this pace, but you can walk with her.

She sends her love and wished me to tell you that she will walk with you." At the end of our run, I shook his hand and hugged him as my grown son faded from my sight.

How can you walk with someone you cannot see? I did that. I imagined walking to and from work, holding her hand and I dreamed of her faithfully every night, until another Terran based week went by, and she was gone! Gone from my daily walk and gone from my dreams. I walked silently to the sleeping quarters, found my bunk and switched to privacy, and I cried myself to sleep. My grief at my loss was eventually complete and one night, I woke in a dream, in a strange place and she was there. She promised to wait for me until I could find her again in that dream that is not a dream.

"We are getting so close," my supervisor informed me. "The ship that will take us to the Stars is almost ready." The Star Ship had been built starting almost from day one — a little over a year ago. Bit by bit, using minerals and metals that were abundant on this planet at the edge of the solar system — having been seen and verified by spectral analysis from Terra before we started the voyage here - most of us in cryogenic sleep chambers. And the fuel the crystal that would power this ship was mined here, as well. Only the non-logical Quantum software that would instruct the special Hyper Drive engine had needed to be created.

"And now we are close."

A week went by, and then a Terran month.

And...

"We did it!" Our supervisor called us all together for a final party to celebrate. "We did it. You did it—all of you!"

We had solved the problem that could not be solved and tested it out. We had used the completed Quantum Drive and journeyed back to Terra, to pick up some scientists and a couple of open-minded theologians (and some that weren't so open-minded).. One moment we were here and the next there! No cryogenic sleep chambers needed. We shared the Quantum Drive technology with the people on Terra - now mined out and nearly as desolated as the planet on the edge of the solar system. Now, we could mine the galaxy - if some people had their way. And then we were back on that desolate planet to pick up our belongings and make that long awaited Quantum Leap to the Stars. In the wink of a Quantum eye!

A couple of the people that came back from Terra had to make use of our busy shrink. Even when they saw it done and participated in the act, they refused to believe.

"What about you, Engine Man?" Our supervisor came around to click his glass with mine. "Did it work for you? Why did you sign on in the first place?"

I raised my glass of ice cube filled wine in celebration. "Well, you know. I came to find something that was missing in my life. I wanted answers to questions that I've only just realized that I wanted to know. You know."

"Always the enigma, Engine Man," he chuckled. "But did you get the answers you came here for? How about that ghost woman who was so hot to trot? Did that work out for you?"

I nodded. "That worked out better than I might have imagined." I answered truthfully.

Just that morning, I donned a jacket to protect me from the bitter cold outside our headquarters and went for one last run. I took it slow at first, not really knowing what to expect, if anything. And then when I reached that critical speed, someone joined me. At first I thought, beyond all possible stretches of the imagination, "she came back?" The young woman who ran at my side was a ringer for my missing love. But something was different, and I could not tell what — except for a strong sense of respect. We ran on together, until she spoke:

"Our people say that I look just like my great grandmother. Is that true?" she smiled slyly.

I nodded in agreement. And I simply surrendered to knowing what could not be true.

"My people—we are moving to another world. I am here to thank you and your people for helping to make that possible.

Thank you, Great Grandfather. We will be forever indebted to you." She moved so easily—she could easily be the one I had given my love to. And we ran on in sync with love and respect.

"What did we do?" I asked. "How are you moving on?"

"With your shared knowledge, we built ships like you."

"Without your help—without the love of your family, we could not have done it," I replied.

"That is what the Sharing of Beauty is about."

"Sharing? I know, but how does Beauty play a part?" I stopped running.

"You will know what you already know." She stopped and kissed my cheek. "Thank you grandfather. Some day we might meet again— out there among the Stars." And she faded away like a ghost, and I clutched my coat around me to ward off the bitter cold.

"Yes. That all worked out for me," I answered my supervisor's question and clicked my glass of watered down wine one more time. "And yes. I did get all that I asked for, and more than I could ever expect."

He raised his eyebrow. And I began to tell him about the people who lived on this planet before we came along—many eons in the logical understanding of time…

"Whoa! Stop right there, Engine Man," he said. "That is more than I need or want to know. Any more of that and I will be off the rails. Just so long as it all worked and will still work tomorrow, and the day after that, is all I need to know."

And you know what? He was right.

Later, within the span of a Terran week we were ready to go. First we boarded a sealed shuttle to make the trip to the sleeping quarters to gather our remaining belongings. Half way there, I noted that a corner of the sky had turned a deep tinge of red, and I walked up to sit behind the driver. "Slow down a bit," I requested. "Until I tell you when." And then, I asked: "keep this speed for a few minutes will you?"

"But this is hardly faster than a man could walk," He complained.

"Actually, it is a good running speed." I replied, as the sky lit up, literally burst into multi-coloured flames.

"What is happening?" The driver of the shuttle was open-mouthed in amazement.

"I believe we are seeing the sun go super nova." Our supervisor's voice sounded beside me. "We are witnessing the death of a Star. Am I right?"

"I believe you are correct," I replied, hardly able to talk from the sense of Awe and Beauty.

"Is this happening now?" our supervisor gasped. "Or did it happen long ago? Or is it still to happen? If it is happening now we should not be here."

We looked at each other in open-mouth wonder and awe.

How could we know? It was not something you can think about, you can only observe. You can only remember that there was a butterfly on Terra that only lives for a day. If you were not there to witness the sharing of Beauty, you would miss the experience. Perhaps we need to slow down, or take time, find a way to be aware of the Beauty that all life has to share, especially those we love. And when we find that Beauty, perhaps when it is our time to leave this world, we will remember and reconnect with that Beauty

"Out There Among the Stars."

CPSIA information can be obtained
at www.ICGtesting.com
Printed in the USA
BVHW050350230622
640452BV00016B/152